THE KENRYK SERIES

THE AVARIS

Book One

WELA KABANE

THE KENRYK SERIES: THE AVARIS

BOOK ONE

By Wela Kabane

Cover design by Muhammad Abdul Momin Arju
                    Nerisha Moodley www.ndesigns.co.za
Formatting and layout design by Saqib Arshad
Illustrations by Veronika Wunderer www.veronika-wunderer.com

ISBN: 978-0-620-94760-2

e-ISBN: 978-0-620-94761-9

ISBN Hardcover: 978-0-6397-8110-5

DEDICATION

To my sisters, Kude and Sive. You're my soulmates in this lifetime and I hope we meet in every lifetime. To my parents, thank you for setting me on this path.

Fleeing home to protect her family, Amari encounters two companions as she journeys through the Great Kingdom of Sagar to fulfil her childhood dream to become the first female Sage Warrior.

A brief encounter with a man who shares her secret fire ability brings danger in the form of the mystical Emori and forces her to journey to Bhrim. Amari and her two companions outmanoeuvre a mercenary and the mystical Emori.

Arriving at Bhrim, her true identity is revealed, one that puts her in a precarious situation. Forced to choose between her desire, a Sage Warrior and her rightful place in the Kenryk tribe of fire, either choice she makes will irrevocably change her life.

Don't miss book 2 of the series:
The Kenryk Series: Rise of the Emoryk

NOTES: THE KAIS

The Kais is a continent currently split into three kingdoms and three independent territories. Before the Kingdom of Sagar, The Mountain Kingdom of Kessariah, and the Kingdom of Elyssia were born, five diverse tribes thrived on this land. Rooted in tradition, culture, and respect for the earth, these tribes had developed a system that worked harmoniously for their coexistence.

In the North, Mer-beings called Za-Aro had the power to manipulate the waters. They could live underwater for extended periods while also able to exist on land. Characterised with smooth marble-like grey skin and hair that changed colour to suit their mood, they were intuitive, diplomatic, protective, but cunning when deeply hurt. Their vengeance came in the form of floods.

In the West, the Taolin, known for their enviable ability to manipulate wind, were fierce warriors characterised by stocky built, wide cheekbones, and black hair. Curious, disciplined, and possessors of the virtue of knowledge, their vengeance always came in the form of hurricanes.

In the south, the pointy-eared and brown-skinned Mbaro reigned. Built to be tall, fast, and enduring, their ability to fly had made other tribes refer to them as fairies. However, there was nothing delicate about this tribe. One angered swoop of their wings that spanned over two metres wide could cause utter destruction when triggered. This destruction came in the form of shards of ice that could kill instantly.

To the southeast lived the Emori, beings with horns that grew from their foreheads. Their blue striped skin, unmatched speed, and ability to draw energy from plants, nature, and flowers meant their vengeance came in the form of famines through destroying harvests.

Just on the border of the Emori lands lay the evergreen valleys of the Kenryk people. Known for their golden-brown skin, long think black hair, fierce warriors, and the ability to form fire from their hands, their vengeance came in a fiery blaze.

The tribes avoided war as it could be destructive. Negotiations were always preferred. A council put in place to ensured that all lived according to the Laws of Nature.

Devastatingly, the balance altered forever by the arrival of invaders in the north and the south within months. The appearance of these invaders five hundred years ago forever changed the shape and territories of the Kais.

The Kingdom of Sagar emerged from the systematic destruction, oppression, and appropriation of the Taolin and Za-Aro people, emerging in the end with its own six fiefdoms ruled by the Great House in Sagar. The Mountain Kingdom of Kessariah was built on the destruction of the Mbaro people in the south and emerged with three territories, the Muir, Shadowvale and Chasewah.

The Kingdom of Elyssia was able to carve up its territory from the unclaimed lands of the Mbaro and received significant resistance from the Kenryk and Emori tribes, who fought defiantly for over half a century to protect their lands. Finally, with the Taolin, Mbaro, and Za-Aro destroyed, only two remained, the Emori and the Kenryk, forced to share their continent with the invaders, yet successfully keeping them off their territories.

PROLOGUE

The Seven Battles of the Kais culminated with the epic Battle of Endric, giving rise to the first Avaris. Driven with insatiable greed, King Kairon of the Kingdom of Elyssia, plunged the Kais into a devastating war that would displace his people forever. Disillusioned with power, words of caution from his council fell on deaf ears, and he sold his soul to the darkness just for a taste of immortal glory. Ignoring treaties centuries-old, King Kairon lay siege on the neighbouring territory of Shadowvale.

Viewing the act as a direct attack on the Mountain Kingdom of Kessariah, the Kessarian King Dratan sent his army from Muir to contain the arrogance of the Elyssians. Kairon crushingly destroyed the army. Drunk on victory, King Kairon extended his reach, attacking the nearby city of Briar Moor under the Kingdom of Sagar. The more territory he usurped, the darker his soul became until eventually, it overpowered him, capturing him whole.

Fear reigned in the Kais as word of his deeds spread. Villages torched in the night, and towns raided without mercy. Smoke blackening the sky from burning homes occurred too frequently, and the scent of burning flesh became a familiar odour. One by one, he executed his councilmen for one excuse or another. No one dared defy him. Only those that encouraged him were allowed anywhere near him. The further his black reach extended, the darker the Kais became.

This act drew the Kingdom of Sagar into the war. King Zaifa II of the Kingdom of Sagar sent his army from Baelyt to take back Briar Moor, and shockingly, the Sagar army was defeated.

Kairon's reach grew, his black heart spreading like vines over the Kais, and terror reigned. When it became evident that something supernatural was the driving force behind Kairon's behaviour, that unless something drastic occurred, the whole Kais would forever be lost in darkness; old enemies became allies.

In an unprecedented show of unity from former enemies, Sagar and Kessariah, the Combined Armies of the Kais lay siege on Elyssia, but the darkness was too intense for them.

As Kairon shed more of his humanity, his entire being underwent a chilling transformation. His eyes glowed red, and his voice sent shivers down the spines of warriors. A cold chill filled any room he entered and grew a demon in the place of a man. He showed no mercy.

When it seemed all was lost, when the greatest armies of the Kais were on the verge of another crushing defeat, help came in the unlikeliest form. In the valley of the Endric, a low-lying area between the Kessariah and Sagar borders, the greatest battle in the history of the Kais took place.

A small tribe of no more than five thousand in population, the mystical army of the Kenryk tribe unexpectedly arrived. Located in the utmost southeast part of the Kais, the Kenryk tribe was known for its supernatural powers and respected as an independent territory. Consequently, it never engaged in wars and kept to itself.

Riding into battle with their red flags flowing in the air, the fire burning in their hands, and a rider leading the army of two thousand men, everything on the battlefield drew to a jolting halt. For it was not the fire burning intensely from the hands of the riders that knocked the breath out of the warrior locked on the battle. It was not even that the Kenryk had joined the fight.

It was the rider leading the Kenryk army who captivated them. With his bronzed skin, his raven hair plaited close to his skull at either side of his head and bound in red strips of cloths, his eyes glowing an incredible gold, he wielded in his hand a large sword wholly engulfed with fire.

He exuded something intangibly powerful, intensely potent, and so incredibly strong that it pulsated across the battlefield. Yet, there was something different about him, something that set him apart from his fellow Kenryk.

In a stunning display of power, the Kenryk army swept through the enemy with their fire. In a battle that many would tell for generations, the rider with the fiery sword leaped in the air. Then, suspended there for a moment, he descended. So intense was his battle with Kairon, the ground shook under their feet, and an invisible force vibrated around them every time he struck. When the rider finally plunged his sword into Kairon's heart, a potent force flared around them like reaching fingers, knocking down warriors to the ground. In a stunning display of power, the Kenryk rider contained the blackness that escaped from the crumbling body of the once formidable King Kairon.

In a moment many shared for centuries to come, the rider extinguished the darkness. And, with it, its power for evil. Then, with one more slice of the sword in the air, he cut off Kairon's head, defeating the Elyssians.

The man with the sword stood before the crowd as the Kessarian and Sagar armies celebrated, powers radiating from him while he held the flaming sword in his hand, blood splattered over his clothes. Zaifa and Dratan approached the man with the Sword, knowing they owed their victory to the Kenryk. The man shared with both kings how every Kenryk, every man, woman, and child sacrificed their powers towards creating the flaming sword. The sword, he said, held an intense concentration of Kenryk powers that could only be wielded successfully by someone with enough force to contain it.

The Kenryk would only use it, he declared, during great strife that had the very existence of the Kais in danger. At that moment, both Kingdoms pledged themselves allies of the Kenryk. So that, in their moment of need, Kenryk would know they had Kessariah and Sagar as allies.

The sword obtained its name that day upon the Endric lands and thus came to be widely known as the Endric Sword. The Elyssians were stripped of their kingship, destroying decades of rich history, and as the Kenryk army rode away from Endric, everyone knew they would never forget the man with the flaming Sword. So, likewise, they would never forget the Avaris.

CHAPTER ONE

"What have you done, Amari?"

The quietly rumbling words instantly brought her down from her euphoria. She gazed up at Arteryn, his mouth set in a hard line as he slapped the reins with more force than necessary. Amari glanced at the walled city disappearing behind her, twisting a little from where she perched in the wooden wagon, its large wheels bumping awkwardly on the rough road. When she had left home before the sun kissed the horizon that morning, sneaking away from the little farm in the dipping valleys of Synia, Amari had skipped with unbridled hope and eternal optimism. Amari's goal had been simple. Go to Simiren, the capital of Orrick, find the infamous fighting pits, and test the skills she had acquired and mastered since she was seven years old.

It had seemed simple enough. After all, Amari had spent the last thirteen years training with Arteryn on the art of fighting. She could wield a sword like a seasoned warrior, and her precision with the bow and arrow was enviable. She had been fourteen when she killed her first mountain lion. The journey to Orrick should have been simple enough.

Furthermore, Arteryn should not have been so enraged with her. Granted, when he first agreed to train her, his conditions were clear. He did not want her to go around picking fights. It may have seemed like a ridiculous request but seeing as he came into her life when she was just five years old, he understood how her mind worked.

Everyone, including her adoptive parents Tia and Joran, knew it. Her adoptive younger brother Crispin exasperatingly knew it and the rest of the farmhands grudgingly knew it. The whole little village of Synia knew it. She was unconventional, they said. What kind of twenty-year-old woman spent her time training to fight instead of looking for a husband? They didn't stop there. No, their whispers behind cupped hands extended to ridiculous and unfounded assumptions about her relationship with Arteryn.

It drove her mad. She would; instead, they spoke about her impulsiveness rather than taint her relationship with Arteryn. The man was only thirty-four years old, but she always felt like he was a second father to her. He had worked at the farm for fifteen years now, and Amari instantly took a liking to him from the first day he set foot there.

At the age of seven, she found a sword under his makeshift bed and pestered him to teach her how to use it for months before he caved in. Arteryn was intensely private about his personal life. So, when she asked how a farmhand possessed such fighting skills, he gave her two options; pester him with questions he would never answer or accept the skills he was about to give her. She chose the latter and what she learned was invaluable.

Arteryn's overprotectiveness was widely known in their tiny village and lit the match for the rumours that circulated about them. While Amari spoke out against them, Arteryn ignored them. She could say without hesitation that, outside of her immediate family, he was the only person she trusted with her life.

Trust wasn't something she gave quickly. Instead, she had a chip on her shoulder brought on by not knowing her origins. As far as she was aware, she had been abandoned with Joran and Tia Leverood when she had been three years old. The only tie to whom she was before that day was the round medallion tied to a leather string that she wore around her neck.

"What do you mean? Arteryn, I just defeated Grantreal." Did he not realise how important this was to her? The hours they spent every single day since she was seven training had been for this. She developed lean, solid muscles and strength behind her kicks and punches because she worked so hard for this. If she was going to become the first female Sage Warrior, she needed to test her skills. Until that afternoon, Arteryn was the only opponent she ever faced. How was she supposed to know if she was good enough to become a Sage Warrior if she didn't test her skills with various opponents?

Not that she doubted herself. Not with Arteryn as a trainer. He had been around twenty-one years old when he had started training her for the first time, but even then, when she had just been a child, Arteryn had never been easy on her. She was used to hard punches and learned very early on to disregard pain and scars. Arteryn trained her with the single-mindedness of someone preparing a warrior. He explicitly proclaimed to her that being a woman did not give her an excuse not to defeat him. She strived for it and rejoiced the first time she disarmed him successfully.

He looked at her now, his hard brown eyes glaring at her. A lesser person would have shrunk under that glare, but Amari knew he would never hurt her. She knew without a doubt that this man would die for her. That was the nature of their relationship. It was confusing to others and yet so simple to the two of them. Her adoptive parents and brother thought nothing of it. In fact, in the Leverood household, Arteryn was treated more like family than an employee. Tia and Joran gave him more liberties than any employee Amari ever met. After all, how many farmhands had the freedom to scold their employer's daughter if she misbehaved?

She valued her relationship with Arteryn above many things, and that had nothing to do with how good-looking the man was.

She wasn't blind. She had seen women and, shockingly, a man or two falling over themselves, trying to gain Arteryn's attention. Their training sessions over the years, attracted an infatuated man or woman or two. After all, the man was stunning. He was taller than most men in the village with a solid muscled body, broad shoulders, and the kind of smile that lit up his whole face. However, that was not what she saw when she looked at him.

In a village of people who were all fair, she and Arteryn stuck out. They both had darker golden bronzed skin, raven hair, and brown eyes. So, it was only natural that in a sea of people who all looked alike, Arteryn drew Amari because he looked like her.

"What do I mean? Do you have any idea what you have done?" The vein throbbing in Arteryn's neck as he pushed the horses at breakneck speed heightened Amari's anxiety. Arteryn had a temper. No one knew that, except her because he kept it so tightly contained most people believed he was easy going. But, on the contrary, he was relaxed, and she admitted that unless her life was in danger, he transformed into a rage-filled version of himself. Amari had only ever seen him in that rage once, and the circumstances were not something she liked revisiting.

"Can you just come right out and say it? I don't know why you have to ruin one of the biggest days of my life. I just defeated two men in the fighting pits. Not even one of those men thought I could do it. They all underestimated me, calling me disillusioned. I showed them-"

"You're proud of yourself, huh, Amari?" His patronising tone did not sit well with her, and before she could tell him off for ruining what was supposed to be a victorious afternoon for her, he suddenly drew the horses to a halt.

She almost toppled over, battling to find her footing at the sudden dead stop. Then, regaining her composure, she glanced around, her mouth hanging open in question because they were about fifteen minutes from Synia. The distance between Synia and Orrick was around an hour and a half by horse. She knew this because the last time she came here, she snuck into the farm wagon when Joran, Arteryn, and Crispin had ridden to Orrick to sell the farm produce at the market. She had been fourteen and livid that Joran had thought it was suitable to take Crispin, aged eleven then to Orrick, and leave her behind. By the time they had caught on that Amari had snuck onto the wagon, it had been too late to turn back. That was the only time she had travelled outside the village in her life.

Well, until today.

When the horses drew to a halt, Amari noticed the beat-up old sign barely hanging on its rusty hinges with the name Synia scrawled on it. The sign was nailed onto a tree with thick roots sprawled out from underground, and Amari wondered why Arteryn would stop in the middle of a forest. She heard enough stories of men who lay waiting in woods to rob people passing by. Not that, between her and Arteryn, they couldn't take anyone down.

Arteryn jumped out of the wagon, tension coursing through him as he paced next to the wagon. Amari frowned in confusion. Arteryn was behaving unconventionally. When she looked up after defeating Grantreal in the pits and found Arteryn there, she felt a sober moment of joy that he had witnessed her victory over such a large man. It hadn't even mattered that she snuck away from home that morning without letting anyone know to travel to Simiren or that Arteryn caught her in a very dubious part of town.

Sliding off the wagon, Amari exhaled as she moved around the horses towards a pacing Arteryn. The frown on his face and his clenched fists were quite an overreaction as far as she was concerned.

"Arteryn, you're overreacting-"

"Amari, do you know who Grantreal is?" he cut her off then rushed to stand before her, towering over her. Most people found Arteryn intimidating. She could see that now.

Arching her eyebrows questioningly, she looked him over, still not allowing herself to react to his behaviour. She was still riding the high of her victory. "You know, I can see why Crispin thinks that when you cut your hair short, you became more intimidating."

"Can you be serious for a moment?" Growling, he held up both his hands between them then folded them into fists. Her head snapped back, and she scowled at him.

"All right, until you tell me what has you so worked up, I refuse to engage with you." Folding her arms across her chest, she stared at him expectantly, tapping her foot impatiently on the ground. He expelled a frustrated sigh, but she waited as he calmed himself down just enough to form coherent sentences.

As though to emphasise his words, Arteryn angled himself a little from her, one palm held up as he began to punctuate each word by hitting the side of his hand on his upturned palm.

"Amari, I will not bother going into why it was wrong of you to sneak away to such an uncouth place. I won't bother going into a list of why it was wrong for you to do that. You know that so much could have happened to you on the road to Simiren alone-"

"No, Arteryn, don't." Her hackles rose. He knew she did not want to talk about it. He knew she never wanted to discuss anything referring to the incident that had happened four years ago that had led to Arteryn being in a rage that had left a man dead.

He closed his eyes briefly, took a deep breath, then when he opened them, she saw the anger still flashing there. Fists clenched to his side, and he failed at taking another calming breath.

"Amari, Grantreal is not a man to be crossed. He leads a mercenary group of men who have a reputation for being paid warmongers. He is ruthless. Over the last five years alone, he has razed villages and homes to the ground. He has a reputation for raping and pillaging villages under the command of warlords. He is petty, he is callous, vile, cruel, and mostly, he is arrogant. He does not allow anyone- anyone- to make him appear weak. He has killed people for sneezing next to him."

Amari's skin tingled and not in a good way, her stomach dropped, and her breath knocked out of her chest at Arteryn's revelation. Her mouth opened, but nothing came out, but her questions were displayed on her face for Arteryn to interpret quickly.

"You just humiliated him, defeated him in front of not just his men, but other people who are undoubtedly telling everyone who will listen right now. He is going to come for you, Amari, and when he does, when he traces you to the farm, the Leveroods and possibly the whole of Synia will suffer."

Arteryn's words were like a sobering bucket of ice-cold water tossed into her face. Denial was at the tip of her tongue, the need to be defensive taking over. She shook her head, still grappling for words.

"It wouldn't matter so much if he couldn't trace you to the farm, but you chose to wear the belt from the Leverood farm! Everyone knows

Joran Leverood's produce, Amari, because it is superior. Everyone knows what that L on that belt stands for. Even if Grantreal doesn't, but someone in those pits probably does, and when they tell him what it stands for, Grantreal will be coming for you."

The euphoria a thing of the past, Amari stared with dread at Arteryn. "He'll come for me? You and I can take him on. I've defeated him-"

"Him and his men while simultaneously trying to stop him from burning the farm to the ground, killing Joran and Crispin and raping Tia? Are you insane? Grantreal will come for revenge and that is the only thing that will appease him."

Her throat constricted, chest tightening, and her forehead broke into a sheen of sweat as dread settled heavily on her. No, no, this wasn't happening. It couldn't happen to her. Such things didn't happen to her. She was supposed to have gone to the pits, fought, and defeated just enough men to prove her skill. Then, in a few days, she would slip away and travel to the Great City of Sagar to compete at the annual Laurean Sage, where she would be victorious and thus become the first female Sage Warrior. She would then live the rest of her days as one of the King's elite warriors.

This situation was no mere irritation. Unfortunately, there were no quick solutions. What Arteryn described could have consequences that could destroy her family. She would rather die than allow anything or anyone to hurt her family. She loved them more than anything in the world, and knowing she was responsible for their demise would haunt her for eternity- if Grantreal allowed her to live before he killed her as well.

She had heard of mercenaries like Grantreal, men who terrorised villages and raided homes. She had heard of their brutality, of the carnage they left behind. After all, the tale of how the younger brother of Lord Gregaria of Orrick had died was well-known. Everyone knew how mercenaries had come upon the homestead and killed everything and everyone. The sole survivor had been Lord Gregaria's nephew, and the boy had only been seven then. Would that happen to Synia because of what she had done? Would it be the consequence of the impulsive decision she had taken that morning to travel to Simiren?

Solutions. Amari needed solutions

"Arteryn, what are we going to do?" They could pack their things and flee to another village. Start over? Her heart tore at the thought of forcing Joran away from a farm his grandfather had earned through bravery over seventy years ago, passed from Joran's father to Joran. How could she make Joran, who had opened his home to her as an abandoned orphan, leave the one thing that separated him from so many people in Synia? The Leveroods were the only family in Synia who owned their lands and employed farmhands. Joran's grandfather had rescued the beloved son of an Orrick Lord without care of his safety from mercenaries over seventy years ago, and the Lord had rewarded him with land and a monthly stipend. How could Amari force Joran and Tia to leave their home because of her actions?

"Wait, if I leave? What if I leave? Would that help?" She asked anxiously, her heart racing as her mind conjured up every worst possible thing that could happen to her family before the day was out.

Arteryn seemed to have calmed down from his anger, but in its place was trepidation. He looked like a man forced to play his hand.

He took a deep breath then ran his fingers in frustration through his short thick hair. Finally, he looked up at the sky, muttering something very much like "this day came far too soon" before he lowered his eyes to Amari.

At that moment, he looked resigned to the situation or whatever decision he had taken. Amari had never seen that look on his face before.

"If you left, it might- might- help. However, there are no guarantees of how Grantreal will react when he arrives. We could tell him you work on the farm and have not returned since you left this morning. He might still seek retribution against the Leveroods, but I will be here, and I will do my best not to let it happen. I cannot make any promises. For their safety, I will have Crispin and Tia hide out somewhere. After that, Joran and I will meet Grantreal." Arteryn paused, his expression changing to disbelief. He ran his hand over his short hair again, resting his hand on his narrow waist as he shook his head. "It's too soon. I thought we had more time." He shook his head then turned his back on her. She watched him make some slight movements hidden by his broad back. After a moment of him doing something hidden from her, the odour of what smelled like burning paper filled her nostrils, but it was gone quickly. He turned to face her resolutely.

"When Grantreal comes, you have to be as far from the farm as possible. He will hunt you down until he finds you. He won't stop until he does. I can't do anything to him if he is in Synia, as that would put the lives of everyone in danger. However, when he tries to track you- and he will- when he is away from the village, I can try to take care of it- of him."

"You will kill him?" The words slipped out of her mouth. She clamped her mouth shut. They already had the secret of a dead Orrick warrior between them. Could she ask him to kill other men for her?

"What alternative outcome can there be, Amari? Let him catch you? Do you know what he'd do to you if he did? Rape you- repeatedly then pass you around to his men to do with you as they pleased. By the end of it, you'd be begging for him to kill you. No." Arteryn shook his head decidedly. "You have to leave as soon as we get home. I have someone very close to me who was travelling to Gildevard from Synia. I will send word for him to meet you. He will keep you safe in Gildevard until the matter is taken care of-"

"Gildevard?" Her mouth went dry, and her jaw dropped. Gildevard would be the furthest from home she would ever be. It would take days to get there.

"Yes, Korrigan left Synia for Gildevard yesterday. He can't be too far."

"Who's Korrigan?" She questioned, cutting him off. Had he said someone close to him? Who could that be? As far as she knew, Arteryn had no family or friends apart from the people who lived on the Leverood farm. Well, and that man he had been intensely friendly with for some years that he conscientiously ignored now.

"Amari, we do not have much time to spend on unnecessary details. I want you to listen to me carefully." Arteryn took a step towards her, and something about his demeanour made Amari shiver as she stood in the middle of the forest with the one man outside her family she trusted with her life. The horse grunted, the leaves swayed in the wind, and the birds flew over her head, but as she stared at Arteryn, an ominous feeling settled over her. She had a sense at that moment that nothing would ever be the same again.

As Arteryn spoke, Amari felt dread wash over her, panic swell within her and her mind started to shut down. Then, without thinking, she reached for the medallion hanging on the leather string around her throat and clasped it. Unfailingly as it had done for her over the years, the moment she reached for it, waves of soothing emotions washed over her immediately. Her heart rate slowed down, the panic subsided, and a sense of calmness washed over her.

"You can trust Korrigan, Amari. That is the one thing I want you to know. Korrigan will protect you as I would. However, I need you to listen carefully. You will have to travel to him alone. I cannot risk you travelling with anyone because they'd either slow you down or be careless. I trust you to keep yourself untraceable on your own. I have taught you everything you need to survive a journey to Gildevard."

"Alone? To Gildevard?" Leaving her family behind without any guarantee of their safety?

"You will have to stay off the road and be as inconspicuous as possible. Avoid engaging anyone who might lead Grantreal to you, and be careful." Arteryn was rattling out instructions, but Amari started to feel the anxiety well up within her again. Alone? To Gildevard?

"Listen to me, Amari." Arteryn stepped forward, resting his hands on her shoulders, and he shook her to the present. Her eyes wide as saucers lifted to his as she grappled for self-control. "When you meet Korrigan, there are only two ways to ascertain he is the man you're supposed to meet. Are you listening?"

She nodded at him vigorously, even though she felt herself tip towards the edge emotionally. Arteryn dropped his hands then nodded at her in return. "He will mention the medallion."

"What?" Her mouth dropped open as her hand slipped from the medallion she desperately clutched. "Why should he?"

"Just listen to me, Amari." He stepped forward again, a sense of urgency settling over him. "Do you trust me to keep you safe? To keep everyone safe?"

She nodded without pause.

"Then just trust me now and don't ask questions. I promise the next time we see each other after this is over, I will answer every question you have ever had for me."

That was a peculiar thing to say, she thought, a frown creasing her forehead. Why would Arteryn phrase it like that?

"When you meet Korrigan, he will mention the medallion and then either before he does or after, you have to say the following words to him. It is important, Amari, that you say the following words. *Tadiamnum Parleum*. Repeat the words to me."

"Tadia... What?"

"*Tadiamnum Parleum.*" Arteryn repeated, and she quickly said the words back to him three times.

"When you say that, he must respond with *Inum Anem Kalhasie.*" Arteryn made her say both sentences repeatedly until they felt ingrained into her brain. And yet, as she said the words, something within her shifted. She couldn't pin it. She didn't know what it was. It was something intangible, indescribable, yet so strangely familiar.

"What does it mean?" Amari asked him, but Arteryn was already shaking his head.

"Listen to me carefully, Amari. Your gifts..." He paused, and that immediately had her snapping her back straight and glancing around in a panic. Why would he mention her gifts now? It was a secret kept only between her, the Leveroods and Arteryn. No one knew beyond the four people she trusted with her life that she could formulate fire out of nothing from her hand. It was a discovery she had made when she was seven. Arteryn had been in the barn with her when it happened. He had told Tia and Joran, and everyone had agreed that her gifts must remain a secret. It had been just one more thing in Amari's life that had made her feel so very different from everyone around her. "On this journey to Gildevard when the need arises, use them, Amari. Use that fire to protect you. Trust it and what it can do."

"You told me-"

"I know. I know what I told you, but you're not seven years old anymore. You're twenty years old and about to embark on a journey alone. The time for self-preservation is over. But, if the need arises, use your powers. You have been practising how to control the flame the last few months."

She shook her head quickly, then nodded again. "Yes." No, this was too much. She had spent most of her life living in fear of discovery, that someone would stumble upon her secret and that she would, as Crispin had once suggested, be burned at the stake because everyone would think she was a witch. How could Arteryn, who had insisted so vehemently all those years ago that she never show anyone her gifts, be insisting that she use them now?

"Amari, look at me." He urged in a voice that had softened. He must have discerned her apprehension, and she lifted her eyes to him absently. "You are about to embark on a journey that will test you. Use everything that I have taught you to survive, but most importantly, trust yourself. Trust your gut feeling."

She could only nod. They climbed back on the wagon and were off within seconds. Words had deserted her. Deep in thought, she didn't even take cognisance of her surroundings. The threat before her was too overwhelming, threatening to suffocate her. She had to work hard to remember to breathe.

Her mind raced with what-ifs. What if she hadn't gone to Orrick? What if she hadn't brazenly declared she wanted to fight Grantreal at the pits? What if she had never wanted to be a Sage Warrior? She sat beside Arteryn, her hand clasping the medallion for comfort as something else entirely plagued her. For weeks now, she had been having the same recurring dream. Houses on fire, rushing feet, bone-chilling cries of pain. There had been so much pain, so much fire. Had that been a premonition of what would happen to Synia because of what she had done? Was that the fate she had set upon the people of her beloved village? She took a deep breath, holding back the tears. Was everyone going to die because of her?

CHAPTER TWO

The moment they reached the farm she knew so well she could navigate blindfolded; Arteryn went in search of Tia and Joran after instructing them to gather necessities to take with her. When Arteryn gathered her adoptive parents in the kitchen, she tried to temper down her distress. If they sensed she was afraid, they could resist Arteryn's suggestion necessitating her departure.

Crispin walked into the house, her lanky sixteen-year-old brother going on thirty immediately sensing something was wrong.

"Tia, Joran, the time is unfortunately upon us. Amari has to leave." Arteryn filled her family in on what had transpired and the decision he had made as a way forward. Amari stood there, confused a little. In the past, Arteryn had been afforded many liberties on the farm and sometimes even regarding her upbringing decisions.

However, she had always found it rather curious how Joran and Tia had deferred to Arteryn at times when it came to her. Not only was he much younger than them, but he was their employee, yet here he stood telling them what he had decided would be the best course of action. And they were not disputing it! She watched their faces as Joran, with his thinning greying hair and tall lean built and Tia, with her dark hair peppered with grey and her round physique, nodded sombrely.

Amari wanted to ask why they agreed to Arteryn's decision and why Arteryn decided about her. Granted, they were not her parents biologically. They had adopted both her and Crispin because they could never have children of their own, but they were still the only parents she had ever known. They were her parents. So why was Arteryn making the decisions?

"Grantreal will come," Joran said soberly, apprehension coursing through him as he straightened. Arteryn nodded at him. Amari watched the look that passed between Tia and Joran. They seemed to be having a conversation with their eyes.

"Grantreal will not harm you. The promise I made to you when you opened your home to us still stands. Crispin and Tia will have to leave for a while until Grantreal leaves. I will be here with you; Joran and I will face him together."

Amari watched Arteryn address her parents and couldn't help feeling like there were things he was saying without actually saying them. There seemed to be an understanding of something Arteryn was saying that Amari wasn't getting. She stole a look at Crispin, who looked uncharacteristically bewildered with everything said. Her usually vocal and opinionated brother seemed at a loss of words.

"I have arranged for Korrigan to meet Amari. He will take her to Bhrim-"

"Bhrim? You said Gildevard?" Amari was aware she should be gathering her things, but if these could potentially be the last few moments she spent with her family, she didn't want to lose them.

"To Bhrim through Gildevard. Amari, you have to understand that it is important to keep as much distance between you and Grantreal, to throw him off your scent." Arteryn replied decisively then continued to brief Tia and Joran on what would happen, but Amari wanted to scream. She felt like yelling and tell him she couldn't go to Bhrim? Bhrim! That was even farther away than Gildevard. That was weeks of travelling on foot. Surely, they wouldn't give her the horse? It was a crucial asset to the operations of the farm.

It took all her strength to remain still, to keep herself from breaking down and crying, yet she knew she had to stay strong. If she fell apart now, Tia, Joran and Crispin would be more frightened for her than they already were. She had to assure them she was confident she would be all right, or they might do something that would put them and the farm in more danger than they already faced.

"Perhaps we could have someone go with her. To ensure she is safe." Tia suggested, looking pale and shell-shocked. It was clear she was trying to keep it together and failing spectacularly.

"Anyone else would be a hindrance to Amari. She is more skilled a fighter than almost everyone in this village." Arteryn slowly exhaled, regarding Tia and Joran with a beseeching look as he towered over everyone in the small kitchen. Amari couldn't remember how many suppers she had over the old kitchen table near the fire heath over the years, of the countless conversations Joran had shared about missing lambs and sheep.

She pondered the many arguments she had with her father about her dream of becoming a Sage Warrior. Joran unsuccessfully tried to talk her out of her dream over the years, and they had butted heads too many times over it. However, she knew without any doubt that they loved her unconditionally. Synia was home, the only home she had ever known, and she was a Leverood through and through.

Joran rubbed his large hand over the spotlessly clean tabletop, wiping away imaginary crumbs; his body held still as he looked up at Arteryn. "Perhaps... perhaps Amari could hide where Crispin and Tia are going?"

Arteryn shook his head slowly. "Grantreal will have someone watch the village for even a whiff of her." Arteryn sat down slowly, looking at the man across him pleadingly, begging for understanding. "I know, I understand it's not easy, Joran, but we both know she has to go. It was coming to this one day anyway. We knew she would leave eventually."

Amari gasped at Arteryn's words. Had he genuinely believed in her dream to be a Sage Warrior that much? Arteryn was the only person she knew who never told her she could not be a Sage Warrior when Amari told him why she was training. Instead, he had responded by saying if she had any hope of defeating the men in the Laurean Sage, she would have to train harder. Hearing that Arteryn had understood her well enough to know she would leave one day to try to be a Sage Warrior was the confidence she needed at that moment. He believed in her.

"Yes, but not this soon. I thought… I thought we had more time…" Tia wiped away tears that escaped down her cheeks, and she shook her head in frustration, wiping the tears away with her well-worn yet clean apron. She expelled a sigh of resignation then nodded. "I will gather provisions for her journey."

"Are you all insane?" Crispin finally spoke. Amari had been watching him, knowing this was coming. "Why are you going along with this? Why is everyone going along with Arteryn's decision as though there aren't any other alternatives?"

"Not right now, Crispin." Joran rose to his feet.

"Why can't we all leave? We're a family. How can we allow one of our own to go off on her own?" Crispin's resistance was something Amari had expected. She had expected Tia and Joran's resistance as well, which was why their easy acquiescence of Arteryn's plan stunned her. However, Amari hadn't expected Crispin's resistance. He had always found what he thought was her ridiculous dream of becoming a Sage Warrior exhausting and constantly reminded her that people would discover her powers if she left home. She would be labelled a witch, and he had been as protective of her as Arteryn.

"I'll go with her-"

"No." The finality of Joran's words echoed around the kitchen that was fast losing light as the sun started to set. "The decision has been made, Crispin."

"By Arteryn? Why?" Crispin went as far as to point at Arteryn dismissively as though he did not spend most of his time hero-worshipping the man. "Who is he to make the decisions?"

"Crispin-"

"No." He protested, cutting Joran off, which was something that never happened. It said a lot about how Crispin was feeling at that moment if he dared defy a father he loved and respected so much. "I know what everyone says. I know people say she has his eyes. I know people in the village think he's her father or something, but Amari is your daughter, and he is the farmhand-"

Amari bit back her words. So that was another rumour about her and Arteryn. Somehow, people couldn't seem to decide whether he was related to her or in a relationship with her. Deep down, silently, she was convinced it was the former even though he had never entertained any questions about it.

"Crispin!" Joran snapped impatiently.

"Crispin, I understand your concern for Amari. It's justifiable, and that is why we won't take anything you say right now personal, but we are losing precious time." Arteryn was the epitome of calm, his arms folded across his chest. He hadn't even reacted to Crispin's accusations.

Tia was scurrying around in the house gathering things, and Amari could hardly move, not after Crispin's accusations. So instead, she watched Arteryn, hoping for something, anything that would confirm what Crispin had said. In truth, Amari had spent many wasted hours over the years building castles in the sky where Arteryn turned out to be her father, but then Amari remembered he was only fourteen years older than her. In such cases, she then built him up as some relative to her, an uncle or older brother or something, but when she had said something along those lines to Arteryn, he had been so dismissive, and she had slunk away in humiliation.

"You mentioned a Korrigan? Is that the man I've seen you with several times over the years?" Crispin questioned, and his words drew an immediate reaction from everyone around the room that Amari picked up on. Tia's scurrying came to a halt, Joran tensed, and Arteryn frowned. "The man who looks like you? Who's older than you? I've seen you with him intermittently over the years, Arteryn. Who is he? Your brother?"

"Crispin, go help Amari gather her things-"

Amari stood rooted to the spot in the small kitchen, unable to move. How had she never seen this Korrigan that Crispin had seen for years? Was this man Arteryn's brother? Could it be? She looked at Arteryn dead on, but he didn't pay her any attention. Except for her and Tia, the others started to move around gathering things. She was leaving her family, and there were so many unanswered questions and revelations hanging all over them. If she could, if the threat of Grantreal did not exist, she would interrogate Arteryn about this Korrigan. Then again, without the danger, would she even know of Korrigan's existence?

"Amari, go gather some clothes, lass. Don't just stand there." Joran instructed, but Amari struggled to breathe, clasping her medallion so tight she was sure it would leave a crease on her palm. She had more questions about Arteryn now more than before. So many revelations in such a short time, and none shook her foundations more than Crispin's revelations.

"No dresses. That will attract attention." Arteryn instructed knowing Amari possessed enough clothes only men wore.

She rushed to the makeshift room partitioned in the house as hers. The Leverood house wasn't big or fancy. It wasn't as though they were of noble birth. They had just been fortunate to be given land and a stipend that had allowed them to build this house. Arteryn had built the extension that would become Amari's room himself a few years ago. Amari was sure she was the only person in the village who had their bedroom. She had thought nothing of it then, but now… there were so many things she had overlooked over the years that suddenly raised her hackles now.

Expelling a deep breath, she quickly changed out of what she was wearing, exchanging the slacks for thick tights and a long tunic slit on each side to allow free movement. Under the brown tunic, she put on a long-sleeved shirt then belted her tunic with just a regular belt.

First, however, she pulled off the buckle with the L and slid it into her things. A piece of home to take with her, she decided. She rolled a wool blanket secured it with a rope before pulling on her dark hooded cloak. Then, stuffing her feet into her well-worn leather boots, she straightened and looked around the tiny room that had been her sanctuary for years. She had entertained many hopes and dreams in this room, but this was not how she had wanted to leave home.

The plan had always been to go to the Great City of Sagar, and as she braided her long dark hair and threw the braid down her back, she decided at that moment. She would not be going to Gildevard. She was not going to wait around for some Korrigan to sweep her off to Bhrim. Honestly, this was too much of a coincidence to overlook. The Kingdom of Sagar would be hosting the Laurean Sage, where five new Sage Warriors would win their place in the King's Elite Guard in a few weeks. This was fate's way of pushing her towards her dream.

She would return home one day waving her Sage Warrior badge, and this would be all worth it- if Grantreal did not kill any of them in the process. Returning to the kitchen, she found Tia had already packed things into a leather backpack. Joran had rolled up another blanket, a thicker one that he secured onto the structured leather backpack. Amari pushed a few clothes into the bag. Tia informed her that she had put in some bread and cheese for her to eat. It would sustain her for a while, but she would have to find ways to get food on her journey.

Joran secured a pot to her backpack tightly and placed a canister of water on the table. Arteryn entered carrying a sword and a bow and arrow. Amari felt like she should say something, but she couldn't. She knew her parents were probably disappointed in what she had done, and the guilt and fear of the danger she had put them in seemed to constrict her ability to express herself.

Joran helped her put on the backpack even though she could have quickly done it herself. Arteryn came to her and secured a belt around her waist. He proceeded to place in two long blades and a sword in their holsters on the belt. Next, he handed her a long knife that she stuffed into her boot. Finally, he strapped on her arrows then draped the bow over her head and across her chest, making sure everything sat comfortably.

"Fire." Arteryn said quickly. Without hesitation, she opened her palm where a flame flicked to life, then he nodded, and she extinguished it. Did he even know what it did to her every single time she opened her palm and fire sprang out? That it felt like coming home? Amari had never told anyone, not even Arteryn, but she had discovered when Amari was fifteen that not only did she not burn from the flame she created from her hand, but no fire could burn her.

"Amari." Joran turned her towards him, his heavy brows cast down as he looked at her sombrely, his hands on her forearms. Emotion clouded his face, and her eyes stung as tears sprung to her eyes. "My little girl... You know, if I could, I would go on this journey with you. But unfortunately, it is physically painful for me not to, and I know for your mother as well that we have to let you go."

A sob escaped Tia's lips where she stood, and without preamble, she pushed herself forward, pulling Amari into her arms and holding her tightly. Joran wrapped his arms around them both.

"Come back to us one day, Amari. This farm is your home. It will always be your home." Joran's words came out broken as he struggled to keep himself together. Amari and Tia, on the other hand, were a mess. They were both sobbing and wiping their tears.

She felt arms come around her waist from the back and glanced behind her to see Crispin, whose eyes were suspiciously glistening.

"You're going to Sagar City, aren't you?" Crispin whispered in her ear, but Amari had no doubt Joran, Tia and Arteryn heard him. She broke down into another sob when he said that because these four people knew her so well. "Stay safe, Amari. Whatever you do, remember you always have to come home one day."

"Of course, I'll come home. The farm and Synia is my home." She wiped her tears away, inhaling sharply then releasing a shuddering breath. Was this going to be the last time she stood huddled in this tiny kitchen with her family? Would she ever have the opportunity to move through this house doing something as mundane as lighting the lamps and helping Tia serve supper ever again?

"Come back to me, Amari. I am your mother, and I will never be happy until you come home." Tia said desperately, and Amari could manage a nod. But, after that, she couldn't speak anymore, not as emotional as she was.

"It's time, Amari." Arteryn's words broke through the heavy silence that had settled over them. If Amari could delay this moment, she would, but she needed to leave.

"How will I know they are safe? That Grantreal hasn't killed anyone?" Amari's heart ached just asking Arteryn that question.

"Once I am certain Grantreal poses no threat here, I will follow you to Bhrim and update you," Arteryn replied as they all left the room, stepping outside into the cool evening air. It was the beginning of autumn, and in Synia, that meant cold nights.

"I'd rather you stayed here and protected everyone." She told Arteryn, but the look on his face told her he had decided already. If there was one thing she shared with this man apart from their complexion, it was his stubbornness. "Arteryn, you have to stay until I return. I need to know everyone is safe, and you're the only one who can keep them safe. Promise me."

"Are we going to pretend I am not going to follow you once I am certain Grantreal is no longer a threat here so that I can ensure that you are safe? Are we going to waste time having a pointless conversation?" Arteryn asked her, and she stood before him, tempted to swat him over the head. He infuriated her with his frankness at times.

"I hate you sometimes." She shoved Arteryn on the shoulder, her emotions threatening to suffocate her as she became conscious of the other farmhands returning from the fields with the livestock. She looked at Tia, Joran and Crispin standing behind Arteryn, each trying and failing to hold back the tears, and she sighed then turned to Arteryn. "You know I don't hate you."

"Of course, I do." Arteryn stepped forward, and just before his face disappeared out of her view as he drew her in for a tight hug, she saw something in his face that resembled the fear in the Leveroods' faces. In her ear, he said, "Use everything I have taught you and everything I know that you are capable of to survive, Amari. You're capable, and you're strong. Do not lose yourself on this journey. Always remember the things you were taught here, at home by Tia, by Joran, Crispin, and me. Trust in your gut feeling. Trust in yourself. Above all, trust in what you can do. And never forget that you are capable of doing it all."

Amari buried her face into his chest, melting into his warmth as his words washed over her. Her hands fisted on the front of his shirt, the urge to throw off her things and refuse to leave weighing heavily on her. She didn't want to let go. She was utterly terrified of what lay ahead. Arteryn made it easy for her, he drew back, and she saw it right there, in the corner of his eye, an unshed tear. She knew then, knew as she looked at this formidable man barely keeping it together, that nothing was ever going to be the same again.

CHAPTER THREE

In the end, much as she tried, she could not leave without making sure Grantreal didn't burn Synia to the ground. So, she hid out in the hills where she would have a clear view of Grantreal should he arrive while ensuring her location remained undetected, and she waited. Eventually, after the sun had long set, a group of men rode into the village. The self-control Amari exercised as she hid out in the hills where she couldn't hear but could see Joran and Arteryn meeting Grantreal and around twelve men was something she would never easily forget. For a heart-stopping fifteen minutes, Grantreal and his men went through the farm, overturning things, shouting her name and pushing the other farmhands around. She realised then that perhaps she should have used an alias in the Simiren pits. If she hadn't, then possibly finding an Amari from Synia would have been harder for Grantreal, Leverood belt aside. Torturous moments went by, and it took everything she had within her to not rush down the hill when Grantreal pushed Joran to the ground.

However, Arteryn remained by Joran's side, and in the end, Grantreal and his men left, hurling threats to return as they took one of Joran's livestock with him. Watching them travel south, Amari quickly slid away from her hiding spot and began on her journey.

She attempted to travel through the night until it became dangerous for both her and the horse. When she eventually slipped through the forest, she decided to risk it and call it a night. There was no point breaking her neck while fleeing.

Deciding to set up camp for the night with the resolution to leave at first light, she tucked herself in behind some shrubbery.

That night, as she lay curled near the tree wrapped in her blanket, she had a dream, one drastically different from what had plagued her for weeks now. It came at her out of nowhere, so fierce, so intense that when she snapped awake, the heavy feelings clung to her like second skin. She struggled to catch her breath, glancing around briefly to ensure she was safe, and the dream played itself in her mind as she lay back down slowly.

She had seen someone, not his face, but his eyes. Light green eyes, but there had been something so haunting about the eyes. She had sensed something looking into those eyes, such horrendous pain. The intense feelings that had washed over Amari as she had stared at those eyes had made her want to break down into inconsolable sobs. Yet, she didn't know what any of it meant. She knew that whoever she had seen in her dream had gone through unimaginable pain, that he- oh, she knew it had been a "he"- had suffered. She had felt his suffering deep into her bones.

Yet, something strange about her dream left her reeling. In a confusing moment, the man in the dream had appeared to be calling out to her. The dream shook her so much it took a while for her to fall asleep again finally.

Two things woke her up the following morning. First was the bug crawling over Amari's face that had her leaping to her knees to swat away anything else that might have thought to nibble on her in her sleep. The second, more urgent than the possible attack by the bug, was the two male voices raised in conversation floating her way.

She ducked her head quickly behind the shrubbery shielding her from view, her brain still scrambling awake. She took inventory of her surroundings, relieved that she was out of eyesight but anxious about why these two men had wandered this way. Why were they not using the roads? Could it be Grantreal's men searching for her? Were the Leveroods still alive, or had Grantreal returned and torched everyone at night? It took everything within her not to convince herself to retrace her steps and return home.

"I feel you are not listening to me, Forde!" One of the men snapped in frustration, and this drew Amari back to her present. Keeping out of sight, she assessed the two men who had stopped walking and were now engaging in an argument. Both men were tall, but one was taller. They both had dark hair, but she couldn't make out their features because she could only see their profiles. The taller one had a muscular athletic built, while the other seemed to be on the lean side. The taller, Forde, had shorter hair, while the slightly shorter one had hair that went past his shoulders and was intricately braided.

"I am listening, Korin! I am listening to everything you're not saying." Forde replied, gesturing with his hands to display his frustration.

They were standing next to their horses, two large breeds that could only come from wealth. Their clothes screamed wealth too. Amari could tell the quality of their shirts and boots was not like the course and cheap material worn in Synia.

"If you were listening, you would not be forcing me to go to Sagar against my will." Korin protested, and in response, Forde crossed his arms over his chest, his impatience showing.

"As opposed to what, Korin? Letting you stay in Orrick and lose you? No. I am doing this for you-"

"You're not letting me make my own decisions-"

"Korin, when you care for someone, you do everything in your power to keep them safe from others and even from themselves. Until you start showing that you're ready to make decisions for yourself that don't lead to you harming yourself in any way, I am going to continue making decisions for you." Forde pointed at Korin's chest for effect, and Amari's eyebrows shot up as she eavesdropped. Forde deflated, running his fingers through his hair before he turned slowly and she saw his face. Her breath caught in her throat. Whoa, she thought distractedly; he was good looking.

Amari, she scolded herself, what is the matter with you? These two could be with Grantreal. Growing up in Synia, she had never paid much attention to men, never bothering with the boys in the village because of her single-minded determination to become a Sage Warrior. As such, she had skipped out on a lot of things. Not to say she was a prude. No. Her determination to become a Sage Warrior made it that nothing, not even the boys in her village, could distract her. Well... that and the fact that Arteryn would have chased them away. This instance was the first time she had felt an instant attraction to any man in her life. Wait, they could be with Grantreal, she reminded herself cautiously.

Though, if she were honest with herself, she instantly knew they couldn't be. Something was gravitating towards her that she couldn't pin. It caused a shudder to run through her entire body as she gazed at the back of the man called Korin. She couldn't define it, she struggled to understand it, but whatever it was, she instantly felt it. Whatever "it" was. It felt familiar, intensely potent and she instantly felt drawn to the man who had his back to her.

"I'm sorry." Forde exhaled slowly then reached out a hand towards Korin. Korin visibly shrank from the oncoming touch, and Forde paused mid-air, a hurt look crossing over his face that he didn't mask. "Korin."

"I can't help it. I'm sorry. It just happens sometimes." Korin apologised, sounding frustrated with himself. Silence stretched between the two men, and Amari watched, waiting for the next move, when something hit her. Wait, they were travelling to Sagar. She was travelling to Sagar. They were using back routes, and if the sword Forde carried and the bow and arrow Korin had was anything to go by, perhaps these men could fight.

"I'm going to find us some food." Forde declared after a pregnant silence, but the reaction from Korin was instant.

"You're leaving me alone in the middle of a forest?" The panic in his voice instantly drew Amari to sit forward curiously. What was going on here? Why would a man who was possibly in his mid-twenties be afraid to be alone in a forest?

"I will stay in your line of vision, I promise," Forde assured him, but Amari saw the hesitation in Korin's body language. Then, finally, Forde took a step forward. "I promise. Just stay here. Don't go anywhere. I won't go far. All right?"

Korin reluctantly nodded, and Forde disappeared into the forest. Korin wrapped his arms around himself, slowly turning to take inventory of his surroundings. Amari wished she had a better view of his face, but she could tell he was young, and she could sense he was afraid. She was intrigued, and that impulsive part of her reared its ugly head. Don't meddle, Amari; she could almost hear Arteryn's words in her head. The truth was she couldn't help it at times. Since she was young, she had always felt the need to fight for the underdog or come to rescue someone in need. It had led to many hair-raising incidents that had given her family nightmares for weeks, but she had never regretted it.

At that moment, she felt an inexplicable urge to push through the brush and offer this man she didn't know comfort. But, instead, what she should be doing was walking away, ensuring she did not run into Korrigan, who might change her course and force her to go to Bhrim with him. Instead, she should leave to ensure she put as much distance between her and Grantreal while finding ways to pick up any news about Synia from anyone she met along the way.

Before she could decide, a cold blade pressed against her throat and chin, and she froze. A moment of utter panic flared within her as she expected to turn around and find Grantreal with his men standing there.

She didn't hesitate, reaching for her sword, she used her arm to knock the blade of the man from her. Then, in one fast move, she turned on her feet, sword in hand and struck. Her opponent blocked the blow, but she did not falter. Instead, she launched into a full-blown attack, metal clanging on metal as her opponent successfully met her blow for blow.

She never had in her life met anyone who was able to match her skill. The sheen of sweat breaking over her forehead was a sign of how much she was struggling. Yet, he did not let up, and he possessed such strength. His hood covered his face so she could not see him, but something about the colour of what he was wearing tugged at her memory.

As she went in for another attack, she stepped on a loose rock and lost her footing. Panic swelled inside as she staggered back. No!

Her arms flailed in the air as she fought for balance, her eyes still desperately trained on her opponent in case he made any further moves.

"Forde! Stop!" The voice that rang out in the air halted any further movements from her opponent as she fell to the ground. However, she was quick to spring to her feet and assume a defensive stance.

"Korin, stay out of this." The man across Amari said through gritted teeth, then his eyes seemed to focus on her, and he paused. Only then did she realise her hood had fallen off, and the man before her had made a realisation. "You're a woman!"

"What a revelation." She said mockingly, still braced in case he lunged at her. His sword was still pointedly facing her.

He didn't care for her tone, so when his surprise turned to annoyance quickly, she realised she could have played this better. She didn't need to torment him if he was not with Grantreal.

Her head jerked as his name finally registered in her mind. Forde? Wait, hadn't that been the name of the man who had been talking with the other man just a few minutes ago. How did he…?

He yanked his hood off his head, and for a moment, she was surprised.

Now that she had the man up close, she looked him over. He was probably in his mid-twenties too, and up close, she could see he had brown eyes, thick dark lashes, a thick head of dark hair, a wide mouth and a chiselled face. If he did not pose an immediate danger to her, she might have even appreciated that he was attractive, but her core focus was to get herself out of the situation alive. She didn't care that his physical built reminded her so much of Arteryn.

His blade travelled lower to capture the leather strap of the gold medallion before he lifted it towards her face.

"What is a woman doing lurking about in the woods at this hour?" Even though he was asking that, she knew the light must have hit her medallion and possibly alerted him to her presence.

Her eyes did not sway from him. Instead, she remained cautious, ready to swing at any moment should she feel threatened, but she did not appreciate his tone.

"Firstly, I do not lurk. Secondly, you came to me. I did not call you over." She challenged him, assessing him to see any signs of whether he was about to attack at any moment.

"Forde, can you stop harassing her, please." The man named Korin that Amari was yet to get a closer look at said from somewhere behind her.

His words seemed to annoy and possibly suck the fight out of Forde. Finally, Forde straightened, dropping his sword to his side and glared at Korin.

"I was not harassing her." He said defensively.

"You're bigger than she is and stronger. You have an advantage here." Korin pointed out, and Amari paused, surprised by Korin's stance on this. It was refreshing to meet a man who was conscious of such things. "She slept here. Look around you."

He didn't have to say that like she had splayed her things everywhere. Everything was tucked away in case she needed to grab and run.

"Only you would go in search of food and find a woman." Korin sounded disgruntled, and Forde let out a scoff.

What was happening right now? Was she not in danger anymore? She straightened, pushing her hair away from her face and instantly saw something flicker over Forde's face. Oh, that was awareness. He liked the way she looked. She could use that to her advantage.

He was taller than she was, perhaps closer in height to Arteryn, though, maybe just an inch shorter than him without a doubt. She could tell by how he stood that he possessed the skills of a trained warrior, and his clothes gave away his privileged upbringing. There was something about his skin tone too. He wasn't as fair as other Orrick people, but he also wasn't bronzed as her and Arteryn. He seemed to be somewhere in between.

"Why are you here?" Forde questioned her, and she glared at him.

"What does that have to do with you?" She retorted, refusing to give any form of advantage to this man.

She started to sense this man was not about to hurt her, but she did not want to make any assumptions, drop her guard, then get herself killed.

His eyes flicked to the gold medallion around her neck, and she hastily moved to tuck it under her clothes. "You can rob me of anything else except this."

"Rob you?" A mixture of disbelief and amusement crossed over the man's face at her words. "A man has a sword against you, and you think the only thing he would think to do to someone so beautiful is only robbing you?"

"So, you think I'm beautiful?" A slow smile formed on her lips as she jutted her hip. His eyes followed the movement, and she knew she had him.

"What? Is that all you caught in what I've said?" Then, amusement went and confusion reigning in the man, she realised if she played this right, she might get away from this man in one piece.

"That you find me attractive?"

"I didn't say I found you attractive."

"You did say she was beautiful." Korin pointed out, and Forde groaned in frustration as if to tell him he was not helping the situation at all.

"Yes, but..." The man trailed off, exasperation pouring from him, and Amari hid a smile. This engagement was almost too easy. Finally, the man straightened his face, apparently deciding he would no longer waste his time. "What are you doing out here by yourself?"

"My business is my own." She responded defiantly, wearing him thin.

Amari finally decided to look at this Korin, who had been passing little comments throughout her strange exchange with Forde. But the moment she laid eyes on him; she froze.

She gaped at the man, utterly astounded. Two things instantly hit her all at once. One, he had the same light green eyes as the man she had seen in her dream and two... Two... He was stunning!

CHAPTER FOUR

S he had never seen anything like it in her life. The only way she could describe what she was looking at was beautiful, in an indescribable manner. Had it not been for obvious male tell-tale signs, she could have easily mistaken him for a woman.

He had a perfectly asymmetrical face with high cheekbones and full plump lips. His perfectly sculptured eyebrows hung over long lashes that framed haunting light green eyes. Those were the light green eyes from Amari's dream. It almost felt like he could see right through Amari. But, instead, Korin's intense gaze drew something within her, something that continued to build from her dream and wrap itself around her in the most puzzling manner.

A few strands of his long thick dark hair framed his shockingly attractive face, and he stood there with the sort of presence that left her slightly dizzy. This man had the looks of someone who would make men question their sexuality and make women envy the sensuality he exuded.

She never had in her life felt so inferior to a man. At least, when it came to looks because it wasn't what was on his face that hit her hard, but what she saw that lingered behind his expression. This stunning lean man in a long-sleeved black shirt, a dark vest and long black form-fitting leather pants with curiously many thin belts crisscrossing over his narrow hips whose clothing screamed wealth gazed at her with the same tortured soul she had seen in her dream. Two things about him instantly made themselves prominent to her. One, the man's colouring was as dark and bronzed as hers and Arteryn's skin. As such, his light green eyes stood out of his gorgeous face. Two, it was almost impossible not to want to reach out to him.

She didn't know what it was, she didn't understand, but something inside her was screaming for her to go to him. It held her in its grip, almost like a force pushing her towards him. If she could explain it, she would say it felt like hands caressing her and drawing her towards him. Yet, it was in no way sexual. Instead, this felt different, familiar, like kinfolk. Its potency stunned her, wrapping around her like home. It was terrifyingly beautiful and welcoming.

"Unbelievable." The word slipped out of her mouth before she could tame her thoughts. "You are unbelievably stunning. I have never..."

The man's reaction to her words amazed her. He didn't seem surprised by it at all. He shrugged almost as though this was nothing new to him. Then again, she thought that compliments must have been naturally expected as the sunrise if she had gone through life looking as he did. If anything, he regarded her with disinterest as he turned to look at his companion.

"Put the sword away, Forde." It almost sounded like an accusation, one that Forde merely scoffed at, and Amari barely managed to pull her eyes from the visually stunning man.

"Korin, not right now, please." Forde lifted his sword, which Amari had somehow forgotten. Seriously, he was still doing this? She returned her eyes to Korin, something else entirely gripping her attention as she looked at him. It was confusing and unbelievable all at once. A radiant layer hung around him that she hadn't seen before. It gave off waves of energy that gravitated towards her, tapping into something within her that she could not define. In a split second, she felt instantly connected to this man in a way she thoroughly failed to understand. Then, almost at once, that glow around Korin seemed to disappear, and she saw once more the irritated man standing there with his arms folded across his chest.

As she looked him over, she couldn't help noticing the exhaustion that seemed to weigh heavily on him. He looked a little on the thin side, but it appeared to be more of a side effect of something rather than a natural built. If he could look pale, she could have said he was because there was an unhealthy look about him. She knew instantly, this man had suffered, and he suffered still. As she stole a glance at Forde, she saw the exhaustion in him as well, and their earlier conversation rang in her head. Something had happened, something significant, and these men were clawing their way back from whatever it was together.

Pushing past Forde, she headed straight for Korin. The inexplicable urge to touch this man, the confusing overpowering desire to soothe him, rushed her. The medallion against her skin suddenly grew warm, something it had never done before, and for a moment, she felt caught in time. What were these strange feelings coursing through her right now? What was this feeling of familiarity she was experiencing as her eyes locked with the light green eyes of the man standing before her?

"This is going to sound ridiculous, but I feel like I should know you. Or rather like I already do but on an intrinsic level. I saw you in my dream last night." Wow, that sounded creepy, she realised as she briefly looked away from him as she cringed. Then, pushing on, she returned her eyes to him, expecting to find annoyance from Korin, but instead, he seemed to be studying her. Goodness, the man was stunning! She had never seen anything like it in her life. He must have had women throwing themselves at him wherever he went. Probably a lot of men too. Waving her hands in the air as she fumbled for an excuse for her rather forward behaviour, she looked at him imploringly.

"I apologise. It's just that you don't feel like a stranger to me. I know it sounds insane. So, ignore me, I tend to ramble a lot of nonsense, but I feel like I should know you. Does that make sense?"

"You're ridiculous," Forde said under his breath behind her, but she ignored him, completely still drawn to the man in front of her.

Korin seemed to be looking her over, assessing her. She crazily thought that, for a split second, she saw his eyes flash, but that had to be the light piercing through the tall trees. Then, while his arms remain crossed over his chest, she thought she saw a little of his aloofness slowly ebb away, just a smidge.

For a moment, a very long moment, he didn't speak. He just stared at Amari, and emotions seemed to play out across his stunning face. It was brief, but she saw something flicker there. Recognition? Was it possible? They had never met. She was sure they had never met. However, something about him was so familiar.

"Your name wouldn't happen to be Amari, would it?" When he spoke to her in that cautious tone, her hackles went up.

"How do you know?" Were they with Grantreal? Had she made a mistake? Nothing about these two men screamed threat to her. At all. Her instincts leaned in the opposite direction, but that this one knew her name? That had her going on the defensive. Did Grantreal have a bounty on her head? It would be too soon for news to have travelled so fast though. It had only been yesterday when she had defeated him in the Orrick fighting pits.

"You were in my dream last night. Your name is Amari." It was not a question. It was a statement, and strangely, the man didn't look as bewildered by the news as she felt.

"And you don't find that strange?" She had never experienced such a coincidence in her life. But, of course, these things didn't happen.

The man released a sigh as he shifted his weight from one hip to another then shook his head. "Not really."

"I..." Her mouth opened, nothing came out, and she closed it. All she managed was a nod to confirm her name. "You're Korin. I didn't get that from my dream. I heard when your companion said your name. You didn't exactly speak in my dream. You just looked at me and felt like you were calling to me."

"This is turning into the strangest encounters I have ever had the misfortune to engage in," Forde commented in exasperation, his sword now sheathed as he expelled a sigh. "Strange and fascinating at the same time."

Amari's heart skipped a beat and not in a good way. Why would Forde say that? He was so blasé about it too, like if that were the case, he wouldn't be surprised. She could tell he no longer posed a threat to her anymore; however, she was still cautious.

Korin's eyes shifted from Forde to Amari, then back at Forde, and his eyes flashed again. A small smile curved his lips for a brief second before he turned back to Amari. "You and I are going to be in each other's life for a long time."

Amari could feel that too. She wasn't even surprised that he said it. It just felt like a confirmation of something she instinctively felt.

"You carry something compelling with you." Korin continued, lifting a long slim hand to brush away strands of hair that the wind had blown to his face. He was so elegant, she thought enviously. He managed to make that simple act so alluring.

His words finally pierced her brain, and she frowned at what he had just said. "The only powerful thing I have with me is my sword."

Korin tilted his head to the side, chewing the inside of his mouth as her words seemed to flicker something in him. "Yes, I think so. It feels like a sword. I'm not making much sense, am I?"

She saw it again that flicker in his eyes, and then his face changed. The curiosity was gone, replaced by a sudden apprehension.

"You're trouble."

"Excuse me?"

"You bring trouble with you."

"I find that offensive."

"And yet it's true. So, who is chasing you?"

"I don't know what you're talking about." This moment was hardly the time to reveal how painfully accurate this man was. It shook her. She had never met someone so forthright. And was it usual for someone's eyes to keep flickering like that?

"Korin, if we are to make it to the inn by tonight, we must be on our way." Forde had reached his limit with this engagement. "And we need to find food because someone finished everything I packed last night."

"You're the only one always telling me I need to eat more, and when I do, you're suddenly complaining," Korin said almost defensively, but Forde's reaction surprised Amari. He almost looked apologetic?

She shook her head then moved towards her things on the ground, but conscious of each movement they made. While she rolled her blanket, keeping her eyes on them, she saw the look Korin trained on her. He was watching her intensely as though he was assessing her.

He tilted his head to the side, showing her his long and graceful neck as she hoisted her bag over her shoulders, then narrowed his eyebrows with suspicion.

"Amari is not an Orrick name."

"Neither is Korin." At least, she didn't think so. "Neither is your complexion. Nor mine for that matter."

He moved towards her slowly, an analytical brow shooting up. She stood still, waiting. He started to move around her slowly, assessing her from head to toe. She didn't feel in any immediate danger, and Forde had abandoned any pretence of trying to impose a threatening stance on her. She should have been concentrating on putting as much distance between her and Grantreal, and here she was wasting time with these two men. Arteryn would be livid at her carelessness. However, he had told her to trust her gut feeling and right then, it was telling her something about these two men that she couldn't quite decipher.

"You're not from here. You sound like you are from here, but you were not born here." It didn't come out as an accusation from Korin but rather an observation. A very accurate one at that.

"I'd say the same for you." She returned, careful to stand still.

He did not respond immediately but continued to analyse her. "You're pretty with no visible scarring of hard lines on your face to show a hard upbringing." He lifted his hand and then shoved it against her shoulder. She yielded but did not stumble. "You're strong." He continued with his clinical analysis of her that was leaving her quite captivated.

"You have long, healthy hair and a healthy glow on your face. You have led a rather sheltered life, but you're bursting with curiosity." He surprised her by taking her hands into his and turning them over in his hands before dropping them. "You probably grew up on a farm because your hands are too calloused to be those of a lady; however, you didn't do so much labour that it would break your back. Beautiful almond-shaped eyes, good posture. A credit to a mother who used to tell you to sit up straight and not slouch? You can fight. Not basic either. Possibly advanced. You have a strong male influence in your life."

What? What was happening right now? How was this man reading her like she was an open book? How could he deduce all these facts about her when he didn't even know her? "How can you tell?"

"The way you were standing when I came upon you and Forde." He responded with a careless shrug of his slim shoulder, then folded his arms across his chest, turning back to Forde. "She's no thief, but she is up to mischief. Probably running away from home for one reason or another."

"You're terrifying." The words were out of her lips before she could think about their implication. She had just unwittingly confirmed Korin's assumptions with that uncalculated response. Forde was standing where she had left him, his eyes on Korin as he watched his companion with what seemed to be disbelief. However, his face suddenly softened as he gazed at Korin. The affection on his face was enough to tell Amari these two men shared a very close bond.

Could it be? She mentally shook her head. Arteryn had once told her of men who preferred the company of other men. Could Forde and Korin be such men? She didn't want to assume because Korin was effeminate in his gestures and looks. However, Arteryn had said it had nothing to do with how someone looked. Besides, Korin had suggested Forde was something of a lady's man with that comment he made when he came upon them.

As much as she couldn't understand the insane need within her to be in Korin's life, she knew it was time she was on her way. But unfortunately, she had lingered here far longer than was wise to do so. As a result, she had wasted precious minutes that could mean life or death.

"Where are you headed?" Forde had pulled his gaze from Korin and was now regarding her with suspicion once more.

"Wouldn't you like to know?" She threw at him.

"I wouldn't be asking if I didn't." He moved quickly and blocked her exit towards her horse with his larger body. She craned her neck and looked up at him, patiently releasing a sigh of frustration. He did not seem fazed by her reaction. If anything, he remained calm and patient, something that seemed like a well-practised reaction.

She met his eyes directly. "Gildevard."

"That would make sense if Gildevard weren't in the other direction," Korin muttered, and she turned an annoyed look his way.

These two men were going to Sagar. She had heard that much. She was going to Sagar, but she had never left home alone before, so she wasn't sure she was even going in the right direction. She knew the journey to Sagar could be dangerous to someone without the proper know-how. She did not want to end up in the middle of Sinagora Forest or the Dewr Mountains by mistake. She had heard many things about those places and the number of men who had lost their lives there.

Would they be a benefit or a hindrance on the journey to Sagar- that is, if they agreed to let her go with them? Confronting Grantreal with two men by her side would certainly be better than doing it alone. Was she wrong to draw these two men into her precarious circumstances? She knew one thing; she was beyond curious to get to know Korin because apart from her and Arteryn, she had never seen someone with their colouring before. Also, there was that pesky supernatural pull the man seemed to have.

"Why are you travelling alone? A young woman like yourself should have a chaperone." Forde's eyes narrowed as his suspicion grew. "Did you commit a crime? Are you on the run?"

"I didn't commit any crime, but I am running from something." She confessed and realised she needed a cover story. There was no point divulging everything yet.

"I'm running away from an arranged marriage. The man is too old and unsuitable for me. So, the plan is to run to Sagar City and start a new life."

"I don't believe that at all." This information piqued Korin's interest, and she froze. His ever-perceptive eyes watched her, and she wondered if he would call her out on her lie. "You seem like the type who would choose her own husband and let him know she had made the decision later."

"You're not wrong, which is why I am on the run. My potential groom is on my trail with his men searching for me, which is why I must stay off the roads. He... he isn't a good man. He has a certain reputation and can be considered dangerous... So, I'm better off making my own life in Sagar than married to him." She trailed off for effect, and of course, it had the desired result. She had seen from the little exchange between Forde and Korin that Forde was a nurturer. A woman in distress would not be something he would be walking away from without trying to help.

The two men exchanged looks, and Forde massaged the back of his neck, then released a sigh.

"Forde and I are going to Sagar as well… Perhaps, if you behaved, we might let you join us." But, boy, did Korin look like he wished he was not extending that invitation.

"We?" Forde pinned Korin with a glare, but Korin ignored him.

All right, so they were getting somewhere, but she still needed to make her terms clear.

"I have to stay off the roads, and I have to travel without detection. So, my pace will be vigorous and not leisurely. Should the man find me, I may have to fight to get away from him. So, what I am saying is my situation has the potential for dangerous encounters." She winced then waited to hear whether Korin would rescind his invitation.

Forde turned to Korin then walked up to him. She watched as they spoke in hushed voices. She could tell by their gestures that they were disagreeing, and when Korin shrugged his shoulders dismissively and nodded, Forde turned back to her then released a sigh.

"Fine. You can come with us because Korin insists. I wanted a very uneventful journey, but I have a feeling with you around, nothing is going to be the same again." Forde muttered, then expelled a sigh. "I have one request. Be respectful."

Somehow, she had a feeling his request was not for his behalf but rather for Korin. She nodded, relieved that she was not going to be alone. She liked talking to people. She never ran out of things to say, and because she didn't know how to get to Sagar, she was thankful she had people with her.

"Great." Relief flooded her because she didn't particularly like being alone. "I have one request."

"And it begins," Forde said under his breath.

She ignored him. "You stumbled on me just as I was waking up. I haven't had the opportunity to take care of a few morning activities…"

"What?" Both men looked confused.

"You know? My womanly things."

The identical grimace that crossed over their faces made her wonder if they were related, but it was the reaction she had been going for anyway. Nothing made men more uncomfortable than a woman talking about her woman things, and they would do anything to make her stop.

"All right, get on with it. We must be on our way. The last thing we need is to have your husband coming upon us." Forde said quickly, and she arched her eyebrows at his tone.

"He's not my husband. I ran away to make sure of that." She waved him away then smiled sweetly at Korin. "Thank you for letting me join you."

"Go away already," Korin told her quickly, and she laughed at him then promptly walked away to take care of business. After what was undoubtedly the most unconventional conversation she had ever had with random strangers, Amari had a feeling that, just as Forde had predicted, nothing was going to be the same again.

CHAPTER FIVE

O ver the next twenty-four hours, Amari convinced herself that Forde and Korin were more than just close friends. The way they interacted with each other was suspect. She had managed to persuade them the night before not to use the inn, which drew a groan from Forde about how she was already making demands. However, there had been nothing malicious in his protests. On the contrary, she found him to be very accommodating. He was, however, intensely protective of Korin. Intensely so.

She noticed little things like how his hackles rose when they encountered men on the road and how Korin seem to gravitate closer to him when someone else happened upon them. Yet, there was something off about their relationship. It was killing her not to ask the questions burning inside her.

This morning as she had returned from tending to her woman things again, she had stumbled upon them standing close and speaking in hushed voices, then Korin had leaned into Forde. A strange expression had crossed over Forde's face before he had wrapped an arm around Korin's waist. Korin had dropped a kiss on his cheek before he had stepped away.

At that point, Amari had made her presence known, but they hadn't acted like they had been caught by her doing something unconventional.

Amari was not sure what she had just witnessed. She may have grown up in Synia, relatively sheltered, but she had seen things. She had seen something that she knew about Arteryn that she had never had the guts to ask him. Maybe Korin and Forde were just close. Perhaps she was reading into it.

As they rode through a flat plain with tall brown grass and no trees for as far as the eye could see, she decided to broach this subject bravely. The autumn winds had picked up a little as they travelled, causing a gentle lean to the willowy grass.

Forde rode behind her while Korin rode in front of her, humming in a low voice. They had ridden hard in the morning to extend any lead she might have on Grantreal but had reduced their pace to a stroll now to accommodate the horses. That impulsive part of her reared its ugly head, and as much as she tried, Amari just couldn't tamper her curiosity about these two men. Something had been gnawing at her since she had seen how close Forde slept next to Korin last night.

"May I be permitted to ask a question that will without a doubt incur your wrath?" She shouldn't ask, but she couldn't help it. It was none of her business. Honestly, she should just let it go, but she was Amari, after all.

Korin turned a corked brow her way. She really shouldn't ask.

"If you know the consequences, why bother?" He questioned, and she shrugged. Sagar was a long way away. Weeks of travel. It was without a doubt that she would eventually get to know these two men she was putting her trust in not to slaughter her at night while she slept. However, this was something she had to address upfront.

"Call me a glutton for punishment." She gave a dismissive shrug, catching the look that passed over her head between Forde and Korin.

Deciding she had to see both their faces when she asked, Amari drew her horse forward to be in front, then turned around to face them.

However, now that she was standing there, she could see just how tense Forde was. She hadn't noticed that before, but now she did. He looked on edge; his teeth clenched tightly.

She sighed. "You know, Forde, if you clench your jaw any tighter, you will be toothless by the time you get to Sagar. You're good looking, but even the most accommodating woman will draw the line at a toothless man."

The sudden bark of laughter from Korin caused Forde's head to jerk back, and Amari watched the stunned look on the man's face. Was Korin's laugh such a rarity that caused such a reaction from Forde? She thought back to the conversation she had eavesdropped on when Forde had accused Korin of trying to hurt himself. She wasn't blind. She could see Korin was dealing with something that was weighing Forde down, but if their conversation was anything to go by, it was much more severe than she realised.

"I said the same thing to him just last week," Korin commented when he tempered down his laughter that, as she looked at Forde, seemed to be affecting him, like a soothing balm on a wound.

"Well, now that you've both amused yourself at my expense..." Forde grumbled, and this only amused Amari. The man was charming when he did that. She had strangely become aware of little things Forde did that she found cute. "What did you want to ask that would earn our wrath?"

Amari took a deep breath then bit her lower lip. Should she? She should, she resolved.

"Are you two romantically involved?"

The moment the words were out, it suddenly felt like everything around them had come to a screeching halt. A lone bird pulled away from the grass and flew away. The silence that followed was deafening.

She waited for their wrath, for the outrage, for the words of fury that would surely follow, but all she received was silence. Forde and Korin glance at each other then looked back at her with mirrored expressions of calm composure.

She rushed to fill in the silence. "It isn't my intention to offend you. I was just curious. It's just that the way you two are with each other..."

"What about it?" Forde asked, still looking calm. She, on the other hand, was sweating under that unwavering gaze. They were going to make this as awkward for her as possible.

"You're quite...affectionate with each other." She supplied cringing. She shouldn't have asked.

"And men shouldn't be affectionate with each other?" Forde continued. A sound of agony escaped her lips as she rubbed the back of her neck with embarrassment.

"They should. I am not saying men shouldn't. They should." Words tumbled out of her mouth as she flailed her hands about awkwardly. "Arteryn once told me about men who preferred the company of other men, and I wondered if you two were such men."

"Because we're affectionate with each other?"

"Forde put her out of her misery. She is so embarrassed it's hilarious." Korin interjected as an amused looked crossed over his face. He turned to Amari and released a sigh. "If only you knew how often we got that question, but honestly, you shouldn't ask people such questions."

She released a sigh of relief. So good, they were not about to send her away for obviously crossing the line.

"I know. Arteryn tells me I need to think things over before I say them at times." She confessed guiltily.

"Who's Arteryn?" Forde asked.

"Just answer the question." The words rushed out quickly.

"Worried we'll grope you in your sleep?" Korin asked, and she let out a sound of exasperation. Why couldn't they answer the question? Korin let her out of her misery at last. "All right, fine. No, Forde and I are not in a romantic relationship. We have never been. We never will be because, despite how stunningly handsome he is, he is not my type. Even though we are not related by blood, we may as well be brothers. We are both protective of each other, we love each other dearly, and no one- not even a woman- can come between us."

Whoa, that was a loaded response, Amari observed, and she frowned in confusion as she processed what Korin had just said. "Wait..."

"Yes, Amari. I am attracted to men and not women. I mean, I appreciate how pretty you are, but you do nothing for me. On the other hand, Forde is attracted to women and between the two of us is the one who finds you attractive."

"Korin!" Forde flushed at Korin's bluntness while Amari blushed. She may have had a sheltered life, but she was not blind. Amari had seen Forde glance her way a few times. Granted, she had equally glanced his way too. However, the man was quite attractive, and his attentiveness towards Korin was something Amari liked. Now that she knew they were not romantically involved, something started to bloom inside her.

"Are you satisfied?" Korin's question interrupted her musings, and she nodded. "And now that you know about me, what do you intend to do with the information?"

She shrugged dismissively. "Eh, nothing. Who cares what I think? It's your life, and it's not like anyone's opinion would change who you were born to be."

Her thoughts gravitated towards Arteryn again. She was almost sure he was like Korin too. It could be because she had once caught him kissing a man in the shed, and he hadn't known she was there. She had never told him about it.

"How progressive of you." There was something on Korin's face that Amari saw even though he pretended to be all casual and relaxed. Relief. He looked relieved.

"Well, Arteryn is a very progressive person, and he opened up my mind to many possibilities."

"Who is Arteryn? I feel like you're always talking about him." Was that irritation in Forde's voice? Interesting.

"I don't know how to explain him. He is everything."

"What does that even mean?"

"Well, he is only fourteen years older than I am, but sometimes I feel as though he's like a second father to me- not an older brother. A father. He likes to act that way. However, I can talk to him about almost anything. We're so close people can't decide if they think we are related or should get married. I should point out, nothing sexual has ever happened between Arteryn and me. As I said, father. He loves me as much as I love him. He has heavily influenced my outlook on many things. A part of me believes we're related because many people like to point out I have his eyes- that and the fact that he and I are the only people in our village who look like this. He is fiercely protective of me- and that is not an exaggeration. He encourages me to be me. He has never tried to make me something I am not. He understands me in a way no one does. He's my best friend and a father figure in my life. Honestly, I cannot imagine life without him. He has been in my life since I was five years old and worked as a farmhand on our farm."

Silence followed again as both men regarded her quizzically.

"What?"

"Are you sure you're not in love with him?" Korin asked, and Amari grimaced, then gagged.

"I think Arteryn is most likely to fall in love with you than a woman. Just thought you should know." With that, she turned and rode off, leaving them stunned.

When they paused in the afternoon to water the horses on a plain with many boulders and rocks, she leaned against a large rock, her eyes scanning the area around them. She was ever alert for any signs of anyone approaching. She missed home. She missed seeing her family. Yet, even her adventurous spirit couldn't tamper down her yearning for the farm.

"Why the forlorn look?" Forde asked as he came up to her, handing her one of the apples they had swiped on a tree an hour ago. She looked up at him, blinking as she pulled herself away from thoughts of home.

She shrugged in response, wishing not for the first time that she had not gone to the Orrick pits. That single decision was the reason she was here now, constantly looking over her shoulder, fearing for her family's life.

"Normally, we cannot get you to keep quiet." Forde continued, and she narrowed her eyes at him in a warning. He smirked in response then bit into his apple. Even though he towered over her, she didn't feel intimidated or like he was towering over her. She didn't know why she felt so quickly comfortable with this man. She knew she liked him.

"You like it when I talk." She challenged, testing to see how he would respond to that.

His smirk slowly disappeared as his eyes caressed over her face. "Missing home?"

Was she that transparent? "A little."

"You know we don't believe your story about the arranged marriage, right?"

When she spoke about Arteryn, she had revealed a lot that she wasn't surprised they would start poking holes at her cover story.

"I can't tell you the truth yet. There is a man after me, a terrible man, but it's not about marriage."

"What did you do, Amari?"

"I...I wounded the man's ego, I suppose. It shouldn't be an issue. It shouldn't have led to me fleeing home. It just doesn't feel that important a thing to cause him to react the way he did. However, it turns out the worst thing a woman can do to a man is hurt his ego- especially when he has a reputation to protect. That's all I can tell you right now."

Forde suddenly looked apprehensive, which quickly gave way to concern. "Is he intending to kill you?"

She looked away from him as she considered the situation. She may know very little of Grantreal, but she knew of men like him. Men like him razed villages to the ground if you so much as looked at them funny. But they were protected by certain lords and were able to do things most people couldn't get away with.

She worried her lower lip as she considered what Grantreal would do when he eventually found her. Had he not gone to the Leverood farm, she might have believed Arteryn was overreacting. However, the fact that he had meant he was in pursuit of her. The influential thing for him now would be to regain his image in front of everyone, and she supposed that would happen at great humiliation at her expense.

"I think maybe when he is done with me, I will be pleading for death." Her eyes suddenly stung with unshed tears as it finally hit her what she was running from. She knew what a man like Grantreal would do to her when he found her. First, he would rape her then probably pass her along to his men. He would then drag her back to Orrick to parade her before everyone she had humiliated him in front of. By that time, she would probably be damaged beyond repair and would have long since begged for death.

She shuddered, the gravity of the situation finally hitting her. What would happen if Grantreal didn't find her? Would he go back to Synia and hurt her family, perhaps have his men hurt Tia.

A breath of fear tore from her lips as she hurriedly turned her back to Forde and shuddered. Then, taking in gulps of air as she blinked rapidly to stay the tears, she tried to push the fear down. What had she done?

She jumped when Forde suddenly placed his hand on her shoulder, but she did not turn around.

"I'm not going to let anyone hurt you. I don't know what happened, but you can rest assured, Korin and I will protect you."

His words were surprising, and as she turned around to look at him, she saw the determination on his face. He meant it too, and she could see that. Despite hardly knowing her, despite not knowing the actual circumstances, this man was still willing to put his life on the line for her.

"There's about twelve of them- the men after me and only three of us." It was better he understood the gravity of this situation before he committed himself to it.

"Well, considering how you were even with me when we fought yesterday, I'd say we can take them on." He patted her shoulder then froze as though he suddenly realised what he was doing. His eyes moved from his hand to her face, and she could tell he didn't seem to know how to proceed from this point.

"I won't dissolve into a puddle of tears just because you touched my shoulder, Forde." She teased him as he hastily removed his hand from her, and he flushed. It was such an endearing reaction.

"If you two are done flirting, can we be on our way?" Korin's frank words caused Forde to throw him an admonishing look while Amari blushed. She had never flirted in her life, wouldn't even know where to begin. However, Amari was keen to learn. In fact, with Forde around, she found she was eager to do a lot of things. Maybe this journey would provide opportunities for her to explore her sexual side too.

As they rode, she found her thoughts gravitating back home but fought the panic welling inside her. No, she couldn't turn around now. She had to continue forward and just hope her family remained safe. Arteryn wouldn't be surprised that she chose to go to Sagar, but he would be disappointed that she had deviated from the agreed-upon plan. Besides, she knew that he would find her wherever she went. He seemed to have a knack for that.

"So, where are you from in Orrick?" Forde thankfully broke the silence, drawing Amari out of her musings.

"Around. You?" She asked, and he responded by corking a brow at her, then he shrugged.

"Simiren, capital of Orrick. Both my parents died when I was very young, and my uncle raised me. He is the Lord of Orrick."

Amari choked at the revelation as she realised whom she was trekking the wildlands of Orrick with. His clothes had hinted he grew up wealthy, but it had never occurred to her that she was with the nephew of the Lord of Orrick. Oh no, she realised as her mind latched on her knowledge of Orrick. Forde was the nephew of Lord Gregaria, who had lost his parents when mercenaries had brutally massacred his village. He had been the sole survivor of that massacre. However, she was not going to bring that up.

"I've never met anyone of noble birth before. I thought you'd be different." She was going to avoid what she knew about his past as much as possible until he brought it up.

"How should I be different?" He asked, and the instant response that almost slipped out and would surely have embarrassed her, died in her lips, and Forde released a sigh of frustration as he drew to a halt. "Amari, it has been obvious since we met you that you're someone who says what is on their mind. Can we not change that? I don't do deception. I like people who are open and express themselves. Be yourself. I am used to people who don't censor themselves. I've had Korin in my life since I was eighteen, and he is known for being very frank. So, please, stop overthinking things and talk."

"Easy for you to say, you never have to worry that something you say will cause you hours of embarrassment later on when you have to overthink everything-"

"Then get over it. Just speak your mind." Forde stated, cutting her off. Left in stunned silence, Amari gasped. Speak her mind? Had he just told her that? Was it possible this man was not put off by her oddities? Something fluttered in her chest, but she quickly tampered it down. This journey was not the time to develop a weird crush on a man purely because he encouraged her to be herself.

She shrugged. "I just assumed noble men were rude, entitled and had no regard for anyone but themselves. But, of course, I haven't known you long, but I think I can already deduce you are not any of those things." She kept her eyes on him, waiting to see if he would be annoyed, but he seemed amused. "Does this make you Lord Forde?"

That amused look turned into a smile that- she almost gasped- caused very unfamiliar butterflies in her stomach. No, she reminded herself, she had a plan for her life, and it did not involve any man. However, there would technically be nothing wrong with experimenting while on this journey if Forde was open to it. This journey was her first journey, her first foray into freedom. Maybe she could let her hair down just a bit and experience things she had tampered down growing up.

"No one calls me that."

"Lord Forde."

"It sounds terrible."

"Yes, it does, doesn't it?" She agreed, and she was surprised when he laughed.

"I'm not much for titles. Just call me Forde."

Mm, that was a first. Amari assumed noble people liked to go about throwing their titles around. "Why are you travelling to Sagar?"

A look crossed over his face briefly, but it was gone before she could decipher it. She thought to what she had overheard earlier on, where Korin had complained that Forde was forcing him to Sagar even though he didn't want to go there.

"Why is anyone travelling to Sagar around this time?" Forde responded and a longing smile formed on her lips.

The Laurean Sage, she thought. She supposed many people were making their way to the Great City of Sagar for the annual games. Every year, men tried their luck, participating in the gruelling tasks in the arena where the king declared only five victors as Sage Warriors at the end of the tournament. However, it came with a steady income, lodgings, the honour of guarding the king and land upon retirement.

She had never seen the Laurean Sage, but she had heard about it when she had been very young. It had planted a seed, and she had dreamed of the day everyone would finally know her name as the first female Sage Warrior and the biological family that had discarded her would hopefully feel guilt when word reached them of her success. If they still lived. It hurt to think about the people who had abandoned her with the Leveroods as a three-year-old little girl.

She had no recollection of them or the life she had lived before being dumped in Synia. Sometimes, she had very vivid dreams, or maybe a scent would catch her nose and tickle a vague memory, but never anything tangible. For instance, she knew the lavender scent meant something important to the Amari she had been before she became a Leverood. Crispin had accused her of trying to become a Sage Warrior to overcompensate for her abandonment issues.

For someone who the Leveroods had also adopted as a baby, Crispin possessed none of her problems. He never wished to know anything about the family he came from. He accepted himself purely as the child of Joran and Tia Leverood, and his dream in life was to take over the farm from Joran one day and carry forth the Leverood name. Amari loved her adoptive family, but the fire that formed in her hand and her colouring made it impossible for her not to realise she was different and to wonder about her origins.

Her hand flew to her chest, clasping the medallion hanging around her neck. This medallion was the only thing she had left from the day she had been brought to the farm, her only connection to the person she had been, and it was her most prized possession. She had always hoped that one day it would lead her to her origins; however, after so many years, she doubted her birth family was ever coming for her again.

"We should probably stop at an inn in Bricklewyn tonight," Forde suggested a while later as they made their way down a plateau towards some brush.

She looked up, wiping away a sheen of sweat. She could tell by the livestock they were passing that there had to be a village nearby, but because they were travelling off the roads, they made their way through the outskirts of the town.

Getting a room at an inn was not an option for her for two reasons. One, she did not have enough money for such pleasures. Her provisions had only been to get her to Gildevard. Two, sleeping over at an inn could potentially leave a trail behind for Grantreal to follow should he start asking questions. She would be easy to describe, primarily because of her colouring.

She bit back a response. She would just sleep outside the village while they slept at the inn and re-join them in the morning. They eventually reached another cluster of trees and brush, the formulations of yet another forest. This forest was thick with very tall trees whose branches blended into each other. Moss grew on tree barks, various mushrooms grew near roots, and Amari spotted several rabbits and squirrels scurrying through the forest.

"My skin is starting to itch," Korin complained, scratching his neck.

"Then put on a cloak," Forde told him. Korin tossed him an annoyed look over his shoulder that barely drew any reaction from Forde.

Before he could even respond, Korin suddenly drew to a halt, his whole body tensing as his head perked up. His eyes scanned the area behind Forde and Amari intensely. His actions drew an immediate reaction from Forde, who paused, tensing as he glanced over his shoulder, and Amari felt panic well within her. Had Grantreal found her? Had that overly muscled, tall beast of a man with a jagged scar running down his left cheek finally found her? Was she about to meet her death?

"What is it?" Amari whispered, looking over her shoulder, then she turned fully, bracing herself for a fight.

"Someone is here," Korin replied; then, quite surprisingly and strangely, both men moved their horses to stand next to her as if to protect her. She felt something warm spread over her. They didn't even know her much and yet were rallying to shield her from possible danger. "I suspected someone was following us for a while now, but whenever I looked, I couldn't see him, but I can sense…something."

"Bad or good?" Forde asked, and Amari wondered why Forde didn't think it was strange that Korin was "sensing something". Did it frequently happen for Korin that Forde didn't need to doubt it or be surprised by it?

"I'm not sure." Korin shook his head, then he suddenly tilted his head to the side, narrowing his eyes as though he saw something that Forde and Amari weren't. Then suddenly, in a loud voice, he called out, "We caught you! Come forth and show yourself!"

Amari's eyes sped around them searchingly, anxiously, trying to identify where the lurking person would come from. Her hand hovered over her long knives at her back while Forde's hand hovered near his sword.

"Wait," Korin whispered to them before they drew their swords.

"Well, I suppose you caught me."

The clear, loud male voice shot through the air, and Amari held back a gasp. It was not Grantreal, she thought, and her eyes immediately latched on the movement to her right. A man suddenly pulled away from the thick tree he must have been standing behind with his hand held up. But, wait, how had he been following them on a horse, and they hadn't even seen him. She frowned as he approached, her eyes scanning over the man, and then her eyes widened when they landed on his face. A face that looked startlingly familiar!

CHAPTER SIX

The man was possibly ten years older than Arteryn, with hair that was starting to turn silver at the temples, but the resemblance between them was unmistakable. Arteryn was maybe slightly taller than the man, but the similarity between them hit her hard. Same eyes, same mouth, same built. A gasp escaped Amari's lips, and her eyes widened as a rush of information filled her head. Crispin's heated accusation that Korrigan was Arteryn's brother came to mind. How had she never met this man, and more importantly, why had Arteryn hidden his existence? If Crispin had seen him intermittently over the years, why had Arteryn never mentioned him?

The man dressed in dark pants stuffed into knee-length leather boots. He wore a dark long-sleeved shirt and a brown cloak with a very curious pattern embroidered on the left breast.

It was that embroidered pattern that sent her reeling. For the very same three dancing flames that were embedded on the face of her medallion were the exact replicas embroidered on this man's cloak. It made no sense. Why would he have that embroidered on his clothes?

What had Arteryn said? If it were Korrigan, he would mention the medallion? Why?

Thoughts rushed into her head while she scrutinised the man who approached them with an air of calmness. Amari had a sense this man was deliberately acting calm to prove to them he wasn't a threat. However, his very presence before her was a threat to her sanity. She had questions whirling in her head, but she bit her tongue and stared at him. The man gave off an air of authority, his dark eyes observing them. Amari tried to remember the words Arteryn had forced her to repeat should she meet Korrigan whom- she stared with disbelief, shared the same colouring she and Arteryn had. This man was family to Arteryn. She didn't need anyone to confirm it to her.

"That is a fascinating looking medallion." The man said as he rode calmly towards them on an impressive horse. This man was Korrigan. She knew without a doubt. But she didn't understand why he was here when he should have been looking for her on the route to Gildevard.

She took a deep breath, her heart thudding in her chest. *"Tadiamnum Parleum."*

She saw something in his face shift, soften and his eyes crinkled at the corners as he smiled then nodded at her.

"Inum Anem Kalhasie."

His response immediately put Amari on the defensive. This man was indeed Korrigan, and if he thought he would sway her from her decision to travel to Sagar, he would waste his time.

"What does that mean?" Forde asked beside her, and she stole a glance at him before returning sharp eyes to the man who stood a few feet away from them. She dropped her hands from her knives then pinned the man with a stern glare.

"You're Korrigan." She stated, and he nodded.

"You're Amari." He moved forward, the dead leaves crunching under the horse's hooves, but he quickly drew to a halt when Forde moved forward threateningly. The man held up his hands to assure Forde he meant no harm, then dropped them again. Amari caught the glint of a sword hilt attached to the man's side, looking him over slowly. She knew without a doubt that if Arteryn possessed such advanced fighting skills, this man would also be as competent. Therefore, he was a threat.

"It is fortunate that I received Arteryn's message before I left for Gildevard. It is also fortunate that he knows you so well that he knew you would simply abandon all pre-arranged plans and choose to travel to Sagar."

Amari ignored the curious looks that Forde and Korin threw her way. She knew the story she had told them about why she was on the road would have them wondering what this was about.

"Is he one of the men sent to find you and take you home?" Forde asked her, and she shook her head.

"No." She answered through clenched teeth, her eyes trained on Korrigan. "He's the man I was supposed to go to who would protect me. Arteryn arranged for him to help me get to Derriane."

"And you what? Chose to go to Sagar instead?" Forde asked her quickly, and his tone forced her to look away from Korrigan and turned to Forde finally.

"I have little doubt that Arteryn knows where I am going. He knows me too well." That at least was true. She returned her eyes to the man who was regarding her with a hint of curiosity.

"Yes, he did tell me to look for you on the route to Sagar." Korrigan folded his arms across his chest. "This is very irresponsible of you, Amari."

"You don't know me. You don't get to judge me." She was defensive, she knew, but Amari was seeing a man who seemed to know of her when she had not known anything about him until Arteryn had mentioned him.

"You're related to her." Korin's sudden declaration had the hairs on Amari's body rising, yet Korrigan remained passively calm. "She has your eyes."

"I am not her father if that's what you're asking." Korrigan ever so casually pointed out as though Amari's world wasn't tilting a bit. It was one thing for people in Synia to assume she was related to Arteryn because they had seen her too many times with him. It was one thing for Korin to find a resemblance to her and this man who looked like an older version of Arteryn. "However, I have known her since she was a little girl."

"I have never met you in my life." Amari denied quickly, and Korrigan merely shrugged.

"I have been to the farm several times. I have seen you training with Arteryn."

"And exactly who is Arteryn to you?" She already had her suspicions, but if he lied to her now, she would know she could not trust this man.

"Why, he's my little brother, of course- though, I hardly think I can use the word 'little' to describe him anymore, seeing as he became taller than me. However, this pesky resemblance between Arteryn and me makes it impossible for us to deny each other." Korrigan was attempting to be more casual and calmer than spook her, but it wasn't working. Her entire body flared as a shock went through her. His brother! Arteryn's brother! Something inside twisted hurt that Arteryn had never told her about this man in the entire time they had known each other.

"He has never mentioned you." So, she accused, more hurt than anything.

"I doubt he ever had a reason to. Besides, I don't suppose his family would mean much to the daughter of his employer-"

"I'm not just the daughter of his employer to him, Korrigan. Arteryn is like a father to me. We are quite close, and I know you know that because it is evident you know more than you are letting on. So enough with the deception and tell me everything." The need to hide who she was and her circumstances from Forde and Korin were long forgotten. The only thing she knew at that moment was that meeting Korrigan screamed at her as the beginning of a shift in her life. "And don't even think of stopping me going to Sagar."

Korrigan smiled slowly then nodded, but the smile didn't reach his eyes. Cautiousness hung all over him. "It was never my intention to. Arteryn did tell me to expect you to be making your way to Sagar. I am on my way to Bhrim through Derriane. I suppose I can just join your company, and we can part ways before the Sinagora."

"You expect me to believe you'd just let me go to Sagar?" This man was not proving himself to be very reliable to Arteryn.

"Let us say I am very familiar with your kind of single-minded determination. You do take after Arteryn, after all. He mentioned your grand ideas of becoming a Sage Warrior. Of course, nothing I say or do will make you agree to travel to Derriane with me; however, he did ask that you let him know when you arrive in Sagar City. I now must see you to the Sinagora." Korrigan's eyes travelled to her companions, and his face changed, looking determined.

"A Sage Warrior?" Forde sounded incredulous next to her. "You are aware only men can be Sage Warriors?"

Amari ignored him. Silence seemed to descend on her, her vision blurring for just a slight moment as a thud began at her temples. Then, slowly, in and out, in and out, she breathed, her head spinning. "I...take after Arteryn? Why would you say that?"

CHAPTER SEVEN

Her heart thudded wildly in her chest. Feelings descended on her, raw, fresh, potent and unforgiving. Fear, panic, and terror all warred within her as images began to play out in her head. At first, it was all vague, and then she suddenly found herself standing in the middle of a burning village, people running and screaming around her. The stifling scent of burning flesh and burning homes filled the air. The screams grew loud, the heavy thud of footsteps approaching behind her. She spun on her feet and froze, her chest heaving as she stared in fear at a tall beast as it came straight for her. Images of tall beings with ram horns, light blue skin with darker stripes and a barrel chest appeared around her. She couldn't move; she was rooted to the spot and couldn't force her feet to move no matter how hard she tried.

A cry tore from her lips as the Emori reached her, and when it would have ploughed into her, as she lifted her arm instinctively to shield her face, it went right through her.

A cry escaped her lips as she whirled around, watching the chaos around her, the people running, men, women and children all seeking shelter. Some were fighting with everything they had, and some gave it all to try to protect their families. But, death, there was so much all around her. Bodies lay in pools of blood everywhere. However, the screams! The screams were getting to her, along with the oppressive heat of the fire all around her.

"Amari!" The large hand on her shoulder shook her violently. "Amari, come back, child!"

Her hand flew to wrap around the medallion, seeking its reliable comfort and the moment she did, sanity wrapped itself around her like the familiar blanket of home. Her heart rate slowed, and her breathing regulated. The terror that had gripped her before starting to ebb away. However, an imminent sense of danger clung to her.

"What happened to her?" She could hear Forde's voice but couldn't look up yet as she fought to banish the raw images that seemed burned into her brain.

She did not remember getting off her horse, or any of them for that matter, but Korrigan now stood before her.

"Just give her a moment," Korrigan told him, then he turned towards Amari, holding her close, his mouth close to her ear. Then, he said the words that snapped her out of her fiery daze in a low voice. "Amari, you have to listen to me. I know about your powers. I know what you can do, not because Arteryn told me, but because I know what you should be able to do. Now tell me, what did you see?"

She scrambled away from him quickly when he said that, her eyes wild with panic as she sought to put as much distance between her and this man.

"We have to go." Korin's voice broke the intense pressure that seemed to be crushing her chest. "We have to go now. Something is coming. It's close. We have to go."

"Wait," Korrigan said with urgency just as Forde started drawing Amari towards her horse.

"We have to go!" Korin said, almost in a panic.

"I know!" Korrigan snapped at Korin. "There are things I have to say first right this moment. They have to be said."

Amari took a step back, right into Forde as Korrigan approached her and something inside told her she was not ready for what he had to say to her. She instinctively knew that whatever this man was about to say would change everything for her.

"The Emori are coming-or at least a bastardised version of them. They are unlike the Emori I knew and fought growing up. There are three of them. I managed to evade them when I changed my destination, but they have found me. If you're going to survive what is coming right now, I have to stay and fight it. That means there is a possibility I may not make it to Bhrim. I need you to take the medallion to Derik in Bhrim should I fall-"

"Korrigan-"

"Just listen to me. You have to listen to me right now, Amari." Korrigan covered her hands with his much larger hands, and he looked her straight in the eye.

Korrigan drew one hand away, then held up his palm, and a flame flicked and danced in the space between them. Gasps from Forde and Korin filled the air while all Amari just stared. Her chest squeezed, her heart thudded, and her head felt like it was going to explode. Korrigan had her powers - but he was Arteryn's brother! That meant one thing.

"I... I am Kenryk, aren't I?" The raw words felt pulled from her constricting throat.

"Listen to me, child." Korrigan grasped her by her elbows and looked down at her imploringly. "I know you have questions. I know this is too much and too soon, but there isn't time. You must go. I have to trust now that Forde and Korin will get you to Bhrim safely."

"We must go! Now!' Korin was already heading to his horse and leaping up without pause.

Korrigan glanced at Korin, then lowered his eyes to Amari again, looking at her meaningfully. "I need you to do something on this journey, Amari. Trust yourself. Trust in your abilities and know one thing, you were never unwanted."

Amari's mouth opened, but all that came out was a strangled cry. Tears brimmed in her eyes. Questions ran wildly in her head, but she was utterly unable to formulate them into words. She could hardly believe what she was hearing. Were it not for Forde, she was sure she would have crumbled to the ground. But, instead, a slight tremble had formed around her shoulders, and it was all she could do not to scream.

Korrigan continued without pause. "Go to Bhrim, Amari. Find Derik. He will provide you with all the answers you seek. And please, don't hate Arteryn, not until you have listened to everything Derik has to tell you."

As Amari struggled, as her chest tightened, air squeezing out of her lungs, eyes wide and panic flaring inside her, Korrigan turned his gaze to Korin. Just as he opened his mouth, the ground under their feet shook. Long fingers of fog crept slowly towards them, lying low on the ground as dread blanketed them.

The flowers and grass the fog touched instantly killed them, and the thump, thump, thump sounded under Amari's feet.

Korrigan looked towards them quickly. "The Emori are here. You must leave. Avoid fighting them. Whatever you do, do not let them get you or the medallion, Amari. Get to Bhrim." He turned urgently to Korin. "You? Trust your instincts, young man. They will need you yet before this is through." He turned to Forde. "Keep them both sane. Now, leave."

Korrigan pushed them away just as a shudder-inducing bellow filled the air. Then she saw it, and Amari froze the same way she had in her brief vision. Ram horns, barrel chest and light blue skin. The Emori were here!

And yet, something was different about the way they had looked in her...vision?

"Go to Bhrim through Derriane!" Korrigan whispered to them as he drew his sword out, glancing one last time at Amari. "Your mother and father loved you, Amari. The only reason you are alive is because of that love. They sacrificed their lives to keep you safe." Korrigan took a deep breath. "Get that medallion to Derik, Amari. If you fail, if the Emori get you and that medallion, we will be plunged into the darkness that wreaked the Kais during the Great War. Now go!"

Amari started to speak, but Forde didn't give her a chance. He began dragging her back, telling her they had to leave. Forde wrapped his arms around her waist and forced her onto her horse, then smacked it. He leapt onto his horse, and they were off. Turning one last time, she glanced over her shoulder to see Korrigan formulate a large ball of fire in her hand as he faced the approaching enemy.

"Korrigan!" She called to him as the Emori rushed towards him. No! She wanted to stay and fight. She wanted so much. How could she lose him when she had just found him?

How could she let him face these beasts alone? The current circumstances took the choice to stay and fight out of her hands because as she glanced at Forde, his eyes told her that if she even tried to go back, he would be pretty unpleased. The last thing she saw before the fog engulfed Korrigan was a blaze of fire shooting in the air and a cry of pain.

She drew her horse to a halt, turning as she stared wild-eyed at where Korrigan had been standing. She couldn't see fire! He was dead!

A sharp ringing sound shrilled in her ears, her mouth agape, and she blinked once, twice, then a tear slid down her cheek. Forde's face came into her vision. He screamed with a panicked look in his eyes, waving at her wildly while she struggled to make sense of what was happening. Everything seemed to be moving slowly around her.

"Amari, we have to leave." It was Korin's voice she heard so close behind her, and it snapped her out of the fog that had rooted itself in her brain. She looked up at him, her mouth formulating Korrigan's name. "He's gone, Amari. We have to go."

It took everything she had at that moment to turn and ride like the hounds of hell were right behind her. She didn't know where she was going, but Korin rode past her, and she followed blindly.

They rode hard through the forest as the loud bellow of the Emori seemed to follow them.

"They're following us!" Korin called out as they sped through the forest, leaping over fallen trees, dashing under heavy hanging branches, slipping on loose soil. Then, with her chest on fire, the need to survive taking over every other emotion that threatened to immobilise her, she rode faster than she had ever thought possible.

"There is a river less than a mile from here. We need to get to the river!" Forde called to them as he deliberately rode at the back, probably so he could face the Emori first if they reached them. The shrivelling of flora around them and the fog seemed to be nipping at their heels. The Emori were in hot pursuit, and the darkness they brought with them threatened to engulf Amari.

She took a chance, glancing over her shoulder, and breath caught in her throat when she saw the beasts gaining on them. It suddenly occurred to her as Korin seemed to be riding faster and further away; her horse slowed them down. It simply couldn't keep up, and Forde had to ride slower not to leave her behind.

The mad sprint down the embankment towards the river had her chest burning, and at that moment, she trivially realised Korin was a much stronger rider than either of them. As they broke through the forest, she couldn't believe their luck. There was a dugout canoe moored on the bank. Whether it would float was yet to be determined. Korin was the first to reach the bank, not bothering to assess whether anyone owned the canoe and, leaping off his horse, started pushing it into the water.

He rushed back to his horse, scrambling to get his things. "We need to leave the horses! We have to get on the canoe!"

"I can't leave this horse! This horse is one of two horses my family owns, and they made sacrifices by giving it to me!" Amari choked out the words as she slid off her horse. Korin was already pulling her things from her horse without waiting for her and throwing them in the canoe.

"I am quite certain they'd rather lose the horse than you. We need to be in the water, Amari. These Emori are fast, and on land, they have the advantage!"

Forde came up behind her. Wrapping his arms around her waist, he carried her to the canoe without waiting for another second. He threw his things in as Korin rushed to untie the canoe. A frightening bellow tore through the forest as the Emori finally cleared it and barrelled towards them. This situation had to be a dream.

Forde pushed the canoe, and leapt on it as Korin started paddling furiously. Forde grabbed the other pedals, and both men set to work, moving them as far away from land as possible.

Amari glanced around, trying to see if she could help, but there were no more paddles. Instead, Forde and Korin rowed at breakneck speed, forcing Amari to sit there helplessly. Another bellow tore through the warm afternoon, and Amari jerked to her side, watching the Emori as they stood on the bank. And what she saw standing there rocked the foundations of her sanity.

Right there on the embankment stood three bone-chilling, frightening and large creatures. The first thing Amari noticed was the sizeable ram-like grey horns that grew from the foreheads of the creatures. Each horn was adorned with gold rings, possibly three or four in each horn. The pale blue skin of the beings tinged with darker stripes all over the visible skin of each beast. They had large, pointed ears that had several gold small hoop piercings on each ear.

Jet-black hair cascaded in large braids down the back, and on each side was a single smaller and thinner braid with a gold clasp at the edges. All three Emori had pierced septum as they stood large, broad, and built like an ox on the riverbank. They each carried a large, jagged sword and a battle-axe in their hands, dark leather armour splayed over their broad chests. Their feet remained wholly shrouded in dusty brown fog, and for a heart-stopping moment, she wondered if they could float on water.

They looked human, and they were human; their features were just startlingly different to what she had been used to growing up. They were also dissimilar to the Emori she had seen in her head. Those Emori had been more lithe than so broad.

Two bronze chains crisscrossed over each chest, and Amari felt her breath hitch in her throat. This situation had to be a dream. Finally, the Emori in front bent his knees and let out a bellow with a mouth that looked far too large with sharp jagged teeth that pierced the air and sent birds fleeing in all sorts of directions. The frustrated cry sent chills down Amari's spine, and she involuntarily shuddered.

She heard them as though they were standing next to her as they breathed heavily, the sound reminding her of a bull that was ready to charge. However, thankfully, and miraculously they remained on the riverbank.

They levelled her with a gaze she realised was very familiar to her. Those eyes had been in the senseless flashing images. They had been in dreams haunting her for some time now and the recent vision she had had.

The air was pungent with fear and death as Korin, and Forde rowed her further away from the shore. Dread gnawing at her bones as she felt like throwing her things down and releasing a wailing cry. She managed to keep it together long enough for them to put enough distance between themselves and the Emori, and she felt tears brimming in her eyes. Finally, when the Emori disappeared, when the river bank and the horses were nothing more than memory, Korin and Forde threw the pedals into the canoe and breathed out heavily. But, as Korin tossed the paddles into the canoe next to her, she immediately realised something was wrong with the way Forde was looking at the man sitting behind her. She turned on the seat where she was stationed between Forde and Korin and found Korin in quite a state.

CHAPTER EIGHT

I t took her a moment to realise what was happening with Korin. She had seen it once before back in Synia, this unrestrained panic that consumed someone to the point where they thought they were drowning or dying.

Korin was hyperventilating, his eyes wide with panic as he looked around him as though he was trapped.

"I have to get off the canoe." He managed through clenched teeth, pushing to his feet suddenly and rocking the boat that thankfully had no leaks. "I have... I..."

He was trembling, his jaw and fists clenched as he seemed to be drowning internally from whatever was consuming him.

Forde dropped his pedals inside and started to move forward. "Korin, no, wait."

"I can't... I..." Korin looked wild, panic-stricken and couldn't seem to be able to catch his breath. Amari could almost relate to how he felt. She may not be acting the way he was, but inside she was a hot mess. Korrigan was dead, and Arteryn was her uncle.

She was Kenryk. Arteryn was Kenryk, and he had never told her. He had never told her she was Kenryk. All these years with him, trusting him completely, and he had been hiding something so important. It was too much, and she suddenly understood Korin's need to get off the canoe because it felt like the walls were closing in on her even though she sat on a canoe in the middle of a wide river. Tall trees lined both sides of the river, and even though the Emori could very well be lurking behind those trees, she didn't care.

She was falling apart. It was too much—all of it.

"Korin." Forde had started to move forward again, but Amari held her hand out and pressed it against his chest, then shook her head. She saw the concern on his face, the panic that Korin might do something, but Amari understood Korin's need at that moment. They had almost just died. They had just been chased through the forest by Emori. They were still alive, but there was so much she was trying to push down on top of that. She pushed their bags away to give herself room, then proceeded to yank off her boots and cloak before she jumped into the river without warning.

When the water surrounded her, warm from the setting afternoon sun, she felt a moment of calmness when everything else that waited for her on the surface did not exist. Down here, Korrigan wasn't dead. Arteryn hadn't omitted the fact that he was her uncle. She wasn't Kenryk. Emori hadn't just chased her down.

None of it existed. She was just Amari Leverood living on a small farm in Synia where she could run down the rolling green valleys, spend afternoons swimming near the waterfall, help the farmhands with the livestock and help Tia bake her famous pie.

Down here, she didn't shoot fire from her hands, and she wasn't some abandoned orphan adopted at the age of three. Only, she hadn't been left, had she? Amari's birth parents had died, and Arteryn, her uncle, stayed around and helped raise her by pretending to be a farmhand. As much as she wanted to stay underwater and forget her problems, the need to breathe took over, and she swam to the top, breaking through the surface.

Korin was still standing in the boat, and she took a deep breath, pushing water out of her face. "Jump in Korin."

He looked at her, his chest rising and falling with each passing second. Then, finally, he pulled his boots off and jumped into the water. Tears mixed with the water dripping down her face as she stole a glance at Forde, who seemed to be counting the seconds as he waited for Korin to break the surface. When Korin did moments later, Amari saw the almost tangible relief that seemed to wash over Forde, but the worry was still there on his face.

She and Korin faced each other and without any words spoken, they both sank underwater and faced each other. Something, she didn't know what it was, flashed past them. A sea creature? She didn't know, but she sensed it and Korin suddenly grabbed her hand and pulled her back to the surface.

Korin was still trembling, but at least he was starting to regulate his breathing somewhat. Amari stared at him as he released her hand, and without thinking, without pausing or considering anything else, she threw her arms around him and held him tight.

He froze in her arms completely, but she could tell that even though he seemed to be coming down from the panic that had gripped him, he was still not all right. She shoved her problems down, focusing on only Korin, on helping him. She drew back slowly then looked at his face that was still pale, his lips trembling while he continued to shake uncontrollably.

He expelled a long shuddering sigh, then drew her into her arms slowly and held her as they floated in that lake with its dark waters. They were probably there for merely ten minutes, but it felt like forever. She stole a glance at Forde, who seemed to be dealing with how own emotions. Korin's trembling died down, and he relaxed eventually.

They returned to the boat silently, Amari instinctively knowing she shouldn't ask him any questions. Once they were on board, the flood gates opened for her. Everything she had pushed down came crashing down on her. Now that Korin was safe and doing better, she caved. She was Kenryk. Korrigan was her uncle. He had formed fire from his hand. Arteryn was her uncle, which meant he too was Kenryk and could create fire from his hand.

Yet, all these years, all this time? She couldn't understand why he hadn't told her any of it, why he had hidden something so vital about her from her. It didn't make sense. None of it made sense, and now she couldn't go back home and demand answers from him because she not only had Grantreal after her but the Emori as well.

Oh wow! She had Grantreal and the Emori after her! The Leveroods could very well be dead, and she didn't know for sure. Korrigan died, and she had just left him. Her birth parents died. Arteryn had lied to her all these years... She heard a sound in the silent afternoon air, a rough sobbing sound, and she realised it was coming from her.

Turning in her seat to look away from Forde and Korin, she stared into the forest as violent sobs wracked through her. As much as she tried, she couldn't seem to stop crying. She wasn't even a crier, and here she was, unable to stop the rushing tears.

It was too painful, too raw. This loss of not just Korrigan she had barely known, parents she didn't remember, but the relationship she had had with Arteryn was just too painful. So much made sense to her now. Tia and Joran had always deferred to Arteryn, and he had been able to admonish her when she misbehaved, how he had decided that it was time for her to go.

What had he said to them before she left? That it was time, and they had all known this day would come? What had he even meant by that? The urge to turn around and go home to confront Arteryn was intense, but only the medallion around her neck kept her on that canoe. Korrigan had said a man named Derik in Bhrim would provide her with the answers she needed. His last request to her was to deliver the medallion to Derik. How could she turn away from that responsibility now? He was dead. She couldn't believe he died.

She almost jumped when a blanket suddenly wrapped around her shoulders, and she looked up to find Forde there. He slipped back to his seat as she looked at him apologetically for her behaviour. She was supposed to be strong, not weak. She couldn't be weak. She inhaled sharply, trying to gather her emotions. She glanced at Korin, who sat on his seat silently, his hair plastered on his forehead as he seemed to be working through whatever was in his head.

"I'm sorry." She muttered when she finally regained the strength to speak, looking out at the water while Forde resumed rowing.

"For what?" Forde asked her after a moment, and she exhaled again.

"Almost getting you killed. Making you uncomfortable with my tears." And the stupid tears slid down Amari's cheeks again. She wiped them away furiously then shuddered. "I just... I was three years old when Arteryn brought me here, and I don't remember my life before I was adopted. I didn't know who I was before I came here. I didn't know if I still had family out there, who I was, where I was from and now...." She trailed off, her voice breaking and tears falling again as she shook her head. "I'm sorry."

"Stop apologising. Unless you knew Korrigan had the Emori coming after him or that he was even going to appear at all suddenly, then there's nothing you could have done." Forde's tone held no judgement, and she appreciated that he was trying to absolve her for something she felt was her responsibility.

"Yes, but now he's dead and... Arteryn is my uncle and...." And she was Kenryk. "I have to go to Bhrim." She announced with another tremble. "I know I said I would go to Sagar, but I... Korrigan said I would find answers there. How could I not do it now...?" She shook her head, frustrated with herself for being so emotional. "Of course, with the Emori after the medallion, I will have to part from both of you when we reach Bricklewyn to ensure they don't come after you-"

"Can you just be quiet for a moment?" Forde asked her quickly, holding up his hand to silence her, and she bit her lower lip, wrapping the blanket tightly around her. Her journey was now setting her right back on the path Arteryn had initially set her on. However, now it was more than just running from Grantreal. It was about finding her roots, finally finding answers to all the questions she had had growing up and, more importantly, questions she had now.

"Korrigan said you're Kenryk, and as far as I know, Kenryk can shoot fire from their hands." Forde began suddenly, and Amari nodded as she continued to chew her lower lip to keep it from trembling. "Can you do that?"

She wiped another stray tear, letting out a long exhale before she nodded again.

"So, you are Kenryk."

"I didn't know." She couldn't help how defensive it came out.

"I know," Forde told her, and when she turned to look at him, she found no judgement on his face, just understanding. He seemed to have reached a decision.

"I mean, I suspected. Deep down, I knew, but I always thought that maybe I created a world in my head where I was something special because I grew up thinking my birth family abandoned me. I always convinced myself that there was no way I could be Kenryk, even though the evidence had always been there. I just don't know what to do with the information right now."

"What do you know of the Kenryk?" Forde asked her as she matched her heart rate to his steady rowing.

What did she know of the Kenryk? She wasn't sure of anything now. "That seventeen years ago, the Emori attacked the Kenryk, and it destroyed both tribes that night. I know no one heard from them again. I know the Kenryk created the Endric Sword that led to the victory of the United Armies of the Kais during the Endric War. I..." She shook her head as her words trailed off.

It was so simple to recite knowledge she had picked up over the years and know that the history related directly to her. How could she not have seen the obvious truth? Seventeen years ago, Emori attacked the Kenryk. Seventeen years ago, she had ended up on the Leverood farm. She was probably one of many Kenryk who had become displaced that night of horror.

Looking at Forde, she found him eyeing Korin, and they seemed to be having a silent conversation with their eyes, then he turned back to her. "We will go with you to Bhrim. The route to Sagar through Derriane is longer, but it still safer than going through the Dewr Mountains with the Emori on our tails.

"We will drop off the medallion; you will have an opportunity to seek your answers from this man named Derik and still have enough time to go to Sagar for the Laurean Sage. However, with not just your potential husband after you but the Emori as well, we will have to quicken our pace to put as much space between the enemy as possible and us. We don't have any horses anymore; therefore, we are already at a disadvantage, but maybe we can secure them at the next village."

Amari looked at Forde in stunned silence. She had not been expecting that. She had expected them to agree to let her go on her own, to shoulder her burdens by herself. They were not obligated to help her at all, despite what Korrigan had said. She wanted to tell them that, but the look Forde gave her dared her to protest.

How could she? Amari didn't like putting these two men accountable to her in danger, but she wanted their company on this journey. She didn't think she could do it alone. If Amari had to, she would try. She would throw everything into trying to get to Bhrim herself, but she didn't want to. She wanted Forde and Korin with her, even if she had only just met them recently.

"Do you mind rowing? I need a moment." Korin spoke after an extended silence from him, and Amari nodded without hesitating. He covered himself with a blanket and promptly fell asleep. Amari didn't ask any questions. She wanted to ask Forde if this happened often, but judging by the look on Forde's face, this was a common occurrence, and he didn't want to talk about it.

She and Forde rowed a little more, and finally, he told her they had to get off the river.

"We're not too far from Bricklewyn. I'd like us to get there before nightfall, preferably." Forde informed her, and this brought about its issues.

"I don't have funds for an inn, Forde." But unfortunately, her family didn't have funds lying around for inns and an unexpected trip.

Forde dismissed her concerns. They woke Korin up, got dressed and jumped off the canoe when they reached land.

Forde turned out to be quite good with navigation because he could tell where they were and how far it would take them to find the road that would lead them to Bricklewyn. However, they were not to travel at night; he insisted as they followed him, trying to keep up with his long strides when climbing the steep hill from the river.

They didn't speak as they walked, and she was thankful for it. It gave her time to wallow in her misery.

She loved the Leveroods. They were her family. They had taken her in and raised her with so much love and happiness. They had even indulged her in many ways other families would never tolerate for their daughter. Yet, Amari had often wondered about her origins all her life, especially when she had discovered her powers. She had wondered about the people who had given her life, her birth family. Amari had wondered about the life she led and the circumstances that had brought her to the Leveroods. She had wondered about her people with the same colouring she had and whether they too could formulate fire from nothing on their hands.

All those answers had been within her grasp. First with Arteryn and then with Korrigan. She had finally met someone from her family, her uncle. He had shown her that he, too, possessed the power. He had spoken of her mother and father, and then he had been swiftly taken away from her. The last thing she would ever remember of him was seeing the Emori barrel on him, and the sharp, piercing pain she assumed came from the stab through the heart. So much had happened. The fiery images she had seen. She wondered if they had been a memory.

Well, if she was Kenryk, then it most probably had been a memory.

She shook her head, trying to clear it to lift this heavy blanket of sorrow that had enveloped her. She immediately reached for the medallion, and it soothed her like a balm on a wound.

"Should you be doing that considering what happened the last time you touched it?" Korin asked, and because she was lost in her thoughts, she ploughed straight into him. Belatedly remembering his aversion to being touched, she immediately jumped back to put space between them. She recalled the fiery hell she had witnessed and quickly dropped her hand away from the medallion.

She glanced around them. They were currently treading along a relatively densely bushy area, but the trees were not so tall or dense in this area. They would soon be on open ground, and they needed to travel quickly through that area, as it would leave them exposed during the night before they arrived in Bricklewyn.

"Why do you think it had anything to do with the medallion?" She asked Korin curiously.

"I noticed that when you're in need, you hold on to it, and it seems to soothe you. And, it has the same crest as the embroidered sigil on Korrigan's clothing. That medallion is pure gold, and looking at your belongings, you don't give off the image of someone who has a family with golden medallions lying around. Therefore, it must be something important. Korrigan just told you to deliver it to a man in Bhrim and firmly told you not to let the Emori get it." Korin noticed the strangest little things about people, she realised, and it unnerved her. He was peculiarly accurate in his assessment.

"I don't think it has anything to do with powers. I think it's just my source of comfort because it is the only thing I had before I was adopted."

She protested, and he arched his eyebrows at her as she suddenly caught on to what he had said. "You said it looks exactly like the sigil on Korrigan?" So, he had noticed that as well.

"Korrigan gave the impression those Emori can sense that medallion, so maybe avoid touching it until we are in Bhrim," Korin told her.

She was relieved to find he was doing much better than he had been on the canoe. Of course, he still looked exhausted, but at least the panic had abated.

Forde was already way ahead of them, not having looked back to realise they had stopped.

"He's going to kill us with this pace." She muttered as she fought to keep up, and Korin glanced her way, then took a deep breath.

"He's angry with you, by the way. I thought you should know." Korin pointed to Forde as he finally came into view, and they had to jog to try to keep up.

She expected his fury. She was, after all, guilty of omission. She should have come clean about her actual reasons for being on the road. However, the Korrigan situation was new to her as well. It had not been something she had known about to be able to tell anyone. She could not explain it to them because she did not understand it herself.

Nevertheless, she resolved to come clean about everything that night. They at least deserved the whole truth because Grantreal might have also been on their trail. Couldn't the fates just put Grantreal in the Emori's way and have them get rid of the man for her? However, she wondered how Forde and Korin would react to her truth. They might decide this was too much for them and let her head to Bhrim alone, but it was a risk she had to take.

Her legs were on fire, but she did not complain. She felt hot, sweaty, and exhausted, but she could not complain, not when Forde was helping her. Then, finally, Bricklewyn came into view at a distance, alerting them with the lanterns that glistened in the dark. Again, she felt hot and stuffy even though her clothes had started drying.

Forde suddenly came to a halt, not descending towards the village, which left Amari and Korin puzzled.

"What is it?" Korin asked him quickly.

"The Emori will expect us to spend the evening in Bricklewyn. It is the closest village. They could easily find us and kill us in our sleep." Forde seemed deep in thought then shook his head.

"What are you saying?" Amari could see the lanterns that lit the scattered homes in the village below.

"We cannot spend the night here. We can stop for food, but Amari will have to do something about the way she looks. We do not want anyone being able to say two men and a woman passed by here. So, I say let us get food and be on our way."

"Travel during the night?" Korin questioned in disbelief, and Forde glanced at him over his shoulder. "In the open like this with what? Do you have a death wish?"

"No, but we have to be realistic about our situation. Staying here overnight is what the Emori will expect, and we cannot do anything expected." Forde started to descend without giving them much time to argue. Amari was relieved that the sense of urgency had finally registered with Forde, but if he kept this pace, they were going to burn out before they reached Golynvale.

CHAPTER NINE

In the end, when they entered the grubby inn and ordered their food, they barely stayed long enough to enjoy it and very soon, they were on the road. As they travelled through the tiny village, Amari peered through windows of homes, knowing inside families were probably enjoying their evening meal in the warmth before the fire. She yearned for home but knew there was nothing much to be gained from what-ifs.

They travelled away from the village, moving along the Tule River into a sparsely afforested area.

Forde muttered something about them finding a secure place to build camp overnight when they had walked for a further two hours. Then, finally, they stumbled upon a shallow cave. Its location on higher ground would not attract any attention from someone travelling on the road located on higher ground just a few minutes away from them.

After scouting the place, Forde declared it unoccupied and safe, and then he turned to Korin.

"Will you be all right in a cave?" Forde asked him, and Korin shrugged, then nodded. He didn't seem too sure, though, and Amari wondered why Forde had even asked the question. "I'll be back. Get a fire going."

"Where are you going?" Korin asked him quickly, and Forde took a deep breath.

"Food for the road to avoid inns," Forde answered, and Amari stepped forward.

"I can help-" Amari volunteered, but he shut her down immediately.

"Just stay put. Your duty on this journey is to keep that medallion safe. Korin and I will handle the rest."

Forde left without saying another word, and Amari wondered if he was insane. Who went hunting for food at night? Or was that just an excuse to get away from them for a moment?

She turned to Korin, who looked visibly uncomfortable.

"Let's get the firewood." She said before he would have to explain himself, and he nodded with relief. They found what little they could before they returned to the cave. Once they had set up the firewood, she took a deep breath, formed a flame in her hand that caused Korin to jump back in shock before she lit the fire.

"I'll give you a warning next time." She murmured to him while he viewed her warily. She sat back on her haunches as he tended to the fire without saying anything, then she took a deep breath. "I saw a stream nearby. Do you mind if I go there? I feel like I need to wash the day off my body."

She saw the brief flash of panic in his eyes, and she got the sense he did not want to be left alone. She couldn't invite him to come along, not without making this awkward for him.

"Uh… Korin…" She trailed off, careful in her approach and trying to find a way around this situation without putting him in a position where he had to say he wasn't comfortable being alone. "Do you mind coming with me? I just… with the Emori out there and… I mean, I can fight, but I just… In case someone has to take the medallion and flee and I can't…."

He nodded, rising to his feet without saying a word, then he looked around, relief washing over him. "What if Forde comes back and finds us gone?"

Amari hadn't considered that, but she doubted Forde would be coming back any time soon. He looked like he needed a moment to gather his thoughts.

"We won't take long, and you can leave your things here while we go. I need to get out of these wet things, and I think you should too." She needed a change of clothes, and she needed to wash off the day and its revelations from her body and mind.

As they walked towards the stream with some things, she was thankful for the light offered by the moon. At least the skies were clear tonight.

When they reached the stream, Korin filled up their containers with water and then filled a pot with water before moving to lean on a tree with his back turned to her. She took a deep breath, pulling off her clothes to quickly wash down her body with soap Tia had packed for her. She should have been self-conscious, standing there naked with a man she barely knew, but she had never had any issues with her body.

As she dried off, Korin, who was still leaning against a tree, finally spoke. "About earlier on…."

"Which part?" She asked, pulling on dry clothes before bending over to wash her hair in the stream. "Frankly, I think the whole day was just horrible. From the moment I woke up to this very moment."

He glanced at her over his shoulder before he turned fully and looked at her. She couldn't make out his expression in the dark, but she could sense he was a little tense.

"It has been a long day," Korin mumbled, folding his arms across his chest, exhaling loudly. "About what happened with the way I acted on the canoe-"

"You don't have to explain yourself, Korin." She said pre-emptively. "I haven't cried the way I did today since I was a little girl, but that was because of the situation we are in at the moment. As you said, it was a long day." She finished washing her hair and tried her best to dry it with one of her shirts. Korin didn't respond while she plaited her hair and tied it back. Finally, she pushed to her feet then walked towards him. "If you want to wash, I have soap."

"I have soap too. I can't stand being dirty." He said almost defensively.

"Fine, then we can swap positions. You can wash. I'll look the other way."

Korin rolled his eyes. "I'll wash in the morning. Let's go before Forde returns and thinks Emori have abducted us."

"Wait, in the water," She paused thinking back to that moment. "Did you see or feel something in the water with us?"

Korin seemed to be thinking it over then nodded. "If Kenryk were not wiped out, maybe the Mer-people are still alive too."

When they returned to the cave, she sat down near the wall, leaning back against the stone while scrutinising the medallion.

"For as long as I can remember, I have always had this. I always viewed it as something that maybe had belonged to my birth parents, my only tie to them. However, after Korrigan's revelations, I am struggling to understand why it could be so valuable." She divulged, relieved that they had returned before Forde. She did not need to aggravate him more than she had. Instead, he seemed to be annoyed with her.

Korin looked up from the fire he was stoking with a long stick, and his eyes narrowed on the medallion as though he was trying to see through it.

"I get the sense its value is not in its medallion form. I don't know why I feel that way, but I instinctively know that its importance is not in its medallion state. I know I am not making sense. I never do most times." He confessed with a shrug then went back to stoking the fire. She frowned in confusion, and when she continued to regard him, he looked up. He sat the stick away. "This Arteryn of yours wanted you to go to Derriane to meet Korrigan. You decide to go to Sagar instead, yet, because this Arteryn knows you so well, he sends his brother to intercept you. Korrigan very casually declares he will not force you to go to Derriane with him but points out he is going to Bhrim- where undoubtedly, he would have taken you. Somehow, he manages to point to your most prized possession, attaches it to your need to attain knowledge of your past and tells you to deliver it to Bhrim. It seems, despite your decision to travel to Sagar, you are now going to Bhrim- as originally planned by your uncles."

Wait, Amari arched her eyebrows at what Korin was suggesting, but before she could voice her protests, he continued.

"Even if you decided to go to Sagar now, two things would ensure you travel to Bhrim; your sense of duty to deliver that medallion and the fact that Korrigan conveniently told you all the answers you seek to happen to come from the same man in the same place you where information about your origins and that medallion-"

"Now, Korin. That does sound a little farfetched."

"Does it?" Corking that perfect eyebrow of his, Korin settled back in the dark, damp cave and shrugged. "I mean, the Emori were probably unexpected, but they worked in Korrigan's favour."

"He's dead, Korin. I'd rather not talk like that about my dead uncle." Her sharp tone took both by surprise, but before Korin could respond, Forde walked into the cave carrying two rabbits. Silence enveloped them for a moment before Korin spoke as he took the rabbits from Forde and started to work on them. "Do you think there are other Kenryk out there, aside from you and…well, your remaining uncle? And maybe me. That would make a whole lot of sense. Or not. I don't have brown eyes that are standard for all Kenryk."

"Thank you for the continuous reminder that I just lost an uncle, Korin. It's not like it's a painful reminder or anything like that-"

"You barely knew him." Korin pointed out quickly, and Amari frowned at him in disbelief. But, seriously, did he not understand precisely why that hurt more than anything? She had met someone for the first time in her life who had displayed the powers she possessed. Korrigan had provided her for the first time in her life with information about her past. He had been ripped from her before she even had a chance to ask anything worthwhile. "Do you think I might be Kenryk? It would explain a lot of things about me."

"Korin, I'd appreciate it if we spoke about something else." If it was even possible, she planned to deny that part of herself as much as possible. If she got into her head that she was Kenryk, Arteryn was her uncle; it could sway her from her goal. And she had one goal to become a Sage Warrior. If she internalised what was happening too much, it might distract her. She should be focusing on what she was going to do when she arrived in Sagar.

However, she had made a promise to herself when she was in the canoe that she now had to fulfil. So, as Forde sat down near the mouth of the cave, pulling his sword out and laying it beside him, while Korin worked the rabbits, she exhaled, a little anxious about how they were going to receive her revelation.

"I have to tell both of you something…." She began, anxiously playing with her fingers, open to the possibility that the very next day, these men could quickly tell her to get lost. She wouldn't blame them, not with all the drama she had brought along even though the Emori were unplanned. "I didn't leave home because I was running away from an arranged marriage. I think it's almost obvious that Arteryn would never force me into an arranged marriage of any sort."

"I had been wondering how long it would take you to tell us the truth because I did not believe a single word of what you said to us about why you left home," Forde stated, and even though his tone was still unwelcoming, she was relieved he was at least talking to her.

She decided to expose it all, leave nothing out and be completely honest. If these men were going to put their lives in danger for her, they deserved nothing but the truth. It was the least she could do. They had to go into this thing with all the facts.

"Since I was a little girl, I dreamt of becoming a Sage Warrior. Everyone said I was insane because women couldn't be Sage Warriors, but I didn't care. I don't care. I can do it. I am good enough to do it." She trailed off then exhaled again. "I was seven years old when Arteryn began my training after I bugged him about it for weeks. He trained me for the next thirteen years and taught me invaluable skills, but I'd only ever had him as an opponent. He's quite good, but I thought if I could stand a chance at the Laurean Sage, I had to test my skill against other people. So, I went to Simiren to the fighting pits."

"The fighting pits?" Forde and Korin chorused simultaneously, and even with the poor light, she could see their surprise.

Their reaction was what she had gotten from people when she had asked for directions to the fighting pits. The place suited its name. Located in a poorly ventilated building with a physical structure that seemed as secure as a frail older man, Amari had immediately been sucked in by the infectious excitement of the spectators. With mere soil on the ground, every time someone stomped, dust flared. The way people breathed on each other; she was almost certain disease was just one more thing people caught at the pits than fights.

"Yes. I had to make sure I was good enough. So, after I defeated the first man-"

"They let you fight?" Korin's mouth hung open, and he seemed to forget the rabbit in his hand temporarily.

"It took some convincing. I can be very persuasive." And determined. "So, after I defeated the first man, I decided to challenge the biggest man there and seemingly the most popular one. I fought and defeated him. That man is called Grantreal."

"Wait, you're the Amari the whole of Simiren was talking about who humiliated Grantreal at the pits? The one Grantreal has declared he will find, rape, maim and kill?" Korin's voice was almost a shrill. "Wait, is he the man chasing you?"

"Yes." The word slipped out quickly. "He hunted me all the way home, but by then, Arteryn had already sent me on my way. I couldn't leave until I was certain Grantreal didn't kill anyone or burn the farm down. That is why I was going to Gildevard. Korrigan would meet me there and hide me in Derriane; at least, that's what Arteryn arranged. Arteryn said he would try to take care of Grantreal, and I'll hopefully return home when he grows tired of hunting me."

"Grantreal will never stop hunting you until you're dead, Amari. What were you thinking? Do you know who that man is-?"

"I didn't know when I challenged him." She had just thought it was just another man. It had never occurred to her she was challenging a mercenary.

"Are you telling me," Forde began, his voice thick with emotion and anger as he glared at her, "that not only do we have Emori nipping at our heels, but Grantreal as well?"

"I didn't know about the Emori. I knew about Grantreal-"

"Does it make any difference?"

No, it did not. Amari and her companions had a mountain of obstacles in their way. She couldn't help feeling guilty that she was thinking in terms of "we". These two men owed her nothing. They could easily pack their things and leave her, moving away from the danger that was following her.

Yet, here they were, sitting in a cave with her in imminent danger. She knew she would be eternally grateful that they had not abandoned her. If she were alone in the cave, alone in this, Amari didn't think she would be as calm as she was at that moment.

"I'm optimistically hoping Grantreal runs into the Emori." That would at least eliminate one enemy.

Forde muttered something incoherent under his breath and shook his head. Korin cleared his throat then leaned forward.

"So, all of this...this entire thing stems from you trying to become a Sage Warrior?" She nodded in return. "Amari, you are aware you have to be a man to compete at the games?"

"Yes."

"Pardon me, but you are not a man."

She rolled her eyes and crossed her legs in front of her quickly. "I am aware that I am not a man." She clasped her hands over her the small mounds on her chest. "I have breasts, among other things that make me a woman."

For some reason, the moment she said that both their eyes travelled to her chest and while Korin seemed slightly amused, Forde's eyes lingered there a little too long. Finally, she dropped her hands to her lap.

"So," Korin continued as their eyes returned to her face, "considering you have...breasts and are, in fact, a woman, how do you suppose you can compete at the Games?"

Amari had given a lot of thought to that over the years. Achieving her goal was the one thing she worked towards all these years.

"I understand they do physical inspections. Why do they when it's supposed to be just men?" That had never made sense to her. What were they looking for?

"To keep out anyone who doesn't belong in the Kingdom of Sagar from competing. That includes Elyssians or people from Bromvile or the Kingdom of Kessariah. So, the Games are only open to those who belong under the Kingdom of Sagar." Forde explained quickly, and she scoffed at the ridiculousness of it all.

"More exclusions. Can one say they are the best when so much of the competition is eliminated based on gender, ethnicity and historical deeds?"

She tried to keep the disappointment from cracking a chink in her dream. She had to protect her goal at all costs. She was going to become a Sage Warrior. "I was going to find a man and convince him to pass himself off as me for the inspections."

"And why would any man do that?" Korin asked her curiously, and she shrugged and smiled slowly.

"Because men tend to have one weakness… most men anyway." She couldn't make such assumptions with Korin around.

"And that is?'

"A beautiful woman."

"You'd planned to seduce someone to pass off as you?" Forde looked incredulous.

"It's not as farfetched as it sounds." She protested. "Don't worry about it. If that fails, I will think of something."

"I wasn't worried about it. It has nothing to do with me if you're so stupid you'd purposefully walk into an arena with men who will undoubtedly pummel you to death." Korin pointed out, her head snapped up at his words, and she scowled at him.

"I can fight men bigger than Forde, Korin, and Arteryn was never soft with me when we trained. I have scars to show for it. But, if I find a way to get into the arena, I will be among the last people standing. I do not doubt my ability." She declared with flaring nostrils, but Korin didn't even react.

"Seems to me this man should have spent more time talking sense into you." He pointed out, and that had her hackles rising. Despite her inner turmoil about Arteryn, she was not going to allow anyone to speak against him.

"He spent more time telling me being a woman didn't make me inferior. He told me that while by nature a man physically was stronger than I am, it didn't mean if I used my skills, I couldn't defeat him. When I told him I wanted to be a Sage Warrior, he never told me I couldn't do it. Instead, he told me I needed to train harder if I wanted any chance to defeat a man twice my size. You don't know Arteryn, so I will thank you not to say anything against him." She snapped furiously at Korin, and for a moment, both men stared at her with stunned silence. She took a deep breath as she realised what she had done. Damn it! What if they decided she was not worth the trouble, packed up their things and abandoned her? She opened her mouth to say something when Korin cut in quickly.

"Well, Amari, it seems to me you don't know him that well yourself. After all, he didn't tell you about Korrigan, did he? Or that you were Kenryk."

"Korin," Forde interjected.

"She's unnecessarily rude." Korin quarrelled. "She's ungrateful-"

"Korin!" Forde's voice was more demanding this time, and Korin glared at him, anger flashing in his eyes. "Can we not do this tonight? We're all exhausted physically, and I can hazard a guess and say mentally as well. It has been a very long day. Emotions are running high. This discussion does not serve any purpose."

"This was all a mistake. One I am regretting with each passing minute." Korin declared, and Amari took a deep breath then chewed her lower lip. It was going to take time to get used to Korin's mood swings, but she was willing to make amends for the sake of their group.

"Korin." She began slowly. "I apologise. I didn't mean to snap at you. I am just handling a lot of information in my head right now, and I am a little overwhelmed, if I must be honest. I am also quite anxious. I don't know what lies for me when I deliver this medallion in Bhrim. I don't know what this man Derik will tell me, and I just found that a man I have idolised my whole life is my uncle. Yet he never told me. Arteryn never once told me he knew Korrigan or that he and I were related, yet he has watched me battle with trying to find my place in the Kais because I have always wondered who I was. I have three Emori and Grantreal with his twelve men after me. I have left behind my parents and little brother, and I have no way of knowing if they're still safe. A man who turned out to be the first blood relative I have ever met just died, and I am just overwhelmed, and I am sorry."

Silence stretched between them, and when Korin continued to say nothing, Amari lowered her eyes to the fire and took a deep breath.

After a while, they decided to turn in, but she could not sleep. The images of the day played themselves in her brain, burned in there for the rest of her life. There was also the glaring matter of the fact that she would have to tell Arteryn his brother had died. Regrets engulfed her, pain that she had only had Korrigan for such a short time before the Emori took him away from her. He was gone now forever and, in his death, had left her with one favourable option; that a man called Derik possessed all the answers to her questions. Whether she was ready or not for anything this Derik had to disclose was yet to be determined.

CHAPTER TEN

When another hour crawled by and she was still struggling to sleep, she pushed her covers aside then slid out of the cave. She glanced around in the darkness, the crescent moon offering some light. Upon a quick assessment of her surroundings, she resolved to perch upon the clearing right above the cave. There were still enough trees to shield her should Grantreal, or those Emori come along.

She assessed the strength of the vines by tugging hard at them and relieved to find they were steady enough to hold her weight before she pulled herself up. Once she quickly climbed to the top of the opening of the cave, she settled in and let out a long, painful breath, her feet dangling in front of the cave.

A movement under her caught her attention, and she leaned forward to see Forde standing there. He glanced around, then turned until he saw her. He effortlessly hoisted himself up to come to sit next to her, and they just sat there for a moment in silence, looking out at nothing. Silence and darkness surrounded them, and while Amari had come out here to think, she still wanted an opportunity to make amends to Forde.

"I am sorry you lost your uncle." The words came from him before she could even start apologising for dragging him and Korin into this situation. He and Korin could quickly leave and let her face the Emori and Grantreal alone, yet here they were, still with her and having pledged to see this through with her. She did not think she could express her gratitude enough. If she had been alone when the attack of the Emori had happened and Korrigan had died, she was sure she would not have survived for too long.

"I hardly knew him." She repeated Korin's earlier said words.

"All the more reason for the loss to be more painful." One of Forde's legs hung over the mouth of the cave as he stared out into the distance. The brush and trees around them blocked their view of the river, and a quiet breeze had settled over the silent night. "I lost my entire family when I was eight years old. In a single afternoon."

That he was even volunteering such information astounded her. Of course, she already knew some of the details from what she had heard growing up, but she had pledged earlier never to bring it up until he decided he was comfortable doing so himself. He had been eight, not seven as people had said.

"I would have died with them, but for some reason, I survived. There was an attack on our village, and the attackers raided the entire place, killing everyone there and burning down the village. Earlier that day, I had snuck out to get berries despite my mother telling me not to do so. I ate so many berries and apples. I was so full, and instead of going home immediately, I fell asleep under a heavy low-lying branch of a tree. I returned late in the afternoon; certain my mother would chew my ears off for staying out so late only to find all the bodies of the people in the village piled up carelessly by the well. My father, mother, brother, and sister, were all dead, their bodies… piled like…bags of grain by the well… There was… blood everywhere, clear signs of a struggle and the smell of burnt flesh hung in the air. The attackers had razed the entire village to the ground, and they slaughtered everything, even the animals."

He paused, his mind travelling to that bleak day that had left him an orphan, the day he had returned to find not a single living soul. She couldn't begin to imagine the horror he had gone through, the unimaginable pain his eight-year-old self had endured. She couldn't survive returning home to the farm to find her family in that position. It would kill her. Wreck her.

"My uncle came for me a few days later. It took a while for word to spread, and I was alone in that village…waiting. I don't quite know what I was waiting for, but I couldn't leave. I just vacantly existed among all those bodies for a whole week. I think I expected everyone to wake up suddenly, and everything would be normal."

He shook his head at the absurdity of it all, but Amari only felt his raw pain. "My uncle had to drag me away from my home because I didn't want to leave my family behind. It hadn't quite sunk in that my family had left me. He took me in, but that sort of thing stays with you. You have thoughts at times, questions of why you lived, and they died. The what-ifs that follow are the worst. You rerun the event in your head, trying to think of what you could have done differently, but the truth is it changes nothing. My parents, my older brother and my sister all died that day, and I lived and whenever I asked myself why I reminded myself that there must have been some reason I was kept alive. I found that reason seven years ago and more so in the past few months."

Seven years ago? When he met Korin, she assumed and once more found herself wondering about the nature of their relationship. She had seen the look on his face when Korin had fallen apart on the boat. That gut-wrenching look of hopelessness on his face still played out in her head. She didn't bring it up, though. She didn't think it was the time, not after he had just shared something about himself like this.

"You may not have known Korrigan long, but he represented a part of your identity and of who you were before you found yourself here. You had questions you wanted to ask him, things you wanted to hear about your birth parents, but he gave you a way forward. He is sending you to Derik in Bhrim."

"Korin thinks it's all too convenient." She confessed to Forde and wished she could make out his face in the dark, or at least his expressions. "He pointed out that my journey is now setting me back on the path Arteryn initially set me on, that, conveniently, the same man I am supposed to deliver the medallion to just so happens to have all the answers I seek."

Forde exhaled slowly, and she felt him shrug next to her. "He has a point."

"Is he always right?"

"Sometimes…he has an uncanny ability to read a situation that can be frightening at times," Forde confessed, and the affection Amari heard in his tone made her smile a little, somehow softening the moment. "He can do things I don't understand at times."

"Such as what?" Amari questioned curiously, and she thought Forde wouldn't respond because he was silent for quite some time. Perhaps he was debating with himself whether to share this.

"Well… he can see in the dark very clearly. He says if he puts his mind to it, he can see as clearly as day. He can analyse a person within moments of meeting them almost accurately. Sometimes his eyes…"

"Flash? I saw that." She heard a gasp of surprise from Forde. "When he casually mentioned that he could be Kenryk then dismissed it, I think he might have been right. Yes, he doesn't have brown eyes, but he looks Kenryk, and he does things that are not normal at times."

Forde took a deep breath then expelled a sigh. "It would make sense that he is Kenryk, but he doesn't have any fire powers. Maybe he is one of the remaining people from one of the other indigenous tribes. Anyway," Forde seemed to realise he shouldn't be having this conversation about Korin, "don't dwell too much on the what-ifs. They will consume you. I know, I've been there. Focus on getting to Derik, and don't forget you still have Arteryn, who can provide all the answers you seek."

Amari wasn't confident she could keep it together if she had to ask Arteryn all the questions she had without resentment. She didn't want to think about him because it hurt every time she did.

"Is he as threatening as Korrigan makes him out to be?" Amari appreciated Forde's attempt to distract her.

"He's broody and watchful. Most people find him intimidating, but I don't. I never have. We've always just had a natural connection between us. Maybe his height, built, and pensive look always makes people a little nervous around him, but when he smiles… You can't help but smile with him. He is very affectionate too, but no one would ever agree with me because well, he was only ever affectionate with me."

"Affectionate?" Forde seemed surprised, chuckling under his breath.

"Yes. Arteryn was never afraid to pick me up and throw me in the air as a child, or hug me, or hold me and kiss my forehead as I grew-"

"And you never thought that was inappropriate? You didn't know he was your uncle then." Forde sounded incredulous, and Amari scoffed. Forde started to sound like the people in Synia who had always had issues with her relationship with Arteryn.

"No, because it was all so…fatherly. There was never anything sexual about it. Things between us have always been easy. He is fiercely protective of me, though, and I suppose now I understand why. He is my uncle…"

Her heart constricted at the thought. She didn't know how she felt about it—conflicted, happy or sad? She was confused.

"Are you happy? That he's your uncle?"

Forde may as well have been peeking into her head when he asked that question and all her cheerfulness evaporated into the night as she shrugged.

"I don't know. I have too many questions running in my mind for me to decide yet. A part of me is ecstatic that Arteryn and I are related. I've always wanted it, hoped for it to be that way because I loved him so much, but now I have so many questions…." She shook her head as she trailed off.

"Well, you have more than enough time to stew over your questions on our way to Bhrim. Right now, you need to sleep because we must be up at the crack of dawn and be on our way."

Knowing Arteryn the way she did, she wouldn't be surprised if he was trailing behind them. She was surprised he hadn't caught up to them yet. Maybe that was deliberate. She nodded slowly, then took a deep breath and pushed herself to her feet.

"Do you remember what your family looked like? I can't help feeling like I should have memorised Korrigan's face."

Forde pushed himself to his feet and towered over her, careful with his footing, so the slippery soil under their feet didn't tip them over.

"You'll forget what he looks like eventually." He said solemnly. "I am almost certain the faces of my family have become distorted in my mind. The only thing I remember quite vividly is my mother's eyes. She had the same eyes Korin has."

"Korin has your mother's eyes?" Her eyebrows almost disappeared into her hairline at that revelation. "Are you certain you're not related?"

Forde didn't seem perturbed by the question. "We may as well be. I consider him my brother. I'd do anything for him, and I know he'd do the same for me."

"You're just more protective."

"I am older by a whole year. I should probably warn you. Korin is working through a few things, so sometimes, he may seem harsh. It's nothing personal. He has built walls so high that I fear nothing can ever get through. He doesn't mean to be rude. He isn't normally like that."

"I know." And somehow, she felt like she did. However, she instantly felt Forde stiffen beside her and thought she should clarify. "I mean, I can tell he is dealing with some issues. This will sound insane, but I had a dream about him before I met him. I woke up from that dream feeling like something pressed heavily on my chest. I felt his raw pain like he had gone through something horrific. I just wanted you to know I didn't take anything he said personally."

Forde was silent for a while, and she thought he might not respond at all, but then he did.

"I dreamt about him too before I met him. I had never had that happen to me before." Forde confessed surprisingly, and while Amari had a million questions in her head, she decided to wait him out. "I didn't see him exactly. My mother appeared to me. In my dream, I was lying under the apple tree near my home in the village, full of apples and berries, but I wasn't an eight-year-old boy in it. I was almost eighteen, the age I met Korin. She came to me, but she wasn't alone. There was a man with her. He had the same eyes, but he never spoke. He just stood there beside her. It didn't feel like a dream. There wasn't any preamble. She just told me to find Korin. That was what she said. 'Find Korin, Forde. Find him and keep him safe.' I asked how I was supposed to find someone I had never met. She said I would know when I met him. When I woke up, I put it all behind me and tried to go on with my life. Then one afternoon, I was walking in the market, and I felt this pull. I can't explain it, but I just felt like something was calling to me, and I have always trusted my gut, so I followed it. It felt like someone was giving off these waves of energy, drawing me to him. Eventually, it led me to a corner where someone sat alone with their knees pulled up and their head buried in them. I walked up to him, and I said, 'What's your name?' When he lifted his head, and I saw his eyes, I knew before he said his name who he was. I took him home that day, and while it took time to gain his trust, we eventually bonded like brothers."

Amari was not at all surprised by the revelation. There was something mystical about Korin, and he constantly gave off this energy that she could not quite place. She could believe that Forde had dreamt Korin. She had done the same thing, and he had been calling to her in the dream.

"Your mother led you to him? Why?"

Forde took a deep breath but didn't respond. She knew there was more to this than he was telling her.

"Was it sexual?"

"What?" Forde's head snapped, and he looked at her in disbelief.

She sighed, her lips curving into a mischievous smile. "Korin seemed to suggest people are drawn towards him sexually."

"Other people are drawn to him sexually, but never me... or you for that matter. I have never felt anything like that towards him. Very few people I know look like he does. He attracts attention wherever he goes unintentionally. It's not just his face. It's little movements, nuances that he does that he's not even aware he does. I know that because I am very good at reading his body language, but as I said, Korin is my brother. From the moment I saw him, I knew we were bound to each other. Whatever pull that draws people to him sexually just never worked on me."

"Why do you think that is?" She asked, and he mulled it over.

"I don't know. Maybe because Korin has my mother's eyes, and he is a man. Also, maybe because I am not attracted to men, and he is a man."

"Korin is not just any man. He is beautiful. I've never seen anything like it."

She felt Forde relax next to her a little, and he sighed. "I know, but he's a man. Don't ever forget that. He hates it when people treat him like he's a woman. So, he will remind you every chance he gets that he is a man."

"Your overprotectiveness is showing." She teased him, and he chuckled. "Don't worry. I have taken everything you have said seriously, and I will not make that mistake."

"Good." He ran his fingers through his hair and sighed. "So, can we put all of this behind us tomorrow and just focus on covering as much ground as possible?"

She was surprised Forde was the one asking her that. He was the one who had been angry with her, and rightfully so, yet here he was holding out the olive branch. This man was full of surprises, and she knew at that moment that he was an honourable man. She nodded quickly then turned to look ahead.

"Amari." He said just as she started to try to find a way down. She straightened and looked at him again. "You're allowed to feel conflicted about Arteryn. You're allowed to feel happy and hurt. He is someone who means a lot to you, someone you already looked upon as a family figure. Yet, he omitted to tell you something crucial. You're allowed to feel betrayed. Just take your time dealing with it."

She could only nod because he was right. It just hurt more because Arteryn had never told her something so important to her. "Forde, thank you. In case I haven't said it before. I know you and Korin don't have to help me. I appreciate that you are taking this journey with me."

"Don't mention it. However, I think you should try getting some sleep. We must be on the road before dawn. I would rather we reach the marshes during the day, so we need to cover some ground."

The marshes. Amari had heard of them. "Is it true there are creatures that live in the marshes who eat Man?"

"We will find out tomorrow. I have so far avoided that route in my travels. I have only ever heard terrible things about it. The alternative is going back and taking the route through Gildevard. With the Emori and

Grantreal on our trail and a medallion to deliver, I would say we should risk the marshes." He suggested, and she nodded slowly. She relied on him to guide her through the Kais. Her knowledge of the lands came from what she had learned through books. He seemed to have the physical experience.

"Come on, let's go to sleep. Elyssians are known to move around at night causing mischief and stealing property from those unfortunate enough to meet them."

She nodded but didn't yet move. "Why do you find it surprising that Arteryn is affectionate? Have you seen how affectionate you and Korin are with each other?"

"Maybe because we're both men and Korin isn't a female fourteen years younger than me. It may be justified now that you know he is your uncle, however we can both admit how problematic your relationship with him is if you were not related. I am not saying that to accuse him of anything. If you were my daughter, I would have been more cautious about the farm hand who has a strong interest in my daughter."

"They knew though. Ma and Pa. They obviously knew, it makes so much sense now. It explains why they allowed him to discipline me."

Strangely, after their conversation, she was able to fall asleep when they went back inside the cave.

CHAPTER ELEVEN

They set out before dawn the following morning, and as they travelled through a rocky path, she could already see the towering Dewr Mountains at a distance. However, she knew that while the eye could see that far, they were probably four or five days away on foot. Two days passed with no further incident, and she was relieved for the reprieve. However, she hated constantly looking over her shoulder, half expecting either the Emori or Grantreal. Furthermore, the sleeping conditions were unbearable. For two nights, they slept under trees with one eye open and on one occasion with a torrent of rain battering them.

Over those two days, she got to know her companions better, but two things stayed with her that she found curious. One, Forde seemed to ensure Korin was never alone. If he had to step aside briefly, he somehow made sure Amari would be right there with Korin. Two, Forde woke up several times at night to check on Korin. Korin seemed unaware of it, or if he was, he didn't seem to react. It made Amari wonder what horrendous thing had happened to Korin to make Forde behave like a mother hen.

At least Korin's attitude towards her had improved somewhat. But unfortunately, it had heavily rained most of the previous day.

This new day did not seem to offer any better conditions, Amari thought when they set out at dawn. But at least the rain had let up. The sky was grey, though, so she was sure they'd spent another night wet.

"If we are lucky, we should be able to go through the marshes around midday," Forde informed them and Amari was glad she had them with her.

As their feet squelched on the wet ground, she glanced up at the sky and grimaced. It was going to rain again if those clouds were any indication.

"So, tell me, Amari, why a Sage Warrior?" Forde asked as they travelled along a dusty slanting route that had clamps of browning grasslands. They had to balance their heels to make their way down the hill without slipping and falling over.

"Why not, though?"

"Well, for one, you're a woman."

They were travelling in a line, with Korin walking ahead while Forde was behind her. She had been watching Korin as he walked and could not help realise he swung his hips as he walked. Amari could not help thinking he could easily pass for a woman. And as Forde had pointed out, she had started seeing the little nuances that Korin had that Korin probably didn't know he had. The man didn't have to do much to appear seductive. It could be a shrug, a hint of a smile, the way he stretched his body in the morning. Amari was ridiculously envious.

However, when Forde made that comment, she stopped, whirled around, and faced him. "What do you mean by that? That because I am a woman, I cannot fight?"

"You hate being a woman?" Korin had stopped as well and was now looking at them, but she quickly shook her head, wondering how to explain this to them.

"I hate the rules that men put in place dictating what a woman can and can't do." She answered and saw a look that crossed between the two men.

"Rules made to protect you?" Forde questioned, and her eyebrows almost disappeared into her scalp as anger and disbelief flared inside her.

"Protect me? You mean oppress me?" She folded her arms across her chest as she looked him straight in the eye.

"Oppress you?"

"Yes, by deciding all on their own that as a woman, I am not good enough to be a Sage Warrior."

Forde stopped short of rolling his eyes and snorted. "I don't think it's about women not being good enough. It is mostly about strength, and being a Sage Warrior is not an easy duty. Plus, I imagine when you have a child someday, you won't be so thrilled to be doing the dangerous work of a Sage Warrior."

Oh, this was priceless! She tipped her head back and released a mirthless laugh before she levelled her gaze with him. "What if I didn't want to have children?"

"Everyone wants children."

"What if I didn't? Not that I couldn't have children and still be a Sage Warrior."

"I'd say you're still young, and one day you'll meet a man and decide you want to have children with him. Besides, this has nothing to do with just that. The duty of a Sage Warrior is physically gruelling."

"So, you believe I am weaker because I am a woman?"

"You are physically weaker than I am because that is nature."

"Yet I defeated Grantreal when some men failed."

"Many factors could have contributed to that; one possibility being he underestimated your skill, and you caught him by surprise."

"So, you don't believe I defeated him because I am good enough-"

"Amari, I know where you are going with this. You are putting words in my mouth, trying to make it appear as if I think women are weaker. They are not. I know. My mother was much more resourceful and powerful than my father. By powerful, I don't mean physically. I mean just her very presence and words. So no, I do not believe women are weaker, I believe men have a higher threshold of tolerance for physically gruelling things than women do, but that does not necessarily mean we are better or stronger. So, you have a real issue about this, I see."

"And you two fight like an old married couple. You're giving me a headache." Korin turned and started to walk. Amari glanced at Forde, and he looked at her for a moment, then turned and started to walk.

"So, Korin, I assume Forde is going to Sagar to become a Sage Warrior. He thinks he can beat me when we compete." She heard him scoff behind her, and a smile formed on her lips. "What is your reason for going as well?"

Korin did not respond immediately, but the way his shoulders stiffened made her pause. It was as though he was choosing his words carefully. Then, at last, he replied. "Because Forde made me. I am not inclined to go anywhere. I don't have inclination much, to be honest, but Forde convinced himself that I need to start over in a new place with new people. Because, somehow, being in a bigger city with more people will make me feel safer." Oh, the sarcasm was just dripping from his tone that Amari couldn't help stealing a glance at Forde walking behind her. "Also, he thinks people in Sagar are more tolerant of people like me."

"Like you? Do you mean beautiful men? I hate to be the bearer of bad news here, Korin, but I doubt many men look as beautiful as you do. Or many women, for that matter." Amari's attempt to lighten the mood didn't seem to work because Korin stopped and turned to look down at her with an unimpressed look on his face. She hadn't been aware that Korin was about to stop suddenly and had to take a step back to keep from running into him. In her haste, Amari didn't see the loose rocks under her feet and stepped on them. The stones shifted under her feet, and she started to slip down.

She gasped when strong hands came around her waist rather unexpectedly, and Forde hauled her upright effortlessly. She glanced over her shoulder to look at Forde and found him smiling at her. Her cheeks burned, and Amari turned forward. Why was she tingling all over from that very brief touch? What was the matter with her? Whoa, no, she could not be having those thoughts. She had only one goal to achieve and could not allow any distractions, certainly not by a good-looking man who seemed like he might be leaving behind a reputation of being a skirt chaser.

What had they been talking about- oh yes, she had been waiting for Korin's response.

"Don't talk about how I look." The way Korin said it, Amari was almost sure he resented his looks.

She nodded because she had already gathered that he felt a way about his looks. So, she would not be mentioning his beauty again then. It didn't seem to take much to annoy Korin, but she was starting to get used to it.

In the short while that she had known them, she now realised with Forde, what one saw was what they got. He did not waste time shrouded in mystery. Korin, on the other hand, well, he carried enough secrets for both.

"Korin, when the Emori were approaching, you also seemed to sense them." It had been nagging her among the various other things she was trying to process in her crowded brain.

"I think the shrivelling flowers gave them away." He said dismissively, and she knew he was not going to discuss this any further. It was like drawing blood from a stone trying to pry the inner thoughts of this man. Impossible.

"I hope they're tolerant. My father says I am not a typical female-though I don't know what that means. If it were up to him, I would be married, settled down as a farmer's wife with a child on the way. Can you imagine such a mundane life? While I have all the respect for what my parents do, it is just not my sort of thing at all. I can't be that female whose place is relegated to just housework, though there is nothing wrong with that for people who want that. I would probably end up doing half my husband's work, and he might not like it. I would want to get involved in the farm's finances and meddle in all sorts of ways. Ma said allowing Arteryn to train me had been deliberate because it was wise to keep me occupied or become a hazard. Besides, I always preferred pants to dresses. I could not do that whole "lady" thing. My father scolded me every time he saw me climb a tree or when I hunted something for dinner."

"You hunt?" Forde and Korin asked this at the same time, and she rolled her eyes.

"I successfully hunted my first mountain lion when I was fourteen, and I would not be going to Sagar if I lacked the most basic skill required for a Sage Warrior. Arteryn used to take me hunting all the time."

"Your parents permitted you to go for days away from home with a man who was not your husband?" The disapproval in Korin's voice was blatantly evident.

The crushing feeling she had started to feel at the very mention or thought of Arteryn since meeting Korrigan descended on her once again. It hurt to consider realising he had lied to her for so long. "Well, clearly, it's because they knew he was my uncle, so that is why they never worried."

"You sound very bitter."

She didn't care for Korin's observation. But, of course, she was bitter! She had been lied to her whole life by people she trusted. Korin knew nothing about how she felt. "You know, sometimes, you don't have to say what you're thinking. Other people have feelings too. Not just your feelings matter. I am dealing with something life-changing here, and I don't need you to make passive-aggressive comments like that."

Korin suddenly drew to a halt, and then he turned around to look at her with a shocked look on his face. She stood her ground. She didn't care just how he could make anyone feel small with just a glance, and she was not letting him walk all over her.

"Did you just-?"

"Yes, I did." She cut him off, not allowing him to continue. "And while I appreciate that you and Forde have come to my aid, it does not mean I will let you just say anything to me. If those are the conditions of your assistance, then I will rather go at it alone."

Silent staring followed with Korin's light green eyes bearing down on her, but she stood firm and glared at him right back. He glanced over her shoulder at Forde, then his eyes returned to her, and he shrugged.

"Noted, but stop being so sensitive." He turned around dismissively and started to walk, and she spurted.

"I am sensitive? Am I sensitive? You're more sensitive than I am. You almost took my head off just for saying you're beautiful. I think you need to take your advice and-"

"All right, no. We are not doing this." Forde interjected as he hurriedly came to stand between them.

"No, Forde, let her speak," Korin said as he came to stand next to Forde, but even though he was not exactly smiling, she got the sense some of the earlier anger was gone. "She has a lot to say."

"I would rather survive this journey to Sagar without any conflict-"

"Which is why we need to have this conversation, Forde. Step aside." Amari waved her hand at him quickly, and then she turned to Korin. "You know what? I like you. I like how your mind works. I even like that you don't indulge me, but you say what is on your mind. However, everything has limitations. You can't just say what you want and expect there not to be any consequences. I am hurt, all right. I am hurting, and the last thing I need is you rubbing my nose into how bitter I sound. I am bitter. Everything I thought I knew about myself is a lie. I just lost Korrigan, and his revelations have made me feel like I have lost Arteryn too. I am going through a lot, and I would appreciate it if you didn't make fun of that."

"I was not making fun of that-"

"You were certainly not holding back in your opinions over how I was overreacting by feeling Korrigan's loss. However, you don't get to tell me how I should process my grief or my situation. That is for me to decide. I have to go through the motions of feeling everything I am feeling to heal."

Silence followed. Forde looked uncomfortably stiff. Korin stared at her. Amari wondered if she may have crossed a line, but she didn't care. She was done tiptoeing around Korin. It wouldn't do them any good to pretend to be something she wasn't.

Korin nodded, crossing his arms over his chest. "All right. I have taken everything you have said into consideration, and I admit, I may have been a little insensitive-"

"A little?"

"All right. A lot. No need for jeer." He waved her off quickly. "Perhaps I have gotten too used to how I say things because I'm mostly with people who may have made allowances for me for too long. I will work on it, and I will try not to be as insensitive. You may point it out to me if I do it again in the future."

She blinked. Wait, what was going on? Was Korin admitting guilt and apologising for it? She hadn't known what he would do. He was the most unpredictable man she had ever met, but this was surprising.

She nodded. "Thank you for that. I truly appreciate it. I am not saying I am without fault, and I wouldn't want you to feel like you cannot be honest with me. Just be sensitive about certain things."

"Are you both done?"

"Stay out of it, Forde!" Korin and Amari said simultaneously, then they looked at each other and smiled. So yes, there were done. Under normal circumstances, she would have offered a hug, but he didn't seem to care about being touched.

"Ugh, you're both going to drive me insane." Forde started to walk off, and Amari sighed.

"Are we fine?" She asked, and Korin nodded, then turned and walked off too. They caught up with Forde, and soon Korin was in front again, and Amari found herself walking in the middle.

"So, out of curiosity-"

"Korin, don't."

"You know I cannot resist." Korin sounded amused. "How were you even able to meet any men with an overprotective uncle like Arteryn?"

Amari almost slipped on the wet grass, but Forde helped her up, giving her a brief smile. She continued to walk, mulling over Korin's questions. "Well, I never really cared about meeting men, if I have to be honest. I decided when I was young that I had to be a Sage Warrior. If I was going to achieve that, I couldn't allow for any distractions. So, I have single-mindedly pursued my goal by training hard every day. Also, no man in the village ever approached me because they were afraid of Arteryn. He can be quite intimidating. In fact, as different as I look, no one dared tease me for it because of Arteryn. He has this quiet way of being threatening."

Korin turned and started to walk backwards, a mischievous look on his face. "So, you have never been kissed?"

She shook her head, not feeling any shame about it. "Not yet."

"Yet? So, you plan to change that?"

"Of course. I said I didn't have a time for men, and I didn't say I was a prude. I plan to do everything eventually."

"Once you achieve your goal?"

She shrugged. "Unless an opportunity presents itself before I get to Sagar."

Spinning on her feet, she turned to face Forde teasingly. "What do you say? Would you like to be my first kiss?"

She expected Forde to sputter at her forthrightness, but instead, he casually shrugged. "Only if you ask me nicely."

Oh, she had not been expecting that. Most men couldn't keep up with her when she was this frank.

"Kiss me then, Forde." She said breathily, and he smiled down at her as though realising she was teasing him. She couldn't decide if she was joking or not. She knew if he chose to rise to her bait, she wouldn't know what to do. Just the thought had butterflies fluttering in her stomach. It had started as a joke, but the more she thought about it, the more she wanted it to happen.

"I don't want your uncle to come after me."

"He will never know."

"I feel like you would tell him."

"Probably."

"Why would you tell him?"

"Just to see how he would react."

"No, thank you. I have way too much to live for."

"Aw, you're scared?"

"Yes. He had you hunting a mountain lion when you were fourteen."

Amari came to a halt, and Forde walked right into her. They would have fallen over if he didn't gain his footing and fumble around to get them upright. Instead, she took the opportunity to tease him, draping her arms over his shoulders and around his neck and looking straight at him.

"Just one kiss."

Forde chuckled as he gazed down at her. "You're trouble."

"I have a feeling she won't stop until you give her the kiss." Korin teased just as Amari released Forde.

"True. I have decided, Forde. You are going to be my first kiss."

"Most women don't talk the way you do. They certainly don't come on to men the way you just did." Forde pointed out, but she merely shrugged her shoulder in response.

"Most women don't kill mountain lions at fourteen. I am not most women." She pointed at him with a look of determination. "You are chosen, Forde. Prepare yourself. I may strike at any time."

"You are insane." He laughed as he spun her around and pushed her forward. She laughed, and they continued to walk.

A strange scent crept into the air within an hour, making it unbearable to breathe without covering their noses. The terrain changed, even more, becoming murky and the soil wetter. Clumps of grass sprung randomly, and the colour of the ground changed from brown to a reddish hue.

"We've reached the marshes," Forde announced.

Fog just lay on the surface of the marshes, with clamps of the earth in the wet area and patches of dead grass growing sporadically all over the place.

"This looks…" She trailed off as she assessed the area. It looked unsafe. If one did not know the proper route, they might find themselves sinking into the waters. "Do either one of you know how to get across? Or how long the path is?"

"Fifteen minutes or less, but we will have to be careful." Korin was standing upright, looking straight ahead, and as she turned to look at him, she saw something flashing in his eyes. It was only there for barely a millisecond, but she saw it, and it caught her by surprise.

"Do you think we can cross?" She asked, and he took a deep breath and nodded.

"I can see the path." He pointed ahead just as she and Forde looked at him in confusion. They had no idea what he was looking at because they stood, and there was just fog and clamps of water and earth.

"Are you sure?" She questioned him, and he turned a hard look her way. Right, she thought, Korin did not like to be second-guessed.

Forde inhaled sharply then started to pull out a rope from his bag. "Look, anything can happen here, so I propose we use this to tie ourselves together, so we don't lose each other in there."

She nodded quickly. When Forde suddenly wrapped his arm around her and drew her close, she yelped at the unexpectedness of it all. He didn't falter. He just started to wrap the rope around her waist. She looked up at him in shock, her eyes meeting his. Then her stomach did the strangest thing. It fluttered. What was the matter with her? She had more significant issues to deal with. She didn't have time for silly crushes. She was going to be a Sage Warrior. He broke the connection and looked at Korin.

"Do you think there are real creatures that are in the marshes?" She asked in a low voice when they finished tying the rope around each other.

Korin pulled out a long sharp knife then he glanced at them. "Can't you sense them? They're there, watching us. They're waiting."

Her eyes darted around searchingly, stunned at his words, then glanced at Forde, who seemed as surprised by Korin's words. She could not feel anything.

"Be very quiet." Korin had become alert and had assumed a commanding stance. They nodded and followed him into the marshes. The first few minutes were relatively uneventful, but the further they walked into the wetlands, the thicker the fog became so much so they could barely see even the ground at their feet. She felt what Korin had been referring to when he had said there were things in the marshes watching them. She felt them all around, watching them, following them, but staying out of sight. She knew then; they were not alone.

CHAPTER TWELVE

Amari and Forde both unsheathed their swords instantly, and in that exact moment, she heard something whip into the thick space around them. A pregnant silence hung over them, and it almost made her heart stop. Her entire body braced herself as she instantly sensed something was about to happen. Before she could take another step forward, a vine-like restraint wrapped around her ankle and pulled. She slipped, going down, but never hit the ground because Forde caught her and cut the vine with one slice of his sword.

A rush of snake-like vines lashed out at them, unseen shadows in the fog. She caught something with her eyes, a short creature barely reaching her waist with a large nose, long jagged teeth, and beady yellow eyes. She held back a scream, determined to keep it together until they passed through the marshes. A vine slashed through the air towards her, and she ducked immediately. It missed her by a mere centimetre.

"Run." Korin snapped at them. No questions were required. They started running through the unstable ground, not trusting in anything else than their senses. Korin seemed to have a clear route that only he could see, and they followed him without question. While running through the unstable wet ground, they fought through vines that wanted to latch on them and drag them down. Amari sheathed her sword and pulled out her long knives. It seemed to make sense to fight with both hands than one when the attack came from all sorts of directions.

As they ran, Amari suddenly became conscious of how quiet it had become. The only sound in the air was their feet squishing through the marshes. Something was wrong. She didn't think for one minute the creatures had stopped pursuing them, but she wondered about the sudden silence.

They didn't stop running, though and unexpectedly, a sound filled the air. There was an unmistakable thumping of footsteps behind them, and from the sound of it, it was more than one creature. Short and fast creatures were pursuing them!

Like a lit match, something unfamiliar flicked within her.

When Forde, tailing from behind, suddenly jerked backwards, they stumbled with him, and Amari fought down the force dragging her back. If she fell, Korin would go down, and they had no hope of fighting if they were all on the ground. She drew from Arteryn's teachings. Remain calm, take inventory and attack. Amari reacted with speed, turning around in the fog and reaching for Forde. A hand wrapped around her wrist, but it was small, slimy with three bony fingers. It was not Forde.

She heard Forde struggle, swinging his sword as he fought the creatures that gripped him, threatening to pull him under, and as Amari pulled her hand forward, something followed. blood drained from her face at what she saw. The creature was frighteningly ugly with an overlarge nose, watery grey eyes, long jagged teeth, and pale fuzzy hair. It came at her with its mouth wide open, and as she readied to swing her blade, she knew she would not be able to stop it before it reached her. The feeling that had flicked within her grew, spread, and burned.

Energy started to radiate around, almost forming a silhouette around her as the feeling within took over. Instinct kicked in. It burned inside her, as natural as breathing. Fire flicked to life in the hand the creature gripped mercilessly, and it released her immediately. She knew it then, understood that these creatures had an aversion to fire. Sheathing her knives, she made a decision.

"Get down!" She called out, and Korin ducked his head. The flame in her hand grew, the energy vibrating around her intensified and when she turned her palms up, fire, hot and intense, shot out from her hand. She blasted the burning ball of fire from her hands in the direction of the creatures. The rope around her waist slackened as Forde pushed himself to his feet.

"Run!" He instructed, pushing her, and they stumbled forward, following Korin's direction.

It appeared she had stunned the creatures briefly, but they were nipping at their heels once more. When she heard Korin yell, "Get down!" She did not hesitate and immediately crouched down. At that moment, a large, winged creature flew right above their heads, and before she could take a moment to digest what she was seeing, Korin was already on his feet, and they were running.

It could have been minutes or hours as they ran; she could not be sure, but the fog started to thin out, the air became clearer, and she felt Korin leap. She followed suit and landed on hard ground, Forde following behind them.

They hit the ground hard and groaned, adrenaline still pumping through their veins, and she jumped up, ready to fight when she realised where they were. Her lungs were burning, sweat drenching her skin, and her heart thudded wildly in her chest. They had passed the marshes. They were on hard ground, and the fog had somehow wholly disappeared. It was as though the wetlands had never been there to begin with. She glanced behind them, and her eyes widened in disbelief. There was nothing there, just low wet ground with a bit of fog. She could easily see where the marshes began, and she was left baffled. Had they imagined it? She glanced at her wrist and saw a bruise forming there where the creature had gripped her tightly. It had not been a dream.

She sagged back to the ground with relief when she realised, they were safe and glanced at her companions, who were also struggling to catch their breath. Apart from a torn shirtsleeve, Forde seemed unharmed.

"We have to get out of these lands fast." Forde rose to his feet and started to untie the rope just as Korin did the same. Amari pushed to her feet then looked at Korin.

"You were unbelievable in there, Korin." She still could not understand how he had seen the clear path through the marshes. "Thank you for guiding us out. How did you even see the path?"

He unwound the rope around her waist and then handed it to Forde, who folded the rope and secured it tightly.

"We need to head out and cross the bridge heading to the Sinagora forest. I think we may sidestep the Dewr Mountains completely." Forde took her hand quickly and started walking, pulling her along with urgency. A while later, he released her hand as they walked as fast as they could through the barren lands, just off the Dewr Mountains. It was different here, so stunningly quiet and an almost cocoon-like feeling wrapped around them as they trudged along.

She still wondered how Korin had seen the path through the marshes when it had been impossible to see anything. Amari glanced up at the sky and realised it was turning darker than expected. It was not just rain coming, but also possibly a storm at some point.

"We're here," Forde announced an hour later after they had entered an area with thick brush. Amari's body was screaming for some rest and the urgent need to catch her breath, but she didn't say anything. The sooner they crossed the bridge and found shelter before the storm hit, the better.

She moved forward and blanched. Forde expected them to cross on that. But, instead, the rickety wooden bridge suspended between two sharp cliffs looked like it could fall apart at any moment. To call it unstable would be an understatement. Did people use that thing? It looked like it would cave in under the pressure of air! Below, pointy rocks jutted out like the very nails of hell waiting to rip anyone who fell into shreds.

She did not think crossing over on a rope bridge with a few wooden slabs tied together was such a wise idea. It looked old, the rope looked rotten with age, and the slabs were almost non-existent.

She hunched on her heels and expelled a sigh. This bridge looked quite dangerous.

"Do you feel that?" Korin was on one knee with his hand to the ground. "Horses. People are coming. From the left, not through the marshes."

"Ya!" She heard the unmistakeably familiar voice and whipped her head around to look behind her. She could feel the thud of several horses behind them and then turned to look at Forde.

"That's Grantreal!" Forde said the words at the tip of her tongue, and it dawned on her at that moment that he probably knew Grantreal. They all came from the same town. "They must have taken the route directly from Orrick through Gildevard. We have to cross now."

"This bridge will not hold us."

"It's a risk we have to take." Forde quickly reached for Amari and pulled her to her feet. "Look, we cannot fight him and his men, not where we are standing. We are at a disadvantage. We are cornered. If we were across with a lot of ground behind us, we might try. Not if he has his men with him, as you said. While I do not doubt our skill to defend ourselves, we need to be wise about our circumstances. This is the time to retreat. Come on, quickly."

She looked at the bridge then behind her. It was probably better to plough to death onto those rocks than to let Grantreal capture her. She did not doubt in her mind what he would do to her if he found her. The man was ruthless. Fear overrode all her other senses. Fear of what being caught would mean. For a moment, she had forgotten about Grantreal, and now that threat was real, and it was back. His pursuit of her was real. He hadn't suddenly decided she was not worth the hassle.

"Amari, unless you want to be captured by that man, have him rape you and pass you around his men before he kills you. I suggest you get on the bridge now!" Forde pushed her forward as his patience slipped, but Korin jumped in before her. It occurred to her as she started to follow why he had gone first. He was testing all the suitable slabs to step on, and she was supposed to follow his lead.

Grantreal and his men pushed through the brush just as Forde started to follow and panic flared up inside her. She noted the moment Grantreal spotted her because he kicked his horse, edging it on to move faster. How had Grantreal found her? How could he possibly have seen her when she had made sure to stay off the roads? How had he gone through the Emori? Had he even encountered the Emori? She was getting tired of running. It felt like that was all she had done since she had met the Emori. She wanted to baulk at Forde's instruction to cross the bridge. She wanted to stay and fight. She wanted this to end now and be done with Grantreal, but there were thirteen men and only three of them. Amari did not see the wisdom in trying to fight. Not when they were this disadvantaged.

Forde was already behind her, trying to hurry her along, but the bridge creaked then swayed. Amari's heart flew to her throat, her head reeled with the bridge, and she had to close her eyes while gripping the rope tightly until the bridge steadied. Her stomach heaved briefly, and it took all her strength to keep her food in her stomach.

"I do not like this," Korin said a moment before a loud snap ripped through the air, almost drowning out the loud war cries of Grantreal and his men.

"Korin, hurry up! The bridge is giving way!" Forde shouted, and as Amari glanced over her shoulder, she saw with horror Grantreal and his men dismount their horses and rush the bridge.

"Wait." Korin pulled at his bow and arrow then turned, balancing on the slab. He pulled the arrow, took aim, and Amari saw gold flash in his eyes.

"What are you doing? You have to move." Forde said in frustration, but Korin ignored him.

"We have thirteen men chasing us, Forde. We need to minimise the number somehow. Don't move." Korin's voice was low, and it dared Forde to argue with him. Amari ducked as Korin let loose an arrow. From the sound behind, she knew it had connected with the enemy. He pulled out another arrow and let it loose. Two more arrows later, Amari glanced back to realise four men were on the ground. Korin's speed and aim were desirable, and she had never seen anyone with such accurate skill with the bow and arrow.

He hung the bow across his chest then began to move again.

"I will reward the first man for bringing her to me!" She heard Grantreal command, but the moment two men stepped on the bridge, it swayed violently, and she froze. They were going to die.

"It would help if you did something about the men right now!" Korin called out over his shoulder as they balanced precariously on the bridge.

"Like what? Burn them to death?" Amari didn't see how that would help. She couldn't take that risk, not with this weak bridge they were walking on.

Korin stopped suddenly, then whipped around, and panic crossed over his face. Amari did the same, and she saw what caused that reaction. A man with a bow and arrow stood on the other end aiming directly at Forde.

Amari didn't pause to think. Instead, forming a hot small ball fire, she hurled it. The bridge swayed violently at her movements, but the ball of fire hit the man hard on his chest, and he fell over. Five down, she thought as Grantreal stared at her utterly surprised, and he moved towards the bridge in stunned silence.

Korin looked ahead, then released a sigh of frustration. "Amari, if we make it through this, I promise not to be so mean to you."

"Thank you." She answered.

"Could you stop talking and move?" Forde said with urgency, and they rushed forward. Amari made the mistake of looking down, and her head spun when she realised how high they were. Her knees weakened, her stomach heaved, and the urge to pass out came over her.

Korin paused, glancing over his shoulder as though sensing her distress. Then, just as her knees started to cave in, he caught her, a strong arm wrapping around her waist before he pulled her up, holding her flush against his front.

"Stop it." He hissed into her face. "Look ahead, not down. Straight ahead, Amari."

Forde had stopped behind them, but Amari's hands gripped Korin's shoulders so tightly, she couldn't even glance behind her.

"I am almost certain between the three of us, Forde is the one suffering the most. He cannot stand heights, Amari. He's still standing. You told us your Arteryn said you were not weak. Prove it. Stand on your feet and move."

Korin set her back on her feet carefully, and she gripped both sides of the bridge as her body threatened to fail her. She closed her eyes for a moment, blocking everything out and inhaled slowly. On the exhale, she felt a calm wash over her. Korin was right. She wasn't weak. Amari was strong, and if she put her mind to it, she could take on Grantreal and his men. She was not a damsel waiting to be rescued. She could protect herself.

As they hurried along with Grantreal hurling slurs at them, another loud snap tore through the air as she stepped on a slab, and it suddenly caved in under her feet, and she found herself sucked down as she sank through the bridge. A scream of surprise tore from her lips, piercing surroundings peppered with insults as she reached out in a panic to try to grab onto anything. All she grasped was air.

She abruptly jolted mid-air, her feet dangling under her, and when she snapped her eyes open, it was to find Forde holding her already bruised wrist.

He pulled her up with one arm; his jaw clenched as he did so while he fought to maintain his balance. The men behind him were almost upon them, but he did not rush as though he did not want to make a mistake. Instead, he bent low, wrapped a strong arm around her tiny waist and pulled her up, setting her on her feet on the slab in front of him.

Looking up at him, completely overwhelmed, she couldn't believe she was still alive, that he had once more saved her life. Turning quickly, she found Korin had already crossed over. She moved forward urgently but with as much caution as possible. They were close, so close to the other side. And Forde said the unthinkable.

"Steady yourself. I'm cutting the rope." He had already pulled out his knife, and it glistened in the sweltering afternoon sun. She had a few feet to go, but he did not wait for her. One side of the bridge suddenly gave way, and she threw herself forward, grabbing onto the rope. The moment he cut the other side, the structure under her gave way. They careened towards the wall of the sharp cliff on the other end where Korin was waiting. The cries of the two men who had been pursuing them cut through the air as they plummeted down, and she closed her eyes tightly as she heard their bodies crash on the rocks below.

Opening her eyes, tightly clasping the rope, she thought for a moment she would die, but Forde had climbed up next to her already. Her muscles ached, her body was on fire, and she was sure she had bitten herself as she crashed on the wall if the blood on the corner of her mouth was anything to go by.

"Are you hurt?" Forde asked her quickly when she didn't move, and she shook her head.

"Incoming," Korin warned them from above, and they turned to look across from where they dangled as a man from Grantreal's team aimed at them with an arrow. "I've got you covered."

Korin aimed, but Amari realised he would be too late to stop the man before letting loose his arrow. There was nothing she could do. If she let go now, she would plummet to her death and possibly kill Forde along with her.

The arrow shot out from the bow, headed straight for them and just as Amari tried to gauge where it would strike, Korin let loose his arrow. Her jaw dropped when Korin's arrow caught the arrow coming straight at them, and both arrows fell away. How had he done that? How was that even possible? She had never done that. She didn't even think Arteryn could do that.

"Move," Forde instructed quickly. "Don't look." He looked up quickly as Korin appeared above them and held out his hand. Forde looked at Amari, who was still clenching the rope with all her might. He was now holding her up with the arm around her waist. Her heart was beating wildly in her chest as fear gripped her. Despite all her confidence when it came to many things, heights were her biggest weakness. "Come on, get up."

Using her upper body strength, she pulled herself up on a rope she did not entirely trust not to break. She was careful about it, too, because she didn't want to make any hasty moves that would hurt Forde, who still dangled below her.

She lifted her eyes to look at Korin, who was holding out his hand to her. She reached up to his hand and grabbed it. She allowed him to pull her up while Forde pushed her upwards, and the moment she climbed over, she turned towards him, but he had easily pulled himself up behind her. They sank to the ground, exhausted, while Grantreal stood across, screaming obscenities at them. He stormed to one of the men and grabbed and bow and arrow.

"Move!" Korin jumped to his feet just, an arrow piercing the air and careening towards them. Amari watched it as it flew in the air and followed its target. It was coming straight at her. She pulled out her knife and, with one swipe of her hand, managed to hit it away. Pushing to her feet, Korin grabbed her hand and yanked her backwards. She turned quickly and sped into the Sinagora Forest.

They did not stop running for at least thirty minutes, then finally Forde called for them to stop. She threw herself on the ground, and as she struggled to catch her breath, her throat parched and her lungs on fire. The realisation of what had almost happened to them, starting from the marshes to the bridge, suddenly hit her. She could not believe they were still alive. She could not believe this was happening to her. Not only did she have the Emori coming after her, but Grantreal had at least twelve-correction- six men on their tail as well.

She glanced at Forde from where she knelt on the ground struggling to catch her breath. She was a sweaty mess, the saltiness sliding down the edge of her lip and stinging her eyes as it cascaded down her face. She felt hot all over, and her body ached from when they had crashed on the wall.

"It will take them at least a day to use the alternative route. After that, we should be able to get through the forest without them coming upon us. But, first, we need to find shelter. The storm is almost upon us. The Sinagora Forest is not a place to be out in when there is a storm like this one coming." Forde instructed, rising to his feet, but he winced and grabbed at his side.

Her eyes widened with concern when she saw the blood oozing from his side. She shrugged her satchel and rucksack off her shoulders as she shot towards him quickly.

"You're hurt." She noted with concern as she reached for him, but he tried to downplay it.

"It's nothing. Just a scratch. I hit the wall hard when the bridge caved in."

"Sit down," Korin said in an authoritative tone that caught Amari by surprise. "Let me look at it."

"No, let us find shelter first, then we can tend to the wounds. I might be able to pick up the necessary herbs to treat the wound as we walk."

Forde instructed, then glanced around to determine the following route to take.

"Let me at least look at it." Korin insisted, but Forde threw a stern look his way. "If you die from a wound I could have treated, Forde, I swear I will never forgive you."

"It's not too bad, and I think we both know I know more about healing remedies than you." Forde insisted, but judging from the way he was standing, Amari could tell he was in a lot of pain.

"I am not very good with plants," Amari confessed, concern for his well-being making it hard to speak.

"I am," Forde assured her, and she stared at him, then glanced at Korin.

They picked up their things and started to walk, but she could tell Forde was in a lot of pain even though he did not stop. A fat raindrop plopped on her nose quickly followed by one that sank into her hair. She looked up as more raindrops started to fall and the wind started to pick up. She sincerely wished they would find shelter before the rain hit because she could not handle another night of sleeping wet. Lightning crackled before thunder roared above them.

Amari glanced around in panic, noting that Korin had started picking up a few provisions for fire as they moved forward with unfailing optimism while Forde picked some herbs and roots.

Amari wished she could be more helpful, but she did not possess any knowledge of healing methods. Her skills were very basic in the least. She was worried about Forde, anxious to see the wound to assess how bad it was. Until she did, she would not be able to relax. Amari glanced around, then she saw it, an opening just up a hill from where they were.

"I think that's a cave." She called out, climbing towards the opening without waiting for them. The sooner they settled down, the sooner she could assess Forde's wound and do something about it.

The last thing she needed either Forde or Korin being severely hurt, primarily because of her. She hoped that it wasn't severe.

CHAPTER THIRTEEN

They made it to the cave just as the heavens opened and rain poured down, followed by another loud crackling lightning. She checked the cave and found it was not too deep, just as Korin set down the firewood.

"I have it. Go tend to Forde." She shrugged her bag off her shoulders, prepping the firewood. She didn't waste unnecessary time. Instead, she used her powers to set the firewood alight. Once it was burning, she turned towards Korin and Forde.

Korin had shrugged his bags off, pulled out a cloth, dampened it with water and turned to Forde.

"Take it off." He turned to Amari quickly. "Clean his wound? I need to prepare this mixture." Amari looked up from what she was doing, then rose to her feet and came to them, brushing her hands against her clothes.

"Wait, wash your hands first," Forde instructed where he sat leaning against the wall of the cave and after washing her hands, she took the water canister and the cloth. He rattled off instructions to Korin about the mixture he had to make, and she found herself wondering how Forde knew about any of this.

Korin moved away to mix the herbs and create a paste Amari was hopeless to decipher.

Forde shrugged off his cloak while Amari struggled to catch her breath. He pulled off his vest then his shirt over his shoulders in one swift move. When she saw his ripped body and hard torso, her jaw dropped, and she gaped. His muscular shoulders flexed as he threw the shirt on the ground. Her mouth went dry as she looked at the beautiful male body before and an unexpected yearning hit her hard.

She had seen more than her fair share of half-naked men with solid toned bodies while growing up. Arteryn was one of them, but she had been too preoccupied to distract herself with men. She had missed so much due to her blind concentration on her goal to be a Sage Warrior. So, the longing that hit her hard when she looked at Forde standing before her with nothing but his form-fitting long black pants on was unfamiliar and potent.

"Amari, stop ogling him, and then perhaps you can clean his wound." Korin cut into her thoughts urgently.

Her cheeks burned as she gathered her thoughts and turned her eyes to the problem at hand, which was the wound on Forde's side. It wasn't as bad as she had thought it would be. It mainly was bruising, and the cut was not as deep. He would live. She poured water onto the wound to clean it, hoping they had something more potent.

Forde did not even flinch as she dabbed his wound clean, yet he stood so still as though if he moved an inch, he might fall apart. She looked up at him from where she bent over his wound, and her eyes connected with his. His eyes were sharp with something Amari had never seen in them before, a fire that seemed to make her feel hot all over her body. She pulled her eyes away from him quickly, focused on her task, and then moved back to put space between them. What was the matter with her anyway? She hugged her middle as she turned away from them while Korin and Forde finished making the paste to put on his wound.

She went back to the fire, adding more firewood and stoking it to keep it alive. It was a poor attempt to distract herself. They had almost died twice, and here she was drooling over a man as though she had never seen a half-naked man in her life. She needed to get a grip.

She decided to scout the cave once she got the fire going, relieved that they had at least a day's travel between them and Grantreal. However, what frightened her was that he had found her. He had tracked her here, and he was hot on her heels. How had she gotten herself into such a situation? How had he even found her?

She knew they would have to spend the night in the cave. There would be no further travelling for the day. It looked like it might rain through the rest of the day and perhaps the rest of the night.

Travelling through a torrent of rain like this would be dangerous. They risked slipping and breaking their necks, among other things.

She glanced at her companions over her shoulder and expelled a sigh as Forde put on his shirt then picked up his things. How could she ever express her gratitude to him when he had saved her life twice already? She moved back to her companions then picked up her things.

"Thank you for once again saving my life. Both of you." She muttered as she looked at Forde, who, for some reason, avoided looking at her. All she got was a grunt in return, and then he moved past her to lay out his things and sit down.

She chewed her lower lip, glancing towards Korin in askance, but he merely shrugged. "Is he angry with me once more, do you think?"

Korin eyed her with a thoughtful expression, and then he shook his head as he gathered his things. "Ignore him. He has a lot on his mind."

She didn't know what to make of that, but Korin knew Forde better than she did, and she had to trust his judgement.

They settled in for the day, aware they were losing precious time putting distance between them and Grantreal. Finally, after a meal, the pouring rain lulled their exhausted limbs, and they all fell asleep.

Their bodies had suffered so much during the day, first through the marshes then the attack from Grantreal. They had walked through lunch, and each was nursing bruises they had acquired through their journey. It was right before dawn when they woke up and immediately set out on their way.

They travelled in silence through the thick forest with its unnerving sounds. The ground and leaves were damp, and Amari ducked under one too many spider webs. The silence settled on them like a heavy rain cloud.

It was not a comfortable silence either. Forde kept his back to her, and for reasons she didn't know, he was suddenly aloof and sharp with her, especially when she tripped and fell, and he made such an issue about it.

He was angry with her; she realised and trudged along quietly, doing her best to avoid further unwanted distraction. Had he not appreciated the way she had looked at him? Was that why he was so cross with her? Korin started to sing as they travelled, his voice soft and haunting. She did not know the song, but the way he sang it sent chills down her spine. Did he have any idea how good he was? She decided not to say anything. She had caused both these men enough grief to last them a lifetime.

Fortunately, the forest shielded them from the sun, yet the dampness around them settled on them, making their clothes clammy and wet. They stopped only briefly for lunch just to get some food, but soon they were on their way, Forde insisting they try to cover as much ground as possible before nightfall. It was when Korin protested towards sunset that they finally stopped. Amari's throat was parched, and her lips were dry. Her feet hurt, and her bruised wrist was still tender. Forde did not even look like he had was injured, and he had still said very little to her. She was relieved when they came upon a stream and quickly washed her face after drinking a little.

Forde had moved forward to scout the area while she emptied her canister with the milk onto the ground then, after washing it, filled it with water. Amari looked at the milk Tia had packed for her and her eyes brimmed with tears. It was already spoilt, but for some reason throwing it out hurt more than it should. It had been part of home, from one of her father's many cows. Cows she had helped tend. Synia seemed so far away now. The only indication that the sun was setting in the thick forest was how dark it was rapidly becoming around them, and she thought about what she would have been doing now had she been home. She would have been dashing across the valley, rushing to get home in time to wash up and help Tia prepare supper for everyone.

She remembered home so vividly, the broken wagon by a tree that had stacks of dried grass on it. That was where their two dogs slept. She remembered the waterfall a few kilometres away from the village where she had bathed under the heavy spray. She remembered the dam where she had swum and played with Crispin. She remembered the warmth of the home she grown up in, the shadows the little pieces of furniture and articles in the house cast upon the glow at sunset. She remembered her room, the window she had gazed out of, praying for an adventure.

As she sat there crying over spilt milk, she suddenly realised adventures were overrated and that she would give anything to be home safe without all of this hanging over her head. She wiped her tears away then released a slow sigh, the urge to reach for her necklace very strong, but she resisted it. So instead, she pushed herself to her feet then followed Forde and Korin's voices where they were chatting somewhere down the thick stream. Korin had unpacked his things near a large tree root and muttered something about gathering firewood.

"I'll do it." She offered quickly because, in all honesty, she was not sure she wanted to be alone with Forde when he was in such a mood. Korin shrugged, and she dropped her things at his feet then went out in search of firewood. It gave her a moment to collect her thoughts and get her head straight, and when she returned to camp, they were in the middle of a conversation. Judging by the topic, it was something only they would know about, something about their home, so it effectively shut her out. They spoke about people she had never met and places she had never seen. It rendered her an outcast in their little group.

She sat quietly eating her supper, and when she finished, she headed to the stream to clean her bowl before she returned, rolled out her mat, threw her blanket over herself and settled in, gazing up at the entwined branches of the tall, sturdy trees. She turned to her side and expelled a sigh but jumped with a start when Korin suddenly sat down next to her.

"Hey, wake up. We have to talk." She shook her head in response because all she wanted was to sleep, but he pulled her to sit up and ignored her protests. "You have had us on this exhausting journey that will surely kill us in the end, so perhaps it is time you told us about these powers of yours, Kenryk."

She took a deep breath, stealing a glance towards Forde to see if he was awake. He lay with his back propped up against a log, glaring at her. He was still angry with her; she deduced then expelled a sigh. Arteryn had told her to keep her powers a secret, but she felt she owed these two men an explanation. After all, they had dropped their plans to help her when they had no obligation to do so. Even now, they could very well pack their things and abandon her- rightfully so. It was only honour that kept them with her. She took a deep breath, sitting cross-legged as she faced Korin, gazing down at her upturned palms. She had never had to explain her powers to anyone, so she didn't know where to start. She lifted her eyes to look at Korin because Forde's glare was a little hard to swallow.

"I can't explain it or how it works, but I can make fire from my hands, as you have deduced." She explained quickly, hoping that was the end of it and they would let her sleep.

"Does it burn you?" Korin looked intrigued. Forde remained silent.

"No." She shook her head as she rubbed her thumb against her palm. "I don't feel anything at all. It feels natural, like breathing. All I must do is think about it, and it happens effortlessly. I can control how much of it I put out."

"Like Korrigan did?" Korin asked her quickly, and the thought of Korrigan and what he could have taught her hit her hard once more.

"I don't know. My knowledge of what I can do with this power is limited. It is mostly self-taught. I have only ever used it to make small fires or for light. So, what I did on the marshes was a first for me."

"Who has powers and never explores them?" Korin looked at her as though she was insane, but she did not answer because, in all honesty, she did not think she wanted to talk about it. She was homesick and missed her family so much. Everything that had happened was finally catching up with her, and all she wanted was to sleep. If only Arteryn were here. She mentally shook herself. She had done such an excellent job of not thinking about Arteryn the past few days, and every time she did, she didn't know how she felt about him.

"I was always afraid of exploring them because I was afraid of being caught. Crispin, my brother, always said if anyone ever found out, they'd likely brandish me a witch and burn me." That single threat, the fear of discovery, had shackled her to that farm. "I only ever explored them when I went to the cave near the waterfall back home. In there, I could practise without fear of discovery."

Korin nodded, looking intrigued. "What else can you do?"

"What do you mean?"

"Well, you're Kenryk, so I'm assuming you can do more than that." He said with a graceful shrug of his slender shoulders, and she stared at him a little annoyed. Did he think she could form things from her hand or move items with her mind? She was Kenryk, not a sorcerer.

"Fire doesn't burn me." She supposed that worked for all Kenryk, although, in her vision, she had seen a few Kenryk burning. It made no sense. She reached out to the dancing flame of the fire burning between them and moved her hand into the fire. She pulled away, completely unscathed and turned back to Korin who looked, surprisingly impressed.

"So, you cannot burn?"

"No. Fire is like lukewarm water against my skin. I don't feel its effects." She had never spoken so much about this in her life. Arteryn had never been very open to discussing this with her, and now she realised he could probably form fire from his hand as well, that liar!

"Not even your hair?" Korin seemed intrigued, and she had to think about that, then shrugged.

"I don't know, Korin. I have never deliberately tried to set myself on fire. I know it does nothing to my skin." She didn't mean to come across as harsh, and thankfully or somewhat surprisingly, Korin did not take offence to her words.

"Can you manipulate it?" Korin asked, and she frowned in confusion at his question. He sighed, reading her confusion at his question. "I saw you make it into a ball. I saw you shoot it out from your hand. I am asking if you can change its intensity or its shape."

She shrugged. "I don't know. As I said, I haven't worked much on it. I spent most of my time training, and apparently, I am an epic failure where that is concerned because I have been nothing more than a burden on this entire journey."

She couldn't help the frustration that coursed through her at how she had been these past few days. Burying her face in her hands, she expelled a sigh, then dropped her hands to her lap and shook her head as heavy feelings washed over her. She hadn't had the opportunity to prove herself at all. Instead, she seemed to be permanently at the mercy of these two men, having them come to her rescue repeatedly. It was starting to chafe at her ego, and she was frustrated, feeling like she had been underperforming.

Korin was observing her face, and because she had never been good at hiding her emotions, he could probably read her frustration easily.

"I think you've been amazing." He muttered, but she snorted at his words. He did not have to lie on her behalf. Korrigan had praised her about her capabilities. Yet Amari felt she had depended on Forde and Korin to get her out of a situation on several occasions. How Korin possibly think she had been amazing? "Well, let's look at this situation in its entirety. You have said you have never left home before, that this is your first time away from your little village. For someone who has lived a very sheltered childhood, you're managing well. You have Grantreal and the Emori after you, and you have taken it in your stride. Most people would have gone into hiding, like in Derriane, as initially planned, but you were going to head to Sagar. You even found out about your heritage on this journey. You could have fallen apart, but you have managed to keep your head above water. If it were someone else, I think I would have been a mess by now, unable to cope with everything happening.

"You saved us in the marshes with your fire. That helped tremendously. You also saved Forde's life with the fire when that man almost killed him with an arrow. You've been able to keep up with us whenever we've found ourselves running. You haven't been an annoying whining companion. You've helped with the fire; you've made sure we always remember to refill our water. Your inability to keep quiet and sink into comfortable silences has made us have some of the most entertaining conversations, and you have not once complained about the brisk pace Forde has set. I don't think you're a burden. I do think you're naïve, though."

Korin reached out and took her hands into his, looking down at her. "Don't feel like you have to perform for us, Amari. We are not in an Arena in Sagar. You don't have to prove yourself to us. Just keep using the fire in your hands when the need arises."

He turned her palms over, inspecting them as though trying to figure out how she formed the fire.

"Your hands are tiny."

She drew her hands out of his and looked up at him with a sigh. "Did you expect me to have hands the size of a man?"

"Your confidence is." He pointed out with another shrug, and she tilted her head to the side as she looked at him.

"I envy the way you move." The words just slipped out, and she knew she stunned him because he drew back and stared at her with an indecipherable look on his face, and she felt the need to explain. "I should explain. I know I should probably stop talking right now, but we both know I won't." Korin didn't reply, but his face was practically saying yes. "You're so fluid in the way you move. The way you shrug, the way you move your hands and gesticulate. It's unbelievably sensual."

"And you want to be sensual? I thought you wanted to be a Sage Warrior."

Huh? Wasn't he offended? She had expected outrage.

"I can be both. I can be feminine and a warrior."

"Are you calling me effeminate?"

Her mouth opened, then closed, and she drew up her eyebrows as she tried to decide if he was offended or not.

"Not quite. I'd say you're a balance of both masculine and feminine, if that's even possible. You know how to be both perfectly. But, on the other hand, you do this thing with your eyes and your body that makes it impossible not to notice you. " Amari winced at her words and waited for Korin to erupt, offended.

He looked at her quietly for a moment, looking thoughtful, then he sat back, his arms outstretched behind him. "I think it depends on your definition of masculine."

Oh, so he was not angry? Amari was surprised. "What do you mean?"

"Well, Amari, when you have lived your whole life told you're not masculine enough, you eventually learn that people's assumption of masculinity is this tough, strong man who isn't sensitive. A strong warrior with broad shoulders built like Forde. Someone who talks and walks a certain way and does things a certain way. I am not masculine enough or man enough by those definitions, which I find insulting and ridiculous because I am a man. I may not walk like Forde, but it doesn't mean I am going to sit here with you and braid each other's hair or gush about how good looking he is."

Amari knit her eyebrows as she digested his words, accepting that she was guilty of making such assumptions, but she also felt the need to point out something to him.

"I suppose we're both guilty of assumptions then, Korin because women do more than sit around braiding their hair and talking about men. Also, no one says I can't sit around, braid my hair and gush about how good-looking Forde is and still be able to take down a man with a single punch. Being feminine doesn't mean weak. I can still worry about how I look and still be a warrior the same way you're allowed to be feminine and masculine as you please."

Korin snorted, then shook his head and glanced at Forde as if to say, can you believe this? Forde did not comment and remain resolutely silent.

Korin turned back to her. "Is this something your perfect Arteryn taught you?"

Her back snapped up, and the need to defend Arteryn rose within her, but she tampered it down. She sagged her shoulders, then shrugged. "He isn't perfect. Not necessarily in the ', you lied about being my uncle' kind of way. He has his flaws as we all do."

"I doubt it. You make Arteryn out to be a god."

"Hardly." Did she? No, way, but now that she couldn't help thinking about Arteryn, she couldn't help offloading the thoughts going through her mind. "He is very patient and calm, but in a way that can be frustrating. Sometimes, he's so calm you don't even know what he's thinking or feeling. Sometimes, I used to act out just to get him to react. While he has always been somewhat affectionate towards me, he can also be very aloof with people he isn't close with, thus why people find him so intimidating. It takes him a while to get angry, but he avoids you for days when he gets there. He was worse when he was younger. When I was a little girl, he was very restless and snappy after coming to the farm. He seemed unhappy, frustrated and he was very standoffish. Then one day, he just packed his things and left."

As the words slipped out, her mind started to unleash memories it must have suppressed over the years, things she had forgotten or left buried in her subconscious.

"I had seen how unhappy he was, but even then, it made no sense for him to be leaving. I felt like he was leaving me, and I tried to follow him. I remember he turned around and told me I had to go back, that he wasn't abandoning me, but that he wasn't well and he needed some time on his own to deal with a few things, to find out who he was. Arteryn+ promised me he would be back but that if he stayed, he would eventually hate himself and me. I don't know why I forgot that conversation." How had she forgotten such a thing? She only remembered being profoundly grief-stricken when he left and had cried herself to bed for weeks. "When he returned eventually, it was like he never left. He was different. Older, I suppose. He had been only twenty years old when he left, and when he came back, it looked like a weight had lifted off his shoulders. He seemed different. I sensed he had come back grudgingly, but then he settled down, and he never left again. Until I met Korrigan, I just assumed Arteryn had no family. He always has this profound sense of loss that you get from him like he lost something and never recovered from it."

"And this man isn't married?" Korin arched his eyebrows at her, and she snapped back to the present, realising she had become lost in her memories and thoughts.

She shook her head. "No." She frowned as she thought back to the past few years then shook her head. "I have never seen him with any woman even though I know most women in Synia clamour for his attention."

"And he doesn't give it to them?" Korin sat forward, and she thought she saw a curious look on his face, but she didn't know why.

"Well, no." She shook her head with a shrug. "Not that I have ever seen. I think he never felt the need to share that part of himself with me."

Korin chewed his lower lip, a small smile forming on his lips. "So, your uncle Arteryn impresses upon you that there are men who like other men. He mysteriously left to discover himself, and you have never seen him with a woman."

She nodded slowly, still not following where he was going. She heard a chuckle from Forde and sat upright as she glanced from him to Korin. "What?"

Korin bit the corner of his lip then winced as a slow smile formed on his face. "Did he frequent Simiren much?"

Amari frowned in confusion. What was Korin getting here? "Normally on every market day with my father for the farm. Why?"

Korin shrugged. "I've probably met him."

Amari's mouth opened at his words; she scoffed, released a sound of disbelief, shook her head, and closed her mouth, then shook her head again. "Is that your way of suggesting you've probably slept with him?"

She wouldn't be surprised. Arteryn had hidden many things from her, and there was that incident in the barn she had seen.

"Hey, I do not sleep around," Korin said with amusement.

"I wasn't suggesting you did. It's just that if you've ever met Arteryn, there would be no "probably" about anything. He is quiet, but he is a potent presence. He isn't the sort of man who is forgettable. So, you'd still be lusting after him if you had met him."

"Now, I want to meet this Arteryn." Korin laughed, thoroughly enjoying their conversation. She had never seen him look so relaxed since she met him. "Now it makes sense why a Kenryk man who has lived years in a tiny village is so unbelievably open-minded. I bet I know what he was doing that time when he was gone from your home."

"Good night, Korin." She shifted around, determined to end this conversation and go to sleep.

She looked at Korin, and something hit her then. He looked different. The last four days seemed to have had a possible impact on how he looked. That sickly look about him seemed to be gone, and his skin had a different hue to it now.

At least this journey was having a positive impact on him.

"All right, don't be angry. I was playing with you." Korin said between stifled laughter, then reached out for her and stopped her movements, indicting they should continue chatting. She found it pleasantly surprising. Usually, he preferred not to talk.

"Fine, but we're not having this conversation again. I have had a long day, and I just want to sleep."

"Don't worry about it. Sleep and regain your energy. I am certain Forde will have us walking tomorrow until our feet bleed." Korin jerked his head towards Forde, who didn't even make a sound to acknowledge their conversation.

Thoughts of Arteryn were crowding her brain that she felt the need to change the topic. She knew she would overthink this whole thing now that Korin had planted the seed in her head. Just great.

"You're exceptionally good with the bow and arrow." She almost groaned because it came out more like a surprise, and she didn't plan for it to come out that way. She didn't know anything about Korin's skills and didn't want him to think she was passing judgement.

"I never miss." He released her other hand, then lifted a shoulder and dropped it. "It used to frustrate Baelin whenever we practised."

"Who's Baelin?"

"Forde's older cousin. He has two cousins. Shorva and Baelin." Korin explained, then shook his head and grimaced. "I miss those two idiots right now."

"You need to teach me how you do it." There was no need not to learn something on this journey. "And perhaps also explain how it is that you seem always to know where to go. The way you went through marshes as if there was some cut-out route to use. The way you found all the stable planks on the bridge. It was amazing."

Korin looked uncomfortable suddenly, and she wondered what she had said to offend him now. She felt him physically and emotionally pull away from her, and when he did that, she shut down.

Growing up, she had always had an outlet for her emotions and Arteryn, Tia, and Joran had always encouraged her curiosity. As such, she seemed to have developed a flaw of not knowing when not to ask questions, she realised. She caught her lower lip in her teeth and chewed on it, her spirits plummeting. It was one thing to have Forde ignoring her and another for Korin, who had seemed to be the only one talking to her suddenly pull back like this. It was best if she kept her mouth shut and went to sleep. Maybe things would be better tomorrow.

"I'm just feeling a little exhausted right now. It's been a long day, and I need sleep." She turned around and curled up once more on her side, yearning for sleep.

She heard Korin shift as he rose to his feet and moved away towards Forde, and she heard him mutter. "This is your fault. Fix it."

She heard Forde grumble and ignored them. Sleep eventually came, but it was far from peaceful. The dream plagued her once more that night.

CHAPTER FOURTEEN

When someone shook her awake the following morning, her instincts immediately kicked in. She immediately went into attack mode, lashing out and fighting, but someone quickly pinned her down entirely within seconds.

"Calm down, would you. It's me."

"Forde?" She peeled her eyes open, and she looked up at the man hovering over her with his hands pinning her down. She struggled to free herself but could not move. He had both her hands pinned by her ears, and he was straddling her. "Get off me!"

He released her immediately, and she scrambled to sit up, pinning him with a stern glare. He was already fully dressed, and the sun was starting to rise on the horizon.

"You were trying to kick me in the face. I had to restrain you. Walk with me." He pulled back then started to walk away from the camp. She wiped the sleep from her eyes, relief washing over her. Then, thinking Grantreal had found her, panic flared within her.

Pushing the blankets aside, she glanced over at Korin, who was still asleep. She forced herself to her feet as she grabbed her cloak. It was a little chilly this morning, so she draped it around her shoulders and followed Forde.

She did not know what he wanted to talk about, but if it led to him ending this torture of ignoring her, then all would be well. However, she could not stand his silence. She found him seated by the stream, his knees raised, and his elbows rested on them. She slid down the embankment then sat down next to him. Silence stretched out between them, and she blew out a puff of air.

"Did you need something?" Why was he suddenly so quiet?

A frown creased his forehead, and he rubbed his palms together; then, he turned to look at her. "I apologise for my behaviour yesterday. I have had a lot on my mind."

She nodded, surprised that he had called her out here to apologise and thankful that they were putting everything behind them. She did not want to fight with him anymore. She considered him a friend now, considering her situation where she was utterly alone; she could do with a few friends.

"Thank you, but you don't owe me an apology. I understand your frustration with this situation. I'm sorry that you and Korin are affected by this situation because of me."

Forde shrugged and a slow smile formed on his lips. "This 'situation' as you call it has had rather welcomed results, especially on Korin. I haven't seen him act the way he has been these past few days in a while." His smile faltered, a haunted look crossing over his face, then he shook his head. "Don't worry about Grantreal. He's hardly the first warlord I have had my run-in with."

"Who was the first?"

"The man who killed my family."

She gasped at his words, her mind jumping to all sorts of conclusions. "You killed him?"

A solemn look replaced his smile, the ghosts of his past settling heavily around them. "I had to."

"For revenge?"

He shook his head quickly, glancing out on the horizon, a pained expression crossing over his face, his wild hair shifting lightly with the morning breeze. "No, it was not for revenge. It was an instinctive reaction.

He was doing something to someone I cared about, something vile, and I stumbled upon it unintentionally, and all I could think about was killing him. Rage overtook me. I had so many emotions rushing through me, but all I could think about was that he had to die. I hadn't felt that overwhelming and overpowering intense emotion, not even when I walked into my village as a child and found everyone dead. It was a mixture of shock, disbelief, rage and something else I can't quite name."

He clenched his fists tightly, the images of that day flashing in his brain. "I didn't ask questions. I took out my sword, and I killed him. I could have done it with one stroke, but the rage that overtook me that day... There was blood everywhere when it was over. I don't remember doing it. I remember hot white rage, and then when I came back to my senses, he was dead at my feet. I only found out after he had died who he truly was."

He inhaled sharply, then ran his fingers through his hair as though trying to shake off the dark feeling that had settled over him. "No one knew who killed him, so I got away with it, and that does not bother me at all. My consolation is that I killed a man who destroyed many families and almost destroyed someone who means so much to me. It's further knowing that he will never harm anyone else ever again."

She should have been afraid to know she was travelling through the Kais with someone who had just admitted to a murder, but she wasn't. For some reason, she did not feel the need to judge him. She knew instinctually that this man had been hurting Korin. She just knew it. A part of her was aware she should have been wary of Forde after his disclosure, but she knew he was leaving out a lot of information that would put the situation in context. If she had walked into a case of someone hurting her family, she was almost sure she would have done the same. Judgement wasn't hers to pass.

"Does that information change the way you see me? That I killed a man outside the field of battle?"

This man who had saved her life countless times on their journey so far, risking his own and not abandoning her even though that would have been the wisest thing to do, thought his confession would make her see him so differently. The same man she had seen over the week wake up twice every single night to check on Korin; the same man who seemed to go into a panic that he tried to hide whenever Korin wandered out of sight? She wasn't blind. She was aware that something was wrong with Korin. He had woken them up twice so far at night from a nightmare he was having. When he had one of his nightmares, he retreated into himself. When he did that, Forde became even more alert, watching his every move. Could it...? Had Korin been...? No, she didn't even want to consider it. The thought was too dreadful to contemplate.

"When I was sixteen years old, I got into a quarrel with my brother, Crispin. I don't know what it was about, and it doesn't seem all that important anymore. I was in a fit of anger and stormed off into the forest. Around that time, there was a group of Orrick knights searching for a runaway prisoner. There were warnings to be on the lookout for him, but in my rage, sensible thoughts fled my head."

She paused, her eyes drifting to the narrow river before them. She had never told this to anyone. Yet here she was about to divulge something she kept so close to her heart. She expelled a sigh, clasping her hands on her lap.

"I remember I was leaning against a tree, too preoccupied with my thoughts when a man suddenly broke through the forest. At that point, I had had about...nine years' experience training with Arteryn so, and you'd think I would have been able to defend myself-"

"Amari." Horror had crossed over Forde's face when she glanced at him, but she didn't want to stop. Instead, she wanted to tell him this.

"Just let me finish." She implored but judging by how he was holding himself, and he didn't seem ready to hear whatever she had to say. "He was a big man, strong, built like an ox. He had me on the ground before I could even think to do anything. I should have screamed or called for help- even used the fire from my hands, but I just... I froze. I couldn't believe this was me, pinned down to the ground by this man and not fighting back. Fear paralysed me. Everything in me screamed for me to fight, to cry out, but my body had gone into complete shock. The man wasn't the person in the issued warnings. No. It was an Orrick Warrior.

"Fortunately, Arteryn had been looking for me. He stumbled into the situation just as the man was trying to rip off my tights. I don't know if it

148

is because I was so terrified that my mind seemed to be all over the place, but in an instant, I thought I saw Arteryn's eyes turn red. What he did to that man…." She trailed off, then chewed her lower lip as she thought back to that day, then shook her head, trying to dispel the heavy thoughts that settled over her.

"Arteryn killed the man. I'd never seen him in such a rage. It was intense, and so was the way he behaved afterwards. He hovered around wherever I was. His normally overprotective streak doubled, and I sensed he was a little angry as well. He had taught me to fight, and when the time came when I had to, I froze. I was mad at myself, and I misbehaved at home because I couldn't process what had almost happened to me or why I didn't fight back.

"So, Arteryn took me hiking for three days, and on that mountain, he broke down my walls and forced me to talk about how I was feeling, and I finally expelled everything that I had been holding so tightly to my chest. It took a while for us to get back to normal, or as normal as you can get after almost being raped. Being here without him, I know it took everything in him to let me go alone."

She paused then looked at Forde, seeing the look on his face. It wasn't pity. There was anger there, just a little bit. Amari realised his anger was directed at what she had shared with him. "So, yes, Forde. What you told me does change the way I see you." When she said those words, she saw the disappointment that clouded his face. "If I were in the same situation, if I stumbled on a situation where someone was hurting my family, I would probably do the same. It's not any different than what Arteryn did when he saw that man attacking me. It affirms what I already know about you; that you'd do anything for people you care for."

He seemed stunned by her words, stunned that she was not judging him for his actions. He seemed unable to process that she was not crucifying him over this.

"What?" She asked him quickly when he continued to look puzzled by her response.

"I'm sorry that man hurt you. An Orrick Warrior of all people." He gritted through clenched teeth then shook his head.

"You don't have to apologise. I was fortunate. Arteryn came before the man did anything. But unfortunately, some aren't as fortunate, and they have to live through the darkness that immediately blankets them when it happens." She muttered, then reached out without thinking, brushing her hand over his back. "It gets better eventually, Forde. It's a very long journey of healing, but it gets better."

She looked deeply at him, knowing that he must have realised she was no longer talking about herself. She felt the weight on his shoulders, the emotional burden he carried like a noose around his neck.

"It's not easy on those around us either, those who have to help us pick up the pieces. They blame themselves, thinking they could have done something to protect us. They allow the what-ifs to suffocate them, but at that point, there's nothing else to do but to try to pick up the pieces. They don't sleep, they constantly worry, they wish they could take away the pain. The sad truth is there is nothing they can do but just be there and show support. We must do all the healing ourselves. We must find the strength to pull ourselves from the darkness and learn to live through the pain. And the pain never goes away. The physical scars heal, but the mind takes longer. The mind never lets you forget, but eventually, one day, you're able to go a few hours without thinking about it, then days and sometimes weeks. Then you encounter a little trigger, a smell, and it takes you back to that dark place." She took a deep breath then withdrew her hand. "He'll be all right one day, Forde."

"Amari-"

"It's fine. You don't have to tell me anything. It's not your story to tell." She assured him quickly and watched a riot of emotions played over his face. He seemed incapable of dealing with anything she had said to him at that moment. The anguish on his face tore at her heart, and before she could overthink it, she threw her arms around him and held him tightly, offering him the support he needed. He had had to be Korin's rock. But curiously, she wondered if he had had someone to be his.

He held her tightly for a moment, then drew back, a look of embarrassment crossing his face as he fought to keep his emotions in check. Her heart broke for him. He was trying so hard to remain strong for Korin that he wasn't allowing himself to work through his emotions about the situation.

"That is not the reaction I was expecting. Your reaction to me being a murderer." He confessed, still clearly processing that she was not reacting negatively towards him.

"What were you expecting?"

"Not this." He confessed quickly, tipping his head to the side to get a good look at her for a moment, and then he shook his head. "I thought that perhaps it might make you feel a little uneasy to know that you are travelling through the Kais with a murderer."

"Well, you have kept me alive so far, and you haven't given me a reason to think you might slaughter me in my sleep." She knew why his revelation did not bother her. In the few days she had known this man, she knew he was honourable and that whatever decision he had made that day had to have some significant reason to it. Forde was not like Grantreal.

She saw a slow smile forming on his lips. She could not help smiling when he did. His smile was infectious. His smile was beautiful. Why had she suddenly started thinking of something like that? She had to be losing her mind, she thought.

She bit her lower lip then looked away from him; her cheeks burned once more. She was smitten with Forde. Plain and simple. What was the matter with her? There was so much happening, so much going on, and there she was, getting a crush on a man she would probably never see again once this journey was over. This moment was no time for such foolishness. She had a goal to achieve. She had been stuck with him for days now, thrust in intense situations that threatened their very lives. It was possibly just her mind projecting her gratitude for him taking care of her.

Besides, having watched the way Forde dedicated so much of his time looking after Korin, she doubted he had time in his life for someone like her either. Furthermore, there was no space in her future for a man.

"We should, uh, we should be heading out. If Grantreal travelled through the night, then he might be gaining on us. Plus, there is the Emori situation...." She felt she needed to bring it up to give her perspective. She could not allow herself to fall for this man. She was already on dangerous ground with the infatuation she seemed to be developing for him.

A look crossed over his face, something she was powerless to decipher, but then he nodded.

"Yes, we should." He expelled a sigh before pushing himself to his feet. He stuck his hand out to her, and she put her hand into his larger one. He yanked her up in one swift move, but she did not know if he pulled too hard or if she had allowed him to pull too hard. Whatever the reason, she found herself flush against Forde's hard chest. It knocked the breath out of her entirely, and her hands flew up to splay over his chest. Amari's hands had only pressed against his chest from instinct, but now that they were up against his hard muscles, his heat and scent enveloping her, she broke into a sweat, and her heart thundered in her chest. For a moment, they stood there breathing heavily as her hands folded over his chest.

"I'm sorry, I didn't...." She fumbled for words breathlessly as she gazed up at him and started to pull back. He did not release her; he held her fast, his arm snaking around her waist to bring her even closer. She lowered her eyes to his chest, her breath catching in her throat. She was not sure what to do. She did not know. She was clueless, and panic flared up inside her. She lifted her eyes to look at him, her entire body trembling out of its own volition. She didn't know what her body wanted, but whatever it was, she was eager for it.

His hands slowly moved up her back, and she almost burst into flames at the unexpected feelings that burned within her. His hands cupped both sides of her face, and he lowered his face towards hers, giving her ample time to pull away. She did not. She knew what was going on, knew what he was doing. He was going to kiss her, and for reasons she could not explain, she wanted him to kiss her. She wanted this so much her body ached, but as she reached for him, something suddenly gripped her tightly. Suddenly, her whole body became alert, the hairs on her arms and the back of her neck prickling. She pulled out of his arms quickly, whipping around, as she knew without a shadow of a doubt that danger was near.

CHAPTER FIFTEEN

"What are you two doing? We have to leave now." Korin was suddenly upon them without preamble. Amari didn't know if he had just come down now or if he had heard them talking. Her face flushed from the tingling in her body Forde had caused, and even though the danger was undoubtedly upon them, her silly heart was still beating fast.

"Can you feel it too? Is it the Emori?" She asked Korin quickly, but he had paused to look between them with suspicion. Please don't say anything, please, she pleaded with him with her eyes.

He shook his head slowly, his eyes narrowing as he looked at them. "It's not the Emori. About three Elyssian men passed us a while ago, but that's not the issue. There's a forest Faun coming."

"How do you know?" Amari couldn't see anything around them that indicated anything was coming. She could sense something was coming but had no idea what it was.

"Listen." Korin held up his hand, and grunts filled the quiet morning. "He's not too far, but he is coming this way. Those three Elyssian men are heading in his direction, and I suspect they will be dead soon. We must go. Unless you both want to sit around here and do whatever you were doing."

"Shut up, Korin." Forde pushed him quickly as he moved past him and headed towards their camp. Amari started to follow, but Korin was watching her, blocking her way.

"What?" She asked him quickly.

"You're not the first woman to fall for him, Amari. I've seen that look on a lot of women." He muttered before rushing up the hill towards their camp. Amari froze to the spot for a moment as his words crashed down on her. What did Korin mean by that? Did she sense resentment from him? Was he giving her a warning? She hurried to the camp to put her things together and quickly hoisted her stuff over her shoulders, and they were moving.

Screams suddenly tore through the quiet forest with unmistakable sounds of bones breaking, grunts and a fight the Elyssians had lost. Amari and her companions drew to a halt as they glanced behind them where the sounds rang out.

"Can we fight it?" Amari asked Korin quickly, seeing as he seemed to have all the information about this creature. If he was still territorial about Forde, he needed to get over it, she thought. Korin turned his gaze towards her. Folding his arms over his chest, Korin regarded Amari with a look that left her feeling like an idiot for asking. "Yes or no, Korin."

"If you want to die then, absolutely, go fight it. I'll have you know that even Sage Warriors avoid Forest Fauns. Those creatures can snap a man in half." Korin answered, and she levelled him with an annoyed glare at his tone. He seemed to realise he was unnecessarily rude because he rolled his eyes. "We run."

Korin was off like a light before Amari could even form a response. Forde shook his head at her as if to tell her not to take it personally. She was behind Korin in seconds as they rushed through the forest.

"I am getting tired of running!" Forde gritted angrily behind them, and to be honest, so was Amari. If it were not for the bloody medallion and the need to get it to Bhrim, she would stand and try her luck against Grantreal, his men and the Emori.

The sounds that followed were clear enough that Amari knew the Elyssians were dead, butchered by the Forest Faun and that it was, without a doubt, coming after them.

They rushed through the forest, determined to put as much space between them and the Forest Faun, but if the thuds behind them were anything to go by, the Forest Faun was hot on their trail. Amari knew that no matter how hard or fast they ran, they were not going to outrun this creature in its natural habitat. It simply knew the forest better than they did. The situation was futile. It was like trying to outswim a fish.

"Stop." She drew to a halt, consciously monitoring the distance between them and the Forest Faun. The creature knew they were there but hadn't seen them yet. That was the important thing. "We can't outrun it. It's too fast."

"It's also stronger than possibly even an Emori and territorial," Forde added quickly, glancing over his shoulder in the thick forest. The damp soil under their feet insulated their footsteps, but it had left tracks for the Faun to follow.

There was hardly much sunlight streaming through the tall and old trees, roots growing thick onto the surface and green moss clinging to barks. Amari glanced around them, taking inventory of their surroundings and formulating a plan. Long branches merged into each other where they stood, but she could see that on their right, the forest sloped towards a stream below and then picked up from across the creek. She hurried towards the sloping area, went down on her haunches, and scanned their surroundings before an idea flashed in her mind.

"Down here." She instructed, carefully slipping down the steep slope by grabbing onto the old roots jutting out of the soil.

"Down where? To our death?" Forde asked incredulously, but she tossed a glare at him as she landed on the ground below.

"There is an opening here, you idiot." She pointed to what she had seen when she had hunched down. The old tree Forde and Korin stood next to on the ground above had a massive hole under it that was too small to be a cave but at least offered some relative shelter from anything that could be pursuing them. If said pursuing creature did not come down the slope, they could hide out in this hole. "Come down here right now or stay there and die."

Forde jerked back, and he seemed stunned by her bossy attitude. Something flashed over his face briefly, and she couldn't make it out. She watched them descend, and the moment they joined her, they slid into the opening under the tree. Amari could hear the loud grunts from the Forest Faun as it approached.

The loud thudding footsteps approached, but unlike before with the Emori, when fear had gripped her so tightly, she had not even been able to think, she remained calm. The thudding stopped directly over them, and Korin's gasp filled the air. She reached out unconsciously and placed her hand on his arm to hopefully still him. She turned slowly, and being she was smaller than both men, she had room to crane her neck and glance through a hole in the tree roots above.

She almost died with horror when she saw the Faun. It was unlike anything she had expected. It was a large creature, grey with yellow obsidian eyes. Its face looked disfigured, and a tree branch grew on its shoulder. The branch even had three leaves growing from it. The Faun had a shaggy old brown sackcloth covering its loins and carried a large axe. It was looking around searchingly, trying to discover their location. She watched it sniff the air, grunting as it tried to catch their scent. Then, suddenly, it went down on one knee very close to where they were, and it took everything in Amari to remain calm.

Amari's breath hitched as the Faun came frighteningly close to where they were. If they stayed there a moment longer, they were going to die. She glanced at the Faun once more, analysing its movements. She pulled her gaze away from the Faun then glanced around quickly to figure out a plan. Forde started to draw his sword slowly, but she promptly stayed his hand and shook her head. "Stop." She mouthed at him, and he frowned, but she repeated it. He looked sceptical but finally nodded.

She knew what she had to do, but she also knew the risk. However, if she did nothing, they were going to be dead in a few seconds.

She took a deep breath, then opened her hand and formulated a hot ball of fire. She disregarded the look of shock that crossed over Korin and Forde's faces. Instead, holding her palm facing the sky, she grew the size and intensity of the fireball. It should have been stifling. It was fire, after all, but it did nothing to her. However, Forde and Korin did draw back from her, squeezing themselves away in the tiny space they all occupied.

Once it was the correct size and intensity, she withdrew her hand, allowing the ball of fire to hover before her in the air. Holding up both her hands up, she focused her attention on the ball of flame then pressed forward, pushing the fireball away from her with force. It flew from her with such lightning speed that when it crashed on the tree across the stream, it almost blew it into smithereens, causing it to catch on fire immediately.

The Faun let out a loud cry then leapt over them to land in a loud thud merely a few feet away from them with its back turned to them. They jumped in stunned silence, and for a heart-stopping moment, they thought it might turn around and see them. Instead, they sat there frozen, unable to breathe, looking at the large, muscled back of the Faun turned their way. It shot to its feet and started running towards the burning tree.

Amari quickly scrambled out from under the tree, pulling herself up with the roots to the path on top. The men were behind her in seconds. Korin moved past her with great speed and agility, and they followed as fast they could to keep up with him.

Amari didn't even know where they were going. She had no idea how she could have possibly navigated this forest alone, and they were not even deep in Sinagora. Amari could only imagine the creatures that lay further within. So, she depended solely on wherever Korin was leading them, and seeing as he seemed to be able to identify safe routes, she was more than happy to let him lead.

She did not know how long they ran through the forest. It felt like hours, but it was probably less than twenty minutes. Putting distance between them and the Faun or anything drawn to the smell of the blood of the dead Elyssians was vital. They followed Korin with complete trust, and because they had only been travelling on the outskirts of the Sinagora Forest, she noted the moment the air became lighter and the sky started to pierce through the thinning trees. When they cleared through the forest, at last, Amari exhaled with relief as they finally slowed down and stopped to catch their breath.

Throwing her things off her back, Amari bent over at her waist, hands on her knees and took a moment to catch her breath. A sheen of sweat covered her forehead and whole body that it stung and itched all over. She saw Forde and Korin in the periphery of her vision as they dropped their things and fought to catch their breaths.

"Everyone all right?" Forde asked as he pushed himself upright. Amari followed suit then nodded, wiping the sweat from her forehead. "That fire… is there a reason you haven't used it to burn Grantreal into a crisp? Or the Emori? It would make travelling to Bhrim so much easier."

"Oh, hilarious, Forde. If it were that easy, then I am sure Korrigan would have done it." She glanced at Korin, who was watching her silently. "What?"

"Nothing." He shrugged then looked away from her, but she watched him visibly relax. "I don't know how many creatures we have to survive to get to Bhrim, but when we get there, I hope they can give me a warm and comfortable bed to sleep in."

Deciding it was time to defuse the situation, she spoke up. "How do you know those men were Elyssian?"

"The clothes they wore," Korin answered with a shrug. "They didn't see me. But, of course, you wouldn't have seen them either, seeing as you were both too engrossed in whatever you were doing by the river."

"Are we still talking about that?" Forde asked in exasperation, pinning Korin with a glare.

"What? I'm just wondering if your obvious similarities to her Arteryn isn't the reason she's making you his substitute." Korin's sudden change caught Amari by surprise. She went from being exhausted to being downright outraged. Korin's accusation almost knocked Amari off her feet.

"Korin, I am very accepting of many things, but what I don't allow is anyone to speak about Arteryn. You don't know him, and therefore you're in no position to make assumptions about him." She didn't care how conflicted she currently felt about Arteryn, and she was not going to allow anyone to talk about him or make any unfounded accusations about her either.

"Oh, I'm sorry that every man you meet has to live up to your saint Arteryn -"

Her usually contained anger slipped, and she rounded on Korin with a heated glare, her hands clenched into tight fists.

"Korin, I don't care that you don't like to be touched. I will hit you if you say one more thing about him!"

"Stop, both of you," Forde said in exasperation, and he looked to the heavens as though seeking patience or divine intervention. Finally, he lowered his eyes to them. "Amari, Korin is baiting you. Deliberately. He likes doing it, and you fall for it every time. I am exhausted, I feel filthy, and I am tired of sleeping huddled to tree barks. If you two are going to keep doing this to Bhrim, I will ask that you stop. Immediately."

Amari turned away from them, folding her arms across her chest as she fought to stay calm. Finally, she closed her eyes, taking slow, deep breathes and exhaling. When Amari felt the anger leave her body, she opened her eyes but still felt a little on edge and glanced at them over her shoulder. If Korin said one more thing, she would not be responsible for her actions.

Korin regarded her with an indecipherable look as Forde picked up his things, preparing to leave.

"Really? Don't you feel just a little pressured to live up to the image of this Arteryn? Apart from her obsession with being a Sage Warrior, he is all we've heard about." Korin picked up his things as well, then watched her as if expecting a reaction. But she couldn't help it. Amari had to say something. Forde had said Korin was baiting her, but for the life of her, she couldn't help rising to the bait. She just wanted to shut Korin up once for all.

"You know, Korin, I am certain if you ever meet Arteryn, you'll want to climb him like a tree. You'll probably throw yourself at him and beg him to take you. I bet the only reason you're so sick of hearing about him is that a part of you is probably lusting after the very idea of a man who is very much like Forde but isn't 'related to you, right?"

"All right, enough! I am not going to keep hearing about this from either one of you!" Forde snapped in exasperation just as Amari watched with satisfaction, blood draining from Korin's face. Whatever he had been about to unleash would have been epic, but Forde didn't give him a chance. "Are you both done?"

"He started it." She mumbled, not caring how childish she sounded at that moment. If Korin planned to continue trying to get under her skin, she would give back just as hard. She didn't care whatever he had gone through. It did not give him the right to treat her this way.

"You are a very peculiar person," Korin told her, but she was stunned to find he didn't appear angry with her. Instead, he said it purely as a statement, not intending to hurt her or anything.

"I get that every day, Korin." She told him. "That's why I am going to be the first female Sage Warrior."

"There she goes again." Korin rolled his eyes, throwing his hands in the air in exasperation, but at that moment, something else entirely different happened. She felt a shift in her relationship with Korin that she couldn't understand. It could be the look in his eyes, but for the first time, Amari got the sense that she had finally earned a bit of respect from him somehow. Even his exasperated sigh didn't come out as an insult, but very much the sort of friendly chiding she and Crispin used to each other. She just knew then that she and Korin were going to be all right.

She shook her head and let out a chuckle that surprised Forde. "I don't mention it that much."

"You do. Every chance you get, which happens to be every day." Korin accused, but the relaxed tone and the slight smile let her know he was just playful.

Forde looked from her to Korin, seemingly trying to make sense of either of them. Poor man, she thought, he was going to lose his mind before they reached Bhrim.

"You two are made for each other," Forde muttered under his breath, but Amari ignored him as she turned to look at the sight before them, and she was captivated.

The fields immediately after the Sinagora Forest was unbelievably stunning.

The view was soothing, picturesque and the air felt refreshing.

"Come on. We have to be on our way. There should be a stream nearby, and perhaps we can refill our water supply."

"I am hungry," Korin said as they started to walk through long willowy brown grass. "And we are out of food."

"We are at least an entire day away from Golynvale, and I think we might have to survive the rest of the journey there without food," Forde informed them quickly as they moved further away from the thick green forest. Amari decided not to argue with him. However, she still had bread and cheese in her bag, and she distributed it out to her companions. They ate as they walked and paused only briefly to refill their water canisters and wash the sweat off their faces.

Forde pushed them hard the whole day, determined to get them within the boundaries of Golynvale by at least dawn of the following day. But unfortunately, there was no shelter available anywhere as they walked a plain with barely any bushes, and as such, he insisted they travel through the night.

"The Emori will find us." Forde kept telling them every time Korin or Amari called for a break. The moon offered quite a bit of light, but Amari still thought it was insane to travel through the night. They could run into anything. It was close to midnight when Korin and Amari protested and insisted on stopping. They sank next to two large boulders and spent the rest of the night sleeping uncomfortably against the rocks. It rained sometime during the night, and it was one of the most miserable nights of their journey. In the back of their minds, they all knew they still had a distance to go before they arrived at Golynvale.

The following morning, they started very early, their stomachs grumbling from the lack of food and muscles aching from overuse. The conversation had dwindled between them as each focused on putting one foot after the other, pushing themselves forward.

Amari almost burst into tears when she saw the walls of the river city of Golynvale. Located at the utmost north-eastern part of the Kingdom of Sagar, the river city was like an oasis in the middle of a desert. Amari was relieved they could rest and get some food.

It was very similar to Orrick, and the people within went about their business not paying any attention to them. It did not look like a city adequately managed, and Forde explained that the Lord of Golynvale was a scrupulous man who squandered all the money and did nothing to develop the city or its people. Finally, they found an inn where they had a bland meal that had been the sole drive to keep moving ahead.

Amari wished she could find a bed to sleep in, but they were so close to Derriane.

The island of Derriane sat across the sea from Golynvale, and she knew they would have to get a ferry to cross. So, while they were having a rest after a rather unpleasant meal, Forde went out to sort out their passage across the river, and when he returned an hour later, he found her and Korin sitting towards the fringes of the city.

"The ferry has already gone to Derriane, and it will be quite a while before it comes back. We have already spent too much time here, so I had to improvise. I have managed to secure a small raft. I know a man in Derriane, and I have arranged with the owner of the raft to leave it in his care." Forde announced, and Amari winced. Forde was incurring too many expenses on her behalf, and she didn't know how she was going to pay him. But, remaining silent, she knew this man was spending so much of his money to help her.

"I've never been to the ocean before," Amari informed them as they walked away from the village towards the seashore.

"I believe that," Korin muttered, but she rolled her eyes at him. "Don't drink the water."

"I know that. I'm not an idiot." She nudged him with her shoulder then cringed, remembering he didn't like to be touched. He didn't react. He just kept walking. "I'm not a very strong swimmer."

"Really? There's something you're not good at? I am certain it has nothing to do with you being a woman." Korin commented, and she couldn't help it; she smacked his arm. He laughed at her, but she knew he was teasing her, so she chuckled along with him.

Forde merely glanced then shook his head, but Amari caught the smile playing on his lips. When Korin spoke again, it was such a departure from what they talked about Amari almost tripped on her feet.

"So, what were you two doing by the river when the Faun came upon us? I mean, I heard everything you said, but I wasn't looking." They could hear the laughter in his voice, and Amari rolled her eyes. She was not touching that topic with a ten-foot pole. Korin knew that Amari and Forde had almost been about to kiss. Had that Faun not intruded, Amari would have overthought every single moment of experiencing her first kiss. The moment was gone, the kiss had never happened, and there was nothing to talk about.

"Just keep walking, Korin," Forde told him, and Korin chuckled at Forde's response.

Their easy camaraderie disappeared completely when a dark feeling suddenly crawled up her spine. Korin came to a halt in front of her, sensing the same feeling going through her. She knew immediately, felt it to her bone, the Emori were nearby.

CHAPTER SIXTEEN

They were barrelling down the valley towards the riverbank when the first thunderous bellow tore through the air. An arrow shot through the sky and landed close to Amari. It was so large, much longer than what she carried. They ran as fast as they could, away from the approaching Emori.

"The raft is down there," Forde called out as they sprinted across the field. "And I am getting tired of running!"

So was she, but while they could fight Grantreal, they possessed no defence capabilities against the Emori. She did not even know if killing the Emori was a possibility. All her focus was on getting on the boat, and the faster they ran, the closer they came to the bank.

They saw the wooden raft that was larger than Amari had expected. She had expected something small, but Forde had other thoughts. She couldn't begin to imagine how much money it must have cost him. Korin reached it first, cutting the raft free and pushing it into the water. They jumped in, grabbing the pedal and rowing away from the bank with as much speed as they could muster. Forde was letting out a string of obscenities out of frustration.

They were already away from the bank when the Emori arrived, and she let out a sigh of frustration as they moved away, relieved that once more they had evaded the Emori. She watched as the beasts disappeared the further; they rowed away from shore. She only glanced around her a few minutes later when she was sure they were safe and expelled a sigh of relief.

"Derriane is at least three hours away, at least at this pace. I'm just relieved Emori do not seem to like water much." Forde muttered, looking a little exhausted as he stretched out his legs in front of him while Korin continued to steer them further away from Golynvale using a pedal.

"Who exactly owns this boat?" She questioned as she sank on the hardwood floor, peeling off everything she was carrying and discarding her cloak.

"It belongs to a man I had met a few times when I made my journey to Derriane in the past. He let me borrow it." Forde leaned over the boat as he responded and scooped up some water. He washed his face quickly, pulling out a cloth to wipe his face.

The rough night they had broadcasted itself on their wrinkled clothes, their frizzy hair and the patches of dirt on their faces. "Am I the only one bothered that we have spent the majority of our time on the run? It is so frustrating. I think about all those hours I spent training to fight, and I cannot even use that skill. At least with Grantreal, we could try to defend ourselves, but the Emori are beyond anything we can handle."

He shed the top layers of his clothes as the sun continued its ascension, and he sat there in nothing more than a blue cotton vest, his pants and boots. He dipped the cloth into the water and tried to clean his grubby skin.

Amari sat there deep in her thoughts, watching his toned sinewy arms and immediately felt her chest tighten as unfamiliar emotions coursed through her body. Her stomach tightened when he stretched his arms above his head to reveal a flash of his taut stomach muscles. Without thinking, she groaned. The heat crawling over her proved too potent to contain. She pulled her eyes away from him to glance at the water all around them. She had to be losing her mind. They had just eluded possible death at the hands of the Emori, and here she was drooling over a man's body. She was losing her mind. She chalked it down to being in a constant state of anxiety since she left home. That had to be why she was acting the way she was.

Silence followed, and when she turned to look back at Forde, it was to find him watching her with a strange look on his face. It seemed he was struggling to understand what was wrong with her and because she could not meet his eyes, she turned to look at Korin, who was having the time of his life.

"Are you all right, Amari?" He had a mischievous grin on his face. She struggled to save face, realising her groan had been audible and the reason for the silence that had followed was because of her reaction to the indecent thoughts racing through her mind. She should have let Sirian kiss her all those years ago when he had cornered her by the river. Then, she probably would not be feeling so hot and bothered over a man's arms and shoulders. Then again, Arteryn had chased Sirian away and threatened him with murder.

She expelled a sigh then nodded quickly, searching her brain for a plausible excuse for her reaction. "I just realised that the Emori must not have been too far behind us. If we hadn't travelled through most of the night, they might have found us before we reached Golynvale."

"Yes, I am sure that is the only thing concerning you this moment." Korin hid a smile as he looked away from her while he continued to row.

Now that Amari had allowed the indecent thoughts about Forde to settle into her brain, she could not stop them from growing and taking over. She was still quite disgruntled and resentful that the forest Faun had disturbed what had undoubtedly been the makings of her first kiss. Amari had to push these thoughts out of her mind. It would not do them any good, and she did not want to make Forde uncomfortable.

She tried to think of other things. If they had not run into Korrigan, the Emori would not have their sights on them, and they would have foregone an attack by the creatures in the marshes or found themselves stalked by a forest Faun. The reason to travel to Derriane would never have existed, and they would have been well on their way to Sagar. But, instead, there she sat on a raft, unable to think about anything else except kissing Forde, and a part of her briefly wondered if her feelings were not a projection of gratitude brought on by the heroic deeds, he had done to save her life.

She glanced at the bed of water surrounding them and expelled another sigh. As strong as she was or thought she was, she would never have made it here alone. Why had Arteryn thought she was ready to leave home alone? At this rate, she never would have made it even to Gildevard.

She turned to look at Forde, who sat across her. He seemed to be deep in thought.

"How do you know how to get to Derriane?" She had never even heard of the place until she had met Korrigan. If she was honest, she had never ventured out much save for those two trips to Simiren. She had lived a relatively sheltered childhood, she realised once more.

"He travelled a lot," Korin responded as he continued to row. He had slowed down now that they were safe from the Emori. "All over the Kingdom of Sagar."

"Really?" Her interest piqued, she sat forward excitedly. She had never met anyone who had travelled a lot before. "Doing what?" She realised that even though he had shared a lot with her, she did not know much about Forde. For all she knew, he might have an intended somewhere back home or a wife and children. Her spirits plummeted as that thought occurred to her. Forde might have had a wife and children back home. How had she not considered that? An unfamiliar feeling of pure jealousy hit her hard at that moment, and she scolded herself for her ridiculous behaviour. What was the matter with her? Amari's thoughts were uncharacteristic of her. However, now that she had entertained the idea that he might have a wife and child, it would not leave her, and she shifted uncomfortably under the sweltering sun. ma

"Tax collector for my uncle. It was the father's responsibility before he died. I travelled to different places with a group of men from Orrick collecting tax then delivering the required portion to Sagar."

Tax collector! He had had the duty of the most hated person in all the Kais. She had heard how disgruntled members of the Synia community had been whenever the tax collector had come around to collect. She could not imagine Forde engaging in such a callous yet necessary job. "Aren't you a little young?"

"I'm almost twenty-six years old, so I am old enough for the responsibility." He looked offended that she had called him 'a little young'. "However, I only did it for about one year with my uncle- my other uncle. He is my father's youngest brother."

She nodded slowly, realising she hadn't even known he had another uncle. "You collected tax from all the villages under Orrick?"

"Yes, to all the neighbouring villages or towns under Orrick, then we would take the required potion to Sagar for the King. While Derriane does not fall under Orrick, my uncle has good relations with the lord of Derriane, and we have travelled there many times."

Her mind was racing, thinking how exciting it all sounded. "So, you travelled everywhere and saw many exciting things."

"It was not all fascinating, Amari. Until you have to force a family who is barely surviving to pay tax, then the euphoria tends to wear off." He looked solemn just thinking about it, and she considered the burden he had probably carried when doing his task. It could not have been an easy job. He probably met with many impoverished families still required by law to pay the very harsh taxes of the King.

"I suppose so, but I never saw you in Synia."

"It doesn't surprise me that you're from Synia," Korin said under his breath, but she caught his words and frowned at him. She didn't know what she had told them. Amari couldn't remember the details of her earlier lie or what she had told them afterwards. However, after everything they had been through, she felt she did not need to remain guarded anymore. She nodded in return. "That explains a lot about you."

Her head snapped to pin Korin with a stern look. "What does that mean?"

"You're very naïve." Korin turned to look her way, his eyes watching hers with a heavy expression on his face, as though he carried the weight of the world. "You don't know the real dangers of the world. Everything is possible to you. Perhaps you should have stayed home and married a farmer, after all."

"Korin." Forde shot him a warning look, but Korin was not remorseful at all. However, he did not say anything.

While his words offended her, she could not fail to see the truth in them. Admittedly, she was naïve to some extent.

"I did go to Synia, but we probably missed each other," Forde answered after a few seconds of silence had stretched between them.

"Aren't you doing it now? Tax collecting?"

He shook his head, quickly running his fingers through his hair. "Not, not for over a year now. I'm an Orrick Warrior, but I usually did that when we were not engaged in battles. Besides, more pressing reasons made it so I couldn't travel anymore. My uncle was not happy, but he understood he could not make me do something I did not want. So, he doesn't even know that I am on my way to Sagar."

"Why didn't you tell him?" She didn't know much about his relationship with his uncle, but she got a sense he admired the older man.

"Because he would have tried to talk me out of it. Baelin and Shorva would have tried to talk me out of it too." A heaviness hung over him as he spoke, and Amari suddenly picked up on what he had said before. Well, no one could accuse her of not seizing an opportunity when it presented itself.

"Pressing reasons not to travel anymore? What were those? Was a woman having your child? You were to be married?"

"Subtle," Korin muttered under his breath, and she winked at him. He smiled her way and shook his head.

Forde missed the exchange between her and Korin. He seemed distracted. His eyebrows furrowed at her assumption, then he wiped the sweat from his brow with the cloth before he shook his head. "No, I have no children or a wife, but the circumstances are the reason I killed that man."

"Forde." Korin's disapproval at the turn of conversation forced Amari to turn to him.

"I told her about killing Earwyn, Korin. You know, because you were eavesdropping. I didn't say why." Forde looked exhausted like he could do with several days of sleep, but the man held on. Amari couldn't begin to imagine what he was going through. Even when they slept at night, he still woke up several times to check on Korin. Forde needed rest. He watched her now with a calm expression, and a part of her just wanted to throw herself at him only to force him to lie down and sleep.

She had pieced together what she assumed had happened to Korin, and she saw every day the toll it took on Forde mentally.

Forde had returned to find this man harming Korin. That was the summary of it. While she was curious about the details, she didn't think it was something anyone asked someone to explain. It just didn't seem considerate.

Looking at how tense Korin appeared, she knew she had to change the subject. She did not want him to make him uncomfortable, especially about this. It wasn't something anyone should force someone to disclose.

Silence settled over them, and she lifted her eyes back to Forde, who had bent over one knee towards him and was trying to stretch his undoubtedly sore muscles. She had welcomed the distraction from her thoughts, even though it had only been briefly. Tia had said she was a hazard whenever she was idle. Now that she was idle, all she thought about was kissing Forde once more and being the person Amari was, and she was less inclined to wait for him to decide to do it.

"Well, we have established that I am quite naïve when it comes to certain matters. But, on the other hand, I am not a prude because I lived with farmhands who never shied away from discussing rather descriptive antics. Would either one of you show me a tongue kiss?"

She knew as she said it that Korin would never kiss her. He did not like to be touched. That effectively passed the task to Forde, and his stunned look was almost comical. He choked on the water he had been drinking, and she stared at him calmly.

"What?" He asked.

She almost felt sorry for him. But, when she set her mind to something, it was virtually impossible to sway her. She had decided Forde would be the first man to kiss her, and it was going to happen before they arrived in Bhrim.

"Pardon me?" Korin sputtered over her words.

She wasn't stunned at all that she had surprised them. She had been having that sort of effect on people around her since she could remember. However, she had just been through one of the most miserable weeks of her life. She had almost died countless times this week. She had slept in some of the worst conditions, and her entire life had changed when she met Korrigan. Surely, she could be selfish and get at least one thing out of this adventure. She had never given men much thought, but since she met Forde, she had found herself thinking more and more about what she could do with him. Now that it was in her mind, she couldn't stop thinking about it.

She had spent a lot of time over the years eavesdropping on the farmhands while they talked about their conquests. They had been very detailed in what they did, and while Amari had listened and learned, she had never physically experienced anything. She was going to have Forde kiss her one way or another and preferably before they reached Derriane.

"Show you?" A look of pure mischief cross over Korin's face as he turned his gaze to Forde. His lips turned at the corners slowly, and she could see he was holding back a laugh.

"Is it disgusting? And wet? The tongue is involved. I imagine it is wet." She had never played a temptress in her life, but she found she had the predisposition for it. Her words had the desired effect on Forde.

He choked when she said that colour seeping down his collar, and he rubbed the back of his neck while Korin seemed to be thoroughly enjoying Forde's discomfiture.

"Forde?" Korin was looking at him, and Forde arched his eyebrows. "Well, take the pedals then while I show Amari what she has been missing out on."

"You?" The words came out more like a strangled sound from Forde's lips.

"She's harmless enough." Korin indicated he take the pedals, but Forde did not move from where he sat with one knee up, and he shook his head. Amari watched them patiently. They seemed to be having a conversation with just their eyes. They had to know each other well to be able to communicate on that level. Korin released a sigh then looked to the heavens.

Forde looked at her, and Amari frowned. "What? Is it that complicated?"

He did not respond, but he seemed to have made up his mind about something.

She saw a small smile form on his lips as his gaze levelled on her, hot and dark and making her feel like plunging into the water to keep from being charred to death. He was doing this deliberately. He was trying to gain some ground.

"Not even one kiss, Amari? With all your talk of knowing the ways of the flesh?"

His words had the desired effect, and she immediately went into defence mode. "It is not from a lack of opportunity. On the contrary, I have been distracted with my training, and Arteryn chased away any boy who looked my way."

His eyes travelled up her body very slowly, dark with intensity, but she did not cave in under pressure. Instead, he grabbed her ankle, then yanked her forward, and she slid unexpectedly towards him, yelping as she did. He reached for her, his arm snaking around her waist as he suddenly pulled her up to straddle his lap. A gasp escaped her lips, ultimately knocking the air out of her lungs at this unexpected turn of events.

Amari could hear a chortling Korin who was enjoying this far too much. "You can still change your mind," Forde told her quickly, his face so close to hers.

She drew back, a little shocked by how close his face was to hers, and her nerves threatened to get the best of her. Maybe she should reconsider this. However, if she did, when would she get the opportunity to try this again?

"What?" Forde asked, pausing to give her a moment to decide. He had drawn back a little bit, and Amari's mouth started running before she could stop it.

"I wasn't expecting you to come this close." And the moment she started; she couldn't stop. "I mean, I knew you had to come close, but I didn't … I couldn't help thinking about a lot of stuff, you see, like should I close my eyes or whether I must hold my breath. I assume I should because it would rather strange to breathe and stare and honestly, the thought of having your tongue in my mouth-"

"Stop, please." Forde waved her off quickly to stop her from rumbling. "If you have to think about it so hard, then you are not ready for it."

"No!" Wow, she sounded desperate, she realised, but she didn't want Forde not to follow through now. She wanted this, and she wanted this experience. Amari was twenty years old and had never been kissed. She just wanted to do it so she could move on to other things. "I am ready for it. I just didn't realise there were so many things to consider."

"We don't have to go through with it-"

"Forde, we're doing it." She declared assertive, sticking her chin defiantly. "I have never done this, so I was just nervous, but I never back down from a challenge."

"A challenge?" He looked offended.

"Just kiss me!" She didn't give him time to overthink it. Instead, she reached for him, grabbing the front of his shirt and plastered her lips over his. Then she froze, not knowing what to do afterwards.

Thankfully, Forde saved her by taking over the kiss. With just his lips moving against hers, it started slow, and then she felt his tongue darted out to lick her lower lip. Instinctively, her lips parted, and after a brief moment of the awkwardness of this new experience, she closed her eyes and lost herself in her first kiss, blocking out any questions that could ruin this moment.

His hand around her waist drew her closer, and out of their own volition, her arms went around his neck, pulling him closer. This was intoxicating, consuming, and she wanted more of it. How had she not done this before?

She was on his lap, straddling him as his and his strong arm holding her in place.

She almost died right there in his arms as the unexpected flood of emotions scorched her entire body. She never had in her life experienced something like this, so intense and primal. Why had she never tried this out before? It was not from a lack of options. The young men in her village had been after her since she had turned fifteen, but she had never paid them any attention, too absorbed in her training. Also, Arteryn had threatened most of them away from her. But, Amari decided, now that she had experienced this, she was sure she wanted to do it more often- and perhaps even more.

Heat spread out all over her, and it took her a moment to realise that the heat within was starting to spread exceedingly quickly so much so that she thought she would break into a blaze of fire. It was building to a point where it became dangerous when she realised the fire building inside her wasn't just lust, but actual fire and that if she didn't stop this, she was going to burn Forde into a crisp potentially. She drew back quickly, scrambling off his lap as she put as much distance between her and Forde. What had just happened? For a moment there, she had thought she would break into a ball of fire- literal fire.

She shifted back to where she had been sitting, breathing heavily.

Korin enjoyed this far too much because he laughed at them both as they tried unsuccessfully to feign indifference to what had just happened. Finally, she cleared her throat as she sat down away from Forde, and he looked a little uncomfortable.

"Well, did it live up to your expectation?" Korin asked her quickly, his laughter bubbling over the surface, and she squinted at him against the sun directly hitting her face. "I am sure it did. I am convinced you were about to burst into fire."

How could he have known? Had he sensed it? And had it lived to her expectation? She had nothing to compare it to, but it was memorable as far as first kisses went. She wanted more. How had she gone through her whole life, never having experienced something so incredible? Now that she had done it, she wanted more. That is if she could keep her powers in check. It concerned her that she had almost lost control. That had never happened to her before.

"I have nothing to compare it to. I'll give you my opinion when I do it again." She had to save face, after all, and couldn't come across too eager, though that boat had sailed already.

"You intend to kiss Forde again?"

"I said I planned to do it again. Whether or not it is with Forde again will depend."

"On what?"

"On Forde and me. I can tell by just looking at him that he would kiss me again."

"How can you tell?"

"His cheeks are all red."

Korin laughed, Forde scoffed, and Amari exhaled as she wondered how she would overcome this fire that threatened to consume her when she kissed him.

"Don't make me regret kissing you," Forde grumbled, and she smiled at him, relieved to see him share in her embarrassment.

"I am exhausted. Forde, can you please take over?" Korin pulled out the pedals from the waters and set them on the raft. Forde grumbled something under his breath while Amari opened a canister and sipped some water. Korin shifted to sit down across her while Forde started to row the raft and exhaled. The silence stretched between them, and the longer Amari looked at Korin, the more her curiosity got the better of her.

She wanted to ask him something. However, she could almost hear Arteryn's voice in her head telling her not to pry, to be sensitive and while she discarded the former, she decided to consider the latter.

"You know Korin," she began as she approached a sensitive topic with cautious bravery. "I have to be honest; I didn't think you would have wanted to kiss me."

"Why? Because I like men?" He rested his elbows on his knees and regarded her with a direct look.

"Yes." If he were going to be direct, so could she.

He shrugged. "It wouldn't have had any impact on me. But, I mean, now that you have kissed Forde, it's only right that when we meet this Arteryn, I- how did you put it- climb him like a tree."

"Korin." She groaned, then shook her head. "Or you could just kiss Forde too."

Korin grimaced at the suggestions, then shook his head. "Yuck." He shuddered at the thought, and Amari arched an eyebrow. "Forde is like my brother. I have never sexually thought of him. I've seen him naked countless times. We have slept in the same bed countless times, but even though he is an amazing person, I have never been attracted to him sexually."

"You've slept in the same bed?"

"Yes," Korin said with a careless shrug. "Have you never shared a bed with Crispin? You're not related to him by blood, but he is your brother."

He had a point, Amari thought with a shrug, then she sighed. "You know, the first time I ever saw someone who liked men was a few years ago. Arteryn and I used to train every day, and every single day this young man used to come to watch us train. It wasn't until I heard the other farmhands talking about how the young man went there every day to watch Arteryn that I realised what was going on. I could understand. I have never looked at Arteryn as anything but a second father, but the man looks amazing. When I asked Arteryn about the young man, he told me it didn't bother him. He said there were people like that, that it was how they're born and couldn't change that part of themselves even if they tried."

Korin chewed his lower lip, a mischievous look crossing over his face. "Was it you or Korrigan who said Arteryn would be travelling behind us to Bhrim? Because I have to say, I am starting to get keen to climb him like a tree."

"Korin." He was incorrigible, she thought. "My point is, although you're determined to drive me insane with your taunts, the fact that you like men than women doesn't change how amazing you are."

The only sound that surrounded them then was the creaking of the wood on the boat and the occasional bird dipping low to the waters. Even Forde had stopped rowing, and he was staring at her with an unreadable expression on his face. She sensed the tension coming from both men and quickly bit her lower lip. The unbearable silence stretched for so long it became uncomfortable, and Amari suddenly wished she had not said anything. When she was about to apologise profusely for talking out of turn, Korin finally broke the silence.

"Why do you think I'm amazing? You know nothing about me." Korin pointed out to her quickly, almost bitterly, but his harshness did not deter her. "Is it because of my face? How I look? Are you drawn to me?"

She shook her head slowly, crossing her legs under her as she gazed at him. "No. Yes, you look unbelievable, and I will admit that I felt instantly drawn to you from the moment I saw you, but not in a sexual way at all.

Like maybe I should know you. That we are destined to know each other, I can't explain it." She shook her head. She was rambling. "I don't know about the man before the person I met on the road to Sagar, but I have come to see the man afterwards. While I am not as accurate as you are in reading people, I have noticed things. I know you were hurt, though I don't know what happened. I sensed it, felt it. I know that you seemed like you had lost the will to live, that you had a lot of weight on your shoulders.

"Yet lately I have seen you fight to stay alive, I have seen you smile a lot, and even though I see a haunted look in your eyes, I have seen moments where you look happy, though what any one of us can be happy about after the journey we have had is a wonder."

She stole a glance at Forde then turned back to Korin, uncertain about how they had deviated such intense and personal conversation. "You said I was naïve, and I admit I am. I have been very sheltered growing up, not exposed to the horrors of this world, but I have seen people who have been, and I have seen the burden they carry, and I have seen them try to claw their way through the darkness. It did not appear like an easy journey, finding their way back, but with a lot of help and support from those around them, they were able to find healing."

Korin continued to watch her, that haunted look she always saw in his eyes still there, but there was also the presence of something else. She could not make it out. He looked anxious, frustrated, and frightened. A myriad of emotions crossed over his face, and finally, he settled on almost being on the brink of falling apart. He exhaled slowly, then chewed his lower lip, glancing out to the sea. She hoped she had not insulted him or said something to alienate him. She valued what little relationship they had built on this journey, and she knew that she would do anything in her power for him.

The heaviness of the subject weighed heavily on them, and Amari realised they needed to settle it. Put it to bed.

"I still don't understand how you can't find Forde attractive, though." Amari's attempt to change the topic to ease away from the heaviness hanging over them only achieved in making her embarrassed. Korin's eyebrows shot up in disbelief, and he let out a bubble of laughter while

Forde let out a groan. "Look at him," she continued indicating Forde. "He looks kissable."

"Yes, to you." Korin shook his head in disbelief. "I don't ever think about kissing him for several reasons. One, he's my brother. Two, he likes women and has no interest in men."

"He's also on this raft and would like it if you stopped talking about him," Forde said in exasperation.

"We know," Amari muttered with a hint of a smile, then she turned back to Forde. "If you need a break, let me know."

"I'm all right." He told her, and she nodded.

The silence stretched once more, and she noticed Forde and Korin were doing that thing again where they talked with their eyes. Korin turned to look at her once more, his intense gaze watching her.

"You once asked why I am going to Sagar."

She knew then that Korin was ready to open up to her and nodded.

"Something happened to me a few months ago. Almost a year ago, to be exact."

CHAPTER SEVENTEEN

O h no, it was that recent! It explained so much.

"Being the way I am, I always attracted attention even though I tried not to. It wasn't just the women. It was men as well. I don't think most men knew what to say or feel when they saw me...."

"Being so beautiful and all?" She could imagine the confusion. He shrugged.

"The older I got, the more they seemed to notice me. Finally, when I turned sixteen, something changed. I wasn't sure what happened. It was strange. Between the people cornering me to cop a feel or being beaten senseless because of the possible anger those people felt inside by feelings I seemed to spark inside them, I practically lived in a state of anxiety. I met Forde when I was seventeen and homeless. He approached me that day, told me I had his mother's eyes, took me home, and never let me leave. I kept expecting him to tell me to leave, but he told me I was going to live with him and his family from that day."

Korin shrugged, lowering his eyes to his feet, and he shook his head, but he continued. "Maybe having the nephew of the lord become your friend makes people a little wary to do you harm. But, while the gazes

181

followed me everywhere, everything else stopped. I was not accosted or beaten by anyone...."

Korin chewed his lower lip for a moment as though trying to find the words. It appeared even thinking about what he had to articulate was invoking intense pain. "Then, on Forde's last trip to Sagar, I was alone, returning home, and a man grabbed me in a dark alleyway and... he raped me."

Even though a part of her had suspected but refused to believe it, the impact of hearing those words felt more painful than a physical blow she might have taken from Grantreal. She could not begin to imagine what he must have gone through. She could tell as the light died in Korin's eyes that he would probably never heal from the violation. Instead, he would carry the emotional scars for the rest of his life. She could tell how painful this was for him and her heart bled for him. She wanted nothing more than to put her arms around him, but she knew he would never allow it, and now she knew why.

"Forde happened on the situation, and he killed the man. It has been difficult living in Simiren. I see that place every time I go home, and I remember what happened, and I can't stop thinking about it. Sometimes, it gets unbearable and being alive feels more of a burden. If I am alive, it is because Forde foiled all my attempts not to be, and I was on my way to Sagar because he thought being away from Orrick might give me a reason to want to live."

Amari tried not to cry, but Korin's words hung heavily over them. He spoke them so quietly and sounded so detached. It was as though he was telling someone else's story, as though he refused to internalise what he was sharing with her, trying to let it not affect him. She didn't think Korin would appreciate her sympathy, but now she understood what had happened. She understood that as a last effort to help his friend, Forde insisted on Korin accompanying him to help him find himself once more. She could tell by Korin's words that he lived with the horror of what had happened to him and that he was dealing with his issues in the best way he could.

"It was not your fault, Korin."

He shook his head and let out a humourless laugh. "I don't know. No one just does something like that if they aren't provoked and something about the way I looked or moved made-"

"Korin, that man was a low life scum who deservedly had his head cut off. Perhaps Forde should have cut his manhood off as well and fed it to him for good measure."

"He did," Korin muttered.

Amari glanced at Forde briefly before turning her attention back to Korin. "It was not your fault. It can never be your fault. No one has the right to put their hands on you without your consent. No one." Her heart shattered into pieces for him. "I am so sorry you had to go through that, but don't give up. One day it will get better, I think."

"I live with the shame. I'm a man. I should have been able to defend myself-"

"You have nothing to be ashamed about. You did nothing wrong, Korin. Man or woman, it doesn't matter. No one should be violated like that. It doesn't mean you're weak because you're a man, and another man did that to you. It has nothing to do with how you look or talk and walk. It is never your fault. That man took something from you, and you need to reclaim it. Focus on healing and get better. I can't imagine it will be easy, but I do believe you can live through it. You are stronger than that Korin, and if Sagar does not work for me, you can come live with me in Synia at the farm."

Korin was holding himself so still and so tightly as though he was afraid that if moved, he might fall apart. She could tell that distancing himself from the demons that plagued his thoughts was probably his coping mechanism, and even though she knew he did not want to be touched, she hurt so bad knowing he was hurting. Therefore, before she knew what she was doing, she had closed the distance between them and had pulled him into her arms, holding him tightly.

"It will get better one day, Korin. You will find your will to live once more," She whispered to him, feeling the shock that was going through him as she held him. She rested her head on his shoulder, her arms wrapped around his shoulders, and the tears did fall when she suddenly felt his arms wrap around her tightly. This was hardly their first contact, but she had a feeling this was the first time he had allowed anyone to touch him in comfort for what he had gone through.

He buried his head into her neck, his arms tightening around her.

She felt the wetness of his tears on her skin as he shook from his silent sobs. She wondered if he had ever allowed himself to come to terms with what had happened to him or whether he had just fought to pretend it had never happened.

She did not ask him any questions, though. Instead, she just let him hold her tightly as he finally let his tears fall and cried his heart out quietly. She did not even know how long they sat like that, but it was quite some time, and by the time he pulled back, she was a mess of emotions and tears.

They looked at each other, him with the look of embarrassment on his face and her with understanding. She leaned forward and placed a soft kiss on his cheek.

"Not all touch intends to hurt you, Korin, and I plan to remind you of that." She glanced at Forde, but he was looking away from them, dealing with his grief over the situation.

"My whole life before I met Forde, people hurt and abused me. I thought it was finally over, you know. Six whole years of thinking I was finally safe, and then it happened, and it broke something in me, I suppose."

Korin exhaled suddenly and wiped the sheen of tears from his eyes.

"Strangely, since I met you, I feel different. Do you know how you said you felt it was our destiny to be in each other's lives? I felt that too, the moment I met you. It was like I had found this part of me that had been missing my whole life- this naive, determined and strong woman who believed she could make it in a world where men created the rules. But, coupled with Forde's enduring support, I now see the world a little differently. I have not looked forward to seeing what tomorrow brings in a long time. These last few days have been amazing for me. I have found myself thrown into situations I have never encountered in my life before. I find myself trusting in my instincts more, wanting to survive one unexpected challenge after the next. I hope if I am ever in that situation again, I will be able to fight. Or preferably to be never in that situation ever again. It is just that history has proven me wrong." He trailed off, then he expelled a sigh and looked out at the long stretch of water.

They sat in silence on the raft for the next hour, each reflecting on everything they had shared on their journey quietly. Amari was glad she had met them. She was glad she had these two in her life, and she was determined to help Korin heal.

"How far are we?" She asked Forde when another good hour had passed, and he looked at her from where he sat.

"Look ahead. There is Derriane." Forde answered, but he and Korin had switched by now, and he was resting. "Derriane is about the size of Orrick, but with beautiful, paved streets, a thriving market and good sturdy homes."

"I wonder how we will find this Derik." Korrigan had not exactly been forthcoming about the details of their trip, not that she blamed him. But unfortunately, he had run out of time.

"I know a man we can ask. It will be a bit of relief to be off the road a bit." Forde informed her, then pushed himself to his feet as land appeared before them, and he expelled a sigh. "There it is."

She pushed herself to her feet, seeing the makings of a city at a distance. But, instead, what caught her attention was the other island, Bhrim, on their left. There was a stunning sandstone castle perched at the top of a mountain. She couldn't understand the emotions coursing through her as she stared at the island.

"Why do we have to go through Derriane to get to Bhrim instead of directly going there from Golynvale?" Amari asked Forde curiously.

"Most people never make it if they use that route. The belief is Mer-people haunt those waters. However, considering history claims all Mer-people were destroyed hundreds of years ago, I don't know if the rumours are true."

"Maybe it is true. People believed the Kenryk were gone, and yet we know that is no longer true." Amari muttered.

When they docked, she realised there was still some walking required to get to Derriane. Why Forde had decided they should anchor miles away from the town, he had not divulged, but if the pensive look on his face was anything to go by, then he was not in the mood for any questions.

She took a deep breath, glancing at Korin as they walked. "So, what did you do for fun in Orrick?"

"Fun?" Korin arched his eyebrows at her. "Do I look like I have had much fun in my life?"

"He used to stalk a man in the market," Forde answered over his shoulder surprisingly, and Amari's eyebrows rose so high they almost disappeared into her hairline. Korin smacked Forde on the back, but Forde ignored him, chuckling instead.

"Oh no, this I have to hear." They could not stop now.

"He was in love with a man he saw at the market, and every market day, he went there to look at him. He never spoke to him. He just found a spot to sit and watch him." Forde divulged, and this earned him another smack from Korin, but Forde only chuckled again. "Since he was seventeen."

"What?" No way. Amari couldn't imagine Korin being in love with anyone, maybe because she had met him as this broken man.

"I think he did try to approach him once."

"Forde-"

"It's not an issue, Korin. Just tell her." Forde looked a little amused, and Korin rolled his eyes and hit Forde hard again, but he took a deep breath and turned to Amari. They had stopped walking where they were along the bank, and he rolled his eyes.

"Fine." He shook his head as though unable to believe he was going to talk about this. "Since I was young, I'd always suspected that unlike other boys my age, I liked them than the girls. So, when I first laid eyes on this man, it confirmed it for me. I was seventeen when I first saw him, and he took my breath away, and every time he would be there on the market day, I would go there to see him. He saw me looking at him a few times, but then things happened at home, and I couldn't go to the market anymore, then a few months later I started going again. Only, this time I didn't let him catch me looking at him-"

"Wait, how long did this go one for?" Amari was intrigued. She understood being obsessed with something. She had been obsessed with becoming a Sage Warrior since she was a child.

"I last watched him two weeks ago. So about seven years-"

"Wait. You've been watching this man since you were seventeen years old, and seven years later, you still haven't said a word to him?" That made no sense to her. She was very proactive about things she wanted.

Korin frowned at her for a moment, and then he shook his head impatiently. "You don't understand. Things aren't that simple for people like me. I could have gone to him, and he might very well not have reciprocated my feelings and possibly beaten me to death. He's bigger than Forde. He could have easily crushed me. Besides, apart from Forde, he's been the only constant thing in my life. I know, every market day, he's there, and there is always something soothing about him, almost familiar. I can't explain it. It's like I look at him, and for a moment, I forget everything, and all is well with my life." Korin suddenly looked embarrassed for even divulging that, but Amari merely shrugged to show him he had nothing to be embarrassed about, and he frowned suddenly.

"What does he look like physically." Not that it mattered, Amari thought.

"He looks like a man designed specifically for my fantasies, Amari."

Amari couldn't help it; she laughed. She didn't know why it sounded so strange to hear Korin talk this way. Maybe because until now, he had hidden most of himself from her. "He has changed physically over the last seven years, of course, but he's the sort of man who could easily pick me up and toss me on the bed."

"Korin." Forde looked at him in disbelief, then shook his head with incredulity.

"He sounds amazing," Amari commented with amusement, and Korin glanced her way, then let out a short laugh. His features changed, and he suddenly looked sad.

"I think he might have a child or wife, though. I've seen him purchase little trinkets or a few things for a woman." Korin said, a hint of melancholy lacing his words.

Amari grimaced. "That's unfortunate. Maybe he has a sister?"

Korin shrugged. "It doesn't matter. He'll never be mine now anyway."

"Why him? Of all the men in Orrick, why him?"

Korin paused, then took a deep breath, hugging himself. He had a distant look on his face as though trying to find a response. When he finally spoke, he surprised her. "I don't know. The first time I saw him, I felt something different. You know that feeling you get when you see someone for the first time, and you instantly feel they're yours. Like there's a part of you that's been missing, and this stranger is that missing piece. I just felt an instinctive bond with him."

Amari knew what he was talking about. She'd felt that bond the moment she had seen him. She had felt instantly drawn to him, and she still couldn't understand why. "Did… You continued to watch even after everything that happened…?"

Korin almost grimaced at her words, but he kept it together. "Looking at him gave me comfort in a way I can never explain to you."

"You should have talked to him-"

"I did." Forde provided, and Amari arched her eyebrows.

"Really?"

"Yes." He glanced at them. "I'd gotten sick of Korin lusting after someone whose name he didn't even know, so I decided I was going to speak to the man. Korin was a mess, of course. He didn't want me going anywhere near him. I didn't listen, so I walked up to the man and introduced myself. I am not going to lie; he is a very intimidating sort of fellow, and he is older than I am—possibly about eight to ten years older than Korin. I never got his name. He somehow managed to hold a conversation with me without giving me his name. What he did do was ask me if I knew Korin."

"Really?"

"Yes. I walked up to the man, and it went something like this; 'My name is Forde.', 'Pleasure to meet you, Forde. I assume that Korin sent you.' I was surprised. I hadn't been expecting him to say that, to know Korin's name or to be so direct about it, for that matter. However, the way he said it made it sound like he was trying to confirm that Korin's name was Korin. So, I asked him what he did. He told me to tell Korin to come and ask him all these questions himself. He stunned me. It's like he saw right through me, and there wasn't much I could say after that. Before I could say anything further, customers came to his stand, and I had to leave. That was about a year ago."

She knew what Forde wasn't saying. The exchange had hurt Korin. "Korin, you never went to speak to him? Not even once?"

He shook his head. "I told you when people see me, something draws them to me, and I think it's supernatural. I just…"

"You didn't want him to want you because of whatever supernatural pull you have. You wanted him to want you for you." She knew by the look on his face that she had hit the nail on the head. Her heart twisted for him. To deny himself something he wanted because he was afraid the feelings would not be natural but coerced because of his supernatural pull.

Korin shook his head quickly. "I couldn't. Not with the way I am. For as long as I can remember, people have always reacted differently towards me. They never quite knew what to think or what to expect, and they usually lashed out at me because of that. So, I didn't want to have to go to him and have him hate me instantly for the feelings I drew out of him that he didn't want."

"You were also always on the defensive." Forde pointed out to him, and Korin's mood shifted so quickly Amari almost took a step back. His face darkened as he glared at Forde in disbelief.

"I was defensive? Well, how else did you expect me to act Forde when for the last eight years of my life, I have had to deal with people touching me, trying to fondle me and even raping me because I am how I am? Again, what did you expect?"

"All right, calm down, I don't need this right now-"

Korin rounded on him quickly. "I don't need to be here right now either, Forde. You forced me to come with you. I didn't want to be here. You forced me to come with you to Sagar, not caring about what might happen one day when you meet someone, and you get married, and I am then alone in a big city with more people to paw me and rape me."

"What are you talking about?" Forde spun around to face Korin. "What is going on in your head right now? Why would you think I would ever abandon you? I have only ever looked after you-"

"I never asked you to."

"You never had to. So, what is the matter with you?"

"The matter with me, Forde, is that I am emotionally exhausted, and you keep stopping me-"

"I am never going to let you kill yourself, Korin! Not if I live. You may have given up on yourself, but I haven't-"

"I don't need your permission-"

"You're unbelievable right now, Korin. You're only thinking about yourself, about how you feel. What about me? Shorva? Baelin? How do you think we will feel if you die? You're my brother. I knew the moment I saw you that I had to have you in my life-"

"Oh please, you took pity on a homeless person because I have your mother's eyes and because of your need to save people-"

"No, Korin, contrary to what you think because of your low self-esteem right now, I didn't approach you because I needed to save you. I am not going to let you die if there is something I can do to change it. This whole thing is not about me. It's about you. It's about making sure you find a reason to live-"

"Right? So, what was the plan then, Forde? Drag me to Sagar, then what? We'd live together? Until when? Until you met someone you wanted to marry, and I inevitably became a tag along in your life-"

"Are we having this conversation? Are we seriously having this conversation?" Forde ran his fingers through his hair, his eyes flashing anger as he glared at Korin in disbelief. "Korin, I wouldn't be here if you didn't come first. I have left my uncle, my cousins and my home because I have to do this for you."

"I didn't ask you to-"

"You don't have to! Don't you get it?" Forde looked on the brink of losing his control. "I don't believe this! I understand you are angry with me because I wasn't there to stop you from getting hurt, and I should have been there to protect you-"

"I don't need you to protect me. I am not another thing you have to save, Forde! I know that since you found your family slaughtered, you have been on a mission to save everything and everyone because you couldn't save them, but I am not a substitute-"

190

"Korin!" Forde balled his fists in a rage, and Amari leapt forward to stand between the two men. She didn't think they could get so angry with each other, and she hadn't even imagined it was possible. They seemed to understand each other so well. This blow-up had just come out of nowhere.

"All right, stop, both of you!" She stood between them, her hand on Forde's chest and the other hovering over Korin's, careful not to touch him. "Look, it has been a long journey. We are all exhausted, and we are nearing our destination, so maybe that is why emotions are at an all-time high. However, I implore you both to keep calm."

Despite her words, Forde continued. He vibrated with anger beside her.

"I have never asked anything of you, Korin! Not once! I have only ever seen you like the little brother I never had from the moment I saw you. I have only ever wanted to look out for you the same way I know you would do for me, but for you to throw my family in my face...! I don't believe this!"

Forde spun on his heel and started to stalk away in a cloud of anger and sadness.

Amari took a deep breath, turning to Korin, who, instead of anger, looked at Forde walking away with panic. Amari reached out for him then stopped just before she touched him because she had seen him flinch just briefly.

"Do you trust him?" She asked him, and this seemed to confuse him. "What?"

"Do you trust Forde?"

"With my life."

"Then why are you both fighting about it?"

"What would you know? You're an immature little girl who-"

"Stop it!" She snapped at him quickly. "Stop lashing out at Forde and me. We didn't do anything wrong. Just take a moment to calm down, please."

Their little group couldn't fall apart now. Amari needed them, not just as companions on this journey but also as friends. She had grown to care very much for both these men, and something about Korin tugged into her soul.

"I am sorry about everything that happened to you, Korin. I am sorry you were hurt, and I know the emotional scars will never heal, but all Forde is trying to do is help you move on from what happened. I can't begin to imagine what you went through, but I know I want you to get better, and so does Forde. We both care about you, and that man loves you very much. For goodness' sake, he wakes up every night to check on you. He wouldn't be here if he didn't care, and you just spat in the face of all of that."

Korin took a deep breath, his anger turning to frustration. He wrapped his arms around himself then shook his head quickly. "You don't' understand. You don't know what you're talking about."

"Then make me understand-"

He seemed to be teetering on the verge of a meltdown, his eyes glistening with unshed tears, but he held back, and when he spoke, his voice was so low it could have been a whisper. "He told me to go with him, Amari."

"Yes, to help you find a place where you could try to rebuild your life-"

"No!" Korin snapped at her, then he lifted his hand and ran his fingers through his hair as his eyes glassed over. "Before it happened…that last time he left with his uncle on tax collection rounds. Forde told me to go with him. He insisted on it. He said it would help me to see the Kais. He insisted, Amari. As if he knew or sensed something was going to happen, and I said no. My training had been improving, and I was so focused on learning everything I could from the scholars in Orrick that I refused, and I told him I would go with him next time. If I had gone with him if I had just… If I had gone with him, then none of this would have ever happened. That man wouldn't have hurt me, and I wouldn't feel the way I do-so used, so dirty, and so empty! He has always trusted his gut, and I should have trusted him that day when he insisted I go with him. I should have gone with him, Amari…."

His voice broke then, and Amari couldn't hold back the emotions choking her. She threw herself into his arms, forgetting his aversion to touch, and she wrapped her arms around his neck to offer him comfort. Tears spilt down her cheeks as he stepped forward, wrapping his arms around her waist and burying his face into the space where her shoulder and neck met and sobbed.

She felt the tortured feelings of "what-ifs" rushing through him, wondering about the many times in the last few months that he had gone through how he could have prevented this from happening to him.

"I am sorry it happened, Korin. I am so sorry." She held him tightly, her own emotions riotous within her. She found herself dwelling on the "what-ifs" as well. What if he hadn't used the route that day that led him to encounter that man? What if Forde had arrived just an hour early? What if he had gone with Forde on his last trip? It was tempting to dwell on them but also pointless. None of the what-ifs had happened. The reality was a cruel thing had happened to him, and he needed to come to terms with it.

"I just want it to be over. I don't want to have to think about it anymore. I don't want to feel the way I do. I don't want to hurt like this anymore." Korin said close to her ear, her cheek wet from tears he was shedding.

"Then don't." She drew back to look at his red-rimmed eyes as tears slid down. "Focus on getting better. Focus on moving on from this, on building your life and becoming stronger. You're already doing it, Korin. You got us through the marshes and the forest. You have shown such strength and a will to live in the time that I have known you, and I believe it will get better. Maybe not now, but one day." She touched his cheek gently, wiping the tears away. "Just…you know Forde just wants you to get better. You know that."

Korin nodded quickly, taking calming breaths, looking down at her, a little embarrassed by his reaction. "No, don't do that."

"What?"

"Hide your emotions. Don't keep it all in. Let it out. Cry, shout, whatever it is. Let those emotions out, Korin. Don't worry about my reaction or anyone else's. Just deal with that thing inside here-" she pointed at his chest, "-that is squeezing the life out of you. Deal with the emotions. Confront them, Korin, and focus on getting better."

He wiped his tears away, calming himself down slowly, then he shook his head. "Do you think I could get better one day?"

"Yes." She nodded quickly, and for the first time, as she looked at him, she knew what he had shared with her was just the sanitised version of what he had gone through. She had a feeling Korin's story was much more profound than what he had shared, that there were more horrors in his life that he had gone through before he met Forde. It wasn't just his eyes that were telling. It was what he was emanating, something she had a feeling only she could sense. "You'll never erase what happened to you. You'll never get over it, but you will get through it. It won't be easy. I can't imagine it would be easy, but if you try-if you find the will to live, not for Forde, but yourself, then I think you can do this."

"You make it impossible to dislike you." He muttered as he wiped his tears away quickly. "You're the first woman I've met who I can't seem to dislike no matter how much I try."

"I'm glad, but I think you should be focusing on Forde right now." She told him, relieved to find him calming down. "Lean on him for support, Korin. You are not alone. He's here, steadfastly, for you. Talk to him. Make him understand how you feel. Don't keep it all inside. You're both keeping it all inside. First, however, you need to talk about how this has affected both of you. Promise?"

"No. We're not women. Women talk about things-"

"I think you'll find it works for men just the same way it works for women." She stated confidently, and he took another deep breath. "I'll go find Forde, and I will give you two some time to talk. All right?"

"No, Amari, I don't-"

"Talk to him. Let it all out. Trust me; it might just be the one step you need to take towards releasing some of that rage inside you that you're allowing to build up." She drew back, away from him, and as she turned, she stopped. Forde had returned, and he had been staring at them. He didn't look angry anymore; he looked determined. Did Korin know how lucky he was to have this man in his life? She knew what having someone like Forde was like. Amari had Arteryn for that. She just wished Korin would find the will to live.

CHAPTER EIGHTEEN

S he gave them an hour of privacy, and afterwards, they didn't mention it again. It was as though it never happened. Amari didn't ask any questions. She knew Korin was dealing with many emotions, and bombarding him with more questions about the situation would only make him feel worse. They walked the distance required to reach the walled-in town of Derriane, and Amari found herself pleasantly surprised. Derriane was as developed as Orrick, though every city in the Kais had a rat and sewer problem. The market was smaller than in Orrick, but it was just as busy. There were people everywhere trying to make a living. There were tents erected where different merchants sold different products, but the stench of fish in the river city was pungent.

She was charmed by the town immediately as she gazed up at the multiple storey buildings built with rock and clay brick, roofed with clay tiles and the narrow streets. She had to dodge a horse-drawn wagon at some point, and when they passed by a pub, her stomach grumbled purely from greed as the sweet aroma hit her nose, but they didn't stop. They passed by several shops, and she made a note of the shops she saw, the butchery, the bakery, a craftsman, the odd weaver or so, and the cordwainer were all going about their business.

The place fascinated her. She realised she preferred towns to villages. They moved through the city, lucky enough to dodge someone who was throwing out water into the street, but her attention was very much engrossed in the giant castle on the hill on the island not too far from Derriane.

"What is that place?" Something about the neighbouring island was calling to her.

"That is where we are going, I think. Bhrim. I hear the only way into Bhrim is through the pass from Derriane. I don't know much about the place. I have never been there before. I don't think many people have. A high wall surrounds the island, and the only thing you can see is the castle perched atop a steep hill. All I know is a very wealthy man bought the island several years ago, and while they trade with Sagar, Derriane and Golynvale, no one has ever been on the island except its inhabitants."

"But, Forde…" She turned to look at him quickly, stunned by his words. "We're going to Bhrim. How are we going to find this Derik?"

He rubbed the back of his neck and expelled a sigh. "I was hoping we might be fortunate to find this Derik in Derriane."

"So, there could be people living on that island that no one has ever seen?" Korin came to a halt then looked at Forde. "Doesn't this worry you?"

Forde winced a little, but he shrugged. "It did cross my mind, but I am assuming Korrigan would not send his niece to her death. Let's hope my old friend, Babaro, will be able to give us direction. We're here."

He pointed to a small house built of wood and brick. He knocked on the door quickly then waited. Now that she was in Derriane, she realised what walking into Bhrim might mean. Was she ready to find out where she came from? Who was she? She should have been worried about Grantreal, but that took a back seat to her anxiety about what walking into Bhrim would reveal about her past. About Korrigan. About Arteryn.

The door opened suddenly, and a short and sturdy man appeared at the door. He had grey hair and his clothing indicated he was neither poor nor rich. His eyes lit up when he saw Forde, and he broke into a toothy grin.

"Forde, my boy. It has been quite a while. Please do come in." The man's excitement at seeing Forde was infectious, and they followed him into the room. Her eyes adjusted to the darker light in the relatively small room that had a table with a few chairs, a shelf with books stuffed in it and what appeared to be a tiny kitchenette. They sat down around the small table, and the man started pulling out cups and saucers. "Would you like to some tea? I was about to put on the kettle."

Forde looked relaxed but having become so in tune with his mannerism since she met him, Amari could tell his mind was racing. "We'd love to, but we are a little pressed for time. Perhaps I could come back later tomorrow for tea and your famous scones." Forde cleared his throat then leaned forward; his long fingers weaved together on the table. "Babaro, I'd like to introduce you to Amari and Korin. Amari and Korin meet Babaro. He has always been very hospitable to me whenever I have come to Derriane."

"It is a pleasure to meet you both." Babaro reached forward to shake their hands. Unfortunately, Korin did not take his hand as expected, leaving Babaro's hand hovering mid-air awkwardly. However, Amari did her best to salvage the situation by shaking Babaro's hand instead.

"Thank you for welcoming us to your house." Amari smiled at him, and then his eyebrows lifted as he turned a knowing look to Forde as though he had just made a remarkable discovery.

"Forde, my boy, have you finally found yourself a wife then?" Babaro's excitement at the ridiculous notion that Amari could be married to Forde was surprising. She heard Korin chuckle under his breath, and she elbowed him in the stomach without even thinking about it. He groaned beside her.

Forde did not miss a beat. "Yes, I have. Amari is my wife, though I had hoped you would allow me to share the news first." Forde nodded though he was scratching his head as he said the words, Amari could not stop the gasp at his outright lie. Why, though, she wanted to ask? He could have introduced her as a friend. It was unlikely she would see this man ever again. "It's all very new, and we are doing a bit of travelling as our first adventure. We have visited most of the great cities of the Kingdom of Sagar."

"You have come a long way, but I suppose a new bride can have a man doing all sorts of irrational things. I didn't think Kenryk allowed their own to marry outside the tribe." Babaro chuckled wholeheartedly, and Forde smiled and nodded. "Is this her brother then?"

"You think I'm Kenryk?" The words blurted out of Amari's mouth before she could stop herself.

"Well, surely you must be. We see a lot of them here in Derriane when they come this way. No one can miss the colouring of a Kenryk. Your brother?" Babaro seemed very keen on Korin.

"Mm, yes." Korin did not even skip a bit as he responded with a nod. Amari gave up on finding reasons for the unnecessary lies. "This is my sister. I love her so much."

Amari stopped shy of rolling her eyes, and Babaro smiled in response.

"Forde, my dear boy, she is quite stunning. She must be a lot to handle if you know what I mean." Babaro commented, but Amari couldn't help noticing that the man was addressing Forde and Korin while completely ignoring her. So typical, she thought irritably.

"I'll thank you not to make such comments about my wife, Babaro," Forde said through clenched teeth, and Babaro immediately sobered and nodded apologetically.

"I remember when I was newlywed. Everything seemed like a great possibility. It is rare to have a wife who does not mind travelling." Babaro's eyes twinkled as he turned to Amari. It was apparent he was not planning to address her directly any time soon. Merely acknowledge her.

She put on a smile on her face, not sure how to play the role of a new blushing bride when she was annoyed at this man's dismissal of her.

"So, is this where your journey ends before you head back home?" Babaro pulled up a seat and sank across Forde.

"No, we still have a long way to go yet before we return home, but while I was here, I thought I could run a few errands," Forde responded casually, looking so relaxed and comfortable, and Amari wondered why he was clouding all of this in veiled secrecy. "I'm looking for a man named Derik. Unfortunately, all we know is that he is in Derriane, but short of asking every random man on the street if he is Derik, I had hoped you might be able to help us."

"Derik?" Confusion played over Babaro's face as he sat upright, the easiness he displayed before slipping away. "Really? Why? I assumed being married to a Kenryk and all, you would know him personally." Babaro brushed his hand gently over the table, dusting away non-existent crumbs.

"Did you make those?" Korin suddenly asked, and then he leaned forward over the table and watched Babaro very closely. Amari watched as the other's man's eyes widened and he suddenly seemed entirely engrossed by Korin.

"Make what?" Babaro's voice sounded different, distant, like he was in a trance.

"Those jars. Such great quality." Korin smiled slowly at the man, his hand travelling across the table slowly towards Babaro's, but he didn't touch him.

Amari looked at Korin in confusion, and then it suddenly dawned on her what was happening. Whatever supernatural pull Korin had, he was using it on Babaro, and if the distracted look on Babaro's face was an indication, he was utterly entranced.

"No, I...I didn't...." Babaro replied, unable to tear his gaze away from Korin. Amari had never seen anything like it. "Would you like one?"

"Yes. I'd like very much, Babaro." The tone Korin used completely floored Amari. The slight smile on his face, the tiny movements with his body and that tone. Korin had gone into a full seductive mode, and Babaro was hopeless against it. "Do you want to give it to me, Babaro?"

"Yes." Babaro's responses sounded automatic, like he would do anything Korin asked of him at that moment.

"Thank you." Korin lifted his hand over Babaro's but did not touch him. Instead, they hovered just over the man's skin, teasing for a touch. Amari watched as Babaro seemed to yearn for the contact, craving it, leaning forward almost unconsciously towards Korin with dilated eyes and a mouth hanging open. "Do you know where we can find Derik, Babaro?"

"He's in Bhrim. He hardly ever leaves the island." Babaro's face was something to behold. He was a man wholly besotted. He was practically drooling over Korin.

"Really?" Korin's seductive voice carried out very quietly across the room, as though meant for Babaro only. "Do you have a boat you can lend us to go to Bhrim, Babaro?"

"Yes. In the pier."

"That's wonderful." Korin leaned forward just a little bit more, parting his lips before licking them slowly. He smiled again, that seductive look on his face bewildering Amari altogether. "We'll take your boat, Babaro, but I want you to do something for me."

"Anything." Babaro looked set to leap over the table and jump on Korin. Amari was baffled.

"After we have left in your boat, you'll know we came here, but you won't remember why? Understood?"

"Yes." A firm nod.

"You won't remember that she was with us. You won't remember that she is Kenryk. And then you'll go to the south shore and get the boat we left there. A friend of Forde's is coming to collect it tomorrow."

"Yes. Anything. I'll do anything you want."

"And then, Babaro, if you're really good, if you do as I say, I will come back for you. Would you like that?"

What was this sultry tone Korin even using? This breathy, seductive tone that had the other man completely at his mercy?

"Yes. Please." Desperation laced Babaro's words.

"Wonderful. Now, take us to the pier and give us your boat."

"Of course."

"And don't forget my jar. I love your jars."

Amari didn't think what she was witnessing was something she would forget very quickly. She glanced at Forde only to find him looking relaxed and slightly amused. This was probably not the first time he had seen Korin play a vixen. After Babaro picked out a jar that he perfunctorily gave to Korin, he walked them to the pier, arranged for them to take his boat, and then, as they rowed away, Korin waved at him and blew a kiss. Babaro looked like he had seen the heavens. Eventually, he turned and walked away.

Once they were on a boat and heading away from Derriane, Amari turned to look at Korin as he rowed.

"What was that? What was that? What happened in there?" Amari was too stunned not to address this. "What you did in there was not normal."

Korin shrugged his shoulder carelessly. "While I hate what this face I have brings my way, it has its advantages."

"Korin, I don't think it's just your face. You had that man in a trance. He looked ready to jump you and lick you all over. It was not just your face. You exuded something that went beyond than how you look." She couldn't believe it. She looked at Forde in askance. "Does he do that a lot?"

"He hasn't done it in a while." Forde looked amused. "He did it to my cousin Shorva once. It was hilarious. Shorva had dared him to do it to be fair because he convinced himself he wouldn't fall for it. So, he lost the bet."

"I almost forgot that happened." Korin laughed, and Amari turned to him, surprised to find him so carefree about something like this.

"That was...mind control, wasn't it? A supernatural form of it. That wasn't just normal persuasion."

Korin paused for a moment, then nodded. "Yes. I've been able to do it to people since I was sixteen. It's one of those things that came to me when people suddenly started being drawn to me. I can convince anyone to do what I want any time so long as I concentrate on it. But strangely, it doesn't work for you. Or Forde."

"Wait, you've tried it on me?"

"Yes, twice. It didn't work. Maybe because you are Kenryk, but then why wouldn't it work on Forde? He isn't Kenryk."

"You've tried it on me? When? Why?"

"It doesn't matter now."

"So, this man you've been stalking for years... you could have used that on him, and he would have been yours so easily." She pointed out, but he shrugged again.

"No. Never. That is something I never considered because I want that man to want me for me. Besides, if this pull I have on people never worked on him, I doubt these powers of persuasion would have. Besides, it isn't something I can just do. It leaves me drained after I have done it. It always leaves me feeling dirty." Korin seemed bored with the conversation then sighed. "At least he won't remember Forde claiming to be married to you, Amari."

"Just row," Forde instructed him quickly, and Korin laughed.

Silence stretched between them for a moment before Forde surprisingly broke it with a statement Amari had never even expected.

"Amari is Kenryk, and we're looking for a man no one hardly knows anything about. We have a medallion we must deliver. We have Emori and Grantreal after us. I did not care to correct Babaro's assumptions." Forde pointed out quickly. "The least he knows about the situation, the better. He can be loose-lipped. If anyone should come across him and ask him any questions about us, he will barely have any information."

Amari knew Forde was right. The least people knew, the better.

"For all it's worth, I think Korin is Kenryk." She declared, and both men turned to her with questioning gazes. She had been giving it a lot of thought over the last few days and what he had just done with Babaro confirmed her suspicions.

"What gave you that idea?" Korin looked incredulous, and Amari couldn't believe he even had to ask.

"Well," she started to list off her fingers, "you and I have the same colouring, and apart from your eyes, you can pass off as Kenryk easily. Korrigan specifically said there were three Kenryk. Your pull and powers of persuasion do not work on me, and I am Kenryk. You also have an uncanny ability to see where no normal person can. I specifically remember Korrigan saying something about your eyes, and what you just did with Babaro was not normal. You are Kenryk."

She didn't know what to expect from him regarding her assumptions, but she braced herself for an outburst. She didn't get one. He shrugged, tilting his head to the side.

"I supposed it is a possibility. Maybe half, at least" Korin chewed his lower lip in thought, then arched an eyebrow. "Wouldn't that be something?"

He turned to look at the looming island. She watched a shudder run through him, so much so that he rolled his shoulders, closing his eyes briefly before he opened them. She thought she saw something flash in his eyes, but it was gone too soon for her to decipher.

Amari had stopped listening at some point, and she was gazing at the island they were approaching. Thick foliage surrounded the entire area alongside the beach, with trees far too tall to give away the secrets that lay hidden behind them. The only thing that stood out for all to see was the sandstone castle perched on the hill. While entirely engrossed by the castle on the hill and something inside her started to change. She did not know when the shift happened, but the closer they rowed, a heavy feeling settled over her, and she could not shake it. Unease washed over her as she gazed up at the castle. She glanced over her shoulder, having noticed that Forde and Korin had become quiet. Korin was watching the castle as well while Forde was focusing on rowing. And in what felt like a split second, she felt something pass right through her. It was extraordinary, a feeling of passing through some invisible barrier of some sort.

"You're both suddenly quiet. It's unsettling." Forde muttered, and they turned their gazes to him.

"I'm just…." Amari battled to find the words to explain how she felt. "I can't shake the feeling that everything is about to change… I don't know why. It's just a feeling."

"Well, Korrigan did promise that this Derik might be able to provide you answers about your history." Forde pointed out, and she pulled her gaze away from him, looking back at the approaching island. "Maybe you're just afraid of finally finding all the answers."

"Maybe she's afraid of what she will hear," Korin muttered, and they quietened again. She could see a pier that led to a paved dock from a distance, yet the whole place seemed to be enshrouded by a forest. After a walk, they would reach the steep stone-paved pathway that appeared to lead to the castle. Once they docked on the empty pier, they shared a look of concern. There was nothing and no one around, no other boats or any sign of life. They walked silently away from the pier, making their way through what seemed to be deserted houses before they reached a steep incline that seemed to lead to the gates of the castle.

"These people leave their ports unguarded?" Forde seemed stunned, shaking his head in disbelief. "This leaves them open to so many attacks."

Amari hadn't even considered that. All she was conscious of was the anxiety going through her body at that moment. She expelled a deep breath to shake off the heavy feelings pressing down on her.

"Well, husband, do you mind carrying me up this entire hill? I am suddenly feeling exhausted." Amari kept her eyes on the castle as she attempted humour, her heart beating a little fast because for reasons she could not understand, she had a feeling her life was about to change forever.

The urge to turn around and flee was inescapable but having gotten this far, and she knew she could not turn around.

She yelped with a jolt when Forde suddenly bent low then picked her up into his arms, straightened then looked down at her. Her eyes widened with disbelief, and for a moment, she found herself stunned; she could barely find words. He smiled down at her.

"I was speaking in jest. Put me down, you crazy man!" She smacked his shoulder as he started to walk, then he paused.

"Oh, I thought you were serious." He put down quickly, and for a moment, she wondered if he had been trying to relieve the anxiety that was weighing down on her in attempted humour. She appreciated the thought. She smiled up at him weakly then they started to climb up the steep hill that was surprising paved.

It took them nearly fifteen minutes to get to the top, and when they reached the large iron rout gate, they stood a moment to straighten their backs. After being hunched over as they had climbed up the steep heel, the relief was indescribable.

They stood in front of the high, sturdy iron gates for a moment, waiting. They were all breathing heavily, overwhelmed by the hike they had taken, but most importantly, they found themselves at a loss of what to do.

"What do we do now? We can't exactly climb over that wall." Korin shielded his face from the sun with his hand cupped over his forehead and looked around. "There aren't any guards at any of the posts. So how will anyone know we are here? Should we shout for Derik?"

"I don't know. Guards usually operate gates. This situation is confusing..." her words died out immediately when they heard a creek and the gate slowly started to lift. She swiftly jumped back, finding it rather peculiar that the gates were opening without any question from anyone. If this Derik permitted no one on the island, why were the gates opening without any sort of interrogation? Suspicion settled over her, and she stole a glance at Forde, who had furrowed his eyebrows with the same worry haunting her. She took a step back quickly as she looked up at the rising gate. "That answers that question. "

As Forde took a step forward, Amari's hand reached out and slid into his. She turned to look at him, but he was scouting the courtyard. She had never seen anything like it. A paved road led to the main steps of the castles, edged by well-trimmed green grass that spread across the courtyard.

"This is quite a curious design. I have never seen a castle built so close to the gates." He started to move forward, but she stopped him when the two solid heavy wooden doors of the castle with large brass rings for doorknobs suddenly peeled open.

Amari's heart lurched to her throat, and the hand holding Forde's tightened. She did not know what to expect, did not know what would come out of that door.

CHAPTER NINETEEN

A man stepped out of the doors of the large castle. It was the only sound that broke the air was of her gasp. There was no one else with him. He came out alone. Dressed in belted grey robes with intricate embroidery, he stood a tall, formidable man somewhere in his late sixties. He approached with the easiness of a man who appeared carefree. However, something about his body language gave the impression that he wasn't as carefree as he pretended.

The man had an air of authority about him, and something about his face was startlingly familiar. She inhaled sharply as she took in the man's features, taking note of the shape of his mouth, of his eyes of his nose. Her breath caught in her throat, and she started to shake her head slowly.

"Is it me, or does he bear a strong resemblance to Korrigan?" Forde muttered under his breath where they stood, unmoving while contemplating their next move.

And a solid resemblance to Arteryn, she finished in her mind, struggling to reconcile the apparent truth that stared her bluntly in the face.

Since meeting Korrigan, the denial she had hidden behind dispelled everything she knew about Arteryn and forced its way into her conscious.

"Breath," Korin whispered next to her, and she tried again, in through her nose, out through her mouth.

The man moved with confident strides then came to stand before them, his hands clasped behind his back and right there on his lapels; Amari saw the same sigil she had seen on Korrigan, and that was on the medallion. Three dancing flames. It took every ounce of her self-control to hold back, to stand there and wait for the man to make the first move. Fire. Dancing flames. How thick could she be? How had she not made the connection? How could she not have realised the dancing flames on her medallion were a direct connection to her powers and thus the Kenryk? She knew why. She had never entertained the idea, not even once. She had always considered herself a discarded orphan plucked out of obscurity by farmers.

She inhaled sharply again, then exhaled, battling to keep her emotions under check and failing spectacularly. No, it was too much. It was far too much. She wanted to turn around and flee. She wanted things to go back to how they were before she stupidly went to the Orrick pits. She wanted to live in denial, continue believing she was just Amari Leverood with grand ideas of being a Sage Warrior. She wasn't ready for this. And yet, as she stood there before the man whose eyes softened when they rested on her face, she realised nothing was ever going to be the same again.

"Amari, I have been waiting for you." The man spoke in a deep voice that immediately forced her to close her eyes briefly then release a sigh. She didn't know how she felt. Terrified? Anxious? Maybe both? The man smiled at them, then he turned to look at Forde and nodded before he turned to Korin. "And the eyes of a Khaiman shall always lead him home."

Korin frowned in confusion, but Amari did not even have time to digest this man's words. All she had latched on was that this man knew her name.

"You know my name?" How could he possibly know her name? Neither Korrigan nor Arteryn could have sent word to this man about her journey, seeing as it had been so unexpected.

"Why, yes. I gave it to you myself. You are Amari Alleayana Kendreka."

Waves of shock went through her at the words the man said, and it took all her control not to react physically. Amari Alleayana Kendreka. Could it be? Was that who she was? No, she was Amari Leverood. Her skin became clammy, her head thudding at the temples and the urge to scream barely contained. Her knees felt weak, threatening to cave under her, but she held on. Her grip on Forde's hand tightened as she unconsciously leaned towards him. Amari Alleayana Kendreka. Not Amari Leverood. She took several deep breaths in quick succession, trying to relieve the pressure building up within her.

"Are we coming in or not?" Korin questioned while she leaned further into Forde, unconsciously seeking his support and protection. Instead, he tightened his hand on hers then looked down at her, seemingly surprised by her reaction.

"I want to go back." She whispered to him, panic flared within her, afraid of what she would discover about herself if Amari stepped over this threshold if she spoke to this man. It didn't make any sense. Any of it. If Korrigan was her uncle, why had she never met him? Why had Arteryn spent years on the farm with her and never claimed her? Why was this man before her who claimed to have named her a stranger to her? She wasn't ready. She just wasn't prepared. She had spent her whole life wondering who she was and now... She couldn't do it. No. She just needed another day or month being just Amari Leverood, being the person she had always known.

She did not know this Amari Alleayana Kendreka. As much as she tried, she simply couldn't dispel the fear that gripped her in a tight fist. She knew deep in her heart that whatever this man shared with her about her past, information she knew was accurate, she would never be able to go back from it. The fear of losing the person she had become was distressing. The fear to bid farewell to Amari Leverood and accept that she was another Amari was too frightening.

"I'm going." She started to pull away from Forde, intent on running as fast as she could away from this place. However, Forde reached for her, turning his back on the man and effectively standing between her and the stranger. He wrapped his arms around her, blocking the man from her view and pulled her close, holding her fast. "Let me go."

He drew back slowly, lifting his hands to cup either side of her face, then he looked down at her with understanding eyes.

"You're not running, Amari, not after everything we've gone through and certainly not after you meet a man who has all the answers Korrigan would have given you. You're strong enough to face this."

Was she? Strong enough? She could face a giant of a man like Grantreal without fear, but this was terrifying. She buried her head into Forde's chest as his arms came around her again, tightened around her.

"Take a moment and breathe." He instructed in a calm yet stern voice.

"I want to go. Just let me go."

"Breathe, Amari." He whispered in her ear, his hand moving slowly up and down her back. She shuddered, inhaling his scent and briefly closed her eyes. Forde placed a hand under her chin, tilting her head up to force her to look at him. "If you leave now, it will haunt you forever. So go in there and find your answers. Give him the medallion, and once you have done that, we can all leave for Sagar, all right. Korin and I are right here for you. We promise. We will not leave you. I will take you back to Synia myself if you ask."

She looked from him to Korin then back at Forde, panic bubbling within her. She could not help it and could not change the instinct, but her hand flew to the medallion that she clutched tightly. Immediately it soothed her, more than any words could ever have. She closed her eyes, breathing in and out slowly. She felt Forde's arms slip from around her, and he took her hand once more. When she opened her eyes, it was not Forde holding her hand, but it was the man in the robes.

"My name is Derik. I believe you are looking for me."

She drew her hand away from his, focusing on breathing, on remaining calm while still clutching the medallion, but she did not say anything.

"Please, come in. You have had a long journey and without a doubt would appreciate some rest and a warm bath." Derik turned and started to walk forward.

"Wait, how can we trust you?" Amari regarded the man suspiciously, and he turned to look at her. "I don't even know you."

Derik corked an eyebrow, and at that moment, Amari almost wailed because it was such an Arteryn thing to do. "You think Arteryn sent you to Korrigan, who sent you here, and then we spent time sewing in the sigil in that medallion on my robes because we intended to bring you here to hurt you?"

When he phrased it that way, it made Amari feel a little foolish for even saying the words. Nevertheless, she still regarded the man with suspicion. "How do you even know Arteryn?"

Derik turned around and began to walk back towards the large doors of the castle without waiting to see if they would follow. Then, mutely, she followed with Forde and Korin trailing behind her.

"Why do they keep referring to eyes when they see me? Korrigan did the same thing. He said the same phrase." Korin whispered to them, but Forde dismissed him quickly as they moved forward, the gate closing firmly behind them.

The moment she stepped over the threshold, she felt something wash over her body. She failed to understand it, but for a moment, it had felt as though she had walked over an invisible high barrier.

As they stepped into the large and cold hallway, she wrapped her arms around herself. She looked up at the high ceilings and intricately carved arches. There were three passages from where they stood in the tiled foyer, one on the left, the other on the right and one heading straight down. The castle was stunning inside, with arched windows that brought in so much of the natural light as possible. They were intricate drawings on the wall that she could not make sense of and patterns she did not understand. There were oil lamps mounted everywhere on the wall, but one thing she noticed was how quiet the place was. The silence was thunderous. One could hear a penny drop and undoubtedly the echo of their thoughts.

"I think you have had a long journey. I understand you still have far to travel, but can I offer you my hospitality for the rest of the day and the night. Perhaps you can leave tomorrow." Derik said as he walked down the passage ahead of them, not pausing to see if they were following.

"Thank you for the invitation, my lord," Forde spoke up before she could respond, and she looked at him over her shoulder, but he did not pay any attention to her.

"Please follow me," Derik called out to them just as Amari pinned Forde with an angry look, but he shoved her forward, utterly unaffected by the murderous look she cast his way.

"You need to rest. You deserve it. Nothing wrong with a warm meal and a bath." Forde continued to push her forward, and she shrugged him off and walked ahead.

"How did you know we were coming? How do you know my name? How do you know me? What did you mean when you said the eyes of a Khaiman shall always lead him home?" Now that she was here, she could not help asking all the questions. But she felt she should get on with it, find out the truth and deal with it. "And I have something I have to give you."

Derik drew to a halt then turned to face her, his expression the epitome of patience. "Allow me to give you a place to sleep, refresh yourselves and get some food before I answer any questions. I can assure you; I will answer every question you have and supply you with all the answers you seek." Derik had his hands clasped in front of him before he turned and walked forward once more.

"Are there people who live here with you?" She had not seen a single soul, and it was starting to scare her. "You cannot possibly live here all by yourself."

"I do not. Your rooms are ready, and you each have a bath waiting for you in your chambers. Please take care of all your needs then meet me in the Great Hall. To get there, you go down the passage, turn to your right, go up a flight of stairs, then turn to your right once more. You will see the passage leading straight to the Great Hall. There's a green door. You cannot miss it. There is a change of clothes provided for each one of you."

A change of clothes? Rooms and food prepared for them? She was baffled. How had they known? How could Derik have known she was coming here with Forde and Korin?

He stopped in the hallway, then pointed to the first door with its arched design and turned to look at Korin. "These will be your chambers. I hope it offers you the peace and solace that you seek. It overlooks the waters, and they can be beneficial when one needs introspection and reflection. It also has a door that locks from the inside."

Derik continued to walk, missing the curious looks that passed between them at his words. Korin shrugged then pushed the door open but did not enter. Forde and Amari peeked in and shared a look. Forde and Amari followed Derik, who had paused in front of another door. He showed Forde his room, which was next to Korin's, then Amari's room across Forde's. "We have allowed your rooms to be in proximity as we believe this will appease any apprehension you may have about where the other is at all times. However," Derik looked from Amari to Forde with a stern look, "I will expect proper conduct from both of you. I will appreciate it if you and your young man keep out of each other's rooms. I will see you shortly."

"He isn't my young man." Amari protested then realised she should not have even responded to the allegation with flaming cheeks because something in Derik's eyes told her he had known that already. Derik walked down the passage with high wooden ceilings, and after turning to his right, he disappeared out of view. Korin cleared his throat as he leaned on the wall next to his chambers.

"He is a very odd sort of man, is he not?" He questioned when they turned to look at him. "And how does he know so much? How did he know we were coming? How does he know our sizes to provide clothing? It must be a Kenryk thing."

"I have so many questions my head feels like it might erupt. And what he said about the eyes of a Khaiman something or the other." Amari was still concerned about that, and she frowned, trying to make sense of it. "Maybe you are Kenryk as well."

"I doubt it. I am not that special." Korin muttered, then pushed the door to his chambers and entered.

Forde folded his arms across his chest while he towered over Amari with a serious look on his face.

"What?" She could see the disapproval in his face, and she took a deep breath.

"Just give it a chance, all right. I know that all your defences are high right now, but calm down and try to relax. Korin and I are here for you, and we are not leaving without you."

He was trying to reassure her, and she appreciated his thoughtfulness, but she was so terrified of what she would find out about herself within these walls. Her biggest fear was that with each revelation from Derik, she could start losing the Leverood within her. Forde stepped forward then opened her door for her before he ushered her in. "See you in a bit."

"Wait, he didn't take the medallion. Why would he not take the medallion?" Was it not that important? Did the fates of the Kais not depend on this medallion?

"You can ask him those questions later." He brushed his hand gently against her cheek before he turned, walked out of the room and closed the door between them.

Exhaling, she turned to view the room, and she inhaled sharply.

CHAPTER TWENTY

Such luxury could not truly exist. As a farm girl, she was used to modest surroundings. This place was just beautiful. She had never seen such architecture in her life, not in Orrick, or Golynvale or Derriane. The arches were nothing she had seen before. She had certainly never seen stained glass before. The

room- or rather, chambers assigned to her were spacious.

An extensive wooden carved ornamentation four-poster bed with a heavy velvet crimson canopy and gold tussles as trimmings stood in the middle of the room. Amari's inquisitive nature got the best of her, and she touched the soft covers, pulling them back slowly to look at the bed. It was a luxurious feather bed with soft linen sheets. She pulled away then took a deep breath. The bed covers seemed so inviting and comfortable that she wished she could throw herself on the bed. She had not done that since Tia had scolded her for it when she had been eleven. There was a heavy-looking oak chest at the foot of the bed.

The large arched window provided natural light into the room. There was a plush crimson rug on the floor, a desk and overstuffed armchairs chairs. A fireplace with slow-burning ambers caught her attention across the room, and as she moved forward, she realised right at the centre of the carved mantelpiece was the same crest on her medallion.

The room itself had white walls, which was shocking. An intricately carved ceiling hung overhead, and where the wall met the ceiling were gilded gold panels that probably cost more than the farm the Leveroods owned.

A large bath in the room with steaming water and cool water in buckets placed beside it stood nearer the fireplace, large towels folded on the bed to wipe herself dry with and the most beautiful dress she had ever seen.

She moved closer to the bed once more, almost afraid to touch the blue and white dress and her throat caught in her chest when she realised it silk. The intricate embroidery with gold threading that she had never seen before astounded her. She traced her hand over it, marvelling at the skill required to achieve such beautiful needlework. She sat the dress down, walking over to the vanity where there were brushes set aside and ribbons to tie her hair. That was when Amari froze because she saw herself in a mirror. Her hands flew to her dirty cheeks, and she cringed. Her hair needed a wash. Her entire face could use a proper wash. She required that bath, she realised. She peeled off her clothes then moved towards the tub, filling the cold and hot water until she found the desired temperature. There were oils placed on a table near the soap and washcloth. She opened one bottle then inhale the sweet aroma. She had read of such bath oils that they left a beautiful lingering scent on one's skin.

She poured a little into the water, then closed the bottle and shoved it into her belongings for future use. She sank into the large and welcoming bath and groaned with utter relief. It felt like she was on a cloud. She started scrubbing her skin dry and washing her hair, determined to look as clean as possible.

When she navigated her way through the castle a while later, she could not erase the smile from her face in the gorgeous dress and a warm cape she wore. The white soft flowing dress with its fitting bodice and flowing A-line full skirt stayed in place with a belt at the waist. Ribbons secured back her hair, brushed it until it shined. She had never felt so clean and refreshed in her life, but she knew that might have something to do with having fewer baths since the time she had left home. Even the soft shoes on her feet were like walking on clouds. She found herself wondering what Korin and Forde looked like now and then wondered what they would think when they saw her. She had never felt this beautiful in her life.

As she navigated through the castle, using the directions Derik had given them earlier, she wrapped her arms around herself, thinking how cold this place was.

She eventually reached the green doors and peeled them open, wondering once more where everyone else who lived on this island was.

When she stepped into The Great Hall, she froze in disbelief. It was a large room, very grand in design with high ceilings, painted portraits hanging on the walls and tables along the wall lined with fresh flowers. It was the most peculiar thing. It reminded her of Tia's flowers under the windowsill back home.

There was a large and long table in the middle of the room. High backed chairs pressed close to a table. The room had high wooden ceilings and large arched windows that offered as much light as possible.

She pulled her eyes away from the ceilings when she heard chairs scrape back on the floor. She turned her attention to the direction of the noise, and a smile broke out over her lips. She rushed forward when she saw Korin and Forde, her eyes narrowing when she saw their clothes. They looked refreshed, and they were in clean clothes that fit Forde's noble station. They look invigorated in their new clothes. Their hair was brushed and neat, and even though Forde looked amazing, she could not help thinking she preferred him with tousled hair.

"Whoa, you're beautiful." The words slipped out of Forde's mouth. Then, as though realising what he had said, heat flooded his cheeks as he glanced around the room. A blush spread over her cheeks at the unexpected compliment while Forde battled his embarrassment. Korin chuckled beside him, and Amari rolled her eyes at him. "Apologies for speaking out of turn. I don't...I just..."

"Oh, Forde, I have never seen you this flustered around a woman." Korin guffawed just as the doors opened once more and Derik walked in.

Forde pulled up a chair for her right next to him as Derik moved to the head of the table.

"Uh-uh." Derik shook his head then pointed to the seat on his right. "She sits here."

Amari almost shook her head at this man's decision, and she moved across and sat down.

An assortment of food displayed on the table hit Amari hard, and she drooled over it. After such a long time, barely eating much while they travelled, the feast before looked delicious. There was more food than Amari had ever seen in her life. They ate in silence, keeping conversation to a minimum. However, Amari's anxiety about what she might find out took her appetite. Once the meal was over Amari, felt the tightening in her stomach because she could no longer delay the inevitable.

"Amari, you remind me so much of your mother, but I think anyone who sees you can agree you resemble your father more than her." He began, but she clenched the wine cup as he began, knowing what he was about to do.

Was she ready for this? She had always wanted to know her origins, but now that they were within her reach, apprehension made her want to flee. She talked herself down, trying to remain as outwardly calm as possible.

"You came here for answers to undoubtedly many questions, and I am going to answer all of them. However, should you have any questions as I narrate, please don't hesitate to interrupt." Derik paused, looking from her to Korin to Forde as though waiting for them to agree. Amari numbly nodded while Forde and Korin muttered the agreement.

"It isn't easy to explain a thousand years of history, but you need to know the beginning to understand how we came to be here. So, first and foremost, I should disclose what you already know, Amari. You are Kenryk."

Even though she had had time to digest this after Korrigan's revelations, it was still a little surprising to have it repeated to her.

"My name is Derik. I am your grandfather. Korrigan and Arteryn are my sons. Korrigan is the eldest, and Arteryn will always be the baby of the family. Don't tell him I said that." Derik smiled at her, even whispering the last end behind his hand as though they were sharing some grand secret. He lowered his hand then took a sip of his wine before folding his hands on the table. "Before I continue, do either of you know about the Kenryk?"

Amari nodded. "Korrigan told me a few things."

Korrigan? Oh no, she had yet to tell Derik that his son had died. Her hand flew to the medallion hanging over her chest, and she clasped it instinctively. "We're aware of their origins as one of the indigenous tribes of the Kais."

"Yes, see, the Emori and Kenryk are the only remaining indigenous tribes of the Kais. I am certain you are aware of the Endric War?"

"Yes, and we are acquainted with the tale of the Kenryk's role in that," Korin added, and Derik nodded in response.

"Azariah the First Avaris. To understand the Kenryk, you need to understand our sigil." Derik pointed to the three dancing flames on his robe. "The triangle represents three things. The first line is the birth of the Kenryk. The second is a line acquired when a Kenryk progresses to adulthood. The third represents the crossing over of the Kenryk to join the Old. Within that triangle are three dancing flames symbolising the three pillars of the Kenryk that must always be in place for the tribe to balance. It was not always so. Before the battle in Endric, there were always two flames, the Leader and the Khaiman. The Leader of the tribe is what I suppose other places would call a King? However, Kenryk do not use such terminology as it seeks to create an unequal and classist society. The Leader represents the first flame in our sigil. The Leader of the Kenryk tribe is responsible for all sacred rituals and rites performed by the tribe. These include the birth rite for children no older than three months, the rite of passage for male and female Kenryk when they reach adulthood and the death rite that unites the souls of Kenryk who have died with our ancestors, who we refer to as the Old.

"The Kenryk are strongly connected to the Old. We see our ancestors as beings whom we reach out to offer wisdom and solace in times of strife. Therefore, it is also essential for every Kenryk child to be introduced to the Old as they acquire their first Kenryk mark during a ceremony called the Umbelechai. Every Kenryk child must have one, or they die when they reach three months.

"The connection to the Old is an important one. A sacred one, and one that is transposed to the tribe by a Khaiman. The Khaiman represents the second flame in our sigil. The Khaiman possesses abilities that no other Kenryk has. He can See where none can. A Khaiman plays the role of medium between the Kenryk and the Old. They can see things that happened in the past and see something that will happen in the future. Because of that gift, the visions of a Khaiman are essential to our tribe. To understand the Khaiman better, you must realise that it isn't an elected role. Someone is born a Khaiman, the same way a Leader is not elected but is born one. A Khaiman has and always will be the first-born son of the first-born son of one specific family in our tribe. It has been that way for over a thousand years. Within the family on the Khaiman, a healer is also born, someone with unparalleled knowledge of healing methods. That person is not on the same level as the people symbolised by the flames, is not always born in every generation and can be male or female. However, a Khaiman is always male, and so is the Leader. The third representative is the Avaris.

"Azariah is the first Avaris the Kenryk tribe ever had. It was a little over four hundred years ago that the first Avaris came to be. During the Endric War, it became evident that King Kairon had amassed powers that no human in the Kingdoms of Kessariah nor Sagar could ever hope to destroy. It called for a great sacrifice to restore peace to the Kais. The Kenryk being an independent territory, did not engage itself in the politics of the Kais, but the dark times of Kairon called for our intervention. On one hot afternoon, the Kenryk resolved to sacrifice their powers to create a weapon that could hopefully destroy Kairon for good. Upon the mountains of Cathraga, the Kenryk surrendered their powers, creating the Endric Sword through the Khaiman. After that Great Sacrifice, Kenryk remained only with their fire powers, having surrendered all the powers that enabled them to do so many things."

Derik paused for effect or to ensure they were following; Amari was not sure, but she was enthralled, and the medallion under her palm seemed to throb with every word Derik said.

"After the creation of the Endric Sword, it became evident that neither the Leader nor the Khaiman was strong enough to wield it. It was simply too powerful, and over a few days, several Kenryk came forward trying to see if they could handle it without being injured in some way. Eventually, two days later, during a meeting where the Kenryk had started to realise they may have made a weapon they couldn't handle, a young man no older than twenty-two got up and took the Sword. His eyes glowed gold and amber that day as the powers coursed through him when he took it. An instant shift reverberated through the tribe, and all at once, everyone felt connected to the Sword and him. They knew they had found the Sword's wielder. That day, Azariah became the first Avaris. Azariah was the last-born son of the Leader of the tribe. As you know, the rest is history."

Derik sipped his wine, then put down his cup, his eyes trailing from Amari to Korin and Forde then back to Amari.

"You are probably wondering why the long history lesson? It is essential so that you can understand what I will say next. You see, seventeen years ago, the Emori laid a brutal attack on the Kenryk, one like nothing we have ever faced. So many people lost their lives that day, so many that only a few thousand Kenryk remained. The attack had been unexpected, and we did not have enough time to prepare ourselves. Nevertheless, they had somehow managed to penetrate our protective wards. Those who survived left our ancestral Kenryk lands, Kenrin, and we moved here to Bhrim to salvage what remained of a very traumatised tribe.

"We call that night the Great Blaze. On the night of the Great Blaze, my third child, Artello, called my youngest Arteryn to his house. It was as the attack began. Artello and his wife entrusted the then seventeen-year-old Arteryn with their daughter, giving him to raise his own because she had to survive. You see, Artello had been an Avaris, and his daughter had the mark of the next Avaris. Artello's focus was to ensure his daughter survived and knew the only person who could ensure that was his brother. So, he surrendered his Avaris powers to his then three-year-old daughter, gave her the Endric Sword, and Arteryn rode off into the night with her. That daughter is you, Amari. I will tell you one day the sacrifice your parents made that night to ensure you lived, but not right now. Raising you outside the tribe was the only way to ensure your safety and the safety of the Endric Sword. No one would have thought that an Avaris lived in the small village of Synia. Arteryn taught you how to suppress your powers to make them undetectable, and he taught you how to fight. He did all he could to prepare you to be the Kenryk warrior you were born to be. On the night of the Great Blaze, our family lost many family members. We lost my wife, my daughter Karla and her husband and two children. Korrigan lost his wife, but thankfully, his two twin sons survived. We lost Artello and your mother, Nessie. Korrigan, Arteryn, me, Korrigan's sons Mox and Keeran, and you were the only members of our family that survived.

"You see, I am the current Leader of the tribe. Korrigan is next in line, and Keeran after him. You were born an Avaris but assumed the role when Artello died when you were three years old. We have kept watch over you these past seventeen years. Korrigan and I have gone to Synia to check on you and Arteryn...."

Amari was numb. She didn't know how to process the overwhelming revelations. So, she remained passively calm on the outside.

"Now, I have told you about two of the three flames on our sigil, namely me, the Leader and you the Avaris, but I haven't told you about the third- the Khaiman. You see, for the first time since the previous Khaiman died twenty-four years ago, all three representatives of our flames are in one room." Derik's gaze shifted to Korin, who had been listening intently. "Every Khaiman, for centuries, has been born with one distinctive feature. Their light green eyes. The eyes that allow them to See where none of us can. Twenty-four years ago, our previous Khaiman, Faegon, died when his son was just six months old. His wife was inconsolable, professing to know who was responsible for the death of her husband. You see, Faegon died due to poisoning. She took the boy and declared she would hunt the person responsible for her husband's death. Being so critical to the tribe, we begged her to leave the boy behind, but you see, she had a gift that other Kenryk didn't have. Any curse she made while in strive came true. She could do a gazimvein, a rare form of a generational blood curse.

"Being in her state, it was best we let her leave, but we sent men after her to watch out for her and hopefully bring the boy back to the tribe. I am still not certain how they lost both mother and son, but we lost all trace of the boy. Then one day, your mother returned, alone, without you. She was dying, and before she could tell us where she had left you, she passed. You were lost to the Kais until...seven years ago. You see, in a market in Orrick, Arteryn stumbled on the Khaiman by chance. You, Korin. He knew who you were the moment he saw you because every Kenryk can feel the presence of another Kenryk when one is around. However, he couldn't approach you. He was not permitted to do so. Remember how I told you the visions of a Khaiman are important to the tribe? Before he died, Faegon had told Arteryn of a vision he had had. Faegon had known the tribe would lose Korin for years, but he had also firmly told Arteryn that he should never intervene when he found him. Your destiny was to return to the tribe by yourself, Korin and bring with you the Avaris and the healer."

"The healer?" Korin's arched an eyebrow.

Derik nodded, then pointed at Forde. "I suppose I don't have to tell you what you have both always suspected. You and Korin are cousins because his mother was Faegon's twin sister. She had light green eyes too. So, I suppose before you two even met, either his mother or Faegon appeared in either Forde or Korin's dream to tell you to find each other."

Amari's couldn't help turning a stunned gaze to Forde because she knew he had told her his mother had appeared to him in a dream and told him to find Korin.

"Because she was the twin sister of a Khaiman, Forde's mother must have transferred more of her Kenryk self into him. That is the only reason the wards around the island did not kill him when you passed by them and the only reason he has been around a Khaiman and Avaris but not affected by it.

"You see, you're all connected by grief. You all lost your parents quite young and somehow found each other and came to the tribe together. It was destined to be that way, how Faegon had said it would be-"

"Wait." Korin held up his hand quickly, his jaw ticking. "You say your son found me seven years ago. Did he not think he should tell me who I was? Did he not think it would be better if he took me to Synia than to leave me in Orrick? Does he know what-"

Oh, the raw emotions pouring out from Korin were tangible. Amari knew what he was thinking. Had Arteryn brought Korin to Synia, then he may never have been hurt.

"As I said, we cannot interfere in how things are supposed to happen, even if a Khaiman has seen it. For one, Arteryn would never have been able to take you to Synia. You and Amari in the same place outside the protection of the tribe would have been a beacon to every single dark thing seeking your powers. You would have been in danger, and you would have eventually had to all come back to Bhrim. You see, Arteryn had his duties that he had to see out in Synia and bringing you home with him would have directly affected the safety of the Avaris.

"Secondly, had he taken you, you would never have met Forde, and it may not make sense now, but you both had to meet Forde. As I said, he has Kenryk blood, and as the direct descendant in the family of the Khaiman, his presence here is as important to the tribe as any Kenryk. In other words, even though he is half Kenryk and his half came from his mother's side, his mother shared a woman with a Khaiman, therefore, elevating how powers. In essence, had we known Forde existed, we would have had to take him from his birth family and raised him as Kenryk."

"Why? I didn't need any of your Kenryk rites." Forde pointed out, and Derik nodded.

"No, you wouldn't have, that is unless Korin died before he had his children, and you automatically became the next Khaiman."

Amari sputtered her drink to calm her nerves and choked. Derik reached over and patted her back until she calmed down. Then, he nodded at her surprised look.

"There must always be a Khaiman, and there must always be an Avaris and Leader. If all three are present certain other factors, come into effect. It gives rise to the need for a healer and a Khosai, but that I will explain to you another time. What I have been trying to say is, no matter what, you three would have eventually found your way to the tribe no matter what path you chose."

"Three and a half Kenryk," Amari murmured as she remembered Korrigan's words to them. However, if Korin was a full Kenryk, why didn't he have any fire powers?

"I don't have fire powers." Korin pointed out as though he had heard her thoughts.

"Suppressing powers is something that a Leader or a Khaiman can only do. I suppressed most of Amari's powers a year after arriving in Synia, but she wouldn't remember that. I suspect, Korin, that your mother tried to do it herself but did it wrong. She suppressed your fire powers, but not your Khaiman. You see, a Khaiman cannot live among non-Kenryk people with unsuppressed abilities. Your powers send out a beacon to everything and everyone around you, drawing them to you. Had she given me a moment, I would have suppressed your Khaiman powers before she left with you, but she was distraught and grieving. I, myself, understand her grief all too well.

"Your Khaiman powers have always been there, and you just wouldn't have known how to use them because you didn't know about them. However, the moment you met Amari, I am certain it triggered something in you, and a lot of it became instinct. Your fire powers will come as soon as I release them. Also, you will need to learn how to use your Khaiman powers. That comes with practice, but most of it is instinct. Amari, on the other hand, needs extensive training. Avaris powers may be the same in every Avaris, but the base powers that lead to someone being the chosen Avaris vary. I cannot confirm this, but I have heard of half Kenryk children who have gone to have fire powers, so maybe that will happen for Forde, or not."

It had been an earful, all of it. There was so much to digest, and yet so many questions still lingered. Finally, Amari didn't think she could take anymore. She had a dull pounding in her head and felt she could do with some rest. Amari was baffled. If she had the Endric Sword, where was it? She had never seen it. Surely, she would have seen a flaming sword! And why had Arteryn not told her she was an Avaris? She could have used these so-called powers to protect herself from Grantreal instead of running from home!

Derik was calm. Maybe his calm manner was the reason Amari had not reacted impulsively yet. Perhaps that was why she was managing to keep it together. Well, as together as she could under the circumstances.

Nevertheless, Amari felt herself coming apart at the seams. She struggled to process Derik's revelations.

"My sons have just arrived. They have been travelling right behind you, careful not to intervene to ensure you made it here purely on determination and will."

"Your sons?" Even as he said it, even though she knew who would be coming through the door as the footsteps approached, a part of her was still in denial about everything. Only one thing would make this nightmare real. Seeing only one face would confirm everything she had heard about herself from the moment she had left home.

The doors were peeled open, two men walked in, and she jumped to her feet when she saw the one face that made it real for her.

"Arteryn!"

CHAPTER TWENTY-ONE

O ne moment she had been standing in the Great Hall staring at Arteryn dumbfoundedly, the next, she had fled the room to the solace of her chambers. Then, finally, she had sunk to the floor and had been trembling uncontrollably since then as tears streamed down her cheeks.

Knowing he knew, knowing he had kept all this a secret from her, the one person in the whole Kais whom she trusted apart from the Leveroods, her confidant, her best friend, a father figure to her. The betrayal hurt. Her heart bled.

All her life, the one person she had trusted outside her family without reservation had been Arteryn. She had looked at him as a second father. Realising that he had been indeed her biological father's brother had made her a little hysterical. Memories of all the time she had spent with him, the countless opportunities he had had to tell her they were related cut through her like a blade.

She did not know how long she sat on the cold hard ground with tears running down her face, but the sun was setting already, so she knew it hadn't been that long. She needed to sleep and block everything out. She did not know the Amari who was supposed to be a part of this family. She did not know the Amari whose grandfather was that man in the Great Hall, who had two uncles who were still alive. She did not know the Amari who was Arteryn's niece!

Picking herself up, she lay on the bed with her back, expelling a sigh, feeling like she had cried herself empty. She knew Arteryn was not going to come to her chambers yet and try to talk to her. He knew her too well. He knew she would need time to process this, to come down from the ledge herself. She did not worry that he could barge in at any moment. She pushed herself off the bed, determined not to see any of them again for the day. Tomorrow she was taking her things and heading to Sagar. There was nothing for her in Bhrim, she resolved. She was simply not in the frame of mind to deal with this situation. She did not know how to deal with this situation. Usually, when she dealt with something meaningful, she always reached out to Arteryn to help her process. Now he was the significant thing she was dealing with on top of everything! She had no one. She changed into the provided sleeping shirt and curled under the covers as the pain refused to leave her. She did not know how to deal with it. Amari did not know if she was supposed to grieve for the parents she had never known, for the people who had lost their lives that day, while Arteryn whisked her off to the Leveroods. Without a shadow of a doubt, she knew that dream that had plagued her had been a memory. The voice speaking in her ear that day had been Arteryn. She did not know if she could accept any of this.

A knock on the door startled her, and she pushed herself to sit up quickly, forcing the covers down to her waist. It was not going to be Arteryn, of that, she was sure. The door opened slowly, and Korin peeked in. Relief washed over as he entered and closed the door. The moment Korin walked in, she immediately noticed there was something different about him. Did he walk a little lighter? Was his face a little flushed? Did he look like the cat who got the cream? What could make him look this way on the day her life turned upside down? Of course, Korin's life was turned upside down as well. She reprimanded herself for her thoughts. Anything that made Korin look like this was a good thing. He needed good moments. Was it perhaps finding out about his parentage? That this was where he belonged? Did it matter? He looked ridiculously giddy.

He moved towards the bed quietly, staring at her, his arms wrapped around himself, but more from excitement than concern. "How are you doing?"

She wiped her tears away then dropped her hands to her lap then released a sigh.

"Numb. Conflicted."

"Conflicted?"

She nodded, releasing another sigh to swallow the lump in her throat. "I've always wondered about my origins. It has heavily influenced who I have become, and finding out all this information is, I don't know if I have the right words to explain it yet. Seeing Arteryn shifted my entire perspective of this situation and made it more real."

She shook her head, thinking she was supposed to be taking this differently. Other people would be excited to finally know their origins, especially something she had been yearning for as long as she could remember. Was she ungrateful? Was she childish? Was she supposed to take all of this in stride?

"Ignore me. I am ridiculous. How are you feeling? Today has been a big day for you as well." She tapped the bed to indicate he could sit. She didn't think he would, but he did, with one leg folded under him on the bed while the other hung over the bed.

"First of all, you are not ridiculous. You have every right to process this any way you want." He began, still looking strangely giddy. "Second of all, I am probably not as overwhelmed as you because anything is better than the family who raised me. I wanted these revelations. I needed to know I was not related to the man who raised me. I needed to make sense of many things about who I am, and the things I learned today have greatly helped. Plus, I now can confirm Forde is my cousin. I have a family—a cousin. I mean, I already looked at him as a brother, but knowing we are related by blood means even more to me. Third, something happened to me a while ago that I need to tell someone. Forde is already asleep, and I just want him to get some proper sleep without having to worry about me, so I am going to be bothering you instead."

229

That he saw her as an alternative to Forde made her smile. They had come a long way. Korin confiding in her was the only light in a dark room at that moment.

"Unless you still want to talk about how you're feeling at the moment, then I won't bother you with what I have to tell you."

Mhm, that was sweet of Korin, Amari thought, then she shook her head. "I could use a bit of distraction."

A blush went right through Korin, and Amari jerked back, wondering what caused Korin to blush.

"Before we begin, I would like to point out that- in my defence- I didn't know you were related when I first saw him."

"What are you talking about?"

"Arteryn?"

"What?"

Arteryn. He's the man! From the market in Orrick! He is the man. The one I watched over these years and never got the courage to approach."

As Amari's eyes widened in disbelief and her breath caught in her throat, Korin looked at her imploringly.

"I know, this isn't the time. So much is going on. There have been so many revelations, but Amari, this cannot be just a coincidence. I happen to run into the niece of the man I have longed for my whole life, we find our way to Bhrim, and he is here? I feel like…."

"What? Fate?" She didn't know how she felt about this. She didn't want Korin to be hurt. While she harboured suspicions about Arteryn's sexuality, there was no guarantee he would even like Korin in that way. What if Korin was sorely disappointed, and Arteryn rejected him? That would shatter Korin, especially considering how much of himself he had invested into his one-sided love. Oh, this was not going to end well. "Korin… I know you're excited, and I don't want to ruin your day, but-"

"I kissed him!"

"What?" Amari could have picked her jaw off the ground with how flabbergasted she was about this revelation. Her hand flew to her mouth as she stared at him. "Korin-"

"First of all, you don't get to judge me. You practically cornered Forde into kissing you. Before you make any comments, just listen to me for a moment." Korin still seemed to be buzzing from the excitement, which was such a foreign look on him. He was positively glowing. "After you fled the room, I realised that it was him. You can imagine how stunned I was, but when he caught sight of me, he didn't pretend like he didn't know me. He acknowledged me with my name. He knew my name. Can you believe he knew my name?"

"Korin."

"Right, I digress. We are adjourned until tomorrow to give you time to recover. Korrigan tried to pull Forde and me aside to thank us for coming here with you, but then I saw Arteryn leave the room-"

"So, you followed him?"

"Of course! I waited seven years already, and I was not going to wait any longer. Besides, I decided I had nothing to lose. I have lost so much already, and I just wanted to do something for myself for a change; consequences be damned. If you know me, you'd know I am not the spontaneous kind. I must think every action through carefully and consider all possible consequences, but since I met you, that seems to have flown out the window-"

"Korin."

"Right." He laughed as he waved his hand away as though to get himself back on track, and she paused. Who was this man before her? This person seemed to be radiating from excitement. "I followed him to his chambers, I assume and- I know, this sounds terrible, but I just needed to say it and get it out of the way. So, I started telling off by introducing myself. I won't lie, he looked a little distracted, but I think that's because he is concerned about you. For a moment, I faltered, thinking maybe this may not be the right time, but something told me to push on."

Korin paused and then took a deep breath; his long hair was usually half braided and tied loosely hung around his shoulders. He looked ethereal, especially with the glow of the lamp shining from behind him.

"Anyway, his face changed, and he pointed out he knew my name."

"Changed?"

"Yes, like usually how people look at me when they see me, especially up close…."

"Sexually awareness?"

"Yes, but with him, it wasn't in that...predatory manner that I normally encounter. Also, I watched him try to make himself look less intimidating, less big than he is, which was...."

A very un-Arteryn thing to do, Amari thought, because he had always used his height and built to be deliberately intimidating. It mainly was to scare all the men away from her but to hear he had done something so considerate for Korin made her realise that Arteryn knew something already. So, she decided not to pursue that line of thought.

"We just awkwardly stood there in silence for a moment because I couldn't exactly say I was the man who had been watching him with his full knowledge at the market for seven years. It is embarrassing after all." Korin grimaced a little, then shook his head as if to dismiss the thoughts. "Then my mouth opened, and I just started saying all kinds of things that, to be honest, I hardly remember. I know I told him I found him quite attractive and that I had never approached him because I was afraid of his reaction. The poor man just stood there and listened to me pouring out seven years of repressed sexual attraction-"

"Oh, Korin, that is embarrassing." Amari found herself chuckling, and Korin laughed along with her.

"Then, he did that thing where he pulled himself up to his full height, and all I could think about was how I just wanted to touch him. Even his clothes couldn't hide his muscles-"

"Korin." She didn't need to hear sexual perverted thoughts about Arteryn, thank you very much.

"Anyway, I just sort of grabbed both his cheeks, pulled his face down and kissed him." Korin suddenly had a dreamy look as he reflected on that moment. "When I released him, I don't know what I expected to happen. Part of me waited for a negative reaction. I mean, I had just kissed the poor man against his will, which is very ironic considering I have lived a life of people touching me against my will. I started to apologise, hoping he wouldn't throw me out, and I got desperate and started trying to use my abilities of persuasion on him to make him forget I had kissed him. He just stared at me like I was insane and said, 'you know your powers cannot work on me, right, or any Kenryk?'. I was mortified, but instead of fleeing, I just stood there, mustered up all my courage and told him he should consider himself blessed to get a kiss from me, that many people would pay exorbitant amounts of money just to be near me."

"In other words, you were just saying anything to save face."

"Absolutely." Korin laughed again then released. "He did the unthinkable. He cautiously reached out, tucked a strand of loose hair behind my ear then looked at me. I am surprised I didn't melt at that moment with how fierce his gaze was. He dropped his hand and said, 'I have waited a very long time for you, Korin.' Then he leaned down and kissed my forehead, but he didn't touch any other part of my body. When he stepped back, he advised me to leave because he was quite concerned about you at the moment and didn't want to say or do anything with his emotions heightened. I nodded, grabbed his cheeks and kissed him again before I ran out."

Amari didn't know what to think about Korin's revelations. Her suspicions about Arteryn were true, she realised. However, Korin's revelations were a lot, but she didn't want to raise any of those questions. Arteryn was never the type to wait on something he wanted. He went after it. She had learned that from him or inherited it, considering she now knew they were related. Why would Arteryn have waited for Korin instead of just pursuing him? It made no sense. However, she decided not to sully Korin's mood with those questions.

"So, on the day I find out my origins, you decide to take your chances with my uncle?" My uncle. Had she referred to Arteryn in that way? It felt so…natural.

"Well, I learned from the best. As I recall, someone cornered a cousin of mine to kiss her on a river-"

"All right, all right. I admit guilt. It's just that… Arteryn has never told me he found men attractive and…."

Concern immediately filled Korin's face, and he looked apologetic. "I should not have told you any of this. But unfortunately, I have unknowingly exposed something he probably was not ready to share with you yet."

Amari shook her head. "I am not bothered that he is attracted to men, but I am a little upset he didn't tell me. I thought we told each other everything. Well, what a fool I was. He hid the biggest thing from me. He is my uncle."

Korin suddenly looked serious, and for a moment, it felt like he was looking right through her. "Amari, you have always known, though, deep down that he is your relative."

Yes, she had, and all she could do was nod. "I wish Arteryn could have told me."

"He doesn't strike me as someone who does something without reason. Perhaps there was a reason he couldn't tell you. You have told us repeatedly on this journey just how close you are with him, how he taught you everything you know, how he protected you. I don't think anyone would do that and deliberately keep your relationship a secret unless he had to. Besides, you resemble him so much."

"Everyone in Synia said that. They always pointed out how I resembled him. I think I have always known. I want him to explain to me why he didn't tell me, why he let me train for years to become a Sage Warrior when he knew I was this Avaris…."

Her mood decline, her chest feeling heavy, and tears sprung to her eyes. "You still want to be a Sage Warrior?"

"I have worked most of my life towards that singular goal!" Amari snapped, then clamped her lips shut and looked at Korin apologetically. "He let me, too. He let me think I could be a Sage Warrior."

"You can be." Korin pointed out, and she rolled her eyes. "Listen to me for a moment. This Avaris role, or duty or whatever it is- is more sacred and more important than becoming a Sage Warrior. You carry with you the most powerful weapon in the whole Kais. From what I gathered, an Avaris plays a very critical role to the Kenryk. An Avaris outranks any Sage Warrior. You're one of the three dancing flames, the core foundation of this tribe. You belong here. You can never deny or outrun it. It is whom you were born to be the same way as I can't decide I don't want to be a Khaiman. These are our people. We are Kenryk and also not just ordinary Kenryk. We have duties and roles that have been bestowed upon us by fate."

"You seem to have easily accepted this."

"It's different for me. Unlike you, my only goal in life was survival. I didn't have grand plans of becoming a Sage Warrior. I just... I think you needed to reflect and understand the magnitude of what being an Avaris is-"

"I'd have to live here-"

"As a Sage Warrior, you would have had to live in Sagar anyway. So, you would have had to leave home." So Korin pointed out, and Amari hated that he was making so much sense.

"Yes, but I don't know these people. I don't know anything about being an Avaris or even being a Kenryk. So, I would have to live here, Korin and assume this role that I knew nothing about until today. At least with being a Sage Warrior, my duties would have been well known and standard."

"But you haven't asked."

"What?"

"You haven't asked what being an Avaris entails. You haven't asked what help you will receive to acclimatise. You haven't asked anything." Korin turned fully, so his whole body was on the bed, his legs crossed as he faced her. "I think I understand your challenge here. You're feeling robbed. You worked your whole life towards this one goal, and you now are told that isn't the path you have to take. You probably feel robbed of the future you planned for yourself. You're not focusing on what you're gaining."

"Which is what?"

"An identity. The one thing you always felt you didn't have. Your family- not to say those who raised you are not your family. You're focusing too much on what you're losing rather than what you will be gaining. Also, because this is something you didn't know and didn't prepare for, you feel overwhelmed by that. You understood the duties of a Sage Warrior, and you prepared yourself for that. However, you never had the opportunity to prepare to be an Avaris because you knew nothing about it."

She felt a little transparent in that moment. It felt like Korin could read her mind, see deep into her fears. For a moment, she couldn't respond because Korin had articulated what she was feeling.

"I'm scared." It came out as barely a whisper. Those were words she had never uttered in her life. "I'm terrified of this entire Avaris situation."

"You should be. That is normal. I am a little afraid of being a Khaiman too. However, because I will be navigating this new life with someone I feel I trust, it makes it less daunting."

"Me?"

"Yes," Korin said with a smile and shook his head. "I think it is obvious you have crawled through my barriers Amari Leverood. It terrifies me that I realise I can trust you with my life, and yet we have spent such a short time together."

He reached out her hand and took it into his gently. "What I am saying is, you are not on your own. I will be here with you, so will Arteryn."

"He lives in Synia-"

"Amari, I think it is obvious he only lived in Synia to protect you. With you back here, he will come back to the tribe. Listen, there is a lot of uncertainty right now, a lot of unknowns. You feel out of your depth. I know what that is like, but just know, you're not on your own."

She nodded slowly, his words making sense, but a part of her still clung to her dream. "I still want to be a Sage Warrior, Korin. That hasn't changed. I worked so hard to become the first female Sage Warrior, and it is within my reach. However, accepting my role as an Avaris means giving up on that dream."

Korin was quiet for a moment looking at her with sympathy, and then he squeezed her hand. "Maybe, you can do both."

"I don't see how-"

"Listen for a moment. Maybe, you can go to Sagar, participate in the Laurean Sage and win that badge, officially becoming the first female Sage Warrior. After that, once you have attained that goal, you return here and assume your duties as an Avaris-"

"They'd never let me leave with the Sword- which by the way, is still confusing. How can this-" she reached for her medallion and waved it towards him. "-possibly be a Sword? Now that I am here, do you honestly think they would let me leave?"

"Maybe you can state your case. You never know. Just try."

She pulled her hand away from him and covered her face with her hands, exhaling in frustration. She lifted her head as she dropped her hands to her lap and sighed. "I think you are right. I think I could ask. If they say no, I'll sneak off."

"I think they'd be expecting that."

"True." She sat back, her back against the wall behind her and released another sigh, but one of resignation. "I just wanted to be a Sage Warrior so bad."

They must have fallen asleep at some point because when she woke up, the only light in the room came from a lamp on the mantelpiece. Korin was fast asleep next to her, flat on his back as he snored ever so slightly. As she sat up slowly, pushing her hair away from her face, she gasped when she saw Forde lounging in one of her armchairs. He pushed himself to his feet slowly and moved towards the bed in quiet steps, and all she could do was watch him approach. Forde's attention was on Korin with a pained expression on his face while shadows from the ambers of the lamp flame in the heath danced on his face. She glanced at Korin, and he was dead to the world, asleep.

"He was holding you when I came in…." Forde shook his head slowly then turned his attention to her due to the poor light from the lamp; she could barely make out his expression. His body language, on the other hand, spoke volumes. He held himself stiffly, as though he feared any sudden movements would disturb the sight before him. "I don't know what you did to him, but whatever it is, I am glad it happened. He has been selective about the touches between us since the incident. Not even a brotherly embrace, and yet today I walk in here to find him holding you closely." He shook his head again then ran his fingers through his hair. "How are you feeling?"

"Emotionally exhausted. Confused and overwhelmed. How do you feel finding out you're half Kenryk.?" She could not find another way to describe it, but she spoke in a hushed tone to ensure she did not wake Korin.

"I don't think it has that much of an impact on me. My mother taught me how to use herbs and plants to heal since I was four, which is a skill I have never lost but have cultivated over the years. The only difference is that now I know about her roots." He continued hovering at the foot of the bed, looking like he had not had any sleep, and apprehension weighed heavily over him. "You've always suspected you're Kenryk? I think the fire coming out of your hands should have been an indication. However, Amari, being Kenryk does not change who you are. So, in a way, I think it might have worked out for the best."

"How so?" How could he think this had worked out for the best?

"While you were growing up with your other family, you had Arteryn around. I think it was to make sure that you would have someone to help you assimilate to your new life when the time came. He trained you himself because he knows what being an Avaris requires. He was preparing you-"

"I just want to be a Sage Warrior."

He folded his arms over his chest, looking thoughtful, and then he slowly shook his head. "And I wish I hadn't lost my whole family when I was eight, but sometimes things don't go as we planned. Life happens, and you must adjust. You cannot, as an Avaris, still strive to be nothing more than a king's guard. You possess something sacred, historic and powerful. Your calling is higher than to be a Sage Warrior. You're an Avaris, a direct descent of a man we read about in historical scrolls. You're not insignificant. You're Amari."

"Korin suggested I ask to be allowed to participate in the Laurean Sage and after that return and take up my duties."

"You can't still be obsessing over being a Sage warrior when you have an essential responsibility."

"I never asked for this responsibility. I had my own goals. I am not an Avaris."

"And yet, that is who you are. You are Amari the Kenryk Avaris. That is your fate, your destiny. No matter where you go or do, that won't change. Perhaps I don't understand why you're conflicted by this because I was raised differently in a place where duty was duty. If my uncle instructed me to do something, then I had to do it. Arteryn raised you to believe you could be the first female warrior, and maybe you can be, but you need to understand this Avaris thing is sacred and more important than being a Sage Warrior. You are home."

"My home is Synia."

"You know what I mean." Frustration laced his words, but he caught himself quickly. "My point is you have to think about it. While you might have decided you want to be a Sage Warrior, that is not who you were born to be."

"I should decide who I am born to be."

He seemed to realise then that he was trying to break down a rock-solid wall with glass and nodded. "All right. If you want to go to Sagar, still you may come with us. However, we both know that is not who you are. Just help me keep an eye on Korin. I'm worried that this revelation about himself might not go down so well. I will let you sleep."

"I think Korin is taking it better than I am." She muttered.

Forde nodded, then drew back. "It must help that the man he stalked in the market turned out to be your Arteryn."

"Wait, Forde." She scrambled to the edge of the bed and knelt. He paused as he had started to walk away then turned to face her. "Please understand that while I understand what role everyone around me in this place expects me to take, I am not yet ready to give up on the dreams I have, goals I set for myself. I need to see it through."

"It is not me you have to explain yourself to." He muttered and started to walk away once more, but she reached out for his arm, and he paused once more.

"Thank you for getting me here safely. I know I would not have made it without you and Korin. Your assistance has been invaluable."

Forde remained silent, seemingly pondering his words carefully.

"You know Korin shouldn't be sleeping here, right?" He asked, and she glanced at Korin over her shoulder. He looked so peaceful in his sleep. She hadn't seen him look like this since she met him.

"He has had a very adventurous night." She crawled over to Korin, then shook gently shook him. "Korin, wake up."

A few more shakes woke him up, and for a moment, he seemed confused about where he was; then, when Korin saw her, he groaned.

"Why did you wake me? I was in the middle of a marvellous dream with Arteryn, and he was-"

"Korin." Forde cut in quickly as Amari sat back on her legs and shook her head. Korin pushed himself to sit up slowly, moving his hair away from his face and a slow smile crawled to his lips when he saw Forde.

"Cousin." He grinned, stretching his muscles. "Why am I awake? Is it morning yet?"

Forde looked him over then his eyes widened. "Oh, my goodness. When you pretended you were in your chambers, you went to see Arteryn, didn't you?"

"Yes. Yes, I did." Korin nodded, rubbing his stomach and looking ridiculously adorable. Then, he shook himself fully awake.

"What did you do?" Forde seemed concerned.

"He kissed him." Amari declared, and Forde looked to the heavens and shook his head before levelling Korin with a look of pure disbelief.

"It went quite well," Korin muttered, then pushed the covers off and rose to his feet, getting his hair under control. Amari watched him as he moved towards Forde and, without pause, threw his arms around the other man and held him tightly.

Amari's head jerked back at the unexpected move, and if the look on Forde's face was anything to go by in the dimly lit room, he was also stunned by the sudden show of affection. Amari smiled at Koirn's actions because she understood what it meant to Forde.

Korin turned his head and peppered Forde's cheek with tiny little kisses, then hugged him again. "Thank you for being the best brother in the whole Kais. Thank you for never giving up on me."

With that, he picked up his shoes and walked out of the room, leaving behind a stunned Amari and an emotional Forde.

Forde cleared his throat as he looked at her, and she could tell how much it meant to him that Korin had not shied away from him.

"Get some sleep. We'll see you tomorrow." He muttered before he turned and walked out of the room.

CHAPTER TWENTY- TWO

When she woke up the following morning, she had a terrible headache and puffy eyes. After taking care of her morning requirements, getting a bath, dressing and having breakfast, one of the guards informed her that she had to report to the Great Hall.

She was stunned to find several men there. She had been expecting to see just Derik, Korrigan and maybe Arteryn. However, these strange men varying in age from anywhere between forty to seventy immediately put her on the defensive. Korin was there too, looking uncomfortable. Forde was surprisingly missing, but Korin had somehow managed to secure a seat next to Arteryn, which was probably the only reason he had not fled yet.

Amari instantly picked up on a negative energy on her left, to a man glaring at Korin with something akin to resentment. The set-up was also unusual, a U-shaped sitting arrangement, but with a singular chair right at the end of the middle of the U-shape. It knocked her back to suddenly realise there were more Kenryk than Korrigan, Derik and Arteryn. She didn't know why her brain hadn't considered this.

"Amari, we hope you enjoyed your breakfast," Derik said warmly, but there was a hint of something in his eyes, an air of seriousness that hung about him. It almost felt like there had been a discussion that had taken place before she arrived.

"It was food." Her voice came out suddenly husky, and she tried to clear her throat quickly as Derik indicated she sit on that solitary chair that would have her in full view of these additional eight men.

"I am certain you are surprised to see the audience that has joined us today. First, I would like to introduce you to the Council of the Kenryk tribe. The Council discusses all matters of the tribe and provides resolutions. By default, an Avaris and Khaiman sit on the Council which accounts for Korin's presence."

"His Khaiman confirmation is yet to take place, Leader Derik. Let us not pre-empt sacred tribal rituals." A man, perhaps one of the younger ones of the tribe, the one who had given off this sense of anger towards Korin, interjected.

"Showell, this meeting is not about discussing whether or not Korin is a Khaiman." One of the men said, and Amari watched the sneer on Showell's face.

"What is this meeting about, if I may ask?" Amari asked, her eyes drifting towards Arteryn, painfully wanting his help but conflicted because he had misled her all these years.

"The Council sat last night and resolved that, due to the uncharacteristic delay in our training, which essentially begins when you are seven, Korrigan must begin your training urgently," Derik replied. Amari blinked because she was not sure she had heard them correctly.

"Wait, it sounds like you think I am staying." They couldn't be serious. And the Council sat? Without her knowledge to discuss her fate.

"You are staying, Amari. You carry in your possession something extremely powerful and something desperately wanted in the Kais. The Endric Sword is not just a weapon. It is a collection of the energies of the Kenryk of Old. You need to start learning how to use your Avaris powers, and Korrigan has the task to carry out-"

"Apologies for my interruption, but should I not have a say in this?"

"You mean, should you have a say as to whether you take the Endric Sword away from the protection of the tribe again? You mean should you have a say a when, for the first time in twenty-four years, we finally have the Leader, Khaiman and Avaris present in the tribe with the Sword safe?" A man with bushy brows and greying hair questioned her, and she stared at him in disbelief.

"I didn't even know I was Kenryk until recently. You cannot be making such decisions on my behalf." Amari protested.

"Your lack of knowledge about your true purpose can be attributed to the particular requests of your father. The Council was very much against it, but a final request of an Avaris cannot be denied." Another man spoke, and Amari blinked again, her hands waving in the air.

"I didn't catch your name-"

"Saulese. However, as per customs, as your elder, you may refer to me as Saulese Kha." He explained to her.

A group of men she didn't know had come together, decided her future without consulting her and expected her to accept it.

"I am going to Sagar to become a Sage Warrior." She stated, smacking the side of her hand on her palm for emphasis. "If your concern is the Sword, I can leave it behind-"

"An Avaris cannot be separated from the Endric Sword. I am Golin Kha, by the way." The man with the bushy eyebrows pointed out. "This is bigger than you, Amari. Bigger than your dreams. This decision is about the tribe. The very essence of what completes us. Our very core. Unnecessary risks won't be entertained because you resolved to be a Sage Warrior as a child."

Amari glanced at Arteryn, and she instinctively knew that he had tried to advocate on her behalf, but the look on his face told her he had failed.

"You need to allow me to at least plead my case. You cannot make such decisions about my life and future without consulting me. What is next? You're going to choose a husband for me?" She had never felt so discombobulated in her life.

"If you will calm down-"

"Calm down? Please, Golin Kha, do not make me out to sound like a hysterical and unreasonable woman. You have all decided about my future. Your tribe hasn't even taken time to introduce me to anything about the Kenryk, and you expect to make such decisions for me."

"Our tribe? The Kenryk your tribe as well." Showell pointed out.

"All right, can we please all just calm down?" Derik quickly interjected the levelled Amari with an intense gaze. "Arteryn did make us aware of your intentions to participate in the Laurean Sage. He explained us to all the work and effort you have put towards that. It isn't surprising that at the age of seven, you asked him to train you. Instinctively, you knew you were supposed to begin your Avaris training, but that is something Arteryn could not give you. We debated this intensely most of last night. However, it is simply too risky. You have never used the Sword. You probably have not even learned how to reverse the transfiguration Artello did on it to make it a medallion. The risks of you leaving outweigh everything."

"My family. My parents-"

"I can assure you, Amari, the Leveroods have always understood your destiny."

Amari's mouth opened, but nothing came out. She was in utter shock, unable to see a way through this.

"You cannot hold me here against my will." She protested but quickly realised that her tactics to advocate for herself were not going to work. She needed a different approach. "I need to do this. I need to go to Sagar and see this through. Arteryn, say something-"

"I see you failed to teach her how to refer to you properly." Showell jeered. "The correct term to use for Arteryn, Amari, is Father."

Amari felt her chest tighten, and she looked at Arteryn pleadingly, and he nodded, his eyes telling her to calm down.

"Perhaps, if you will allow me to explain a few things to Amari-"

"What's there to explain-"

"Then perhaps she may have a better understanding of why you decided that she must stay." Arteryn continued as though Showell had not even interjected him. He completely disregarded the other man and faced Amari, looking at her imploringly. "I need you to listen to me, all right. You may ask questions where you feel you need more clarity. Agreed?"

She nodded, her hands clasping the handles of the chair tightly as everything in hr fought for her to flee.

"Artello… my brother, your birth father, called me on the night of the Great Blaze. Both he and your mother Nessie were there with all your things packed. The tribe was under attack with no time to prepare our defences. My brother asked me to take you to Synia. He had somehow found a way to change the shape of the Endric Sword into a medallion. He had already, by the time I entered the room, transferred his Avaris powers to you." Arteryn paused to be sure she was following. "I knew instantly walking in that he had transferred his powers already; therefore, I knew my brother intended to stay and fight. The two of them gave you to me and told me strictly where to take you. The Avaris had to survive, and the Endric Sword had to be kept safe. The Emori knew Artello was an Avaris. He would have been their target. I had to leave that night everything and everyone, riding off into the night during the attack to ensure your survival. The reasons you were raised in Synia? There are two. Firstly, the Emori would never have found you there because they wouldn't expect an Avaris in a tiny village in Orrick. Secondly, my brother had explicitly expressed that he wanted you to have what he never had; the freedom to be a child and find your own goals. You see, the training of an Avaris begins when they are seven years old. While other children are playing, an Avaris is training. He told me how he wished he had just a little freedom before becoming an Avaris.

"He and I knew the Leveroods because once when we had travelled outside Kenrin, our ancestral lands, we were caught in Great Storm in Synia. The Leveroods sheltered us, and we thanked them afterwards by helping them repair the damage to their property. So, for two weeks, my brother got a taste of what not being an Avaris meant. He could be like any normal young man, and he loved it there. Artello told me he wished he could go there often. Therefore, when he told me to take you to Synia, I understood what my brother wanted for you and of me.

"He wanted you to have your childhood, but because it is ingrained in you, at the age of seven, you came to me and asked me to train you how to fight. But unfortunately, the training you were supposed to receive as an Avaris is not something within my capacity. So, I couldn't prepare you to be an Avaris, but I could prepare you to be a warrior because an Avaris must fight to keep the Sword safe.

"I didn't tell you that you were Kenryk or an Avaris because I knew that would have an impact on you. I know you. You would have become obsessed with finding the Kenryk and coming here. In allowing that, I would have broken a vow to my brother that I would only ever let you come here when the time came. You see, Artello's Khaiman was Korin's father. Korin's father could see the future, and he told him many things that my brother never could share with me. I know that my brother made me understand that I had to keep you in Synia until the time was right for you to come here. He said that a man with a scar and sharp dagger would be the catalyst of your return."

"Grantreal." She said breathily.

"Yes. That is how I knew the time had come for you to return. However, I also knew I could not interfere with your journey here because the prophecy from Faegon Kha was that the Avaris would return one day with a Khaiman and a Healer. It had to happen that way. You had to meet Forde and Korin. You all had to come here. That was fated, and I could not interfere with that fate even if I could easily take care of Grantreal."

Of course, Arteryn could have quickly taken care of Grantreal, and his men included. That was the level of skill the man had. She hadn't even thought to ask why she had to leave Synia and not stay and fight alongside him.

"Artello wanted you to have a normal childhood so you could develop your own goals, but he knew that eventually, you would have to return to the tribe and assume your responsibilities.

"Why didn't you tell me we were related?"

"Amari, you knew we were related. You've always known."

"I asked you several times, and you'd ignore me."

"Because I had to give Joran and Tia the respect they deserved as people who raised you as their child-"

"Arteryn, there are times when you didn't do that. There are many instances when you would be the one disciplining me instead of them. There were many instances when they allowed you to have the final say about me. You were already acting like we were related. Why couldn't you just tell me? Why couldn't you just say you were my uncle?"

"You wanted to hear the words, or you preferred the actions?"

"That is not fair! You're telling me that behaving like we were related counts more than telling me we were related when you knew how much I yearned to know of my origins-"

"You wouldn't have understood."

"That is an insult."

"No, it is a fact. You wouldn't have understood. I stopped being your uncle when Artello handed you to me. From that day, according to the laws of my people, I became your father."

"And you could have explained-"

"And what would it have achieved?"

Frustration and anger rose within her, and she glared at him. "You of all people saying that to me…."

"You already had fire coming out of your hands. You've known since you learned of the Kenryk that you were one, but you deliberately chose not to acknowledge it. Instead, you chose to focus on becoming the first female Sage Warrior. That was your goal, the thing you had decided you wanted to achieve in life. Telling you everything would have changed that."

"I can't be a Sage Warrior anyway! I must be this Avaris! You let me grow up thinking I had a choice to become anything in life. You're the one who consistently told me being a woman didn't mean I was weaker, that I could achieve whatever I wanted. You told me that, Arteryn knowing it wasn't true. All along, I was going to have to come here and be an Avaris. So, tell me how what you did was to my benefit?"

"Amari, you must understand-" Korrigan interjected, and Amari shook her head quickly, quivering with repressed rage.

"I don't have to understand anything. You kept important information about me from me. Something that effectively changes everything about the future I had planned for myself. I trained since I was seven for this one thing, to be this Sage Warrior. That was my goal in life, the one thing I strived for and right next to me, Arteryn was telling me I could be anything I wanted to be. He encouraged me all the way only to now turn around and tell me all of it was a lie."

"It was never a lie. I still believe you can become the first female Sage Warrior; I just didn't think the year you had to return to the tribe would coincide with the year you had decided you were going to sneak off to Sagar and try to compete in the Laurean Sage,"

Amari chewed her lower lip, her hands gripping the armrests tightly as she stared at Arteryn. Her heart shattered. Had he hoped that she would be able to go to Sagar, become a Sage Warrior, then one day give that up to become an Avaris? Had he been hoping she would achieve that goal first before the time came to return? She took several deep breaths, pondering the situation, analysing it in her mind. She knew Arteryn. He would have let her participate at the Laurean Sage. He would have allowed her to become the first female Sage Warrior. Amari had defeated Grantreal in front of hundreds of men, and that set her on this path. She had to acknowledge the part she played in this situation, but it still didn't excuse keeping something so important to her.

"So, what do you want me to do, Arteryn? Give up on the goal you encouraged and allowed me to nurture? Do my needs no longer matter? Am I no longer a Leverood?"

Arteryn didn't respond. He lowered his head and looked at his clasped hands on the table.

"What is important now, Amari is that you begin your training as soon as possible. With the Emori having found you and followed you, we may face an attack again. You need to be prepared to protect the Sword-"

"I apologise for cutting you off, Derik, but that isn't what is important to me now. What is important to me now is what happens to my family in Synia when Grantreal cannot find me. Arteryn is here. They're defenceless on their own. Secondly, what about the dream your son had for me? The one where I develop and achieve my goals. Does that no longer matter-"

"You were young when the Great Blaze happened, only three. So, you didn't see the catastrophe that was left when the Emori eventually left." Korrigan cut her off quickly, his tone serious. "You're not aware of what it has taken for our people to rebuild here, in a land that isn't even our own and adjust to a climate that is vastly different from our indigenous lands. You don't understand the grief they faced, that we all met, and the losses of lives that came with the Great Blaze. Therefore, you wouldn't understand what it would mean to the Kenryk to hear that both the Avaris and Khaiman have returned.

"Artello's wishes are fulfilled. You grew up in Synia even though the whole tribe was against it because Artello believed it would make you a stronger Avaris. We didn't have to wait seventeen years for you to come here; fate dictated that we wait until circumstances brought you here. The Emori have been attacking lower lands, extending their power. They now know you have the Sword with you. I am not quite certain how they know, but they have been pursuing you because they have found out somehow. They were not after the chest. They are going to be planning an attack. They will try to get the Sword, and when they do, you need to be ready. Your training needs to resume immediately-"

"No." She interjected, slowly taking deep breaths to calm herself down. "No. My Avaris training is not going to begin immediately. I am aware that you are trying to manipulate my decision by bringing up the Great Blaze. While I express my condolences for the suffering and loss that everyone experienced, you still can't force me into this. I know myself. I know what I want and what I want is to become a Sage Warrior. It may sound ridiculous to you, but I need to do this. I need to achieve this goal for myself so that even if I decide to return here and assume my role, I would have already achieved a goal I have had for ten years. I may not know how to use Avaris powers or the Sword, but I know how to fight. I have kept the Sword safe my whole life, even though I thought it was just a medallion. Even when a group of boys in Synia once tried to take it from me, I instinctively knew I had to protect it without even knowing the medallion was a Sword. I need to go to Sagar. I need to compete in the Laurean Sage, and I need to do this on my own.'

"We cannot allow it-"

"With all due respect, Derik... or should I call you grandfather, you cannot stop me. The only way to do that is to lock me up in a room I will simply burn down. You see, fire doesn't burn me. External fire does nothing to me. I am immune to its heat. I would eventually find a way out, and I would sneak off to Sagar. That is why I am here asking that you consider allowing me to do this one thing for myself before I return here and assume the role of Avaris."

"A compromise?" Arteryn suggested, letting the words hang in the air.

"Arteryn, this is a non-negotiable matter. She cannot go to Sagar, not with the Emori already on her trail-"

"She wouldn't be going alone. I would go with her." Arteryn cut Golin off quickly, looking at the older man boldly. "Who else in this tribe can kill three Emori on their own except me?"

"To bring that up-"

"It is valid, is it not. You all know me. You know what I can do." There was almost a hush in the room as though Arteryn was painting a picture that looked horrific. "I take her to the Sagar, and once she achieves her goal, we return, and she resumes her duties. In the meantime, I will train her on how to use her fire powers-"

"This is ludicrous...."

Saulese's words died out when something strange and unexpected happened. Korin, who had been sitting there silently, suddenly sat up slowly, elegantly in his way, but that was not the issue. No, the shock was that his eyes had changed. They were not still. They swirled, and he stared ahead as though in a trance, unseeing of anything before him. Energy radiated from him that she had never felt before, but she could tell every Kenryk in the room felt it.

He was gripped tightly in whatever was happening to him, then he suddenly sighed and sagged back against the chair. Arteryn was quick to help him sit up, and even though his eyes were not swirling, Korin seemed to be vibrating.

"She must go to the Laurean Sage. It is only through this journey will her Avaris powers be unlocked and the Sword transformed." His voice sounded flat, emotionless and then he blinked and seemed to snap back to reality. However, he visibly shrunk when he realised everyone was staring at him.

"You had a vision!" one of the other councilmen exclaimed in disbelief, and there was almost this sense of joy that suddenly flared in the room. "That was a vision! He... The Khaiman has truly returned."

"Excuse me." Derik indicated for Korin to come closer to him. Korin rose gingerly, then walked over to Derik, where they had an inaudible conversation, then Korin returned to his seat quietly. Derik ran a hand over his face, his frustration visible. "She must complete her journey to Sagar."

"Leader Derik-" Showell gasped.

"The Khaiman had a vision, Showell. Amari's Avaris powers will remain unlocked unless she completes this journey-"

"Or you're just accommodating your granddaughter."

"Watch your words, Showell!" Saulese snapped at the other men. "Leader Derik has always shown impartiality when carrying out his duties even when it related to his family. So do not insult him and this Council by suggesting that he is biased because she is his granddaughter. You know we all want the Avaris here. He wants the Avaris here! However, the Khaiman has had a vision, and we cannot ignore the vision of a Khaiman."

What was going on? Amari sat forward as she watched the men argue back and forth with Showell.

"What about the impartiality of the so-called Khaiman. He could have said those words to help her go to Sagar-"

"Showell, you of all people should be accustomed to what happens to a Khaiman when they have a vision. You felt it. We all did." Golin pointed out with a sneer.

Derik cleared his throat. "It appears, Amari, that this journey to Sagar is something you need to complete and the only reason this Council would allow it is for the benefit of the tribe. Therefore, Arteryn will accompany you to Sagar and return you instantly upon the end of the games."

"Wait, you're letting me go?" Amari was still at a loss for words.

"Only because you will have Arteryn with you. Perhaps we should add a few more warriors on your detail-"

"No. We travel light. More people attract attention." Arteryn argued, then he turned to his father. "I swear to return her the instant the games are over."

As she sat on that chair, she had a sudden flash of images in her head, yet these images were not painful and harsh.

She could hear a woman singing softly in a sweet voice before she suddenly came to vision. She grinned and immediately rushed forward to sweep Amari off her feet. The details of the room were vague, but she heard a man chuckling from the door, muttering something she did not quite catch before he came towards them, and she saw his face. He kissed the woman's cheek, then plucked Amari from the woman's arms and threw her into the air. She laughed with exuberance, enjoying being in the air and having no doubt that he would catch her. He always caught her.

She exhaled sharply as the images disappeared as fast as they had appeared, and her hand flew to clutch her chest as unimaginable pain tore through her soul. She knew those people in her vision had been her birth parents, and tears slid down her cheeks without notice as she finally lost her resolve.

"What did you see?" Korrigan asked tentatively, giving her a moment to collect herself.

She sat there quietly as something else entirely assailed not her memory but her sense of smell. It tugged at her nose, connecting it with a memory.

"I remember lavender and a woman, older with dark hair and dark eyes." The words slipped between her lips before she could censor herself, and she saw the immediate reaction from the three men in her family. "And being taken for a swim on a hot day. I remember I broke someone's treasured vase, but instead of being scolded, I received comfort because I was so upset about it."

"That was my mother," Arteryn muttered as he lowered his head. "She always smelled of lavender."

Her heart twisted as more memories of these people started to emerge from her brain. It was becoming increasingly evident that this was indeed her family, especially considering she had just had a memory of a grandmother. She took a deep breath, knowing there was no denying what they had told her but also knowing that she had to leave. "Thank you for your hospitality, but if we are to make it to Sagar in time, we have to leave today."

There was silence across the room, Derik looking a little rough around the edges, Korrigan looking frustrated, and Arteryn looking thoughtful.

She swiped her hand over her face and expressed a sigh of frustration. She could not go forward denying the truth she had found out about herself. She could not pretend she was not carrying around her neck the most powerful weapon the Emori sought. She also could not ignore the obvious fact that she was a Kenryk and this Avaris. She understood the responsibilities that came with it, and she knew that maybe deep down, one day, she might have to accept her duties.

However, before she tied herself down for the rest of her life to guarding the Endric Sword, she needed to do this one thing for herself. She needed to participate in the Games.

With a heavy heart, she looked up at the three men and sat forward. "Thank you all for affording me this opportunity. I understand now that I carry with me something significant, and I will protect it with my life. After the Games, I will return. I promise, but I also have a condition. Whether I am victorious or not, I will be allowed to go back home to Synia. I need to talk to my family and explain everything to them. I want them to understand why I would be leaving home."

"They know. Tia and Joran have always known." Arteryn at least had the decency to look embarrassed.

"I still need to see them, Arteryn. Please."

She could not believe she was even contemplating returning here and living among people she didn't know.

"That is something we can negotiate on upon your return." Derik nodded as he pushed to his feet along with his sons.

So, she still had a shot at becoming a Sage Warrior, even if in name only.

CHAPTER TWENTY-THREE

W hen she eventually returned to her chambers an hour after going for a walk to clear her thoughts, she found Korin sitting cross-legged in the middle of her bed and Forde lounging on a chair by the window.

"We didn't know what your reaction after the meeting today would be. So, we thought we would wait here." Korin explained, and Amari noticed his eyes light up as she sat straighter when Arteryn walked in and shut the door behind him. It scared her a little how Korin seemed to be so captivated by Arteryn. He didn't need any more disappointments in life. However, she had more pressing issues at hand.

"What are you both doing here?" Arteryn sounded stunned to walk into her chambers and find two men waiting there for her. He was still the Arteryn she had always known, she thought. She turned around slowly to face him.

"Arteryn, don't. They kept me safe all the way here. I don't need you doing your Arteryn thing right now." She waved him off quickly.

"We're just here to make sure that now Amari has been allowed to continue to Sagar, we will be going with her as promised," Forde replied as he stood up, but something in his tone had Amari looking his way. The three men in her room were by no means short, but Arteryn was still the tallest and, to be fair, more intimidating to strangers than Forde and Korin. He was also more muscled. The chamber that had seemed big before felt smaller now with three men in it. However, Arteryn still stood with his back facing the door, so whoever had to leave would have to go through him.

"You do not have to. I will go with Amari." Arteryn pointed out quickly, then seemed to realise how that would come across. "I would like to thank you both for being with her all the way here. As much as I know she would have been capable of getting here on her own, I know the major role you both played to get her here. That said, the Council has agreed that I can accompany her-"

Forde folded his arms across his chest and sighed. "As I said, I promised to get her to Sagar, and I intend to keep that promise."

Amari watched in stunned silence as Forde stared eye-to-eye with Arteryn with a daring expression. She never had in her life met anyone who dared challenge Arteryn.

"You do not have to."

"And yet I will."

"Why?"

"One," Forde folded his hand into a fist and propped a thumb up, "my uncle has a house in Sagar that is well protected. It will ensure Amari has accommodation within a protected environment. Two," he lifted an index finger, "I made a promise, and I intend to keep it."

Arteryn stared at Forde, a tense silence stretching throughout the room. "I should probably let you know now that if you harbour any romantic notions towards her, you should discard them now. You are of the Khaiman bloodline. Your family and my family's bloodline are not allowed to mix."

Forde gave a humourless smile as he looked at Arteryn. "If I harbour any romantic notions towards her, then I think that will be between Amari and me to decide. No?"

"Actually, no." Arteryn gave a condescending smile. "I am the only one in this tribe who can ever consent with whom she engages romantically with according to the laws of this tribe. Fortunately for you, as the son of a twin to a former Khaiman, you have inherited the healing abilities that can only come with your bloodline. Having been around Korin and Amari, it is only inevitable that you will get your fire powers soon. You're more Kenryk than your other non-Kenryk side. In other words, you can live with the tribe as Kenryk should you wish to. I am letting you know that because henceforth, both Amari and Korin will be living here. If you are going to be living here, you need to understand that unless Korin bears a son, you cannot be with Amari in any way because should Korin die before he sires a child, you become the Khaiman. So, if you thought the only way you can get to live here with Korin is to use my niece, then you do not have to."

"Arteryn. You don't know Forde; therefore, you cannot lay your unfounded accusations on him. He does not deserve this verbal attack from you, who has, by the way, been an absolute gentleman towards me. He doesn't require your warnings or threats, and I am not going to let you attempt to intimidate him." Amari interjected quickly.

"One kiss," Arteryn stated, and her eyes widened.

"You saw that?"

"I have been following you since you left Synia. I just couldn't intervene." Arteryn looked at Forde once more. "That is all I will let you get away with. Consider yourself fortunate."

"She orchestrated that kiss." Korin pointed casually from the bed. "I think you might need to be warning her instead of Forde. You're the one who raised her. You should have known she would have her first kiss on her terms."

Arteryn looked at Korin, opened his mouth, paused, and seem at war with himself, then clammed his mouth shut. He turned to Amari, then shook his head, then grimaced. He turned to Forde.

"Right, I owe you an apology."

Korin chuckled.

"What's so funny?" Amari asked.

"Arteryn knows you well if he didn't even question that you orchestrated that kiss."

Well, that was true. No one knew Amari as Arteryn did.

"I am going to Sagar with her." Forde reiterated, and Amari wondered why he was insisting. He didn't have to. They could part ways now, but she didn't want that. No, a part of her already knew Forde was someone she would give her heart to. The thought of never seeing him again was painful to consider.

"And I may kiss him again," Amari said, deliberately baiting Arteryn, who did not fall for it.

"Fine, you may come with us if you wish." Arteryn capitulated then turned to Amari. "We need to talk.'

"Yes, we do." They did.

"And to correct you, Amari, I do know Forde. I know him probably more than you do. You just both didn't realise it."

"How could you possibly know me? I only spoke to you once." Forde questioned.

"You think I wouldn't take the time to learn about the person the Kenryk Khaiman was living with? I know you, Forde. I know of your history. I know of every up and down you have had since the moment you met Korin. It was my duty to know." Arteryn pointed out factually rather than with any animosity. "I am not concerned about the kind of man you are. I know the kind of man you are. This tribe knows the kind of man you are, based on my reports. However, the matter remains. You're from the Khaiman bloodline, so even if you were worthy, you could not be with Amari. I thought that was something I should let you both know. Now, of you will both excuse us, I owe Amari a much-overdue conversation."

"Should we prepare to leave today?" Forde asked Arteryn, but more as an equal rather than a follower.

"That would be best." Arteryn nodded; then, as Forde moved to walk past him, he grabbed his arm and stopped him, then looked down at him. "I've never said this to anyone, but you are the only man I have ever met whom I think is worthy of Amari. Thank you for everything you have done. I can only hope that upon our return, you do decide to live as Kenryk as I think both Korin and Amari would benefit from having you in their lives."

Forde looked up at Arteryn, but he didn't say anything. Instead, he left the room quietly with Korin. Amari moved to sit where Korin had been sitting cross-legged in the middle of the bed.

Arteryn moved to take a seat then took a deep breath.

"Before your parents were married, Artello and I travelled to Orrick to look for your mother, Nessie. Her father had wanted her to marry someone else, and, being the person she was, Amari had decided she was not going to marry a man she didn't even like. So, she left the tribe and Artello, decided he would look for her and bring her back. See, my brother had been in love with her since he was fourteen. The love was mutual. We found Nessie near Gildevard. The tribe still lived in Kenrin then. However, as we were travelling south, we were caught up in the Great Storm. We found shelter on a farm and the respect and kindness the Leveroods showed us that day, complete strangers we were to them, was something your birth parents never forgot.

"We stayed a week, helping them rebuild some structures destroyed by the storm, but I knew your parents had fallen in love with the place.

"When we returned, they married. Artello was eighteen, and Nessie was just seventeen then. After that, I never thought about the Leveroods again until the night of the Emori attack. During the attack, my brother summoned me to his house where…." Arteryn drifted off briefly, pausing to catch his breath as though the memories were pressing hard on his chest. This wasn't easy for him, Amari realised with surprise. "… he and Nessie gave me strict instructions. They asked me to take you to Synia, to the Leveroods. They said under the guise of ensuring your safety if you were away from the tribe if no one knew where you were hidden, but I knew the real reason.

"My brother didn't want you to grow up in the tribe, like how he did. I had gathered that much from the conversation we had had even before you were born. He didn't want you to grow up with the heavy responsibility of being an Avaris from a young age, and it is quite a responsibility, Amari. He wanted you to grow up "normal" and have the childhood he never had. He wanted you to choose who you wanted to be, to choose this instead of having it forced on you. He wanted you to have that decision even though it wasn't really a responsibility you could ever walk away from.

"It was a condition he set when gave you the Endric Sword and surrendered his Avaris powers to you that night. The power he displayed that night when he moulded a sword into a medallion is still by far the most spectacular thing I have ever seen." Arteryn shook his head as though he was trying to keep himself from being distracted, but he sat there so tensely, a frown on his face as he revisited memories that tortured him. "One cannot change a condition made on the Endric Sword. Even if the tribe wanted, they couldn't have gone against it. It's not something Avaris are encouraged to do. In fact, it is frowned upon because it forces the hand of the tribe, but I think it was my brother's last act of rebellion against his responsibilities.

"So that night, when I was seventeen years old, and you were three years old…when my brother relinquished his rights to you as your father, I became your father. And I took you to Synia. I had to leave with you while everything was burning and keep you safe. I didn't even know if anyone in my family had survived. I didn't even know if anyone in the tribe had survived or whether you and I would even have a tribe to go back to one day.

"The Leveroods were very accommodating. The support they showed me that day I walked into their farm and asked them to provide us with a home is something I will never forget. When I was confident you were safe with the Leveroods, I returned, and I found that not only had I lost Nessie and Artello, my sister and her whole family but that I had lost my mother as well. I hadn't been there to protect them because I had a more significant responsibility. You.

"It took longer to help the tribe settle down here, and when I returned to the farm, you didn't remember me anymore. It seemed like the best way to help you live the life Artello had wanted, unburdened with Avaris responsibilities. If you didn't remember me, I wouldn't have had to tell you everything. If you didn't know anything, you wouldn't have had to spend your life from the time you were five years old looking over your shoulder, thinking the Emori were after you. I didn't want that, and I am not good with training anyone regarding their powers. However, I could teach you to fight, and that is what I did.

"This…" Arteryn paused, then shook his head, "this wasn't some great ploy to hide the truth from you. It was my brother's last request to me for what he wanted for you, and he wanted you to have freedom before you had to spend the rest of your life here."

Many emotions were rioting through Amari, and most of them had her on the verge of tears. She wanted to stay angry. She wanted to lash out, but how could she now that she knew the truth. How could she spit in the face of everything Arteryn had gone through for her? He had left his family behind during a siege to protect her, losing precious last moments with his mother. How could she remain angry when now that he had offered this explanation, she realised it had all been for her benefit. Growing up not knowing was a double-edged sword, though. She found herself unprepared, clueless about what being an Avaris was, and she was the sort of person who liked to be ready for something. Yet, as he said, she was walking into this having been afforded the freedom her birth father had never had.

She chewed her lower lip, digesting everything Arteryn had said about Artello and Nessie, parents she couldn't remember and didn't know anymore, and her heart broke. However, she managed to keep it together, to remain strong.

"Why did you have to stay in Synia? Why didn't you stay here and leave me with the Leveroods? Also, why did he ask you and not Korrigan? Or your father to be responsible for me?" It seemed terrible to have asked someone so young to take such a responsibility. "You were just seventeen years old."

Arteryn took a deep breath the shrugged his broad shoulders. "For several reasons. Korrigan was already married and had two children. So was our sister Karla. My father, on the other hand, is a traditionalist. He wouldn't have subscribed to Artello's need to get you out. He chose me because my brother knew me better than anyone I have ever met in my whole life. Artello knew I needed to find myself away from the tribe, that I had things about myself I needed to deal with without being here. In a way, he gave me my freedom too. He gave me a chance to live on my terms away from the tribe."

Amari stared at Arteryn because of his carefully said words, and her eyes narrowed. Korin's words popped into her head about Arteryn.

"And as for why I stayed in Synia...." Arteryn continued as though not wanting to give her time to ask him any questions about what he had just said. "As I said, that night, I became your father. In this tribe, when someone relinquishes their parental duties to someone, it is not said in jest. It is binding. From that moment on, you become the parent. So, when Artello did that, I became your father that night in every sense of the word." He jerked his head to the side, and a small smile formed on his lips as he straightened his head again. "Essentially, that means the tribe cannot make any decision about you without me. You can't marry anyone without my consent. No one can make any decision about you without my consent. However, the Council can override me on certain matters."

Amari's jaw dropped. Arteryn's revelations were more than she had expected to hear. Of all the things she had considered since Korrigan told her Arteryn was her uncle, this was not one of them. So, the Kenryk tribe considered him her father? Could it...?

"You negotiated for me to go to Sagar to the Council before I arrived. Korin's vision may have allowed them to agree, but you fought to me to go to Sagar." She realised with clarity.

Arteryn nodded slowly, looking at her meaningfully. Emotions flooded her, and a tear slid down her cheek, and she wiped it away because, at that moment, she realised nothing between her and Arteryn had changed. He was still looking out for her best interests. He would always fight for her, no matter what.

Amari took a deep breath, completely overwhelmed. This was a lot of information to process, and all the anger she had drummed up on her way to Bhrim slowly evaporated. If anything, an overwhelming need to cry overcame Amari as she looked up at Arteryn. She had looked upon Arteryn as a second father her whole life, who had encouraged her to strive for more, want to be more, who had never treated her as anything lesser than an equal was in this tribe considered her father. It was reassuring to know that she had him with her throughout all of this.

"Do I have to call you Father now?" She asked him, and he sighed and ran a hand through his hair with a grimace.

"Would that not be strange for us? You can in front of the tribe, but you don't have to when we are together."

"Yes, I suppose me calling you father would make you appear quite old for Korin when there are only ten years between you."

A look of almost panic came across Arteryn's face at her words, and she sat there calmly and smiled at him.

"It's fine, Arteryn. I saw you once in the barn with a man, and I know about you and Korin. I don't know why you didn't think you could tell me, why you hid such an important part of yourself from me. Were you simply not ready to tell me?"

Silence enveloped them. Arteryn looked like someone out of their depth for a moment before he collected himself and rubbed the back of his neck. She waited him out as he processed, then finally clasped his hands together on his lap.

"I've never said the words to anyone. I've never said that I- I knew I was since I was fourteen years old. I acted on it, but I have never had to tell anyone that I was. Korrigan, Karla and Artello found out because they caught me. I think they told our parents about me. I've never had to verbally explain that I...."

"Prefer men to women?"

"Preference? I don't know if that is the right word. It makes it sound like I have an option, an alternative. Like it's a choice and could easily be swayed to consider something else. There is no alternative for me. It's just men. It's not an either-or kind of situation." Arteryn released a sigh and looked away from her for a moment before turning to look at her again. "I am attracted to men and not women."

"And Korin? Do you find him attractive?"

Arteryn took another deep breath like he was struggling with this conversation then responded. "I should probably let you know upfront that it is possible for men who are both attracted to men not automatically to be attracted to each other. However, I do not think there is a human being alive who would not be attracted to Korin from a physical point of view...."

"I don't want Korin to be hurt, Arteryn. If you do not want to pursue anything with him, then do not give him hope-"

"Oh, if only you knew how long I had to wait for him, Amari," Arteryn said in a tone Amari had never heard before from him. Yearning. Desperation. "It is a conversation for another day, but one day I will tell you why Korin is mine, and I am his. I would never intentionally hurt him."

The words floored Amari. She wanted to ask more questions, but this wasn't the time as Arteryn had explained, and she sat there, chewing her lip as she realised that Korin and Arteryn had been yearning for each other from afar.

"Stop chewing your lip."

She looked up when Arteryn 's words broke into her thoughts, and she smiled because he always said that to her.

"I love you, Arteryn." She scrambled off the bed quickly, and he rose to his feet as she threw herself at him and wrapped her arms around his neck. "Thank you. For everything."

"I love you more," Arteryn whispered into her ear, then drew back and looked down at her. "Seeing you grow up carefree was my absolute pleasure. I loved my brother, Amari, more than anyone in the world. Losing Artello was like losing a part of myself. It's not something I ever healed from. However, seeing the person you have become, so strong and determined, it makes up for the pain because it means I kept my promise to him."

"You're going to make me cry." But the tears were already falling, and she tightened her arms around him. It would not be easy, being Kenryk, being an Avaris, but she would have Arteryn with her. She was going to be fine.

CHAPTER TWENTY-FOUR

S he stepped back, realising at that moment that she had never said
the words to him because she couldn't have been able to. Certain
boundaries were in place because he had been a farmhand, and she
had been the daughter of his employer.

"I know." Arteryn brushed his callused palm across her cheek, then
dropped his hands and smiled at her. "You know you have to win at the
Laurean Sage, right."

"Oh, without a doubt." She had been preparing for this event for
years. "But I think it has become even more important now. I'm not just
doing it to become the first female Sage Warrior or have my name
immortalised in history anymore. I'm doing it for you and my birth
parents. Also, it will help to come into this tribe having achieved a great
feat."

She was already at a disadvantage because she hadn't known anything
about her parentage or her responsibility. As a result, she felt ill-prepared
for this new task. Being an Avaris still felt rather abstract to her. It was
one of the reasons she was so apprehensive about it. She hated walking
blind into a situation, and this seemed to be a lifelong commitment.

"Well, I should be on my way. The Laurean Sage waits for no one." Amari declared, somewhat relieved she and Arteryn had been able to weather this bump in their relationship. It also helped that she knew that whatever decision she made, he would be there with her. However, the thought of moving here, of leaving the farm for good, of leaving her family behind… How could she leave the Leveroods? How could she? "Arteryn, please don't make things awkward between Forde and me. I think I like him."

"Good luck with that." Arteryn walked towards the door. "I'm off to pack."

When they met up in the corridor, packed and ready, Amari immediately noticed that Korin wasn't there. Korin peeled his door open, and she realised he did not look like someone packed and prepared to leave. Instead, he beckoned the three of them into his room, and they followed. Once he shut the door, Korin stood before them, looking anxious as he twisted his hands, his face giving off that he was about to say something important.

"You're not packed." Forde pointed out, looking around.

"I have something to say." Korin broke the silence, and something about his tone made them all turn to look at him. "I was planning to do this privately out of respect for Forde, but with the revelation of my parentage and my duties as a Khaiman, I suspect the four of us are going to be in each other's lives moving forward. Besides, doing this in front of the people in this room ensures is it acknowledged. Also, there are things I want to say and address that I never want to talk about again and feel it's better just to let it out now."

Amari straightened, then stole a glance towards Forde, who seemed apprehensive by Korin's words.

Korin took a deep breath then looked down at his hands before he looked up, a pained expression on his face, that haunted gaze falling over his face.

"Forde… You know I would have gone to Sagar with you…."

"You're staying, aren't you?" Forde cut him off, looking bewildered and almost panicked.

Korin nodded, running his hand over his face. "You know what I have gone through, Forde. One of my earliest memory is of the man I thought was my father locking me in a cupboard because I made the mistake of sneezing around him. I lived through his physical and verbal abuse for years. I lived through him trying to change me, and I tried to change for him. I hated myself for a very long time because I couldn't be what everyone around me wanted me to be, what he tried to beat into me with fists and words. I don't have many happy memories of my childhood. It was mostly me trying to survive. I lived through being homeless, where I would spend days without food. I lived through trying to make myself invisible, living in shadows because being seen meant being touched by people I didn't know." Korin shook his head, and he lowered his eyes briefly; then, he looked up and took a deep breath. "Until I met you, Forde, I didn't know that someone could care about me and not want anything in return. I didn't know that someone could care about me at all. And the last seven years, you have been my rock. You've continuously given me so much of yourself, and I learned to open up because of that.

"But you also know how hard it has been for me this last year. You saw me at my lowest when I gave up on myself when I didn't want to be here anymore, and you never gave up on me. Ever. When I couldn't stand, you stood for me. When I couldn't breathe, you breathed for me. You gave me such unyielding support." Korin shook his head then looked up at Forde, his eyes glistening with unshed tears. "You never gave up on me. You never tried to change me. You never wanted to make me something I am not. If anything, you always encouraged me to be true to myself and through the environment you built for me in your life, I learned to look in the mirror and not hate what I saw. I learned to accept myself for the way I was born. I learned to live. You didn't care what people said about you for being friends with me. You didn't care about the rumours about us, about you by being associated with me. You never allowed anyone to talk wrong about me, sometimes even at your own expense. Instead, you accepted me, and when you realised the environment I was in was no longer conducive to my recovery, you were willing to give up your whole life in Orrick for me and move to Sagar for me. For me.

"You've done so much for me, Forde. So much, and I am not going to stand here and insult you by calling it a burden because I know you never saw me as a burden. You never saw me as anything but your family. You took the time to teach me how to fight and defend myself when you realised people constantly accosted me. You taught me to read and write. You taught me that there was more to life than terrible memories. But Forde..." Korin trailed off, taking a deep breath as emotions threatened to overwhelm him. "I need to learn to stand on my own feet. I need to get better not just for you but also for myself. I need to deal with what happened to me. I need to learn to find the will to live again. To find me through this unrelenting pain in my chest that I've lived with for almost a year."

A single tear slid down Korin's cheek, and he wiped it away. "You know I would have gone to Sagar with you, but we both know I would never have been happy there. Too many people to fight off, too many people to hide from. I need to stay here for a while and just work through getting better, and it also helps that whatever draws people to me doesn't work on the Kenryk. I'm not disillusioned to think they'll accept me the way I am. I can't change how I am. I tried before and never could, but at least I won't have to walk around looking over my shoulder, thinking some man will shove me against a wall and fondle me. I can't live through that again.

"I feel terrible that I am doing this. I feel like you uprooted your life for me, and I am abandoning you." Korin wiped away another tear then shook his head. "I want you to know that this isn't the end of our friendship. You're my family, the only family I have ever known, and whatever you decide to do from here, I will always be here for you. I'll visit you in Orrick as much as I can, and you can come to see me whenever you want. But... I think I need to stay here...."

Amari sniffed and realised in that moment tears were running down her eyes, her heart twisting as she got a glimpse into the life Korin had endured. She knew there was so much more and things Korin hadn't said. A history of memories from his past that only he and Forde would ever know about, but that he trusted her enough to share even this little part of himself with her was emotionally overwhelming. She wanted to wrap her arms around him, but she didn't want to say or do anything to temper with this moment, especially because she could see how Forde was struggling. His whole body was tense; his shoulders held stiff, his eyes never wavering from Korin as he focused on breathing in and out slowly as though struggling to keep himself together.

Seconds passed before he seemed to shake himself out of the trance that was threatening to suck him in. He inhaled sharply, then shook his head; a slight panic splashed over his face, his eyes wide with realisation. "You...don't know anyone here, Korin. I don't... I can't just leave you with people I don't even know."

Korin inhaled a ragged breath and wiped a rogue tear again. He was barely keeping it together, Amari noted. The man was on the very edge of falling apart, and perhaps that was why Korin had wanted to do this with an audience. If Amari and Arteryn were there, then he could try to remain strong for Forde, keep up the illusion that he was strong enough for this.

"It's fine, Forde. It's time to let go now. It's time for you to live without feeling like you have to take care of me. I'll be fine. I want to live. I want to take control of my life for a change. I've lived so much of it on other people's terms." He buried his face in his hands and released a shuddering sigh.

Forde shook his head, opened his mouth and nothing came out. Instead, his eyes were bloodshot red, and Amari knew he was on the verge of surrendering to his emotions.

"I don't know if I can, Korin. I don't know how not to worry about you or your safety. You're asking me to pretend that the last year didn't happen, that we didn't go through so much. You're asking me just to let go. I don't know if I can."

Korin dropped his hands then quickly walked towards Forde before he settled down in front of him, gently touching his shoulder as he looked at Forde straight in the eyes.

"But you have to Forde. You and I are a family. We have always been family, even before we knew it. You're everything to me, but I can't continue to use you as a crutch anymore. I need to stand on my own feet, and the only way I can do that is for you to let go. I know it's not going to be easy for both of us. I've learned to depend on you for so much. I know about how you wake up every night to check on me, but Forde, you're young. You need to live, to get married and start and family, and if I don't learn to take care of myself, if you have to take care of me, you'll never be able to." Korin dropped both his hands on Forde's shoulders just as Forde dropped his eyes to the floor and shook his head. Korin forced him to look up again.

Forde let out a shuddering breath, emotions coiling through him. "If you feel this is what's best for you and what you need to get better, I will support you. The most important thing for me is to see you get better, Korin, to see you live without reservations and boundaries. I want that so much for you. I want…I want you to be there when I am old with grey hair and weak knees, and if this is the only way to ensure that you have a long, happy life, then I have to let go. I'm not comfortable with this, but I have to listen to what you want."

Korin leaned forward, wrapped his arms around Forde, burying his face on his throat, and then exhaled as Forde held him. Then, he drew back and looked at Forde again.

"I think meeting Amari has made us both sentimental."

Amari found herself chuckling amid the tears and snort and heavy emotions running through her. She moved towards Korin and pulled him into her arms, holding him tightly.

"I'm glad when I come back here; I will have you with me." She whispered to him, wiping her spilling tears away furiously. "Focus on getting better, Korin and I know you both won't say it, but I know you and Forde love each other very much. Besides, he's half Kenryk. So, he can live here too."

"I'm not Kenryk. I don't belong here." Forde said through clenched teeth as he took several steps back and left the room without another word. Amari watched Korin's face flutter shut, and he chewed his lower lip.

"He's hurting," Korin told her, pain and sincerity on his face. "Take care of him for me, please."

Amari nodded, then took a step back and as she turned, she saw Arteryn standing there staring out the window with an inscrutable expression on his face. He looked calm, relaxed, as though he had not been listening, but she knew him so well she saw the tick in his jaw and knew Arteryn was processing what he had heard. He was affected by what he had heard.

"I hope when I see you again, you will be on the path of recovery. You already are, in a way." She said, and Arteryn turned a stunned look her way, but she didn't want to get into this, so she moved towards her things, keeping an eye on Korin, who still sat on the edge of the bed looking distraught. A part of her wondered if he would change his mind and come with them to Sagar. Instead, he suddenly leapt off the bed then rushed out the door, closing it behind him, but Amari heard him call out Forde's name.

She exhaled as Arteryn turned to face her, a frown creasing his forehead.

"Will he be all right? Safe?"

Arteryn nodded. "Korrigan knows his situation. He will be allowed to stay in the castle until he feels comfortable joining the tribe. Korrigan will work with him on his powers in the meantime and perhaps help him through the grief…."

She wondered what Forde was feeling. It couldn't possibly be easy for him just to let go. After everything he had been through with Korin, he was right to worry. She knew he was perhaps wondering what would happen if Korin tried to hurt himself and he wasn't there to stop him.

"There's just…some things about Korin… a reason why Forde watches him so much…."

"I know," Arteryn said quickly, looking pained as he said it. "I know, Amari. I know what happened to him. I should have protected him. I know, and I hate that I wasn't there to protect him. I have wondered over the last few months if bringing him to stay with us in Synia wouldn't have been the best thing to do, but I couldn't do that and protect you at the same time. You and Korin in the same place would have been a beacon to all Emori. A concentration of such intense powers outside the tribe in the same place would have drawn so much to us, but it's no excuse. I feel like I should have done more, especially because I should have been protecting him. He is mine to protect. It should never have been Forde's burden alone to carry."

Amari was about to ask why he thought he should have been protecting Korin. Then she remembered what Arteryn had said, that he had known Korin was Kenryk, a Khaiman and how he had kept tabs on him.

"Forde says it doesn't help to dwell on what-ifs. It happened, Arteryn, and now he wants to get better. The only thing we can do is help him get better." Amari muttered and then blurted out something she had decided she would only address after the Laurean Sage. However, it didn't help to keep her head buried in the sand. When she returned, she wanted there to be no more lies between her and Arteryn. "Arteryn, nothing is ever going to be the same again, is it? I know…I'm aware that I can never go back to pretending I am just Amari Leverood. I know when the Games are over, I will be coming back here…." She paused and looked at him hesitantly, worrying her lower lip. She sighed. "I want us to be honest with each other, to start this new chapter of our lives with nothing but the truth. The truth is I'm terrified because I feel ill-prepared and may not live up to the expectation of an Avaris."

Arteryn nodded, turning to look at her with understanding. "First and foremost, an Avaris is a warrior because you need to have the skills to defend that Sword. Avaris powers are different, and they serve their purpose only when they are needed. You'll just be a normal Kenryk who sits on the Council and has to deal with people that try to get that Sword once in a while. You're not going to be alone here. I will be here, and so will Korin. I suspect Forde, too, because I can't see him allowing himself and Korin to be separated. Korin is the only thing he has left of his mother; this tribe is the only thing he has left of his mother, and he has a special Kenryk gift of healing. You won't be alone. I will help you."

She nodded, but because this was Arteryn and she thrived on pushing his buttons, she smiled at him. "Full disclosure, I will probably seduce Forde before I return here."

Arteryn threw his hands in the air and rolled his eyes. "With me around, good luck with that. Then again, your mother is the one who pursued Artello, and my sister did pursue her husband, so it's to be expected. You just cannot sleep with him because you are not allowed to have a child with him until Korin has a son."

"How do you expect Korin to have a son? He's…" she trailed off and corked an eyebrow at him. "Like, how would you have a child?"

"That is not a conversation for today, unfortunately, but keep your heart guarded because Forde is officially the spare Khaiman."

She nodded, then sighed. "I'm sorry you couldn't live your life because you were bound to me."

"Being bound to you is the only reason I was able to live my life on my terms without the rules of tribe hanging over me."

"Have you?"

"What?"

"Lived your life as you wanted? Were there men?"

"Amari-"

"Please, just… I just need to know that while you wasted so many years of your life living in Synia because of me, you at least got something out of it."

Arteryn opened his mouth as he stared at her, looking stunned by her words before he closed it and nodded. "First of all, being with you in Synia wasn't a sacrifice, and I didn't waste my time raising you. You're my niece, and I was your guardian. By your side is where I should have been. Second, yes, Amari, I was able to live how I want without any restrictions even if none of those interactions led to anything permanent."

Amari nodded slowly, staring up at him and still unable to believe she had never suspected this important thing about Arteryn. "You were very discreet."

"I had to be." He dropped his hand and released a sigh of frustration. "Anything I do reflects on you."

Amari nodded, then folded her arms across her chest as she digested this new reality.

"Would you ever pursue Korin?"

"Amari-"

"Would you?"

Arteryn looked to the heavens then lowered his eyes back to her. "Obviously, but it's not because of the way he looks."

"What do you mean? He's gorgeous. If he liked women, I would have tried my luck-"

"Amari-"

"Oh, please. We've already established I'm no longer a child. Besides, considering I have known him longer than you-"

"No, you haven't." Arteryn shook his head at her quickly. "I was almost ten when he was born. I knew both his parents personally because his father was Artello's Khaiman. Although, I will admit his father did creep me out a little because he had a bizarre way of looking at me like he knew something I didn't. Korin was six months old when his mother left with him. I may have only seen him once because I was almost ten, I had no use for babies, but when I saw him in Orrick…."

"He was seventeen."

"I know, which is why I didn't go after him. He isn't seventeen anymore."

Amari arched her eyebrows at Arteryn 's tone. "He has issues he's dealing with."

"I know, but he isn't fragile either and treating him like he's about to break isn't going to help him heal. Besides, I am almost certain he told you he kissed me last night."

"Of course, he did. Korin is going to be my best friend. He just doesn't know it yet." She had known it the first moment she saw him.

"My point is, I may pursue something with him, but I don't want his recovery to be around me, and I don't think it will be. Everything he said to Forde today is a sign he wants to get better for himself. And I can't believe I just had this conversation with you."

Amari smiled at him, watching the relief that flowed through him now that he had finally confessed everything to her. "If refusing to live here to ensure you get to live your life is what I have to do, I will gladly walk away from being an Avaris."

"You cannot walk away from being an Avaris, but I appreciate your sentiment anyway." He told her, then took a deep breath. "I can't believe I just told you all of this."

"It doesn't change anything, Arteryn. It's just one more important layer of you that I have always wanted to know more about all these years. It doesn't change how I see you. It doesn't make you any different in my eyes. You're still my hero."

Arteryn flushed at her words which was not something he often did-ever- if she was honest. She must have caught him by surprise, she realised. He nodded slowly, then jerked his head back. "Just… you're an Avaris, and the next Avaris will come from you, so again, don't get pregnant by Forde, please. And if you don't plan to be with him, don't get emotionally attached."

Amari rolled her eyes. "Admit it. You like Forde."

"Not in the way you like him."

"That would be strange if you did because I'd fight you for him."

"This conversation is over."

Amari laughed again. She had missed Arteryn and the blunt honesty they had always shared between them.

He wrapped his arms around her and planted a kiss on her forehead, cupping the back of her head protectively. "You find new ways of making me proud of the person you have become every single day; Amari and I wish Artello and Nessie had been around to see it."

She rested her head on his chest, and her heart twisted. A part of her mourned for parents she would never know, but another part of her would never trade the love Tia and Joran had shown her for anything. The Leveroods were her family.

However, now she had to focus on what lay ahead in Sagar.

Two Kenryk men prepared provisions for their departure. Amari hadn't seen Korin or Forde since they left her chambers, and she was starting to worry about them. She understood why Korin had wanted to be so open with Forde in front of her and Arteryn. It was his way of letting Arteryn know that he came with his emotional baggage and a way to let Amari see that he had accepted her into his inner circle. She didn't need a more significant endorsement than seeing Korin allow her to see him so vulnerable. Her heart broke for him when Amari realised that he had grown up so terribly, abused as a child and suffering as an adult. She hoped that Korin would find what he sought in Bhrim. More importantly, she hoped, even though she was still trying to wrap her mind around it, that he and Arteryn would find something in each other as well.

It was probably too soon for Korin to open up to someone in such a way, but if there was anyone with the sort of skill set and personality designed to deal with Korin, it was Arteryn.

Forde appeared just as she was about to knock in his chambers. Korin came out of his chambers with Forde behind him, and Amari quietly waited as Forde gathered his things. When he joined her out in the passage with Korin, who looked like he had been crying, she decided to ignore the elephant in the room and not make it awkward for him or Korin.

"Derik has prepared a boat for us with provisions to see us through to Sagar... if you're still going. Arteryn and I are ready to leave" She had worried it over the last hour, wondering if Forde would see the need to travel to Sagar now that Korin was staying behind. A part of her felt selfish for even being worried that he would turn around and travel back to Orrick. Forde didn't owe her anything. He didn't have to travel with her to Sagar. She hadn't been his motivation to go there anyway. However, she wanted him with her. She valued him, trusted him even.

Forde frowned slightly at her words. "I said I'd get you to Sagar, didn't I?"

Whoa, she jerked back at his harsh tone, but because she knew what he was processing at the moment, she decided not to take offence. He was letting go of Korin. It was not something easy for him to do.

"Yes, thank you." She replied, and they made their way to the Great Hall. Korrigan, Arteryn and Derik were there.

They travelled down a steep staircase that eventually led to a courtyard near a river. Then, their group descended another set up of steps until they reached the moored boat at a small port. The small ship already contained all their provisions, and she turned to look at Korin, who stood quietly next to Korrigan.

It was strange that at that moment, she thought she heard him ask her to take care of Forde, but that couldn't be possible because his lips hadn't moved. However, his face said it all, his fear, determination, and hesitancy... he was at war with himself.

"You will come back to us?" Derik asked hopefully.

"Yes.' She was terrified, but she had made a promise. "I will return. Besides, with Korin staying, I have no choice but to ensure he is well cared for. How can I do that if I don't return?"

"We should be on our way," Arteryn muttered, setting his things on the boat before he turned towards Korin. "Korrigan can be very pushy. If you reach your limit for the day, tell him you want to stop."

"Arteryn," Korrigan scoffed but without malice.

"Take care of yourself." Arteryn lifted his hand rubbed gently against Korin's cheek in a move so daring and shocking that Amari caught the concerned look between Derik and Korrigan. She expected Korin to pull away from Arteryn's touch, but he didn't. Instead, he stood there, almost leaning into the touch before he nodded. Arteryn dropped his hand then got onto the small boat.

Forde didn't say much. Instead, he walked over to Korin, stood before him then grabbed him by the back of his neck while regarding him with a stoic expression.

"Look after yourself, little brother. When the Games are over, I will come and see how you're fairing." Forde pulled him in for a brief hug that Korin seemed to want to prolong even as Forde drew back and turned to Korrigan and Derik. "Fire and powers or not, if I return and something has happened to Korin-"

"Nothing will happen to him," Derik reassured Forde. "Don't worry; we will look after him for you."

"The fact that you are saying that is why I'm worried," Forde muttered under his breath, a frown on his face as he turned back to the boat and jumped in. Amari could tell it was taking every ounce of his self-control not to reach out to Korin and convince him to go with them.

She walked over to Korin and pasted a weak smile on her face as she looked up at him. She was standing before him, but she missed him already. She wasn't blowing hot air when she had said to Arteryn that Korin was her best friend in the making. She felt a connection to this man that transcended anything anyone could explain. They were bound to each other. An Avaris and a Khaiman. Even though she hadn't known him long, she felt as though she had known him her whole life.

"I am going to miss you." She told him, then lifted her hand and paused before she touched his cheek, waiting to see if he would jerk away from her touch. When he didn't, she went up on her toe and kissed his cheek. She brushed her hand against his cheek as she settled back on her heels. "Do everything I would do. I mean everything."

"I have a feeling there's nothing you wouldn't." Korin smiled at her weakly as well, looking anxious.

"Exactly." She nodded and then turned to Derik and Korrigan. "I will see you soon, as a Sage Warrior."

She turned and walked towards the boat to join Forde, who was still simmering with anger. He was not going to be fun.

CHAPTER TWENTY-FIVE

Amari endured three hours of utter silence with Forde as they rowed away from Bhrim and reached land. Forde was there physically, but emotionally, he was not present. He was too lost in his thoughts and his concern for Korin. Amari went against the ingrained need to fill in the empty silences. Instead, she gave him his space to deal with his issues. She missed Korin too, but she had to concentrate on the upcoming Games.

Shortly before they reached land, she tried to break the silence that had descended uncomfortably over them.

"When we were in Bhrim, I only saw a handful of people who are not from my birth family. So where is the rest of the tribe?" Her preoccupation processing the shocking revelations of her past hadn't given much thought to the people who had survived the massacre she had escaped seventeen years ago.

"If you were interested, you should have stayed and asked those questions yourself." The snarky comment from Forde left Amari cold, but she decided to let it go. It wasn't always about her. Forde's concern for

Korin was the reason he was snappy. It couldn't be easy for him to continue to row away from Korin.

"There is a whole village, built in such a way that you cannot see it from the castle, in the middle of a forest with wards around it," Arteryn informed her, and she nodded.

By the time the sun started to fall, they finally reached land, and Arteryn suggested they find a suitable place to spend the night to find their way to Sagar the following morning. All she did was agree.

After they had set up camp for the night in a cave that had an entrance concealed by hanging vines and shrubbery, she decided to talk to Forde. They would be safe there for the night; they had a small fire going that they were going to let die out, and he sat across her on the other side of the fire.

"Your ability to ignore someone is legendary." His ability to go an entire day without saying a single word apart from necessary instructions was unbelievable. It was new for her, especially since talking was one of her favourite hobbies.

He looked up from the fire he had been staring at absently, and an eyebrow shot up as he turned his attention in her direction. He had been sitting across her for the past hour, just staring at the fire deep in thought. He had not even said one word to her even as they ate, and she had used the time peppering Arteryn with questions about the tribe.

"I'm not ignoring you. I just have a lot on my mind." Forde muttered, running his fingers through his hair before he leaned back on the wall of the cave and expelled a sigh of frustration.

"I understand, Forde. I was not expecting you to be chatty, but you've been treating me like I'm the enemy the whole day. If you'd rather go back to Bhrim, then go ahead. Arteryn will get me to Sagar. I can get myself to Sagar." She hadn't meant to sound irritable, but in the last seven hours, he had been nothing more than an ogre to her. She was surprised Arteryn hadn't called him out on it. Instead, Arteryn seemed to have been quietly observing them. There was so much she could tolerate, especially because she knew what was bothering him, but if Amari had to deal with Forde's behaviour to the City of Sagar, then she'd instead go at it alone.

Guilt crossed over his face, and he stretched his legs in front of him, nodding her way. "I apologise. I didn't mean to mistreat you. I just have several things I am dealing with right now…." He trailed off, and she could see him pulling away from her once more.

"I know you don't approve of me leaving Bhrim." No, she thought, what was bothering him had nothing to do with her. It was all his concern for Korin, but she would rather give him something to think about.

Lifting one knee, he rested his elbow on it then shrugged. "I just don't understand you, that is all. You grew up with your adoptive family, always wondering who you were. Then, after discovering who you are and the integral role you play in the Kenryk tribe, you chose to leave anyway. You learned about how precious to your birth family you are that not only did they whisk you away from an attack on their tribe to ensure your safety, but also that your uncle spent years working on a farm to stay close and keep you safe. We're talking fourteen years of farm work here when he could have been living in that castle. He trained you, he didn't even stand in your way when you expressed your need to be a Sage Warrior, yet here you are. You turned your back on your responsibilities because of a goal you set as a child. You have the most important task in the Kais, and you walked away from it. You walked away from your responsibilities, and that does not sit well with me. I don't understand it."

"You keep talking about responsibility as though this was something I have always known about my whole life." She was defensive, and she knew it.

"Responsibilities are things we acquire every single day, Amari, so finding out today or years ago is beside the point. It is your responsibility, and you're running away from it-"

"So, you want me to what? Forde? Stay in that castle cooped in there all day. I have already lived a life where all I knew was the small village of Synia, and I have always said I wanted to go out and see more of the Kais. You're asking me to go shut myself up in a castle for the rest of my life without even doing this one thing for myself."

"You would not be living in the castle. You're going to live with my father while our house while they build our house. After that, you will live with me, in the village. No one lives in the castle. It's used as a front to negotiate with traders without making the presence of our tribe known. Even the clothes worn at the castle are a façade of what people in Sagar wear. The way the Kenryk dress is very different." Arteryn, who had been keeping himself out of their conversation, interjected, but he was carving something from wood, and she didn't bother asking what he was doing.

Forde's jaw ticked, his eyebrows narrowing as he regarded with an intensely frustrated look on his face. "I feel your decision was selfish. You may have set a goal for yourself as a child, but life never goes according to how we want it."

"Korin had a vision-"

"He has never had a vision in the entire seven years I have known him."

"Forde, Korin had a vision. I felt it."

"You're just too focused on your needs and less on the fact that you carry with you something your people died because of seventeen years ago."

"All right, enough," Arteryn interjected. "Firstly, if you think this is the first vision Korin has had in his life, you have not been paying attention. Secondly, please refrain from guilting Amari about what happened seventeen years ago. She had nothing to do with it. Thirdly, the only reason we are even going to Sagar is so that she can finally unleash her Avaris powers. Finally, you are entitled to feel angry and frustrated that Korin is not here, but you are not going to take it out on Amari."

Silence descended on them, with Forde choosing to ignore Arteryn. Amari turned to Arteryn, trying not to take anything Forde had said personally. "Can you tell me how the tribe ended up in Bhrim? I know it is not the original Kenryk lands."

"Despite the heavy losses, a lot of us survived, Amari. Using the fortune the tribe had amassed over the years, the Council decided that moving to Bhrim would be the safest option while we regroup. The previous owner of the island of Bhrim was an egotistical noble who lost his wealth and was keen on selling to acquire more money to gamble and waste on women and rum.

It was an adjustment for the five years, I understand. Different climate, soil that couldn't produce what was our staple foods, but our people adjusted. They rebuilt a new village, put up even stronger wards and, for our sake, self-isolated in a way. I spent the first two years there with them as we tried to adjust, detached from our ancestral lands, our sacred temples. It was not easy. We were adapting while grieving the loss of so many. However, no discussion to bring you and Korin back to the tribe arose because the previous Khaiman had already stated that the Avaris would return with the Khaiman and the Healer. It had to happen that way. For years, we have wracked our minds wondering how Artello transfigured the Sword into that medallion, and no one in the tribe was able to come up with an explanation. The only thing they could do was wait and hope that when you returned, you would instinctively know. Korin's powers have were not bound, unlike yours, which is why when he came within the tribe, his Khaiman powers easily allowed him to have that vision.

This journey is a risk. All we know is you going to the Laurean Sage will unleash your Avaris powers, but it could also risk exposing us, but for seventeen years the Endric Sword has laid dormant-"

"It was never dormant." Amari pointed out, and Arteryn corked a quizzical brow, and she took a deep breath. "I always knew there had to be something special about it because whenever I felt overwhelmed, I would only need to reach for it, and something about it would soothe me immediately. I just never told you because I thought it might be my mind convincing me it was something special because it was all I had of my birth family. When I was injured, I've woken up overnight with the wound completely healed with traces of gold coursing through my veins. I didn't tell you that because you had always told me to be cautious-"

Arteryn had pushed himself upright as she spoke, and she registered the shocked look on his face. "Those were your Avaris powers, Amari. Not your basic Kenryk powers. I thought I had been able to suppress them all these years, but they managed to come through. Faegon Kar wasn't lying when he said your Avaris powers would be stronger than anything we have seen before."

Amari took a deep breath then looked at Forde. "I'm not running away from my responsibilities, Forde. That isn't who I am, and I am offended that you think that about me. I wouldn't have promised to return if I didn't intend to. To me, what happened seventeen years ago isn't just words. I have seen it repeatedly in my head for years. I just didn't know what it was. I have lived that moment so many times in my sleep. I have walked amongst the chaos, fire and burning flesh. Making me out to be this selfish person who doesn't care about the Kenryk people and what they suffered in pursuit of my chance to be in the Laurean Sage shows just how little you know me. With that said, I think I'll go to sleep before I say something we would otherwise not be able to come back from."

Turning over, she covered herself with her blanket and laid on her side in silence. She was upset, she was angry, and all she wanted to do was sleep. But Forde didn't have a right to take out his frustrations about Korin deciding to remain behind on her.

"Amari." She heard Forde shift where he sat and listened to the reproachful tone. Then, biting her lower lip, she slowly turned to sit up and look at him. "I apologise. I had no right to say the things I said to you. But, yes, most of the emotions I feel right now are because of Korin. I feel abandoned."

"By him?"

"Yes," Forde answered, then exhaled loudly, leaning back against the wall of the cave and shaking his head. "I can't explain to you what Korin means to me. When I say he is everything, maybe it sounds dramatic, but until I met him, I was lost. His very existence gave me purpose and cause; someone to look after because…."

"You feel you had not been able to look after your family? You were eight years old, Forde."

"I know, but my mother came to me in a dream and told me to find him. That had never happened to me. Time had already distorted her image in my head, but that day, I saw her as she had been with those light green eyes. And a week later, I found Korin, with those light green eyes, and I knew in my soul who he was. So, I took him home, and I found someone to tell all the things I felt I couldn't tell anyone in the world. I thought we were going to be together as brothers for a long time, and now…."

"Forde, you do know you are allowed to live with the Kenryk, right?" Arteryn asked him.

"That would mean turning my back on the responsibilities my uncle gave me."

"And at what point are you going to start living for yourself and not other people and your perceived responsibility to them?" Arteryn questioned quickly, and Forde was bewildered for a moment. "You see, you and Korin may have saved each other, but as he said, you need to find your purpose besides taking care of him... besides taking care of people. You're doing it now, with Amari, even though you don't have to. You could have chosen to return to Orrick, but you insisted on coming with us to Sagar. Your need to save people is strong, and while it's admirable, it cannot be how you choose to live the rest of your life. So, it would be best if you found your purpose, the Forde you are, aside from being Korin's protector. It took me a while to find out who I was besides being Amari's guardian too. So, that is your task on this journey. Look for Forde, the Forde that Korin's existence doesn't define."

Forde ran a hand over his face, exuding frustration and confusion. Arteryn was right, and Amari hoped Forde took Arteryn's words with sincerity and seriousness.

"I failed Korin before. I didn't protect him and-"

"You think you must protect Amari now? She's capable of taking care of herself. I am also more than capable of taking care of her, so your reason to come on this journey isn't just about taking care of her. The truth is, a part of you knows Korin is going to be fine, but you can no longer use the excuse of going to Sagar for him anymore. I should reiterate. You are allowed to live with the Kenryk as one of us because of your mother's lineage. You don't need to be married to Amari for that to happen-"

"Arteryn." Amari flushed at what Arteryn was suggesting.

"And as I said, your bloodlines cannot mix anyway. So, the Council would never allow you to be together. Not until Korin has a male son, which won't be happening any time soon, I assume. You may carry on an affair, but you may not have a child together because that child will be the next Avaris. Amari is marked already to be the one the next Avaris will come from. The man she has that child with will be intensely scrutinised and challenged, not just by me but also by the Council and the tribe. I thought you should know what you're getting yourself into should you decide to pursue her- or rather, she pursues you."

"I thought you said he was the quiet brooding kind," Forde said to Amari in exasperation, and Amari fought hard to fight her blush.

"Did I mention he can be brutally honest?" She asked helplessly.

"And he thinks he can be with Korin? That will be interesting to watch."

Arteryn sighed unbothered. "Don't try to understand my relationship with Korin. Ours is fated. You're the one who has to prove himself worthy of even kissing Amari."

"Good night." Amari turned over, horrified, and covered herself with the blanket again. Then, she shook her head and sat up again. Finally, she rose to her feet and gathered her blankets.

"Where are you going?" Arteryn asked her as she walked towards Forde and laid out her blankets next to him. Forde looked frozen for a moment, his eyes darting between her and Arteryn.

"Last night, when I was feeling horrible, Korin did the most amazing thing for me. He held me the whole night. Forde is suffering so..." She threw a daring smile Arteryn's way as she slid under the blankets then turned to look at Forde, "You know we will get warmer quickly if we're both under one blanket."

Again, Forde's eyes darted to Arteryn, who took a deep breath, put away his carving, put out the fire and slid down to sleep.

"Do not try anything funny." That was all Arteryn said, and Amari turned a sweet smile to Forde, who still looked stunned. She didn't wait for him. Amari threw her blanket over him, shoved him backwards on the one he was sleeping on and slid right under the same blanket with him. Facing him, she sighed and relaxed.

"He doesn't bite," Amari muttered, gesturing to Arteryn, and Forde groaned.

"Stop talking, Amari." She felt his hands reach out for her of the darkness, drawing her near; then, she tried to wiggle until she found a comfortable position next to him. She ended up with her arm wrapped around his middle, her head on his shoulder and a heart that was racing faster than it should. He was still on his back; his breathing having quickened just as hers had.

"Is this comfortable?' She asked.

"No," Forde said in a strangulated tone, and she smiled slyly. She wasn't clueless; having her so near distracted him, and that had been her intention.

Silence stretched between them slowly, but with each passing second, she started becoming aware of the man plastered against her, every single hard line, his scent, his chest under her hand. She just wanted to bury her nose into his neck and inhale him. She wanted him more than she should, and it should have overwhelmed her, but it did not.

She wanted him to kiss him. She had never wanted to be kissed the way she did at that moment, and it was so overpoweringly potent. Her heart was beating fast, her leg itching to cross over his, her fingers just barely hanging on from not exploring his chest. It was all too much. What had she been thinking? Where had these thoughts come from? Why could she not control the strong urges that were currently making her feel hot all over? Her breath hitched when he suddenly inhaled sharply then exhaled.

Her head moved of its own volition, and she found her lips very close to his neck, the urge to inch just a little closer unbearable. Her hand slid upwards slowly to rest on his chest, and she thought she heard him audibly gasp. She froze, unable to move another inch in case she combust right there in his arms.

"Amari, I don't want your uncle to kill me." He whispered, his voice giving away that he was also battling with himself just as she was. It told her that he was as affected by their nearness as she was by his. But even though he was giving her this warning, it did not change how she felt. She covered the inch between her and his throat and pressed a kiss against his hot skin.

She heard him groan, and then he was moving. Within moments, he had her pinned under him, and his lips crashed down on hers. A gasp escaped her lips at the unexpectedness of the kiss, and he deepened it. She wrapped her arms around his neck, trying to pull him closer even than he already was.

All coherent thought fled, and she only lived in that moment, wanting more though not certain what more was. While she had listened in on the conversations of the farmhands, she had always had questions she could never ask. Now she wanted them answered. She wanted Forde as much as her next breath.

While completely lost in his kiss, it was hard not to react to his hands as they explored her body. She desperately clawed at his shirt, wanting so much to peel it off his body, but she had the sense not to try. His hands somehow slid under her shirt, and the moment they touched her skin, she almost burst into flames hotter than the searing fire she could shoot from her hands. She writhed under him, wanting more, but he suddenly stopped, and she let out a mournful protest. She could have died at that moment, and as he pulled away from the kiss, she kept his arms around him and refused to release him.

"Forde-"

"Arteryn…." His words forced through clenched teeth, he unwound her arms around his neck, and his hands were in tight fists as he fought for control.

"Ugh? Arteryn, am I ever going to lose my virginity with you around?" She groaned and heard him chuckle.

"Never. Why do you think I made certain I would be coming with you both? Someone has to make sure you don't something you shouldn't- like what you just did while I am a stone's throw away." Arteryn didn't even move from where he lay. The cave was dark enough that she couldn't see him, but she wished he would disappear at that moment.

"I think you should move back to where you were sleeping," Forde said hastily, and Amari looked up at his shadowy figure in the dark and frowned. "Look, just do it. Please."

She didn't know how to interpret this. Was Forde rejecting her? That would be humiliating. Was he forcing her away because of Arteryn? Hopefully, however that inexperienced part of her brain only saw the rejection, and she pulled her blankets away and curled up on her own, confused.

CHAPTER TWENTY-SIX

The following morning, she woke up before Forde did because she had barely had any sleep. By the time both men stirred, she was packed and ready to go. She sat by the mouth of the cave outside because suddenly the cave had felt too small.

She had pulled out the book Derik had given her and was now reading it, more to avoid talking to Forde than any other reason. The book proved informative, holding detailed descriptions of the Kenryk. She knew that before the Kenryk forged the Endric Sword, the Kenryk had had various powers such as the ability to move things with their minds, some had super strength or speed, and to formulate things in their hands from nothing, to name a few. After the Great Sacrifice of their powers for the Endric Sword, that power diminished to solely fire powers. Every so often, a Kenryk might have one of the old powers flare up, such as the powers Korin's mother had. She also learned that even though other members of the tribe had only firepower now, the Avaris and the Khaiman powers had remained consistently powerful.

She was pretty curious to see how a Kenryk who had a complete understanding of their powers wielded them. Suddenly staying on in

Bhrim started to make sense to her than being on this adventure. However, she still had a goal to achieve.

She yelped, the book falling out of her hands to hit the ground hard, releasing a puff of dust as hands gripped her forearms and yanked to her feet. For a fleeting moment, her heart stopped beating when she thought that Grantreal had found her, but she was relieved to look into Forde's eyes.

"Are you going to avoid me the whole way to Sagar?" He questioned; his face marred with his displeasure.

She stared up at him in confusion. She had not even realised he had woken up and had pulled his things together. The book proved to be engrossing, and as such, she had lost track of her surroundings. "I wasn't avoiding you." So much, she finished in her head. She knew she had been avoiding him. She was still suffering from the shame of throwing herself at this man and how he had rejected her.

He paused, confusion creasing his forehead, then he looked down at their feet and saw the book. Embarrassment washed over him, and then he released Amari quickly.

"I thought that after last night you might...." His difficulty in expanding on those words only caused her further embarrassment by the situation.

"That what? I would be avoiding you because you rejected me?" Minimising this whole situation and bluffing her way out of this was the only way to save her pride.

"I didn't reject you. Your uncle is here. What did you expect me to do?"

"Whatever, Forde."

She rolled her eyes and started to bend over to pick up the book, but he reached for her suddenly, and before she could tell him to get over himself, he had pulled her flush against him and was kissing her senseless. She melted in his arms, responding immediately, but she fought the urge to wrap her arms around him. She would not put herself in a position for rejection ever again.

When he released her, they were both breathing heavily, and her eyes fluttered as she looked up at him, her hand flying to her chest in a useless attempt to try to stop her heart from beating so hard.

"What was that for?" She had assumed he did not want to touch her in front of Arteryn. So why was he kissing her now and in such a manner?

"To prove to you that this thing between us is mutual, but that this isn't the right time." He took several steps back then glanced around. "We have to be on our way."

She could not believe this. She bent low, picking up the book then stuffing it into her carrier as Arteryn exited the cage. Strangely, he smelled of burnt paper. They started on their journey, and she shared with them what she had learnt from the book thus far.

"Korin would have loved this stuff, I think." She told them hours later as they had no choice but to get on the road now that they were nearing Sagar and had left the forests well behind. They had secured a ride on a wagon moving east, but as it was not going to Sagar, they had had to jump off at a crossing where their destinations parted. Forde had suggested they take the ride. He had pointed out that she would ruin her feet which made Amari and Arteryn roll their eyes simultaneously.

"Korin is going to be taught all that stuff." Arteryn pointed out.

They had travelled for most of the following day, and on the third day, Forde had finally started to relax around Arteryn and would even tease her.

"I miss Korin so much. I've known him a short while, but I feel like I have known him my whole life." She could feel the vacancy he had left in their little group.

"Have you never wondered why I never let you go to market with us?" Arteryn asked her, and she shook her head. "Firstly, you two would have been instinctively drawn to each other. Secondly, a Khaiman and Avaris together would have been a beacon for anyone out there with powers, especially because Korin's powers were unrepressed."

That made sense. Amari could never understand why she was never allowed to go to the market while Crispin could, and he was younger than she was. She also recalled how she had become instantly drawn to Korin the moment she laid eyes on him.

"And how do you feel about being half Kenryk?" She asked Forde.

He shrugged. "Surprisingly… not surprised at all. My mother had something very mystic about her. She never spoke about her past, but she had an uncanny ability to heal even the worst ailment. I always knew she was not originally from Orrick, and in a way, finding out where she came from, about her twin brother and knowing Korin and I have found our way to each other eventually makes it less painful. Korin is all I have from my mother's side of the family. However, it wouldn't have mattered even if Korin and I didn't share blood. I always considered him my brother."

"I know what you mean about family. I'm not really a Leverood and Crispin, and I don't share blood, but he will always be my baby brother."

She drew to a sudden halt, her face breaking out into a grin as her eyes widened with disbelief. "Forde, is that the Great City of Sagar?"

Her eyes were as wide as saucers as her gaze feasted on the high walled structure that stood empirically in the horizon.

"Yes." He smiled, looking at her amazed expression as she clasped her hands over her mouth, completely enthralled by just the realisation that she was so near. "The Games are the day after tomorrow. We will sleep at my uncle's house. You also have Grantreal on your tail, so I would advise against going anywhere. I'll see about finding a man to stand in for you for the inspection before the Games, but no risks."

"Wait, I am going to stay inside a house the whole time? So, I won't get even to see the city?" She had been hoping to explore a bit.

"This is not an excursion, Amari. You should be focusing on practising and your meditation before the games. I agree with Forde. You have to stay indoors." Arteryn said without missing a breath, and she suddenly wished she had come here alone.

"I doubt Grantreal is still after me. We haven't run into him in quite a while-"

"I thought I taught you better than that. You're allowing your excitement about being here to cloud your judgment. You're a Kenryk Warrior. Start acting like it." Arteryn stated. He pulled out a scarf and wrapped it over her head, then covered her face. He had never called her a Kenryk Warrior before, and it jarred her a little bit.

"How am I supposed to assess my competition if I don't at least look around-"

"You don't have to assess your competition," Arteryn said dismissively. "You're good enough to win."

"Corky." Forde pointed out.

"Facts," Arteryn stated without hesitation. "Amari isn't trained to defeat your average man. She's trained how to fight Emori, who are bigger and stronger than any man who isn't an indigenous person of this continent. Every Kenryk is trained to fight Emori. So, defeating a man like Grantreal would be nothing to her."

"I bet she can't beat me," Forde said conversationally, and Arteryn rolled his eyes at him. "I'm part Kenryk, and you do roll your eyes a lot."

"You have Orrick skills of fighting, not the Kenryk way. You'll need to learn that." Without preamble, Arteryn launched an offensive attack on Amari. However, because she had been watching him, she was ready and blocked his blow quickly. They sparred for a short while, then he stopped and turned to look at Forde, whose mouth was hanging open. "That is barely half of what she can do. You decide if she can defeat you or not."

"I want to hate you right now, but I also want you to train me how to fight the Kenryk way," Forde said under his breathe at Arteryn, who ignored him and started walking ahead. Forde moved towards Amari as she caught her breath. "You really didn't need Korin and me to get you to Sagar."

"I did." She answered easily. "Knowing how to fight and knowing how to survive this journey are two different things. You were able to source our transportation and push us to travel routes Grantreal would struggle to use. Korin was able to sense the Emori and help us through the marshes. I know how to fight, but I know very little about the world outside Synia."

A smile broke on her face when she watched Forde visibly blush, and she pointed at him. "I think you like me."

"What a revelation. It's not like I have kissed you several times or anything."

"So, you do like me?" She had been bluffing, trying to pretend she wouldn't mind if he said he didn't.

"Amari, you're driving me insane. Just walk."

"You're both nauseating," Arteryn said under his breath and walked ahead.

***

She was simply not prepared for what she found when she walked through the high walls of the great City of Sagar. Sharp white walls, horseshoe arches, stucco roofs among the arches, large domes and intriguing geometric designs characterised the City of Sagar.

Forde had explained many riads with courtyards that had lavish gardens for the wealthy were typical and more modest homes for the poor.

The Great City was also quite fortified with a high outer wall that would almost be impossible to climb. The one thing that threw Amari was the sheer size of the city. She had never been anywhere so large and with so many people.

However, while excitement hummed through her body for finally reaching Sagar, the crowds of people all fighting for space within the city walls diluted the experience. There were so many of them that within moments of walking through the gate, she was certain she would have bruises from being bumped into and shoved so many times.

Even as early as the hour they arrived at the City of Sagar, there were already drunk patrons. Somehow being drunk induced a level of excitement that was causing them to sing boisterously and dance. In her effort to sidestep several people, she bumped into a few who were not too thrilled that she was stepping on their toes.

She muttered her apologies as she tried to find her way through the many people. She whipped around, trying to find Forde and Arteryn, but it seemed she had lost them as the crowd swallowed her.

Panic flared inside as she realised why there were so many people. Different people from the various villages and cities in the Great Kingdom of Sagar, participants and spectators, had descended on the City of Sagar for the Laurean Sage games. As someone who had grown up in a small village with a small population, she was not used to many people in one area. She had thought Simiren had many people, but this was madness. She could barely hear herself think, and as she spun around to find Forde while the bodies around her continued to bump and press against her, the panic grew.

She was not used to this, was not used to so many people misbehaving all at the same time. For an instant, the loud crowd swallowed her completely. Then, when hands wrapped around her waist and she was yanked back, she struggled. It did not matter what she tried to do; the way the person had her in a grip, she could not fight, not with so many people around her, certainly not with the lack of space. Whoever had her grabbed both her arms and twisted them behind her, and she yelped with pain. The person dragged her to the side of the street, his hand immediately covering her mouth, and nothing she did helped free her. More hands grabbed her, restricting her movements. Dragged farther away from the crowd, she struggled, and just as she was about launch into an attack, something hard struck the back of her head. Right before darkness swallowed her, she heard Grantreal's voice in her ear.

"I knew I'd find you eventually.

You should have ditched the nephew of the Orrick Lord. His presence gave you away."

***

Peeling her eyes open, she didn't know where she was or what time it was. The searing pain of her pounding head and aching bones hit her immediately. A dirty cloth gagged her mouth, her arms and legs bound as she lay on a cold hard surface. Releasing a groan of pain, she tried to turn from the uncomfortable position she had was in, but her eyes hadn't focused yet.

"Ah, you have finally woken up."

Her body jerked, her heart leaping to her throat at the unexpected voice in the poorly lit room that stank of urine and old wood. Memories of what had transpired when Grantreal had kidnapped her at the market square flooded her. She struggled, trying to untie her bonds, but she only got a condescending laugh in return from the man.

"Do not even try it. My man made sure your bonds were tight."

A dirty, weathered boot appeared before her eyes as he suddenly crouched down in front of her. Grabbing a fist full of her hair painfully, he forced her to look up at him, a cruel smile on his scarred face. Her eyes finally focused, and she glared at him in response. Never show fear, she thought.

"After spending so much time chasing you over Sagar, I knew you'd eventually make your way here. All I had to do was wait. It is too good to be true, and yet, here you are. You covered your face, but you forgot to conceal the nephew of the Lord of Orrick. We have been patiently waiting for you, and when we saw him, finding you was easy."

Grantreal breathed heavily down on her, and she fought down vomit from the stench of his mouth. "While I enjoyed hitting you around a little bit, I wanted you awake for what I planned next. I want you to enjoy every single moment when I peel off your clothes and teach you not to mess with a man like me. After that, when I am done, I will hand you over to my men to do with as they please. Then, when they are done, I will slowly peel off your skin and leave you to die. First, however, I think I will have my meal to give you some time to mull over what will be the last day of your life. I will return, I promise."

He laughed with an evil glint in his eyes. "What I will do to you requires a lot of stamina and strength." He cast her back and walked out of the room whistling and thoroughly enjoying himself.

The moment the door closed and she heard the lock turn, she immediately started to take inventory of her surroundings. She had to get out. She had to get out now. She knew the man was going to carry out his threats. She was in a room with a single old dirty bed that dipped in the middle, a rickety old chair, a pitiful looking table, grubby walls and a little window that barely offered any light.

Her entire body was on fire from the pain Grantreal had inflicted on her. What kind of person beat an unconscious person who was not able to defend themselves? He had no honour! She twisted, with each movement further inflicting pain on her battered body

She should have been more alert and aware of her

surroundings. Instead, she had let her guard down. As a trained warrior, she should have known better. Was she even worthy of being a Sage Warrior if it had been this easy for Grantreal to catch her?

No, it hadn't been easy for him. No. He had been waiting. Had Forde's face been covered, he would not have found her. Many people and being overwhelmed by the crowd were something she had not considered in her plans. Many factors had come into play to put her into this situation. It boiled down to her allowing herself to be distracted by being finally in the Great City.

Worrying about being caught now was no longer the priority. The primary concern was how to get out of here. Amari took inventory of her surroundings and tested the strength of her bindings. Rope. That was easy enough. She formed a fireball and anxiously awaited as it burnt through the rope until she was free.

Painfully, she pushed herself to sit up and quickly untied her feet, then gingerly rose to her feet. It was not easy. Pain shot from her head, arms, and chest, but she managed to force herself up.

With willpower she had hadn't known she possessed; she carefully made her way towards a boarded-up window. As she tried to find a latch, she realised she had a cut on her forehead. Her body ached terribly, but she fought through the pain with clenched teeth and determination.

She did not waste time taking stock of her wounds, but she suspected she might have had a cracked rib.

The window was so old that it had moulded onto the wall, and it did not budge no matter how hard she pushed against it. Furthermore, it was simply too small for her to get through anyway. She glanced around the room, trying to find something else to use as a weapon, but there was nothing else. She would have to be ready when Grantreal came in. She would have to fight for her life.

She was in so much pain that she had to sit down. She had to keep up her strength for the fight that was about to happen, and there was no point standing around.

She inspected the wound on her forehead and tested her flexibility with all the pain she was in. Then, in a panic, her hand flew up to her neck, and relief flooded her when she realised the medallion was still there. Wait.

She was Kenryk. She had fire. No matter the size of the man she faced, no one could stand against fire. It was pointless to try to fight Grantreal physically. She was already too injured. Yes, she risked exposing herself, but this was not the time to prove she was a trained warrior. She had already done that when she defeated Grantreal in the Simiren fighting pits.

Taking a deep breath, she calmed herself down and focused on the powers she felt coursing through her.

She never had a warning. The door crashed open with a bang, and the seconds it took her to jump to her feet cost her. Her entire body felt heavy, and she even swayed on her feet as she struggled to collect herself to focus on scorching this man to death.

Grantreal leapt forward towards her, knocking her back when he realised she had managed to free herself. She stumbled back, falling hard on the ground, and a cry of pain tore from her lips as her body suffered.

He slapped her hard across her face, and she saw stars but did not pass out this time. She refused to pass out as she struggled with the big man who was now towering over her. Despite the horrific pain she was in, she still fought with everything she had, kicking, scratching, biting, and screaming to attract any sort of attention.

A man and a woman suddenly appeared at the open door, and she called out to them for help as they stood there in shock. Grantreal's men suddenly appeared behind the couple questioning what was happening and started threatening and intimidating them. The couple cowered under the verbal assault.

Amari was calling out to them for help, but Grantreal used his physical power to bind both her wrists in his hands and held them over her head, her lower body immobilised by his heavy body sitting on top of her.

"Now, I am going to teach you a hard lesson on crossing me." He ripped her tunic down the front with his free hand, exposing her flesh and continued to tear it right through to her naval. The vile wanton look that crossed over his face when her chest was entirely exposed completely paralysed her with fear as she realised this was truly happening, that this was not some bad dream. She knew one thing. She was not going to plead with this man. She was not going to beg him to stop because his sort fed off the fear of their victim. Instead, she was going to fight with everything she had. This time, she was not going to wait for Arteryn to save her.

She bit back a scream the moment his hand completely covered her exposed breast, allowing the anger at his audacity to grow within her along with something else entirely. It just lit inside her without notice, igniting as fast as it spread all over her body. It was rage mixed, with something inexplicable that threatened to engulf her, she realised as she still struggled with this man. When he bent down and licked the side of her neck, the scream that tore from her lips almost caused the window to rattle, and before she could control whatever was raging within her, fire flared out over her entire body engulfing her in one fell swoop. Grantreal was so stunned he pulled back, scrambling away from her, but the fire kept building and raging on. The medallion around her neck grew warm, unbridled power raging within her as intense fire swirled around her body, and it latched on to him.

He cried out as he stumbled back, but he had already caught fire, and as his men hurried forward to try to get the fire out, Amari rose to her feet in a blind rage she had never felt before. No longer conscious of the pain in her body or that her exposed breasts, she zoomed in on Grantreal. Amari took a step forward. His men stumbled back as they saw her with flames dancing around her entire body while she remained unhurt. The blind rage within her propelled her to raise her hand towards Grantreal.

"You will never hurt anyone again!" Fire, white-hot, intense and scorching shot from her hand in its glory, and it hit him hard on the chest. The fire engulfed him, eating away at his skin, and his cries of pain loud as he shook violently on the floor, trying in vain to put the fire out. His guttural screams seemed to go on forever until he was scorched so intensely that all that remained of him was charred ash. She turned to his men, but they turned and fled the room.

She stood there for a moment, expecting them to return, then when seconds ticked by and she realised they had fled, adrenaline abandoned her and relief washed over her.

Amari swayed, and her legs caved under her. Her eyes moved to the ashy remains of the man who had tried to hurt her. The last thing she saw was the stunned faces of the man and woman as she hit the ground hard and passed out.

CHAPTER TWENTY-SEVEN

S he heard a voice saying her name above her head, a male voice and instinctively, as she came to, she started to lash out to defend herself, but she found herself hastily restrained.

"Let me go!" She cried out, fighting with everything she had.

"Amari, it's me, Arteryn! Open your eyes and look at me!" He implored.

Arteryn? Arteryn? Was he here? Was it real? Her eyes flew open, and her eyes connected with his. Then, she burst into tears as she threw herself at him, wrapping her arms around his neck tightly. Could it be true? Was he here?

He held her tightly, allowing her to cry her heart out as everything suddenly came back to her, about what had happened and what could have happened, about how she had burned Grantreal to death, about how she had used her powers. She had never done that before, had never been able to formulate fire beyond just her hand and had never been able to shoot out a ball of fire that big and intense from her hand.

Arteryn sat her back from him slowly, and glancing around, she realised she was in a room expensively furnished. Forde hovered near the bed with concern on his face.

"How did you find me?" She asked, suddenly noting with confusion that the pain in her body was completely gone.

"Everyone is talking about the woman who burnt Grantreal into ash in an inn. We followed the trail and found you there." Arteryn answered, the concern on his face tangible, his eyes roaming over her.

"How bad are my bruises?" She asked, afraid to look, and both men looked at her with mirrored looks.

"You don't have any," Forde answered, and she frowned in confusion.

"How long have I been out? Has it been weeks?"

"What?" Her words seemed to have confused him, and he glanced at Arteryn.

"Have the Games passed-?"

"Could you stop thinking about the Games for a moment?" Arteryn thundered, then he paused. Taking a steadying breath, he closed his eyes for a moment, and when he opened them, he seemed to be in control, although anger still simmered just below the surface. "I apologise. I lost control. I have anger issues."

Arteryn? Anger issues? She ran a hand over her chest and found there was no pain whatsoever.

"When we found you, Amari, after following Grantreal's trail, you...you were lying on a bed, covered, but... your dress was ripped open... Did...?" He closed his eyes tightly, then opened them, clenching his fists tightly then releasing them. "Did he...?"

He was expecting the worst. His entire behaviour was because he was so scared of what Amari would say about what had happened. She reached out for him slowly, turning Arteryn's face to look at her with her hands on his cheeks, feeling a strange calmness in the wake of his frenzied panic.

She shook her head. "He hit me. When I woke up, he had beaten me very badly that I think I broke a rib. When he tried to...." Arteryn closed his eyes, but she shook him gently, and he opened his eyes. "He didn't rape me. I stopped him."

He looked at her intensely as seconds stretched between them, and she watched his face as he digested her words. "You're certain?"

She nodded quickly, and even before she could say the words, he had wrapped his arms around her waist and pulled her tightly to his chest, holding her closely. With her head against, she could hear the rapid beat of his heart.

"I thought I'd lost you, Amari. When I found out he had you, I thought...." His voice was hoarse with emotion as he kept his arms around her, just holding her. She took the comfort he gave her, holding him tightly as she buried her head in his neck, tears of relief finally rushing through her. She could not believe she had survived the ordeal. It seemed impossible somehow, yet she had managed. She remembered what had happened, remembered that Grantreal was dead, then pulled back slowly to look at Forde and Arteryn. Grantreal was dead. He was dead. Would his men come after her?

"I have to tell you something." Immediately concern crossed over their features when she said that, and she bit her lower lip as she struggled to say the words then took a deep breath. "I killed a man. I killed Grantreal."

Relief washed over them, and Forde finally sank onto a chair. "If you hadn't, then I would. But I'm more concerned about word spreading about the fire powers you used. If word reaches the King, this could be a problem."

"Why?" Amari asked in confusion as she shifted to sit back against the wall behind the bed, and Forde scratched the back of his neck.

"Amari, you're aware Sagar views people with powers as a threat to their power and sovereignty? The previous King may have been more tolerant of the remaining indigenous tribes, but not this King. King Eldrian considers Kenryk and Emori a threat. When he came into power, the whole Kais assumed the Kenryk and Emori no longer existed. His only threat was the Kingdom of Kessariah. People know very little of the Emori because they seemed to have gone silent in the past seventeen years. The assumption has been that none of the indigenous tribes existed anymore. Knowing that a Kenryk is still alive is going to be brought to the attention of the King. That man does not hesitate to cut down his enemies.

I know him. As a nephew of one of the Lords of Sagar, I grew up coming here. I met the King before King Eldrian. I played in the castle with my cousins. I know this King, Amari."

Arteryn took a deep breath then looked at Amari. "Forde has raised a valid point. I think we should leave before the King comes for you-"

"Have the Games passed?"

"No-"

"I need to participate in the Games."

"Amari, stop this! Your life is at risk. The King probably has his Sage Warriors out looking for you. When they find you, they will bring you before the King. You will be jailed and then killed." Forde argued as he rose to his feet quickly. "You can always come and compete next year if it is so important."

"No." She shook her head with determination. "I have to do it this year. Forde, I promised Derik I would return after the Games and assumed my responsibility as an Avaris. If I don't do it this year, I doubt the Council will let me go next year, especially after exposing that a Kenryk is still alive. So, I must participate in the Laurean Sage this year. But, more importantly, when I burnt Grantreal, I felt something unleash within me. I feel I am very close to unleashing my powers."

"Amari-"

"Forde, please. I must do this. I feel it. I must do it. I have to." She knew she did not have to explain it to Arteryn. He would understand, but Forde wouldn't think the Kenryk way. He was thinking like an Orrick man. It was no longer about the badge or being a Sage Warrior for her. Something was raging within her that wanted to come out, and she knew the only way it would be released was if she put in an environment where she had to defend herself. She looked at Arteryn. "I have to do it, Arteryn. I can feel it."

He looked at her, clearly warring with himself. Yet, leaving made sense from Forde's perspective, and his concerns were valid. It would keep her safe but leaving also meant taking the risk of not allowing her to unleash her Avaris powers.

"For the tribe, the best decision would be for you to unleash your Avaris powers. However, if unleashing your powers happens during the

Laurean Sage, the repercussions will have a rippling effect on the tribe." Arteryn thought out loud, then ran a hand through his hair. "What are you feeling?"

"I can't explain it." She heard a gasp from Forde as she said those words, and he was staring stunned at her arms. Then, when she looked down, she saw what had shocked him. Her veins had gold particles coursing through her, and it was slowly spreading across her body. It only happened after her body had healed itself.

"What is happening?" Forde asked
with concern.

"Her Kenryk and Avaris powers are unleashing," Arteryn said, then took a deep breath and looked at Amari. "You have to compete in Laurean Sage... Artello's veins used to do that when his Avaris powers came forward. If we leave now, we risk blocking the progression."

"The King might behead her!" Forde pointed out, and Arteryn rose to his feet.

"He can try. The Games are tomorrow. Forde, you need to find someone to stan in for her physical inspection. I need to monitor her powers so she doesn't burn your uncle's house down."

"This is a bad decision," Forde said as he reached for his jacket. "She should leave. I was seen leaving with her. But unfortunately, it is only a matter of time before the Sage Warriors come knocking on our door."

A sudden commotion outside drew their attention, and they turned to face the door moments before it burst open. Four men rushed in without preamble just as Forde and Arteryn turned to the door. Amari rose to their feet quickly, thankful to see she was clothed in something not torn. Three of the men were carrying crossbows aimed at them. The one in front had a sharp sword.

"You are Amari?" the man standing in front asked her, and as Amari looked at this man and saw the badge he wore sewn onto his black leather uniform, she realised she was looking at a Sage Warrior. She had never met a Sage Warrior before, only ever heard of them and their feats. These men were so large, strong, broad, and intimidating. How could a Sage Warrior possibly even know she existed? She nodded just as Forde asked why the man was asking. "Amari, you are hereby ordered to appear before the King on charges of witchcraft. You are to come with us this instant, and should you resist arrest, please be informed we will be required to use force."

Her jaw slackened, her eyebrows narrowed, and she was rooted on the spot as she stared at the men in disbelief. This situation was ridiculous. She had come here to be a Sage Warrior, and a Sage Warrior was now arresting her. For witchcraft! As if these men didn't know Kenryk had existed! The audacity of brandishing her a witch!

"Witchcraft? How absurd!" Forde had somehow stationed himself between Amari and the guards. "She is Kenryk, not a witch."

"Tell that to the king, Lord Pembrick." The Sage Warrior told him, and Amari arched an eyebrow at how the Sage Warrior had addressed Forde. The Sage Warrior was so calm, and his eyes levelled on Amari as she peeked over Forde's shoulder. "It is reported that last night, the lady Amari was witnessed formulating fire out of her person with no assistance from an outside resource. Amari, we will provide you with a moment to put shoes on immediately as we would like to refrain from further embarrassing you by dragging out of here in nothing more than what you are wearing."

"You know the Kenryk can formulate fire from their hands without an outside resource, right?" Forde looked stupefied by the actions of the Sage Warrior before him.

"Kenryk were all wiped out seventeen years ago, and I would caution you from doing something that will have an impact on your uncle and his standing in the Kingdom, Lord Pembrick." The Sage Warrior rebuffed with such annoying calmness.

"Not seeing something for seventeen years does not mean it no longer exists. Are you dense? Surely, the fire coming from her was an indication she must be Kenryk and not a witch." Forde argued further, refusing to move between Amari and the Sage Warrior.

The Sage Warrior took a deep breath, a hand on his waist in front of him as he stared at Forde. "A man is dead killed by that woman with fire."

"No, that's not what you said when you came here. You said you came here because Amari is a witch who formulated fire without the aid of an outside resource. You said nothing about this being about a murder—"

"I do not have to explain myself to you. Word has reached the King, and the resolution was that we must bring the woman before him. We are here to carry out those orders. Of course, we can do this with as little violence as possible, but I can assure you that if you insist on fighting, there will be bloodshed." The Sage Warrior declared, his long dark hair tied at the nape of his neck as he stood there imposing and resolute. Amari took a deep breath, bewildered. How disappointing that what should have been her first meeting with a Sage Warrior had turned into a bittersweet moment. Nothing had gone right since she left Synia. "Now, if you will step aside...."

"You lay one hand on her, and it will be the last thing you ever do." Arteryn's voice suddenly interjected into the conversation, but there was something different about it. It sent shivers down Amari's spine, and as she turned to him, she thought he had somehow become physically bigger. Were his eyes flashing red? Was this real? "Amari will not be appearing before the King. She is not a witch, and how dare you insult my people like that and me. Of course, if you want to get to her, you are welcome to come through me but be warned, you will feel every single moment of your last breath."

The look that crossed over the Sage Warrior's eyes was something Amari had not been expecting. Concern, a hint of fear mixed with indecision.

"You came looking for Amari. You did not find her. She had already left. That is what you will tell the King." Arteryn took a step forward, and everything about him, the energy vibrating through him, sent shivers down Amari's spine. She had never seen him like this, so threatening, so dangerous. "You're welcome to try to fight me, but I am Kenryk and fire forming my hands is the least of your worry in what I can and will do to you if you do not leave. Try me."

Something was different with Arteryn, and it reeked of untold violence. Amari watched as the Sage Warriors took a step back when Arteryn took another step forward. The room had gone ice-cold, the danger looming over them all. In an instant, Arteryn looked like a man capable of ripping these men into shreds without breaking a sweat, and she suddenly wondered if there was something he hadn't told her about his abilities.

"You came looking for her. You did not find her. She had already left." Arteryn repeated, and the Sage Warriors seemed to be weighing their options. Then, in a millisecond, Arteryn's hands broke into hot balls of flame, and Amari knew in that instant that the dangerous air she sensed around him had finally made itself apparent to the Sage Warriors.

"I'd advise you to leave tonight then. The King will send men out to search for her. He will not rest unless she is brought before him. So, to make our job easy by leaving now." The Sage Warrior standing in front said, probably to save face, and Amari watched in disbelief as the Sage Warriors left.

"Arteryn-"

"Sh," Forde quickly said as he stared at Arteryn, who seemed to be battling to control whatever was raging within him. It took a minute, and when Arteryn turned to face Amari, the fire in his hands gone and looking somewhat like the Arteryn she had always known, he exhaled.

"Forde, find someone to help her pass the inspection. Amari, I need to help you centre yourself in preparation for tomorrow. And no questions, please."

***

When Forde returned and told her he had secured someone who has passed the inspection on her behalf, Amari had been excited. However, now that they were on their way to the arena for the Laurean Sage, everything felt surreal. It had been a strange twenty-four hours. Arteryn had worked hard to bring her powers under control, and the fact that she had no bruises or pain made it feel like the Grantreal incident had never happened.

"Are you alright?" Arteryn asked as they rode on the wagon to the arena, and she shook her head. "Nervous?"

She nodded. "It's finally happening. It was an obscure possibility that didn't feel real when it was nothing more than a goal. Now that I am here, on my way to the arena, seeing all these people making their way there...

I am just… It's surreal. I don't think I have yet convinced myself that it is actually happening."

"Afraid?" He asked, and she shook her head.

"Not of the competition itself. More of when these Avaris powers will unleash themselves. I don't want to win this because of my powers. I want to win it as Amari Leverood, the girl from the farm in Synia."

"Don't think about them. Just do what you came here to do, get that badge and remind us for the rest of your life that you are the first female Sage Warrior."

"We're here," Forde said and jumped off the wagon.

"Wait, I brought something for you," Arteryn said before Amari could get off. He drew out the sack he had been lugging around. "Basic Kenryk armour. Not the whole thing as that would give you away, but our technique is unique, and this will give you maximum protection and still the ability to move freely."

"Thank you." It was silly, but she felt like crying at that moment. To have him here with her when he had been with her when she first began this journey as a seven-year-old was overwhelming and something she would treasure forever. Thirteen years of her life had been dedicated to this one moment and knowing he had even brought her armour. "You're the best uncle in the world."

"It's as if I don't exist," Forde muttered under his breath, and Amari turned to look at him with a smile.

"I wouldn't have done this without you."

The cry of the horn incited exuberance, and the crowd roared with excitement. Amari's heart raced with unadulterated fear and excitement. She turned to Forde, who was watching her face as they stood outside the arena.

"I'll be waiting and watching. I will not at any point intervene. You can do this yourself. You said you could." Arteryn said before he rode away from them.

Her amour fit like a glove. It was black and burnt orange made with the strangest leather she had ever seen in her life. It looked solid and sturdy, yet it was so light on the body with intricate trimmings. She recognised the trimmings immediately. She had seen them on Derik's robe. The top half of her armour was panelled and layered with three fastens on her chest and three on her naval. The sleeves had intricate curling vine designs. She reached into her bag and pulled out a pin she had not looked at in a while. It was the one from the Leverood farm. She fastened it to her armour. It represented a piece of home, of Joran, Tia and Crispin, of the place she had grown up in and trained for this very moment.

With her hair tied low on her nape, the helmet fit well and hid her features. Forde was dressed in full Orrick colours of black and red, donning his armour that had been in his uncle's house. He looked like a formidable warrior, and a part of her wanted to tell him he did not have to participate because of her. However, she doubted that would help. Forde was seeing her through all the way. It had also been fortunate that he had armour in the villa.

"You look beautiful." Forde looked down at her then as though realising this was not the time for such thoughts. He quickly shook his head, pulled out the paint that he applied around her eyes and towards the side of her face, then he helped her put the helmet on again. Again, he looked down at her, brushing the side of her face before he leaned in and kissed her. She wished this was not a goodbye, that they both survived the Games.

The emotion and intensity he poured into that kiss made her knees tremble, and she clung to him with everything she had. If this was possibly goodbye, she wanted it to be memorable. He drew back then looked at her. "If you win- when you win, remember they will bring you before the King. Good luck, Amari. I believe in you."

She looked up at him, unable to say anything but wanting to say so much to him. The past few days had given her perspective. Suddenly becoming a glorified guard was not so important to her anymore, especially now. This man had risked his life so many times to help her, and even now, as they stood there, he was still willing to put her needs first, still ready to have her reach her goal even though it had been made clear to him that he couldn't be with her.

"Forde." She began, but he was already handing over the parchment that had her registration for the Games.

"I registered you, and I paid a man off to do the physical inspection for you, so that is out of the way. So go in there and fight."

"Forde." She reached out for his arm quickly and shook him, the need to tell him what was rushing through her at that moment imperative, forcing him to give her his complete attention. "I don't want to be a Sage Warrior anymore."

He looked at her face searchingly, seemingly unable to believe her words. "Is that fear talking? You're already here, Amari, next to the arena, registered to participate. You can do it. You have put your mind and time into this, and you are not going to turn back now, all right?"

"Do you want to be a Sage Warrior?" She felt it was important she understood this, and he took a deep breath and shook his head.

"I've never wanted to be one. I never planned to come here to compete to be one. I needed to get Korin away from Orrick...." He trailed off, then shook his head as if to dismiss his thoughts. "However, we are both here now, so are you ready to go in?"

"Maybe I should go home."

"No, Amari, you are not going home. You must do this for yourself. You must go in there and show them what you can do. So, stop dallying and let us go inside."

"You're not listening to me, Forde." She protested as he started to walk off.

"I am, Amari." He whirled around to face her; his face clouded with emotion. "I am listening to you. I have done nothing except listen to you.

Do you know what I have heard? You, going on and on about the goal you set yourself to become a Sage Warrior. It was all you talked about all the time. It is the reason we are here. So come along."

He turned and stormed off in quick strides that forced her to jog to keep up with him. "I'm frightened."

"I know you are, but you will do great. Don't worry about it." He took them to a door off the main entrance, and they slipped in. They sat their things against a portion of the wall that had caved in and hid them there. She clasped the necklace in her hand as they walked down the dark passage with low ceilings and a beam hanging over their heads.

"Forde, if something happens to me, take my medallion to Arteryn." She instructed him, and he looked at her over his shoulder but didn't say anything in response.

The further they walked, the louder the crowd became, and she realised they were right over them on the stands. Her heart started to thud wildly in her chest when she saw the two lines of the participants standing behind a closed iron-wrought gate waiting to enter the arena. They were so tall, so strong looking and very intimidating. She felt a panic set in and gripped the necklace even tighter, and it started to soothe her once more as they joined the line.

A tall, broad man carrying a whip and a heavy moustache came to them, but Forde spoke.

"Apologies for being late. The nerves kicked in, and we had to go take a piss."

The guard grunted as he took their cards and moved to the front of the line. "Listen up, all of you! We are all going in there in one line. You will turn, and you will face the King. Each round has its own set of instructions. Adhere by the rules. If you don't, you will be disqualified. Rules apply until the last round. That one is a free for all. Whatever works, use it to your advantage. No shields or weapons are permissible in the first round. The first round tests your agility and your physical strength. It's designed to wean out the weak. The second round will test your stamina and your ability to think quickly on your feet. The third round focuses on your mental strength. The last round will test your fighting skills. We induct only five into the honourable call of Sage Warriors every year. The last five men standing will be this year's Sage Warriors. The rest of you will possibly be dead or severely injured. Should you be victorious and then decide against being a Sage Warrior, you will be fined. You may try the following year again. Now, ready yourselves to go in."

Amari was trying to breathe as she fought to steady her nerves. She was truly here. It felt surreal, like something out of a dream. The joy and euphoria within her was diluted by disbelief and fear. She could very well die here today. Something was dizzying about it and infectious about the crowd chanting above them in the arena, and she itched to step outside and finally do this. She stole a glance at Forde, who looked intensely focused.

"Forde."

He turned his head to look at her quickly as she reached for his arm, ensuring that her knives remained securely encapsulated in their holsters and that her sword was perfectly in place. She did not want any unwanted surprises.

"Promise me that you won't intervene. Even if things are looking bad for me."

He turned to look ahead as he stretched his neck from left to right. "I will not make such a promise, Amari. You might be going in there to be a Sage Warrior, but I intend for you to come out in the end alive. However, I will only intervene if you give me a sign that you are spent. Will that work?"

She nodded, then turned to look ahead as the gates opened before them, and they started moving forward. The anticipation coursing through her body and the adrenaline pumping as she approached the doors was something she would never forget in her entire life.

***

The sound of the crowds cheering, stomping their feet in wild and abandoned excitement was enthralling. It was infectious, giving each participant that boost in confidence required for such gruelling tasks to come.

Standing in a single line to face the King was a new experience for most, knowing he was standing there, addressing them, and letting them know that the victors would be joining his elite team of warriors. Further encouragement was that the current Sage Warriors were in attendance in their reserved space, giving each participant grand ideas to fill that seat themselves one day.

Amari was glad to see a few short men who were participating, so she did not necessarily stick out, and the way her armour was designed was to hide any tell-tale signs that she was female. Finally, they walked into the arena, and the crowd went wild. Everyone jumped to their feet, shouting and clapping with excitement that immediately erased Amari's apprehensions. A smile broke over her lips as she looked up at the oval arena and took in the excited faces in the crowd. Once the King declared the games open, the crowd burst out in another song of cheers. An official came to stand before them, and Amari counted thirty-six participants. She knew they eliminated quite a few participants during the physical inspection at times on minor technicalities.

"Listen carefully." The man who had met them before they entered the arena turned to the participants. "This purpose of this round is to test not only your physical strength but also your brevity. If you cannot face what comes through those doors, then you have no place among our elite Sage Warriors. Twenty-four of you will advance through this round. The next round will only have eighteen spots. The last round will have ten. The rules for this round are simple. Use any means necessary to survive, but the victor is he who holds the head of the beast in the end. Six of you will go at one go. The first six are the last six that entered the pit. The rest of you head behind the gates with me."

Beast? Amari's eyes widened at the words. She had heard of the tasks, but this must be a new round. What beasts could the official have been alluding to?

The official moved down the centre of the arena, followed by the men waiting for their round to come while leaving behind Amari, Forde and four other men and locked himself behind the iron gates.

The official moved down the centre of the arena, followed by the other men while leaving behind Amari, Forde and two other men and locked himself behind the iron gates. The arena, built in an oval design with the crowds seated in rows upon rows, was impeccable infrastructure, with a clear view of the main stage and sandy pit in the middle. The public occupied the majority of the audience. The right side of the arena with a lavish tent was reserved for the King. The King's guard and the lords of the Kais under Sagar and the Sage Warriors sat around the King.

Erected closer to the audience stands stood an obstacle course in preparation for the second round.

"My uncle is seated close to the King. On his right. It's the man with greying hair in red and black robes." Forde whispered to her, and she followed his gaze to see the man who had moved to the edge of his seat when he spotted Forde. The man looked to be in his sixties and dressed in his elegant official robes with his guards behind him. "And my cousins. They are going to have words with me for not mentioning my intention to participate."

She glanced at Forde and noted that he was under pressure not to only perform for victory but to do it in front of his family as well. He could not afford to fail now that his uncle and cousins were there.

"Is that where you used to sit to watch the Games?" When he nodded, it further dawned on her what this man was willing to give up. Meeting the King of Sagar was not a novelty for Forde. He had done it countless times growing up. He had played in the castle. He had sat with the Lords of the Kingdom of Sagar. Yet, he was willing to walk away from that to live a quiet existence in Bhrim. That alone proved to be motivation enough to succeed. "He'll be proud when you are victorious."

She turned to look at where the nobles sat with the Sage Warriors seated on either side of the nobles. She saw his cousins nudge each other as they recognised him and seem to break into a grin. They were two strapping young men. One seemed to be older than Forde and the other younger.

"You're close?" She asked, and he shrugged and nodded.

"Very. My uncle raised us as brothers, not cousins."

The gates at the far end of the arena peeled open, and the men around her started to move apart, readying themselves for whatever came out of there. The crowd descended into a hushed silence as anticipation hung in the air.

The sound that came from the other side of the arena alerted them to what was coming. Mountain lions! When the first one leapt into the arena followed by another one, all the men seemed to move back in shock, and she glanced at them, thinking this was unbelievable. Arteryn had trained her precisely for this. She remembered his words in her head as though he was standing beside her and whispering them himself.

Mountain lions target the head and throat. They kill by disabling the prey through strangulation. The first thing they will try to do is knock you out. If you want to kill them, you must fight. The claws and teeth are sharp, and its main aim is to kill you. You must fight to the death, Amari. If you are going to cut its throat, target the centre of the throat right above the collarbone. It will not be easy. The animal is fast, and it aims to kill you. Alternatively, aim for the heart, but if you're going to do that, you need to use as much force as possible.

She immediately reached for her long knife, knowing it was the only weapon suitable for this fight. She sized her prey, focusing only on it and blocking everything out. She could not hear the crowd and was not even conscious of the other people she was in there with.

The mountain lions moved forward, stalking them and Amari kept a close eye on her prey. Unfortunately, there were only three mountain lions and six competitors. That meant not only did they have to compete with other participants to get to the mountain lion, they also needed to face the mountain lion. She could not linger around and wait for someone to attack first and take the opportunity from her. Now that she was in the pit, all her training and her need to succeed kicked in. Her heart twisted a little when she realised these majestic beasts were being used for sport, but Arteryn had taught her how to make a quick and clean kill.

The mountain lions let out a hair-raising cry as they started moving towards them. Amari moved to the side to attract the attention of one, and sure enough, the beast caught her and zeroed in on her. The crowd had become deafeningly quiet, and she wondered if they feared the mountain lions might attack them if they made a sound. Amari counted in her head and could not believe the number of beasts sacrificed for sport.

She decided she would have to try to ensure her beast suffered the least possible amount of time. She rounded on the beast as it stalked her. She prepared her knife then bent her knees, ready to attack. The beast pounced, running towards her. She stood her ground, waited for it, and braced herself, then at the last moment moved forward as it leapt into the air. The angle was all wrong, and if she tangled with it, she would be dead in seconds. She had no choice but to try to dodge it. Its claws caught her arm and ripped her leather armour. She hissed but bit down hard to keep a scream from her lips. She turned quickly to face it once more, biting her lip with concentration, and the large cat eyed her once more. It pounced on her, a pregnant pause hanging in the air as she advanced as well. Using her full power, she launched herself at the animal, her blade finding its mark in the heart, and she twisted the knife. The mountain lion gave out a strangled cry before it fell on the ground in a thud, a cloud of dust springing up around it.

An audible gasp echoed through the crowd, and as she turned, she realised a mountain lion had just mauled a man. Forde attacked then, and after a struggle that had her biting down a scream, he managed to bring down the beast. But unfortunately, he had blood running down his shoulder at that point and several scrapes from the run-in with the mountain lion.

The crowd erupted then as the third man took down his mountain lion. The other two stood in frustration, eliminated so early in the Games was humiliating. The sixth man groaned on the ground. The master of ceremonies moved forward as the crowd erupted, announcing that Amari, Forde and the third man would be moving to the next round. Of course, he was using numbers because they were nothing but numbers at this point.

They were ushered out of the pit quickly for the next round of fighters. As they passed through the group of men waiting their turn, they met them with congratulatory pats on the back.

They made their way to the back silently, each not able to believe they had come out of that alive. Finally, Amari and Forde moved to sit on a hard bench in the dimly lit waiting room corner. The waiting room wasn't much, just a large room with a dusty floor, several long benches and no window except the large iron wrought gate.

A man came carrying cloths and water to help tend to their wounds, but Forde told him they would handle it. The man moved away from them quickly as they both sat down, still a little dazed from what had happened.

"You..." Forde began, then stumbled over his words. He shook his head quickly then tried again. "You were amazing. You killed that beast in one move. Amari, I can't believe you did that."

"So did you." She pointed out as she reached for the water first and told him to pull off his armour.

"Yes, but I had physical strength on my side."

"I had prior experience. I was fourteen when I killed my first mountain lion."

"First? How many have there been?"

"This would be my third. The first time was practise. The second time it had come into the farm, and I had to do something." She started to clean his wounds. One was quite deep, and she took the needle and threaded a knife through it. "I have to sew this."

"Wait, have you done this before?" He held her hand quickly to stop her, and she arched her eyebrows. He sagged back, then grabbed a cloth and shoved it into his mouth. She glanced around, then used her powers to heat the knife.

"This is going to hurt."

He clenched his fists the moment the knife dug into his skin, but she told him to relax his arm in a hushed tone so that no one would hear her voice. Once she did the gruelling task, she washed off the wound on her arm, assuring him that her injuries were not deep.

"I can't believe we survived that," Forde muttered under his breath.

"I can't believe we're still alive."

"I think I underestimated you."

"I think you did, too."

The man around them started to move, parting away to make space for the approaching people. Amari and Forde pushed themselves to their feet, and Amari was stunned to see his uncle and cousins.

The older man approached first, looking at Forde straight in the eye with an unreadable expression on his face. Nevertheless, Amari could see the resemblance between Forde and these three men. They were, without a doubt, related.

"You did not speak to me about your intentions to become a Sage Warrior." His uncle began in a harsh voice, and Forde took a deep breath. "You just left with merely a note saying you had to leave. You didn't even say where you were going."

"I know. I was wrong. I should have said something, but the need was urgent." Forde explained quickly, and they stared at each other for a moment before his uncle took a step forward.

"Now, you listen to me, Forde. You come from a long line of strong men. The blood of the Cambridge-Pembrick runs through your veins. Honour and Unity is our motto. You wear the colours of the people of

Orrick. You stand here not as a representative of yourself but of me and, most importantly, your father. You make him proud, son. You go out there, and you come out of this victorious."

"I will make you proud," Forde muttered with a nod.

"And you live. Don't you dare die, or I will never forgive you if you do, Forde. You have the responsibility to carry forward your father's line, and there is still so much you have to achieve." His uncle nodded quickly, then clasped Forde's shoulder, shaking him gently. Forde nodded as his uncle took his hand into his and shook it, then his uncle turned to look at Amari. "That was astounding, young man. If you are not victorious here, I want you in my army." His uncle nodded, then he turned and walked out of the room.

Forde's cousins moved forward, and they hugged him, expressing their excitement at what he had just achieved.

"I am surprised to find you here without Korin? Is he in the crowds?" One of his cousins asked, a man as tall as Forde with thick dark hair. "Is he all right? I can find him and get him to come to sit with us as usual. How is he?"

"Korin is with friends," Forde responded and stole a glance at Amari. "Go back to the stands."

"Forde, is he all right?" The younger of the men asked, and Forde took a deep breath while Amari registered the concern in the man's tone. She realised at that moment that these three men had carried the burden of seeing Korin through his dark times. She didn't know why she hadn't considered that Forde's cousins were just as close to Korin.

"He will be," Forde replied with an affirming nod. "Now go back to the stands."

"You could have told us you were leaving with him. We could have come with you." The older of the two young men said.

"Baelin, I can't talk about this right now," Forde said defensively, but the two young men seemed hardly impressed.

"He wasn't only your friend, Forde. He was our friend too, and you had no right just to leave like that without saying something to us. Not after everything we have all been through with him this past year." The younger man looked visibly upset, and Amari stood there silently, watching this with keen interest.

"I know, Shorva, I didn't really think any of it through. I just decided to leave because I thought it might help him. I know you would have come with us, but the way he was… he just needed some solitude-"

"That he couldn't get with us around?"

"No. That's not…." Forde bit back his response, then took a deep breath and shook his head in frustration. "Korin is all right. We found his family, and they are going to help him get better."

"His family? We are his family, Forde. We're the ones who have been with him for the last seven years. So where has his family been all this time?" Shorva angrily questioned as he stared at Forde. "The least you could have done was to tell us you were leaving with him. Do you know what I went through when I went to his chambers and found him gone before we found your note? I thought he'd-" Shorva cut himself off then shook his head, as though realising this wasn't the time for such a conversation. "You'd better live through this because you have a lot of explaining to do."

"I intend to," Forde muttered, then folded his arms across his chest as he looked at his cousins. "I did it for Korin. I did all of it for Korin. I couldn't stand to see him suffer anymore. I was willing to try anything."

Amari watched the pained expressions on Shorva, Baelin and Forde's faces and realised Forde's cousins cared deeply for Korin.

"We know. Now, go out there and prove Orrick Warrior are superior." Baelin petted him on the shoulder.

"Good luck, brother." They hugged him once more and quickly left the room.

She saw the emotion on Forde's face, knew his family's words had been precisely what he had been hoping to hear.

"Did Korin and Shorva ever…" She trailed off. She didn't know what she was asking or why she would even ask this now, but the way the young man acted said a lot to her.

Forde glanced at her, then he sank onto the bench again and sighed. "Yes, though they'd never admit it to anyone. Shorva doesn't discriminate when it comes to men or women. He likes them both. It was never going to work, though, because Korin has been in love with Arteryn since he was seventeen, and Shorva plans to only settle down with a woman. So, it was never anything serious, but they do still care about each other, and they only sought each other out in that way sporadically over the years."

Amari had questions, but she was not going to ask any of them. She was just stunned to realise Korin had not exactly been living a chaste life these past seven years. She didn't know why she felt slightly jealous on Arteryn's behalf.

Time passed with the two of them sitting there quietly facing each other as they watched men come in either victorious or writhing in pain. One man lost his life.

Amari pushed herself to her feet as they were all called up to the front. The official once more looked at them.

"This round is an obstacle course. The purpose is to test your strength and stamina. The first eighteen to go through will advance to the next round. The rules are simple, do whatever you can to get to the finish line first, which includes ensuring your opponent does not reach the line before you do. Now get out there immediately."

They all hurried outside as Amari realised this round was going to be tough. If the participants could sabotage each other, she might be in a bit of trouble.

She took a deep breath as they stepped out to a cheering crowd that was anticipating the next round. Amari tried to pay attention to the master of ceremonies and caught on that they had to go around the obstacle course twice. She assessed each point, taking in the task and calculating in her mind how she would do it.

Eleven obstacles completed twice were all that stood between her and the following round. It was a daunting task, but she refused to go down at this level after killing a mountain lion. This course would not require just speed, but upper body strength and a certain level of fitness.

The official told them all to line up in one straight line, and then he started counting down. When he drew his flag down, they all sped down the arena towards the first obstacle course. The crowd went wild as one of the men stuck his foot out and swiped at her. She had not been expecting it, and she hurtled to the ground, landing in a dusty thud.

She looked up as the dust settled while other men left her behind, and she lost a lot of ground. She picked herself up then ran forward to try to catch up. She knew she had lost precious ground, but in a way, it would serve as a blessing. Being at the back did not make her an immediate threat to anyone. They would eliminate each other at the front while she fought to catch up.

The first part of the obstacle course was to climb over three relatively high walls. Due to Amari's height, she had to launch herself high to reach the top of the wall and hurl herself over. Next, she jumped over and did the same with the two remaining walls. The next part had two ropes ties on two poles. She had to hoist herself up and swing to the other side without touching the ground. Two stations of the same obstacle were set up so as not to delay participants.

She jumped, swung her legs until she latched onto the next rope, and she swung herself to the other end. Her arms were burning at that point, but she did not dally. She reached the next level, where she had to swing herself across a pit on the ground. She grabbed the rope and swung herself over the pit. One of the participants lost his grip and fell into the muddy waters. She could not help thinking whoever had planned these games had a sick mind and derived pleasure from other people's pain. The course proved challenging, but she still pushed as hard as she could. She spotted Forde right in the front as he dodged a swipe from an opponent who tried to take a swing at him. She pushed with everything she had, trying to catch up. She jumped over a person sprawled on the ground after someone caught him with a hard punch on the face and had fallen hard on the course, injuring himself. Then, she picked up the pace, climbing over things, balancing on beams, dangling in precarious positions. They started the second round with three men down, and she pushed with everything she had, ignoring the burning pain in her chest, the shortness of breath and the pain shooting through her muscles.

Eventually, she just had to pass one person before she could make it to the top eighteen. She needed to make it to the top eighteen. Elimination after having come so far would be painful. The man before her was so near, and they were fast nearing the end of the course. She realised Forde had already completed along with two other men and the others were about to cross over the finish line.

Digging in with everything thing she had, she pushed even further, pushing through the pain and the crunching muscles as Amari swung with a rope, her arms burning as the man did the same beside her, and she knew as she landed on her feet that he was going to cross before she did. She recognised the man by his armour. He was the man who had tripped her at the beginning of the course. She lunged for him, rolled with him on the ground, pushing herself over him, then kicked him hard in the stomach. He groaned as she detached from him and ran to the finish line. The crowd went crazy with roaring excitement. She lost her balance as she crossed the line and landed on a heap on the floor, grazing her cheek on the dirt. She struggled to catch her breath as she slowly pushed herself to sit up. Forde came to Amari and pulled her to her feet quickly as the man she had overtaken moved past her in anger, letting out a string of curses.

"You had me worried there," Forde whispered to her as the crowd cheered for them. The remaining eighteen participants waved to the crowd while the disgruntled eliminated contestants walked off with their heads hung in shame and their shoulders slouched.

"I was worried myself." She confessed as she swallowed, trying to catch her breath.

Without even giving them further pause, the masters of ceremony came forward where he stood.

"And now we will commence with the third round."

"I need water," Amari whispered to Forde, but she had a feeling the lack of pause between the two rounds was deliberate.

"The third round is designed to test the strength of your mind. A man's strength is his mind, his ability to withstand any sort of pain under any circumstances. Ready yourselves, men!"

"I really need water," Amari muttered but knew there would be no water. For the first time that day since she had stepped into that course, she started to doubt her ability to finish this thing. Amari was so parched and so tired, but she refused to cave in. She had made it to the third round. There were men Amari had beaten out for the position she was in. Even if she lost now, it would not be a failure on her part.

She took a deep breath, her hand flying to her necklace, and it immediately soothed her.

She was going to complete this competition even if it killed her.

CHAPTER TWENTY-EIGHT

The next task left her somewhat perplexed. Eighteen short poles stood erected firmly on the ground. Two thick iron nails were wedged horizontally deeply into the poles, and the expectation from them was that they stand on those nails for as long as they could without falling over. The catch was that they had to be barefoot, and after hours of being under the sun, the thick nails were possibly hot.

She turned a determined look at Forde as she realised what they had to do, and they all pulled off their boots off their feet.

"We can do this. Just stay focused and don't fall off."

All she could do was nod as they all moved to their posts. Finally, the official came to stand in the middle of the arena. "At the count of three, you will all climb onto your posts. I will then count to ten to give you time to be settled into a position, and the round will begin. The last ten on the poles will proceed to the last round."

Amari took a deep breath then looked at the pole that was a few feet off the ground. The official started to count, and they all climbed on when he reached three. She wobbled a little bit, trying to find her footing as he counted to ten, and just as he reached ten, she stabilised herself.

Under the hot sweltering sun of Sagar with parched throats and chests still heaving from the obstacle run, they all tried not to allow their minds to fail them.

Amari knew this was not a test of physical strength but a test of willpower. First, she had to clear her mind and focus. Amari knew not to think about the searing pain under her feet or the sun beating down on her. She had to overlook her thirst and block out all distractions.

It took her two minutes to find a comfortable position, she settled in, and heat beat down on her. She was sweating profusely under the leather armour she was wearing, but she kept her eyes glued on one spot. Whenever she started being conscious of an itch or uncomfortable pain on her toes, she thought back to the village in Synia, of the green valleys and the friendly people. She went through pieces of her training with Arteryn, went through conversations with Crispin in her head. She even thought about funny moments she had shared with Korin and wondered how he was getting on. She promised herself that she would see him the moment the Games had ended.

A sudden thud had her looking up, and she saw a man who had fallen off his pole and was currently unconscious on the ground. She started to sway herself, struggling to find her balance and the crowd seemed to latch on to that and cried out as though they had the power to keep her on the nails.

She settled in again then glanced at Forde, who had his head down and was looking very relaxed and comfortable. He was in as much pain as she was, but his level of concentration was admirable. An hour passed, and by then, even Forde was starting to look like he was feeling the pinch. Three men had fallen off at this point. The last round only had ten spots. Two men had fallen over, and she knew only a few more had to go before this round could end.

Her legs were on fire, her feet had gone numb, and the urge to step off was becoming more attractive by the second, but she knew she couldn't give up. She had given up so much to get to where she was. Giving up now would almost be an insult to everything and everyone she had turned away from to be there.

She took a calm and steadying breath, her mouth so dry that she would give anything for a sip of water as three men fell off. Another hour passed of her letting her mind wander to all sorts of things, and just when her knees started to wobble, when she thought she could not take anymore, two men suddenly lost their balance and fell off at the same time. The crowd erupted in cheers, knowing the round was over and the fun was about to begin.

The ten remain contestants gingerly stepped off their posts then immediately sank to their knees in pain. The crowd was excited, enjoying every moment as Amari looked at Forde, who was two poles away from her. They had made it, but she had no idea how the last round worked. Amari just hoped whatever it entailed; she did not have to fight Forde. She knew he would let her win.

She pushed herself to her feet as the gates opened, and they were all recalled to the waiting room. Of course, the first thing they all did was gobble down water to quench their thirst before sinking onto benches to rest the sore legs. Amari tried to wipe the sweat off her neck, but short of taking off her armour- which was not an option- she had to stay in that hot suit while they waited for the last round. Fortunately, the King had decided to take thirty minutes recess for refreshments.

Forde sat on a wooden bench hunched over as he inspected the base of her feet. There was an angry red welt on each foot. All of them had the same markings. Nonetheless, he shoved his feet into his boots then looked up to find her watching him. The paint on her face had started to melt away, and she wanted nothing more than to throw off her helmet, but she had to keep it on. He beckoned her to come over, and she expelled a sigh and moved to sit next to him.

"I have to fix the paint." He rose to his feet and walked off to get it from his bag where he had left it. He returned shortly then started to reapply it. Once done, he glanced at the other men, having to lean forward because they were in an area that gave them a little privacy. "We might have to fight each other in the next round."

"I know."

"There are ten of us. It means we each have one person standing before us and victory." He supplied, and she nodded. "The problem is I know five of the other eight men. I have seen them fight. They have reputations for being brutal. They are going to come out swinging hard, Amari, with everything they have. We could get hurt. I should have brought you a shield. I don't know why I didn't think to bring you a shield."

She nodded because she had deduced that anyone who could kill a mountain lion had to be brutal on some level. "I don't need a shield. Stop frustrating yourself about this."

"Listen to me." He shook her quickly, and she returned her eyes to his face. "You're not dying here, all right. I know the law of the Kenryk about us, but when this is over, I am going to Bhrim."

"You've decided to move to Bhrim?" Was there ever a doubt.

"Yes. See, there's a man there I love dearly - my very own little brother who isn't little at all, and there is a woman there that I can't imagine a future without. So, you and Korin are stuck with me." Forde told her, and her mouth hung open as she stared at him in surprise. "I've been lost for a very long time Amari, wandering through life without a real purpose. The only thing I have ever been certain of was my healing skills, which was sacred to my mother. I want to explore that more; I'd like that to be my purpose."

"Helping people? Why am I not surprised?" She smiled, knowing Forde could never fight his need to do what he couldn't for his family and help. It shaped who he was.

"I never could quite understand why instinctively I knew what to mix or brew over the years when my uncle and cousins fell ill, but now I know it's in my blood, and I don't want something so valuable that I inherited from my mother to disappear. So, I must use it."

She opened her mouth, but before she could respond, she saw him lean forward. He said something harshly under his breath, and she followed his gaze and found a few men looking at them.

"What is it?" She frowned in confusion as his frustration started to rub off on her.

"Think about it. There are ten of us left, and five will become Sage Warriors. All that is required is for five men to band together and eliminate the rest of us. By sitting here together, we have just given everyone the impression we will be working together." He pushed to his feet quickly, crossing his arms over his chest as he looked down at her quickly. "I need you to promise me something."

"What is it?" She felt broken the way she repeated that.

"In there- in that pit- when we are fighting… it's going to be brutal, Amari. The sort of thing you probably have never faced, and I do not doubt that you can pull through, but if I think you're in danger and I jump in to help, don't hate me."

She pushed herself to her feet, not expecting anything less from Forde, and she smiled at him. "I could never hate you, Forde, not as long as I live."

"All right then, good luck. Don't panic, stay calm, use your mind and trust your instincts." His breath hitched as though this whole thing was not settling well with him. "Amari, just promise me you'll come out of this alive, please."

"You too."

"I promise."

"Me too."

The horn blared out a while later, and the crowd erupted as they made their way to the middle of the arena. The master of ceremony came forward once more, looking a little less animated than he had that morning. It had been a long day for everyone, especially the participants.

"This it is, everyone. The final round! When this round is over, we will have our Sage Warriors. It has been a long day, and you have all come here to be entertained by the spectacular!" The crowd erupted in cheers once more. "We have finally reached the stage where our warriors finally engage in physical combat."

The crowd enjoyed this bit of information as well. Amari sized the men she was competing with, and she was by far the shortest person there. So, the odds were stacked against her.

The men around her mumbled, and Amari glanced at Forde, who was looking up at the Masters of Ceremony.

"Unlike in previous years where we had a draw to determine who fought who, this year, it will be a free for all." The master of ceremony declared, and Amari released a sigh of relief. At least this guaranteed she would not be forced to face Forde.

The official came out to the pit one last time and assessed them. "All right then, you all have your weapons? We have reached the final round—the last five men standing win. The rules are simple, disarm and get your man out of the game by all means necessary. These are games of honour; therefore, only one rule applies. No killing. We still want these great men who made it so far this year to come back again, next year hopefully."

"Did you consider that before you set mountain lions on us?" One man asked from behind Amari, and she could only concur with his words.

"Anyone eliminated in the first round is not worth a moment of our thought. Good luck, men."

The official made his way off the arena as they spread out. Amari glanced at the man eyeing Forde. He was built large and muscular with a sword and an axe as his weapons of choice. Forde had his sword, and she knew he had two sharp blades on his person. She had her sword with her, one knife at her back and another shoved in her boot. She was ready for the man she was about to face. He was about Forde's size, tall, lean, solid muscles, and he was sneering at her. She realised that while Grantreal's size had slowed him down and given her an advantage, she might have met her match at last.

The horn blared, and she immediately became alert, her legs spread out as she and the man rounded each other. The man unsheathed his sword, and so did she.

He cried out as he attacked and immediately put her on the back foot. The force with which he brought his sword down forced her to stumble back as she blocked the blow with her sword. He was strong, she noted. She steadied herself as they rounded each other once more, their eyes never leaving the other. He had a shield, and she did not, which put her at a disadvantage. The man advanced quickly and swung his sword. Once more, she had to be on the defensive, and then more blows came. She spent the next good twenty seconds blocking blows that would have grievously injured her.

She was so focused on blocking the blows that she did not see the fist that came flying to land squarely on her jaw. The impact was so hard and unexpected her head turned violently to one side; she stumbled and fell to the ground. The crowd grew excited. The man did not let up. He advanced, ready to end this fight, but she rolled on the floor to her left as he brought his sword down and had to dodge again when he brought his sword down. She realised then that this man planned to injure her grievously.

She couldn't roll down on the ground forever, and when he approached once more, she swung her legs behind his legs and knocked him off his feet. She jumped to her feet quickly to gain lost ground once more as he rolled to his feet. Her cheek stung painfully, and it would surely bruise, but she refused to let the pain define her. With speed and agility she had not expected, the man lunged for her, attacking with everything he had, and he forced her to take steps backwards as he continued with his onslaught. However, she remained resolute in her technique. Eventually, he was going to tire himself out at this pace, but before that happened, another fist came, but she saw this one and intercepted it by blocking it by swinging her arm towards him. It left the man exposed, but all she could do was punch him in the chest.

He stumbled back, his shield falling out of his hand, and then attacked once more. He was very skilled, and he did not even give Amari a chance to gather her bearings. She was stunned when he kicked her so hard, she fell, and her sword flew out of her hand to land pathetically a few feet away.

He was already coming for her, and as she rolled to one side, he anticipated her moments and drove his sword down. She reached up and managed to block him from ultimately driving the sword through her shoulder, but it went through her armour, and the tip cut her skin. She knew he would twist the blade and cause possible irreparable damage to her body, so she used her feet to knock him off his feet. She pulled his sword out, throwing it aside as her other hand immediately went up to the injured shoulder. It would probably hurt later, but the adrenaline pumping through her at that moment was intense. She pulled out her knife and, without waiting for the man to recover, attacked.

They sparred intensely, blocking and attacking until she was able to slice him across his chest with a sharp blade.

He stumbled back, her sharp blade had cut through his leather armour, and she felt satisfaction at having drawn blood. She heard the crowd cheer and knew one of the men had been defeated, but she couldn't look, wouldn't lose her concentration even though she longed to ensure that Forde was all right.

She attacked once more and, using her arms and her legs, attacked and blocked her opponent. This time he caught her with a fist across the chin that made her bite herself, and blood started to ooze from the cut lip.

She wiped it away as the crowd cheered once more. Another man had been victorious. Enough of this, she thought. It was time she finished this fight. She hadn't come this far to lose. She had not left home, faced certain death, and kidnapped by Grantreal to lose now. She wanted to go home, and she refused to go home, hanging her head in shame. In her mind, one image had always reigned. She had replayed repeatedly in her brain; of a day when she returned victorious from the Games, and she would walk into the farm and show her family the Sage Warrior badge. Tia, Joran and Crispin would be proud of her. She refused to go back home a failure. She was going to fight with all she had.

The crowd erupted once more, and she realised then that it was just down to her and this man. She started running forward, and the man crouched, expecting her to attack his lower body when instead she leapt in the air. She saw the stunned look on his face as she wrapped her legs around his neck, swung her whole body, bringing the man down with her. Then, before he could gather his bearings, she lashed at him, driving her knife into his shoulder before she swung her fist and knocked him out clean. She heard his jaw crack under her fist and then silence.

She watched him, waiting to see if he was completely out cold.

He didn't move. He lay there, unconscious and defeated. Amari's eyes widened, stumbling back and unable to comprehend this fully. She was probably dreaming. Was this real? She breathed heavily, the pain in her body replaced by a growing sense of euphoria.

She had won! She had defeated this man! She stumbled backwards, sinking onto her bottom on the dusty ground, her heart beating fast as she struggled to make sense of what was happening.

She achieved her goal and had was a Sage Warrior! It seemed surreal, insane, and unbelievable!

She pushed herself to her feet, turning to look at the crowd that had erupted into such frenzied excitement that some were hanging over the stone railing of the border separating them from the fighting pit.

She didn't know what to do with herself. She laughed, but an intense urge to break down into tears settled on her. She shook her head again, unable to accept that she had been victorious. Her whole body trembled slightly, her feet moving towards where Forde was standing, looking at her with pride and joy on his face. That was the moment she realised he, too, had become a Sage Warrior. She leapt in the air and started to run towards him when a feeling of cold dread settled over her.

Raw, biting, stinging like pins, the cold seeped into her, and she staggered to a halt. Fog crawled into the arena, mouths that had been crying with jubilation emitting white cold air from their lips. She heard the loud cry before she saw them, and her eyes widened as she staggered back. The iron gates flew open; the official hurled unceremoniously across the air to crash down in a dusty heap.

When the large creatures stepped into the arena, panic flared up within her.

"It's the Emori!" She heard someone cry out in disbelief.

"Impossible! They do not exist anymore!" Another person responded, but Amari could not move. She was rooted to the spot, grounded as though shackled to stone underwater.

"Protect the King!" Someone called out, but she was oblivious to everything happening around her. No! Why was this happening? Why now? In front of everyone? Were the Emori that brazen? She hadn't even had time to bask in her victory. She didn't know why she hadn't given the Emori any more thought after leaving Golynvale. She had just assumed they had lost her once she arrived in Bhrim. Had she unknowingly led them to Bhrim as well? Was Korin and the other Kenryk all right?

A hand clasped around her arm, and she realised someone was pulling her back.

She turned to see Forde trying to get her to safety, but something snapped in her that she had never experienced before. The feeling was so instinctual that she dug her feet into the ground and stepped away from him.

"No, Forde, I'm done running." She pulled the sword he had been holding out of his hands and started to turn.

"No, Amari, they will kill you!" Forde's panic and fear on her behalf were welcome, but these Emori were responsible for killing so many of her people. Her birth parents had died because of Emori, and she knew it in her heart that if she ran now, she would be running for the rest of her life. She should have known using her powers would lead them to her, but suddenly she didn't care anymore.

"No, they won't, Forde. I am Avaris, a Kenryk warrior trained to fight Emori. I kill Emori." She pulled out of his grasp, not even considering the Sage Warriors that had immediately readied themselves to protect their kingdom with their lives.

Stomping to a halt in the middle of the arena, the Emori in front pointed directly at her. He clenched his fist, making his intentions clear, then let out a loud cry.

It was evident to everyone that she was their target and an uncomfortable silence pregnant with terror settled all around her. Amari pulled off her helmet and cast it aside. Gasps filled the crowd with whispers as they saw her face. She was a woman. She moved slowly, dragging the sword behind her with lazy confidence, but Forde grasped at her quickly.

"Amari, please."

She looked down where his hand gripped hers with intention, growled, and he released her immediately. She looked up at him.

"Forde, I just became a Sage Warrior, something we all thought was impossible. I am an Avaris. That is my duty, more than what I just achieved in this arena. I must prove myself to the Kenryk and myself to be certain that I deserve to be an Avaris. I must do this. If anything happens to me, take my necklace to Arteryn." She reached for the clasp of her armour, unfastened it, and the upper half came off.

"Amari-"

"Please, Forde." She handed him the armour, the evidence of her gender evident for all to see as she stood there in her light cotton vest and the lower half of her armour. "And Forde, I'll be fine."

"Your amour-"

"I don't need it." She assured him with a small smile. She looked at this man once more, watching him fight his urge to protect her, yet understanding this was the one thing he could not protect her from. She was facing her fate.

As Amari stepped away from him slowly, she knew she could very well be walking to her death, but at least she had succeeded in her one goal. She was now a Sage Warrior, and no stunned gasps from the crowd when they realised, she was a woman could take that away from her.

CHAPTER TWENTY-NINE

A mari glanced towards the King, who was now on his feet, a stunned look on his face while one of his council members spoke to him rapidly in his ear. The council member was probably advising him to let this play out. However, it was evident that she was the Emori's target, and she did not cower from a challenge.

A part of her hurt that she might never be able to go back home and show her family that she had succeeded in becoming a Sage Warrior; that all those years of training had been for nothing, but she was through with running. She now knew what the Emori sought, it dangled on her necklace, and they would have to pry it out of her cold dead hands.

"Amari!" She heard Forde call. As she turned to him, he threw a shield at her, and she caught it quickly, thanking him by nodding her head. The pit cleared, and she stood there with the Emori, alone with nothing more than the skill that had just helped become a Sage Warrior and a body exhausted from hours of participating in the Games.

The Emori in the front said something in a language she could not understand. It was not a tonal language, but she could easily deduce they were talking about her. Immediately the Emori on the left, the one who was big and carried an axe, assumed a position of one ready to attack.

She had thought Grantreal was big, but seeing the Emori so close made her realise they were unnaturally bigger than the average tall and broad man.

The terrible smell they emitted was enough to make her gag, but she held it back as the Emori with the helmet that had three openings on it for the eyes and nose suddenly bared its jagged, sharp teeth and let out a loud cry. She had never seen a mouth so big and with so many teeth.

Don't overthink, Amari. Just be present in the moment. Arteryn's words echoed in her head as though he had whispered them to her ear in that moment. Unfortunately, the crowd did not cheer. Instead, they cowered away with both shock and dread at what was happening. It was too bad, she thought; she could have fed off their good energy.

The Emori came at her with speed she had not imagined someone of the height could manage. Once more, she could not see their feet, clouded in the fog that hung low to their ankles. The entire arena had grown bone-deep ice cold.

The Emori came at her so fast she barely had time to come up with a strategy. He jumped, his axe held high in the air, and he brought it down fiercely. All she could do was hold up her shield, easily perforated by the axe. A gasp escaped her lips when the axe stopped short of her nose. Moving swiftly, she jumped out of the way and cleared space between her and the Emori. Throwing his axe away, the Emori pulled out his jagged sword with intricate carvings on it. She could smell the fear that hung over the crowd.

The Emori attacked again, his blade thinly slicing her arm. She survived because she had managed to dodge the sword that had been coming for her stomach.

The crowd let out a collective gasp as the Emori drew blood, and she hissed in pain.

She bit back a cry, and he came for her again, this time delivering a blow so hard on her stomach it sent her hurling across the arena to land on a thud on the ground. A loud cry filled the arena, and she groaned as pain seared through her body. She tasted blood in her mouth, and her head spun.

She looked up to see the Emori already about to deliver a final blow on her when she lifted her arm in a lame attempt to protect herself. She knew this was it, that she could be dead in the next second. Everything around her had slowed down somehow. She became conscious of Forde running towards her to rescue her; she saw the sword coming down towards her and could tell it would pass through her arm and chest.

Every way she looked at this situation, she knew she was going to die. Amari's next thought was how warm her necklace had become against her chest, and in an instant and something clicked in her brain. The emotions coursing through her were unknown yet surprisingly familiar to her. She didn't know what was happening to her. Something was churning through her entire body at that moment, an alien power coursing through every vein and pore in her body. It enveloped her, engulfed her in its potency, and her entire body started to vibrate. She watched as the blade came down then heard the collective gasp from the crowd. Amari looked at the Emori's sword, her entire attention centred on it. It came down, and it would have touched her skin as gold grains appeared in the space right over her arm, started to spread out and without any notice burst into golden shards that shot straight to the Emori. The impact on the Emori was so strong; it threw him half across the arena to smash against the sides.

A fire burned within her, boiling over in a way she hadn't felt before. It was an intensely inexplicable feeling of something that had been inside her for far too long, and it threatened to come out. In fact, it was starting to spill out, and with her in the middle of the arena, she was in full view of everyone.

Already her body was starting to heal as fire poured from her hands. At this point, she had shut her mind to the reaction of the crowds. She glanced at Forde, held her hand up and felt an invisible force shoot from her hand to strike him. He fell on the ground then groaned as he rose to his feet quickly.

"Stay out of this, Forde!" She snapped and was relieved when he did not advance even though his body strained to do the opposite.

The leader of the Emori made another cry as the one she had hit rose to his feet.

She wasn't even conscious much of what was happening around. What was overpowering was what was happening within her. She had never felt power so strong, and she had this burning need within her that she could not understand. She could feel her body calling- yearning for something, trying to tell her what to do, but she didn't know what it was. The medallion on her neck became hot like molten lava, and that was startling considering she was currently starting to have flames around her that were not burning her at all. While the orange fire was cool on her skin, the medallion was on fire.

She reached to her chest and pulled at the medallion. It came away easily from the strap, and she looked down at it. Her eyes danced as she gazed down at the gold medallion glowing in her hand. There was a pounding in her head. She thought she heard a low humming from a crowd of many. It grew louder and louder until once voice was suddenly isolated, a man's voice and she heard him clear as daylight. Be the Avaris, Amari. It is what you were born to be.

She gave in to the fire raging within her, and it overtook her, engulfed her, and the moment she did, something exploded within her. From out of her fiery hand, the medallion began its swift transformation. It began to morph, first formulating the silver and gold hilt, and then the blade sprang out. It was the Endric Sword! The flaming sword of the Kenryk! She looked at the weapon with its golden blade. It had many inscriptions on it she could not read. The hilt was silver and gold with intricate carvings. However, the inscription was startlingly similar to words she had seen at the castle in Bhrim.

The small inscription written down the centre of the blade was in a language she had never seen before, but one she immediately understood. *Inum Anem Kalhasie.* In you, we offer our service. In you, we will live forever. She understood it now, understood the many Kenryk who gave up their powers to save the Kais from the demon king. That inscription was engraved in her heart. She could not fail those people. She refused to be the Avaris who allowed the Kais to plunge into darkness once more. It was not going to be under her watch that the same Emori who had killed her people would not have in their possession the Endric Sword.

She felt her entire being become one with the sword, blending in her power, essence, and soul to the sword as the powers of the Old coursed through her entire body. It engulfed her, and she felt whole as the fire blazed around her. On some level, she heard the comments around her. The Sword of Fire! The Fiery Endric Sword! She is an Avaris! Yet those words meant nothing to her. The very people sitting on the stands stood to lose their lives if she failed today.

The fire died around her body but continued to burn around her feet in intense flames and from the hand holding the burning sword. An inexplicable breeze flowed around her as she lifted her head to look at the Emori.

They came at her then, in one go, all at once, and she braced herself. Those watching would talk for years of the woman who stood in the middle of the arena with golden eyes. She took just a moment to collect herself then advanced. What followed next was something people would talk about for centuries to come. Before them, the crowd watched as a young woman fought three Emori, blow for blow, matching them, blocking them, attacking them. It was so intense that teeth were gritted, fists were clenched, and everyone was gripped with the fear of making a sound lest they disturbed her. The spectacular part was that every single time the Endric Sword met the sword of an Emori, the clash let out a loud sound that vibrated through everyone, and it let out sparks of gold.

Seeing the woman wielding the fiery sword, leap, kick, spin, duck and retaliate had everyone on the edge of the seat. The King himself was so mesmerised he forgot to breathe.

The Emori large; they were strong, three of them, and Amari fought them with everything she had. She had realised that even when she connected with the Emori, they were not harmed and knew there was one way to kill them. Cut off their heads.

She rolled on the ground to dodge another swipe of an axe and jumped to her feet. Her body did not feel like hers. It was lighter than usual. She was able to jump higher and move faster than before. She knew she could not continue fighting them all at once. She had to cut down her opponents.

She could not continue to fight these Emori indefinitely. She had to try to end this now. Her muscles were already aching from the strain of the Games.

She found her opening when they all attacked her at once, surrounding her. She saw the swords coming from all three angles at her and leapt straight into the air. Their swords met in the middle, and as she descended, she balanced briefly on the joined blades long enough to swing her sword and decapitate two Emori in seconds.

She did a backward flip, landed on her feet, then swung around quickly, dust collecting around her as she turned to face the leader.

The bodies of the Emori remained upright before they started to shake violently, and right before her eyes turned into ash and sank to the ground. The heads shrivelled up, turned to ash, and mingled with the dirt on the ground.

She twirled the sword in her hand, then put one foot back as she turned sideways to face the leader, the sword held in the air close to her shoulder as she breathed heavily, waiting for the next move.

With teeth tightly clenched and bared, she glared at the enemy.

The Emori let out a loud, harsh sound, anger emanating from him in droves as he faced her. His eyes glowed red beyond the mask. She straightened and took a step back, knowing, feeling it to her core that this was it. This was the moment. She channelled the power within her, channelled the energy of the sword as the wind whipped around her uncontrollably.

Those who were watching were stunned by the transformation that happened before them. They watched as Amari's eyes swirled gold. Fire wrapped around her fiercely, her hair coming loose as red layers of clothing started to plaster themselves on her skin, the fires hiding the clothes that fell away from her. The mixture of the fiery red smooth leather armour and leather pants mixed with the blazing orange of the fire that was burning around her in circular motion flashed before everyone's eyes.

She started to formulate a ball of fire in her left hand, large and so intense those in the first row had to cover their faces. She started running forward at the same time the Emori rushed straight at her in full attack mode. Just as she was about to reach him, she fired the ball of fire, spun in the air to land on the shoulders of the Emori and drove her sword down the Emori's skull. She yanked her sword out, did a clean backflip, swung her arm behind her and effectively cut off his head seamlessly.

She landed on the ground, spun around with one hand splayed on the dusty surface and a knee on the ground and hissed at him. She watched as he crumbled before her eyes and disintegrated into ash. The head did the same just moments later, and she remained in that crouched position, fire blazing around her. Then, the sound of the crowd erupting around her snapped her out of her profoundly focused state, and her eyes returned to normal, the fierce red armour falling away to be replaced by her old armour, and the Endric Sword shrank in her hands. She watched in disbelief as it morphed into liquid gold, then proceeded to slip under the skin on her wrist, travelling up her arm and disappeared utterly—the Kenryk sigil formed on her wrist like a golden tattoo.

She swayed, sinking to her knees as the sound of the loud crowd swallowed her. Then, as she tipped back about to pass out into the ground, the last thing she remembered was being caught into the arms of someone who had slid fast next to her, and as Amari looked up, she met Forde's eyes, knew that she was safe and welcomed the blackness that swallowed her.

"Amari!"

His voice was calling to her, she heard it faintly, but he kept calling out her name repeatedly, the crowd's jubilation dying out as silence fell around them.

"Amari, don't you dare die!" he shook her once more, violently, and she let out a sigh as she slowly opened her eyes to look at him. She lay there in his arms, gazing up at him, her body spent.

"Take me home, Forde." She whispered at him; his face filled with tormented emotion as he shook her again.

His eyes looked around searchingly, and then something crossed his face, urgency, concern, the need to get her out of there.

"We need to leave now." He declared, pulling her into his arms and rising to his feet.

"Why?" She didn't even know why she was asking; her mind and body felt numb, spent and utterly depleted.

"Because you have the Endric Sword, Amari, a weapon the King of Sagar might feel he wants."

Forde carried Amari out of the arena, and his only focus was to get her to Bhrim as fast as possible. Unfortunately, she looked depleted, and her lips started turning blue.

He met his cousins just as he entered the tunnels in the arena, and he paused long enough to tell them to bring his and Amari's bags.

"Forde, where are you taking her?" Baelin asked when they reached the horse-drawn wagon he and Amari had taken to the arena only that morning. Shorva lay down a blanket on the wagon, pulling off his robe, folding it to make a makeshift pillow and helped Forde set Amari down. They covered her with a blanket quickly.

The King came out with several Sage Warriors just as they covered her, laying out their bags on either side of her. "Where are you going?"

In his forties with dark hair and brown eyes, King Eldrian stood tall and imposing in his expensive robes.

Forde moved towards the front of the wagon, intending to get out of there.

He knew everyone's interest would be piqued. If Amari was, according to them, the last Kenryk alive, everyone would strive to ally with her to secure their positions. He had to get her out of there before becoming a pawn in a game she had not trained thirteen years for.

"You are not taking her anywhere-"

"Try and stop me!" Forde snapped at the King. He didn't care at this point that he was shouting at the King of the Great Kingdom of Sagar or that his actions would have consequences.

"I am your King, and I order you to stop at once. We will give the Avaris the treatment she deserves and shelter-"

"She doesn't need any of those. She has a place to go." Forde pointed out quickly then turned to look at the King. "Thank you for the offer, but I have to go. You can give my uncle our Sage Warrior badges to carry home."

"Forde." His uncle came out, hurrying towards him quickly, looking incredulous.

"Sage Warriors, make sure he does not leave the city!" The King demanded, and Forde stopped and turned to the King as more people started to come out of the arena towards them.

"She is dying. No medicine you have can treat her. She is a Kenryk, and they treat their own. Avaris do not align themselves with any king. If you do not let her go, she will die, and you will be responsible for killing a Kenryk!"

"Forde." His uncle said in a warning tone, but Forde was past caring about protocol. He had to get Amari to Bhrim as fast as he could. She might not even make it past this first night, and they still had a long way to go. He did not need to be standing there arguing with the King.

"I have to go, and any man who tries to stop me will lose his life!" Forde snapped at them, and at that moment, relief washed over him when Arteryn jumped off the wagon and turned to face the others. Forming a giant ball of fire, Arteryn stood there, threatening, imposing, and exuding something deeper than danger.

"If you try to stop us, I will burn this city to the ground." Arteryn threatened, then looked at Forde. "Get us out of here. I will administer temporal aid."

Forde leapt onto the wagon and grabbed the reins as Arteryn jumped onto the back of the wagon. The Sage Warriors approached, but Arteryn did something that even shook Forde to the core. He growled, a growl so menacing, so terrifying that it brought everyone to a halt.

"Any man who wants to lose his life may approach me." Arteryn's words came out fierce, terrifying and Forde could only stare at him as he watched something happen to Arteryn, a change in his body, both in size and appearance. His hair had gotten longer, and were those fangs? His eyes flashed red, and he looked like an animal ready to pounce on its prey.

Forde shook himself out of his stupor and slapped the reins hard. The horse sprang into action, and they sped through the city.

"Is she dying?" He asked Arteryn, who looked at him gravely then nodded. Arteryn's appearance had changed again, looking normal, that Forde wondered if it had been a figment of his imagination. As they rode through the city, Forde glanced behind him as he watched Arteryn trying to use his fire powers to revive Amari.

Forde glanced at Amari as they sped out of the city, but she was so still. His heart clenched as he stole a look at Arteryn, who did not carry an encouraging look on his face.

"Why is she dying? Why are her powers killing her?" He failed to understand how this was possible.

"She is dying because she used powers she has not trained to use yet. With practice, the body of an Avaris develops the strength to control and withstand the Endric Sword powers. However, what she did today... I have never heard of the Endric Sword coming with its armour before. She used too much power than she was ready to. It is the reason she had to stay in Bhrim to train. An Avaris' powers are stronger than an average Kenryk. If we do not get to Bhrim on time, she is going to slip into an Avaris sleep."

"What is that?"

"Neither alive nor dead. More dead than alive.'

CHAPTER THIRTY

I f it were possible to sleep on a cloud, she would have said that was where she was at that moment. She rolled to her side slowly in her dreamy state and expelled a sigh of contentment. She wanted to bury herself further into the soft bed and disappear.

"Wake up, Amari." A very familiar voice said impatiently somewhere nearby. She groaned, reluctant to leave the peaceful haven she languished in. "Come on, wake up. I have so much to tell you. Wake up!"

"You're starting to annoy me." Another very familiar voice pierced through her subconscious, and she frowned though still reluctant to open her eyes. Why couldn't they just let her sleep?

"She's been in this Avaris sleep for a whole month." The first voice pointed out quickly, and his words forced her eyes open. She bolted upright, inhaling sharping, her body snapping awake in an instant. She sat suspended in time for a moment, her body catching up with her mind in an instant, and she released a slow exhale. She blinked once, twice, and her eyes darted around her searchingly. It took a moment, but everything came rushing back to her in an instant, and as her mind registered that she was in fact in the chamber she had used when she had been in Bhrim, the words about an Avaris sleep lingered in her mind.

She turned her head to her side, where Forde and Korin sat on low backed chairs next to the bed, watching her cautiously.

"Should we call Arteryn?" Korin whispered to Forde, who swatted him away quickly as he surged forward. "Wait, no sudden movements."

Korin drew him back roughly and forced Forde back into his chair. Forde turned his head in annoyance towards Korin, who merely shrugged.

"We don't know if she's altogether herself." Korin pointed before he rose to his feet slowly and approached the bed. "Do you know who you are?"

Amari's scrunched up her nose as she wiped the sleep from her eyes, her brain fully awake now. She frowned at Korin's words. "Korin, why wouldn't I know who I am?"

He broke into a smile then released a sigh. "You've been asleep for a month. I was starting to think you'd never wake up. But I will have you know that I played a very active role in ensuring your hair remained tangle-free. I brushed it every day."

"He actually did." Forde nodded quickly, and Amari's gaze turned towards him, and a rush of emotions filled her as she looked at this man who had stayed with her through it all. Through it all? Wait, what had happened after she had faced the Emori? How had she ended up in Bhrim? How was it possible that she had been asleep for a month and was still alive? Had any of it been real? She looked down hastily at her right arm where the sword had liquefied and sunk beneath her skin and stared in surprise. A tattoo in the form of the Kenryk crest was still emblazoned on her wrist. Memories rushed in. She had become a Sage Warrior and then fought Emori.

"Can you tell me what happened before I lose my mind? Please." She could feel her chest tightening as panic started to sink in.

"Wait, just pause for a moment." Korin raised his hand. "Breathe in and out slowly."

She followed his command, and the tightness started to wane, but her eyes remained wide. If she had been here for a whole month, Joran, Tia and Crispin would have been beside themselves with worry. She needed to go home.

Korin sat on the bed, facing her, ignoring Forde's cough that basically told him to get off the bed. She looked Korin over, and she saw the change in him. He looked healthier. He had picked up a healthy amount of weight, his hair had grown a little more, but what she noticed immediately was that the look that had been in his eyes, that haunted look, was gone. He seemed rejuvenated.

"I have to go home. My parents will be beside themselves with worry." She looked down at herself then realised she was in a nightgown and the blanket covering her made her feel a little hot. Sunlight streamed through the large arched window, and she could hear a bird singing through the window.

"Take a moment," Forde instructed, and she turned her gaze to him. "Let us tell you what happened over the last month first before you panic."

So, something had happened? "Was anyone hurt? Is my family all right? The Emori-"

"Are still dead." Forde cut her off quickly, then he smiled softly, and it did things inside her that made her relax. "First things first, after your battle with the Emori, you slipped into an Avaris sleep. Apparently, that happens when an Avaris has spent their power. In your case, you used too much power that you had never trained to control, so it depleted you. However, the Endric Sword, in your arm, kept you alive this entire time. We were assured that in an Avaris sleep, one doesn't need food or water or anything. You're neither dead nor alive, and that once you had recovered or healed, you'd wake up."

"Of course, no one knew when that would be. Apparently, it's not something anyone can determine. Arteryn has been beside himself with worry. He comes in here every day and sits with you." Korin added, and Amari caught the glint in his eye when he mentioned Arteryn. "Oh. And Forde made this concoction for you that he helped you drink every day. You responded every day by scrunching your nose every time he gave it to you, but I think it may have sped up your healing process."

"Wait, what happened after I fought the Emori?" She asked anxiously.

"Well...we have good news and bad news." Forde grimaced, and she got the sense he didn't exactly want to tell her what the bad news was. He must have caught the wild panic in her eyes because he quickly raised his hand to ask her to calm down. "No one died, rest assured. Only the Emori."

"Give her the good news first," Korin said impatiently, and Forde nodded.

"Well, after you defeated the Emori, Arteryn and I rushed you here-"

Korin scurried to pour water into a tin mug that he quickly handed over to her before perching back on the bed.

"After we brought you here and while you have been in your sleep, Arteryn rushed to Synia and brought the Leveroods here. Tia stayed by your bed for hours, but eventually, they had to leave because they couldn't leave the farm alone. We assured them you would go home for a visit the moment you recovered."

"They were here?" And she had missed them? Her eyes brimmed with tears. She hadn't seen her family in such a long time her body ached from it. She missed her family.

"Now for the bad news," Korin said dramatically, drawing Amari away from her musings, and she frowned at his theatrics.

Forde sighed in exasperation at Korin and gave him a look that told him to be quiet. "Right. So, Amari, you did become the first female Sage Warrior, but unfortunately, you will not go down into history as one."

She frowned in confusion. What was Forde talking about?

"After Forde and Arteryn brought you back, we received word through Derriane that the King was holding Baelin captive unless Forde returned to Sagar to answer for his crimes against the King."

"Crimes?" Amari asked, and Forde nodded slowly, a frown creasing his forehead, a sense of anger settling over him.

"Yes, I disobeyed the orders of the King. This man who has known me since I was ten years old pulled rank on me." Forde supplied, then he released a sigh. "I knew I had to go back, but I didn't exactly know how I was going to handle the situation. Korrigan went with me.

"You were in a vulnerable state, and it wouldn't have boded well for the whole Kais to know your true identity without somehow implicating the Leveroods. We didn't want to bring them into this situation. We wanted to keep them safe. Who knows what the King might have done if he knew they had been harbouring a Kenryk all these years?"

Oh no, she had never considered that at all.

"When we arrived in Sagar, Korrigan reminded the King about the treaties signed centuries ago that clearly stated that Kenryk were independent of any state or King. Korrigan reminded the King that an Avaris could not align itself with any king. The King proceeded to be stubborn about it, pointing out that the security of the Kais was at stake if there was someone like you out here where they couldn't monitor you."

"Monitor me?"

"Well, come on, Amari, the King thinks if you align yourself with the Kingdom of Kessariah, he might lose his advantage, and that would threaten his position," Korin explained quickly, and she shook her head in disbelief.

"Eventually, after days of Korrigan working on it- while I was in a dungeon, I should add- the King finally capitulated and agreed to set Baelin and me free. However, he did make a declaration that seeing as you are an Avaris, you would have had an unfair advantage over the other competitors in the Laurean Sage. So, he rescinded your Sage Warrior status, but I stole your badge for you. So, unfortunately, you may have won in the arena, but you're a Sage Warrior in name only." Forde explained, and for a moment, all Amari felt was just numbness. She had heard everything Forde had said, but it did not register. Amari's heart twisted in her chest, knowing how hard she had worked, how much she had sacrificed, the danger she had face all to become a Sage Warrior, and now it had all been taken away from her.

"Korrigan pointed out to the King that as an Avaris, you would never have served under the King's guard anyway. So, the King made us pay a fine- including me because the King felt my behaviour towards him also deemed me unworthy of Sage Warrior status. After that, we came back, and we have been waiting for you to wake up since." Forde rose to his feet then and moved towards the bed, his hand slowly reaching out to hers. She slid her hand into his larger hand, and the touch instantly soothed her.

"I know how much you wanted this Amari, how much being a Sage Warrior meant to you, but I do not regret how I handled the situation after you collapsed. My only objective was to ensure your safety and protect your identity. I never wanted to be a Sage Warrior, but I know this loss might mean a lot to you."

She inhaled sharply, still battling to believe her every effort to become a Sage Warrior was reduced to merely an unfair advantage over other competitors because she was an Avaris. However, as Amari sat there staring at Forde and Korin, she chose to focus on the everlasting friendship she had created with these two men. Another priority was the duty that came with being an Avaris and what was best for the Leveroods. Suddenly, she found that she was all right with not carrying the title of Sage Warrior.

She sighed then nodded as she reached a decision. "Do I have the badge here?"

Korin nodded along with Forde, and she exhaled again. "Then that means the goal I set for myself as a seven-year-old girl has been realised. I know that I didn't use any powers against my opponents. I know I earned my badge fairly, and that is all that matter to me. The King may dismiss my feat, but the people in that arena realise I made it, I know I earned it, and the people I care about know I deserved it.

"That chapter of my life is over now. I was going to become a Sage Warrior by choice, but I was an Avaris by birth, and that duty takes precedence over everything. Nevertheless, I am proud of what I achieved. I went in there; I competed against men much bigger than I am, and I succeeded. I know I succeeded, and that is enough for me."

The myriad of reactions that flowed across Forde and Korin's faces was almost comical. It appeared this was not what they had been expecting her to say. However, as she sat there, she made peace with her past, present, and future. If the Leveroods were safe, then that was all that mattered.

"I think I am proud of you." Korin sounded still in shock as he said it, as though he was saying words he had never thought he would say to her. "You've grown up, Amari Leverood."

She flushed under the unexpected compliment from Korin and realised that yes, she had grown up a lot since she left Synia.

"I should probably let Arteryn know you're awake. He will be thrilled to know you're finally back." Korin slid off the bed quickly, then paused and turned to Amari once more. "We didn't ask, but how are you feeling?"

How was she feeling? She didn't know. "Physically, I feel fine. But, in other ways, I am processing. I am also famished."

Korin brushed his hand over her ankle over the blanket the nodded. "I'll have someone bring you food, and maybe you might want to soak in a bath as well. I'll leave you two to kiss each other or whatever."

"Korin, really?" Forde threw a glare his way, but Korin merely shrugged before he walked out of the room. Amari bit her lower lip, feeling nervous suddenly, although she didn't know what she had to worry about. This was Forde. This man had seen her through many things, and he was still here. He had stayed by her side through it all.

He moved closer to the bed, closer to her, and she exhaled slowly, pushing the blanket aside and making an executive decision to do something.

He reached for her the exact moment she reached for him, and within a moment, they were in each other's arms, their lips sealed against each other. Forde's arms wrapped around her middle, drawing her closer. Her arms tightened around his neck, and within seconds she was flat on her back, and Forde's weight pleasantly pressed down on her. She couldn't get enough of him. Despite the new challenges that came with her new duties of being an Avaris, the uncertainty of moving into a new community staring down at her, she decided to enjoy this one moment in time.

The door crashing open had Forde pulling off her quickly, and before she could catch her bearings, he was shoved aside, and she was enveloped in a solid warm hug. She knew his scent instantly, and a smile broke across her lips while she struggled to recover at this sudden change of tone.

"Arteryn." She murmured as he squeezed her tightly then dropped a kiss on her forehead. He looked down at her, his chest rising and falling as though he had rushed here. He looked her over, his eyes roaming over her as though to satisfy himself that she was awake. He touched her face and her hair and exhaled. Then, finally, he drew back slowly and released a sigh of relief.

"You're awake." He looked like he couldn't believe it. It appeared he was finally releasing a weight that had been on his shoulders.

"Did you doubt it?" She asked him as she settled back on the bed, noting that Korin had walked into the room again.

Arteryn suddenly looked serious and nodded quickly. "Yes, there is an Avaris who never woke up from their Avaris sleep. Your condition was a serious one, Amari. I thought I'd lost you forever. When days turned to weeks to a month, I thought... I thought you might never wake up again and...."

He trailed off, and Amari was caught off guard by the emotion on his face. She pushed herself to her knees again and threw her arms around him, holding him tightly. Tears prickled her eyes as Amari buried her head into his neck, allowing him to envelope her into another hug. She took several deep breaths to calm herself down, then drew back and looked at him.

"I did it." She knew she didn't have to explain to him what she meant. He knew what her goal had been, and to be able to sit here and proudly tell him that she had succeeded, that all the hours and hard work they had put in over the years had given rise to her success at the Laurean Sage was something she would forever treasure.

"I know, I was there. I saw you." He rested his hands on her shoulders, then took another breath and smiled. "You were amazing, and I am so proud of you."

Pleasure spread all over her at the acknowledgement, and she wiped the solitary tear that slid down her cheek as she laughed.

"It was worth it. All of it. Every scar, every time ma scolded me for coming home late because I was training, being chased down by Grantreal and then the Emori... it was all worth it, Arteryn. I don't regret any of it." How could she? Amari recalled that brief moment when she had stood in the arena, victorious over her opponent, knowing she had become a Sage Warrior, and she knew it would live with her forever.

"I would have rather not seen you almost die, but if it made you happy." Arteryn smiled down at her before he seemed to notice Forde, who was still standing a little behind him, staring at him. Arteryn flushed then rubbed the back of his neck as he stepped back. "I didn't interrupt anything, did I?"

"You did," Forde told him quickly, moving closer to the bed to link his hand with Amari. "But I will forgive it because I know how unbearable it has been to be around you these last month because of your constant worry for her."

"This even though I told him Amari would be fine. I even said she would wake up today. Did any of you believe me? No." Korin moved towards the bed, carrying a tray of an array of foods. "I brought you something to eat to tide you over while they prepare something solid."

"Thank you." Amari took the tray then set it on the bed. "I would like to get off this bed, but you're all hovering...."

The three men shared a look then turned to her with indignation. "We've done nothing but hover the last month. We didn't think you'd ever wake up, and now that you have-"

"You didn't think she'd wake up. I did." Korin corrected playfully, and Arteryn shoved him on the shoulder quickly. Korin smiled up at him sweetly, a smile Arteryn returned, and Amari turned a corked brow towards Forde, who shrugged and shook his head as if to say he was not getting involved.

"Can you both leave? I'll stay with Amari while she waits for the food and the bath." Forde said quickly, and he was met with a frown from Arteryn that he returned.

"Don't let them fool you; they love each other now," Korin told her before he nodded and reached out for Arteryn's arm. "Come on, let's give them privacy-"

"Privacy? Korin-"

"Privacy, Arteryn." Korin started to move backwards, dragging Arteryn along with him, who moved forward reluctantly. "This is what happens when children grow up."

"You're still not allowed to sleep with each other. To be clear, no one can ever know. So, you two will have to be discreet." Arteryn pointed out, and then he looked at Amari over his shoulder. "I will let you eat and bathe, and then we are having a conversation."

Amari nodded quickly, and just as the door closed, it opened, and she watched as two women walked in carrying buckets of water towards a large bath she hadn't even realised was in the room. The third woman came in with food. Amari sat there quietly, watching them work, and she stole a glance at Forde, who looked just as amused.

"I'll let you eat and bathe too. I'll be back shortly." He announced, then surprised her by leaning in to kiss her cheek.

Once she was alone, she sat on the bed for a moment and exhaled. She was alive. She had killed Grantreal and the Emori but still couldn't decide how she felt about it. It stung that her Laurean Sage victory was tarnished and stripped away from her, but there was nothing she could do about that now. She swung her legs to the side of the bed. She expected her legs to be weak after a month of inactivity, but surprisingly they were sturdy. She was a little winded by the time she made her way to the bath, and after washing, dressing and eating, she gingerly made her way back to the bed, still feeling a little lightheaded. A single knock on the door was followed by Arteryn sticking his head in. When he realised she was decent, he entered, still looking at her as though he couldn't believe she was real. He moved towards the bed, reaching out for her hand, and he held it for a moment.

"You're not a child anymore." He sounded surprised, and Amari nodded. "And I have to let go, I suppose."

"Not completely." She still needed him. She would always need him. "Are my parents here?"

Arteryn shook his head. "They left a week ago, which is what I have to talk to you about. They saw the badge, Amari. They know you succeeded in the Laurean Sage, but as your identity and existence has been exposed, the Council has decided that you shouldn't travel outside of Bhrim for some time."

She blinked in confusion as his words hit her. "Are you saying I cannot go back to Synia? Not even briefly?"

Arteryn shook his head. "It would be too dangerous. I know you wanted nothing more than to go back to Synia and show everyone the badge, but things have changed. The whole Kais is talking about you. Some think you're a threat. You know how those who invaded this land feel towards us indigenous people and our powers. So, you should stay here at least until something else comes along that everyone else can talk about."

"But I wanted to see my parents, Crispin-"

"I know. I understand. You know I do, and you know if it were up to me, I would take you to Synia at least one last time, but it cannot happen. The decision is above me. Your life is here now, and I have spent the past month building the house we are going to share because I will be damned if I have to go live with my father."

Tears sprang into her eyes as she stared at Arteryn rather dejectedly. She understood. That was what annoyed her the most. She understood the situation, and she understood why she couldn't leave Bhrim right now. She understood. She just wished things were different.

"Will I ever see them again?" She asked as a tear slid down her cheek, and Arteryn nodded.

"They can come to Derriane, and you can meet them there. It is a bit of a challenge to let them through our barriers at the moment because everyone is so vigilant. They were only permitted through because we had hoped their presence would wake you up."

"I can never travel south again?"

"Just not for a while."

She took a deep breath, digesting the words, then nodded. "I understand. I just feel like I traded one restriction for another. I could never leave Synia before, and now I cannot leave Bhrim. I suppose I should be thankful you're here with me, but I miss them."

"I miss them too, Amari. They were our family for seventeen years. It's just that, with everyone looking for you, it is safer for them if we do not go to them."

She understood that too and nodded. "So, I will be living with you?"

"Yes. You're unwed, so you have to live with your parents."

"I am not calling you father."

Arteryn grimaced. "Please don't. That would be strange for both of us."

"And you and Korin?"

"Amari."

"Tell me."

Arteryn rubbed the back of his neck and expelled a sigh. "We're...taking things slow. Or at least, I am trying. But he is not letting me."

"He's not ready?"

"No, it's the opposite. I've never been pursued before."

"Wait, Korin is the one pursuing you?"

"And I am trying to slow us down because I am trying to be considerate of his past, but he won't have it, and I am too weak to say no to him."

"You? Weak?"

"When it comes to him. I just feel like I waited years for him, and now that he is here, I don't want to ruin things by rushing. But I think, for him, it's more about all the repressed feelings he had that he just wants to let out."

Amari looked at Arteryn for a moment then her eyebrows narrowed. Finally, she gasped, covering her mouth with her hands. "You have slept with him!"

"Amari!"

"You did. I can tell."

"How can you possibly tell?"

"You have a glow about you that I have never seen before."

"Don't be ridiculous."

"You did!"

"Fine! I did. A lot. It's been a month. A lot has happened, and he is quite irresistible-"

"Yet you won't let me be with Forde!"

"That is the law. But, should you decide you want to sleep with him, make sure you do not get pregnant. You cannot have a child with him until Korin has a male child."

"How is Korin supposed to have a male child when he is with you?"

A sad look crossed over Arteryn's face, and he shrugged. "Things aren't going to be easy moving forward, Amari. We all have to make adjustments and do things we are not comfortable with."

She frowned at him. "You...you're saying you will have to let Korin be with a woman to bear an heir?"

"Let's not talk about it. You just woke up. My father is excited. Poor man still thinks you're going to live with him. Absolutely not. The rest of the tribe cannot wait to meet you, and your confirmation has to take place soon."

"My what?"

"Utrirecha. It's the ceremony where an Avaris is confirmed once their Avaris powers are unleashed and they're set. You will also have to go through the female rite of passage to adulthood. Korin will have his confirmation for being a Khaiman. He chose to wait for you so you can go through it together. Artello did tell me the part where the three flames appear on your skin marking you the Avaris are painful, but only for a while then it goes away."

"I'll get markings?"

"Yes, but these aren't markings we draw ourselves. The Old bestow them on you. It's a confirmation. If they don't appear, then you're not an Avaris. If they do, you are. However, there is no question that you are. Only an Avaris can use the Endric Sword. It will appear on the back of your left shoulder. Same with Korin."

"The Old? Our ancestors."

"That's what we call those of us who have departed but live among us in spirit. Our ancestors, those who came before us, those who were with us and no longer here in the flesh."

Amari didn't think she was ready. It all felt and sounded daunting. This was unchartered territory for her, a challenge she was not confident she was prepared for, but one she had no choice but to accept.

"Nothing is ever going to be the same again, is it, Arteryn?"

He shook his head. "This is the beginning of the rest of our lives as Kenryk."

"Are you terrified? As I am?"

He looked down at their joined hands and played with hers thoughtfully. "Yes. More so because I know what living here as Kenryk means for me."

"What do you mean?"

"You don't have to concern yourself over it." He forced a smile on his face then gently touched her cheek. "Come on; it is time for you to meet everyone."

"Arteryn, can I do it tomorrow? Today, I just want to take it all in." But, first, she needed to prepare herself. Her life was about to change irrevocably. She needed time to prepare herself mentally. He nodded, then rose to his feet.

"I will see you later. Walk around a bit."

She nodded and watched him leave, knowing without a doubt that there was a lot Arteryn was not telling her. When Korin entered an hour later, he moved to sit on the bed, facing her and just stared at her.

"I'm glad you woke up. I was afraid of walking into this without you. But, knowing that I am assuming this important role of being a Khaiman to an Avaris, I like feels less frightful. So, we'll navigate this new life together."

That was probably the closest thing to him saying he cared about her that she was ever going to get, she thought. However, she understood what he meant. "I'm glad you're here too, Korin. I'm scared if I have to be honest. I'm walking into something I am not prepared for at all. And there seem to be many rules, a lot of cultural differences. I don't know if it's going to be easy, but having you, Forde and Arteryn here will make it less frightening."

"I've been here for a while. I have only gone down to the village a handful of times. I don't know if they accept me the way I am. Unlike Arteryn, I can't hide who I am behind a masculine image. However, I have resolved. If they don't like me, then it's their problem. It has taken me a long time to get to where I am, Amari. I hated myself growing up. I wanted to be like everyone- 'normal'- until I finally realised, I am normal, and normal doesn't come in one specific image. I'm not willing to sacrifice myself for this place, and if that makes me selfish, then so be it. If they want me to change who I am to fit in, then I will gladly move to Derriane and convince Babaro to take care of me for the rest of my days."

They bought laughed at Korin's words, but Amari knew there was a seriousness to his tone. She understood his concerns. Amari had them too. She had been a pariah in Synia because she did things women were not supposed to do, and she had a feeling it might become the same problem here.

"Well, the good thing is they need us, so they cannot throw us out." She declared, and he nodded immediately in agreement. "And we have each other."

"Yes, we do."

"And you never told me about Shorva."

"What?" Korin's perfectly sculptured eyebrows went up quickly, and she folded her arms across her chest and eyed him. He shrugged. "Forde said you met them in Sagar, and I suppose he couldn't keep his big mouth shut about my past, could he?"

"To be fair to Forde, it was the way Shorva was acting that sort of gave it away."

Korin groaned, then shook his head. "There isn't much to tell, really. We were together for about a year and a half, and he may have wanted more, but I always knew it could never happen. He was the son of a Lord. I was a nobody, and he was also susceptible to my pull. I found it hard to believe he wanted me for me and not because he was supernaturally drawn to me. But, most importantly, I could never love him because I was in love with a man I had never even said a single word to. Fortunately, it did not affect our friendship."

"Does Forde know you were together that long?"

"No. Forde travelled a lot at the time, so we could pretend it was nothing serious when he returned. Also, I am rather glad it didn't work out because now it would be just strange. Shorva and I share a cousin through Forde."

"Well, I suppose I am glad too because Arteryn seems different now that he's met you." Her uncle was in love. She could see it in his face and the way his eyes seemed to follow Korin whenever he was in the room. She still wasn't used to this Arteryn, but she was ecstatic that he was happy.

"He's been amazing." Korin turned to look out at the sea. "I won't lie, he can be irritatingly stubborn at times, but I like that he knows when not to push me. I've never met someone so in tune with my emotions. It's almost unnerving. I am worried though about something."

"What is it?" Her mind leapt to all sorts of conclusions.

"Well, aside from you, Forde and myself, no one seems to know about him, and he doesn't seem all that keen on letting anyone know. So, I just don't know where that will lead us in the long run."

Arteryn's words rang in her head, and she could already see the problems looming above Arteryn and Korin.

"I'm just glad you're thinking long term."

"Well, I have several motivations for wanting to be alive. Of course, I have terrible days, but I seem to be having more good days than bad lately, so at least that is something. I should probably let you know something."

She arched her eyebrows quickly in question.

"You and Forde… the rules around are clear. You cannot risk having a child with him unless I have an heir."

"But that would mean…."

"I know." Korin nodded grimly. "He loves you; you know. Forde. The only thing standing in the way of you two being together is me. I must have a child, and I don't know if I can do that. I don't know if I want one. My life has been such a mess. I have nothing to offer a child, and what would that mean for Arteryn and me. I feel caught. I can't give Forde the one thing he wants, which is you, which makes me selfish because he has given me so much but giving him that one thing he wants means possibly losing the one thing I have always wanted, which is Arteryn. I don't…."

She touched his hand and squeezed it. "Don't do that to yourself. Don't make it your burden. We will all find a solution to this situation together. So don't make it your burden to carry."

The following morning, a woman assisted her in dressing in clothes she was not familiar with, braided her hair in a way she had ever seen before, and painted her face in markings she had never seen. Amari realised that this was indeed her future, that this was the moment she had never known was coming.

She was about to start a life in Bhrim, living as a Kenryk, but most importantly, she was about to begin a life as an Avaris.

THANK YOU

Thank you for going on this adventure with Amari. I hoped you have enjoyed her introduction into a world and responsibility she never knew she was a part of. More challenges will come as she struggles to navigate this new life and its rules.

Make sure you get the next book where Amari, Korin, Forde and Arteryn adjust to life in Bhrim and discover whether it will build or break them.

Look out for: **The Kenryk Series: Rise of the Emoryk**

Reviews are vital to authors, and all reviews, even a thumbs up, can help a reader decide whether to pick up our books. If you have enjoyed this, please consider leaving a review on the site you purchased from.

ABOUT THE AUTHOR

Since I was ten, I would cut A4 books into smaller-sized pieces to write my stories for my classmates. As years have gone by, I continued to write. However, those stories remained files in folders, unpublished because I was terrified of the critiques. This one has finally seen the light of day, and I hope it inspires all those who have been writing in their little corners, afraid to let others see their stories, to find the courage to do so.